HEARTBREAK HOLLOW

FRANK F. WEBER

A TRUE CRIME NOVEL

HEARTBREAK HOLLOW

This book is dedicated to my son, Preston Weber. Brenda and I had you involved in music at an early age to keep you interested in school when academic work became tedious. You could have been successful in so many professions but selected the challenge of making a living in an arena where many of the most talented receive little reward. If this wasn't demanding enough, you also stepped into the challenge of teaching in a world of budget cuts and political insanity. Through all this, you excel and bring such positive energy. It's always a pleasure to be in your presence. Thank you for your gift to us!

Emily Piller, my amazing editor, has once again challenged me to elevate my work. Emily is insightful, and as a result of her feedback, I feel this book is another step forward for me as a writer. I have enjoyed our hours of reflection on characters and scenarios, which ultimately led to the finished product. Emily is able to graciously guide in a manner that fuels excitement about the project.

Thank you, Mikayla Dulz, for your cover model work! I have been fortunate to work with Mikayla as a colleague in the forensic world, and she is impressive! It's great knowing you and working with you!

Thank you, Kelsey Wesenberg, for your mapwork and Allie Toenies for your technological guidance!

Most importantly, thank you, Brenda Weber, once again for allowing writing to work in my very demanding life. Sharing my life with you is the ultimate reward!

This story was based on a true crime case.

Other works by Frank F. Weber:

Murder Book (2017)
The I-94 Murders (2018)
Last Call (2019)
Lying Close (2020)
Burning Bridges (2021)
Black and Blue (2022)
The Haunted House of Hillman (2023)
Scandal of Vandals (2024)
The Sun (2025)
Heartbreak Hollow (2025)
A Superior Affair (2026)

This story is told from the viewpoints of Jon Frederick, Eliana Castillo, and Lorenzo Turrisi Caruso. The narrator's name is listed at the beginning of each chapter.

List of Characters

Eliana "Ellie" Castillo, *Single mother*
Luis Castillo, *Eliana's five-year-old son*
Lorenzo Turrisi Caruso, *Eliana's partner and Roan and Catania's son*
Roan Caruso, *Entrepreneur and convicted murderer. Spouse of Catania; Lorenzo's Father*
Catania "Cat" Turrisi, *Mafia boss and restaurateur. Spouse of Roan; Lorenzo's Mother*
Donny Nguyen, *Father of Eliana's son, Luis*
Eve Fang, *Donny's spouse*
Mike Haney, *Police officer*
Carmel Cano, *Pearson Assessment employee and Eliana's friend*

Larry McBride, *Incel & Lorenzo's acquaintance*
Ross McBride *Larry's brother & Lorenzo's friend*
Molly McBride, *Larry and Ross's mother*
Dante Peterson, *Ross's partner & Lorenzo's friend*

Jon Frederick, *Bureau of Criminal Apprehension (BCA) Investigator*
Serena Frederick, *Private Investigator*
Nora, Jackson & Cami Frederick, *Serena and Jon's children (ages 9, 5 & less than 1 in 2024)*
Billy Frederick, *Jon's father, Navy veteran*

Candy Zapzalka-Ahles, *Heroine*
Steve Lee, *Detroit Lakes Chief of Police*
Todd Miller, *Becker County Sheriff*

Heather Hilton, *Attorney*

Halle Day Therapist, *Roan's daughter, Lorenzo Turrisi Caruso's half sister*

Tug Grant, *Former attorney and convicted murderer*

Cheri Wilde, *Exotic dancer*

Bina Kaplin, *BCA Digital Forensics Examiner*

Timeline

May 17, 2018	*Eliana Castillo acknowledges she is pregnant, to her lover, at Como Park High School*
July 26, 2024	*Eliana and Lorenzo's engagement date in Detroit Lakes.*
August 5, 2024	*Jon Frederick investigates in Aurora.*
August 9, 2024	*Cheri Wilde, of Inver Grove Heights, is connected to the case.*
	Eliana Castillo is released from the hospital.
	Shooting at Eliana's home in West St. Paul
August 16, 2024	*Serena and Jon Frederick's tryst in Nisswa.*
August 18, 2024	*Jada Anderson, of Minnetrista, becomes involved.*
August 23, 2024	*Jon Frederick and Eliana Castillo return to Detroit Lakes.*
September 13, 2024	*The texts begin…*
October 11, 2024	*Texts continue at Reds Auto in Pierz.*
October 15, 2024	*A clue is uncovered in the woods North of New York Mills.*
November 19, 2024	*What will the court decide?*
December 14, 2024	*Serena and Jon at the MAC in Pierz.*

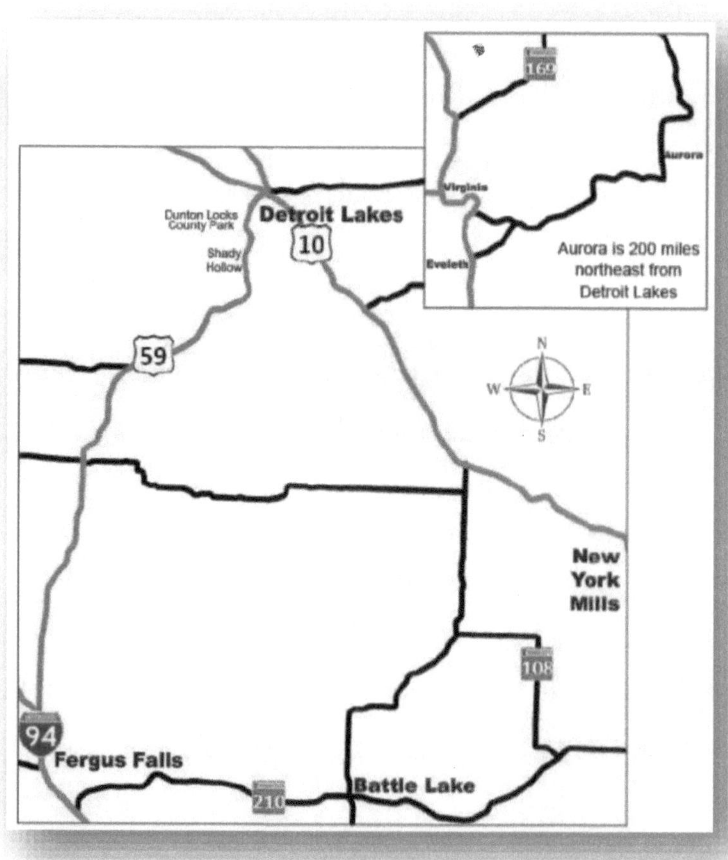
169
Aurora
Virginia
Eveleth
Aurora is 200 miles
northeast from
Detroit Lakes
Dunton Locks
County Park
Detroit Lakes
10
Shady
Hollow
59
N
W E
S
New
York
Mills
108
94
Fergus Falls
210
Battle Lake

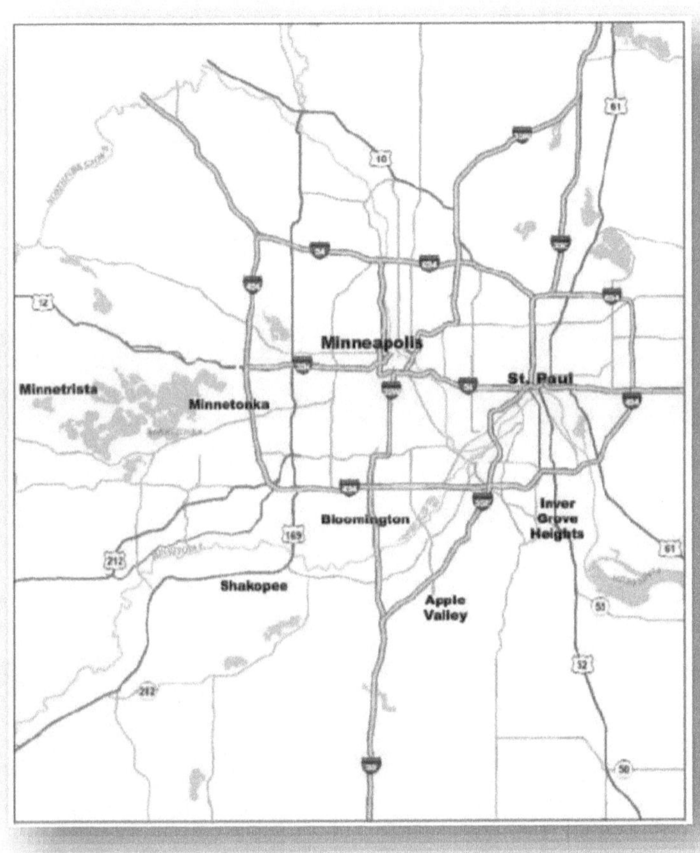

61
10
94
694
12
694
Minneapolis
St. Paul
Minnetrista
Minnetonka
94
94
494
494
Bloomington
Inver Grove Heights
169
61
212
55
Shakopee
Apple Valley
212
52
50

1

ELIANA CASTILLO
MAY 17, 2018
COMO PARK HIGH SCHOOL
740 ROSE AVENUE WEST, ST. PAUL

I should have been dressing for our softball game, but instead, I was waiting for the senior class to be dismissed so I could meet my boyfriend, Donny Nyguen. The final bell rang, and the cage doors opened. Students rushed to the exits as if their lives depended on it. Fortunately, today it did not. I sat at a cafeteria table, pulling the string back and forth on my gold hooded sweatshirt, which read "Cougars" in thick black letters across the front. I think our moms liked wearing the school swag more than we did.

Finally, I spotted Donny coming toward me. He was handsome, tall, and thin, with straight black hair. He glided smoothly into the seat across the table from me. Seeming bored, he asked, "What's so important that you need to tell me before tennis practice?"

His awkward teenage voice was higher than mine. Donny told me he loved my sexy husky voice. I wasn't sure how much he'd enjoy hearing this. I teared up and bit my lip. "I'm pregnant."

"You sure?" His eyes quickly darkened, and for the first time, I felt unsure about our relationship.

"Pretty sure. Tested three times," I muttered.

"Damn it, Eliana!" His resentful hostility silently poured over me. I realized at that moment this boy would have given everything he owned to have never met me. He looked around the commons, then quietly declared, "I can't be a father."

My whole world was falling apart, but in our little glass globe, we were ignored by students rushing past to catch their buses. I managed, "You are."

"I won't be. My family will disown me. I'm going to college. And you, Ellie. You're a petite, dynamic fireball. You light up a room, girl, with a passion that's contagious. You're okay turning into a pathetic blob baby carrier?" He whispered, "I'll pay for the abortion."

"I don't want your money." I hung my head to hide my tears. "I can't have an abortion."

"Of course you can."

"I won't." I looked up at him with pleading eyes.

"Then you're on your own. I'm sorry, but I've got to get to tennis." Donny tapped the table. "It's a woman's right to choose, right? So, make the right decision. Either way, we're done. My family would kill me if they found out. I can't do it. This is serious shit. You're sixteen. You going to drop out of school like your cousins? Don't call me until you've changed your mind."

I'm not sure how long I sat before my bestie, Carmel Cano, pulled me to my feet and dragged me away. Carmel was a platinum-blond Christina Aguilera lookalike. She was already wearing our uniform—a gold jersey with black pants. With her arm around my shoulder, she walked me toward the locker room. Trying to comfort me, she said, "Hey girl, you've been thinking about it for weeks. Donny's only had five minutes after school. Give him some time."

There was no coming back to it. The line had been drawn.

But Carmel continued, "We've got playoffs tonight, so get your shit together and be ready to play." Carmel was ambitious and fiercely competitive.

"I don't know if I can," I said, my head hanging.

Carmel spun me and faced me. "You can! And you will. We've got those Vis bitches, and I don't want to lose."

Her reference to the all-girls Visitation Catholic High School as "bitches" struck me as funny since they were the politest team we played. But Carmel was right. Life goes on, and I needed to go on with it. We had won the St. Paul City Conference this year, and the Pioneer Press sportswriter referred to Carmel and me as "double trouble" for our ability to turn double plays. Carmel played third base and turned on a dime to make the throw to me at second, and I released my throw to first just as fast. Playing third in fastpitch is like volunteering to be the poor soul shot out of a cannon at the circus. The protective mask they wear isn't enough to ever get me to play that position. They cheat up, close to the hitter, when they think someone might bunt, risking that the person might turn on a fastball and line drive a ball at them at rocket speed. Carmel was a friend who would kick someone's ass for me, and she lived just down my street in St. Paul. Having her on my side was everything.

1:30 P.M., FRIDAY, JULY 26, 2024
(Six years later)
CESAR CHAVEZ STREET, DISTRICT DEL SOL, WEST
SIDE, ST. PAUL

Carmel and I bought houses in the neighborhood where we grew up, and we still lived just down the block from each other. We lost that game to Visitation, 13 to 12, and I went hitless. It was a hard lesson on how life can get in the way of our dreams. We were going to be college athletes who roomed together, but the Vis game was my last. After I had my son, Luis, I knew I wouldn't give him up for anything. I did go to prom my senior year with a friend. When Carmel heard a guy saying to my date, "You're lucky. She's already had a baby, so you know she's giving it up," Carmel interrupted the conversation and told my date, "If you do anything with my girl that she didn't ask you to do, I'll cut your dick off." She was my protector, and it never bothered her to always have Luis tagging along with us.

I had to stop over and say hi to my friend before heading off to Detroit Lakes to spend the weekend with my boyfriend, Lorenzo Turrisi Caruso. Lorenzo was a fit Italian man with thick black hair and coffee brown eyes. The man could be a romance novel cover model. He was infatuated with me, and I was excited as I dreamed about how my life could change this weekend.

Carmel was still platinum blond, and now in her early twenties, she absolutely glowed. She offered me a Diet Coke, and we sat on the couch.

I told her, "My parents have Luis for the weekend."

"I would have taken him," Carmel offered.

"Thank you, but you need to get back on the horse, girl." She had dated a jerk named Larry McBride, who had attempted to assault her, and I hadn't heard of her being with another guy since. Lorenzo spends time with Larry, which bothers me, but he says guys don't need to get along to hang out. He claims Larry is very mechanical, so he's useful. I can't picture a group of women ever inviting an obnoxious jerk along based on that criterion. But I also don't think Lorenzo has deep conversations with anyone but me.

Carmel leaned into me as she asked, "Are you sure Lorenzo's right for you? It doesn't bother you that he's been unfaithful? Girl, that would torment me!"

My nerves tingled as I said, "That all ended over a year ago." It still hurt. "We're taught to forgive."

"Okay." She stood up and stepped away. Carmel turned back, "I don't trust him, but it's your life. Your call. Do you ever think of Donny anymore?"

"No," I laughed. "I was infatuated for a bit. But he didn't want to parent, and I do fine without him."

"Do you ever wonder what he's like now?" When I didn't respond, she added, "I'm still pissed at him for costing us that game. You loved him until the moment you told him you were pregnant. I always wondered what would happen if you spoke to him again."

"I think I'm the one who cost us that game. Too much going

on in my head." The game was a nonissue now.

"It's funny," Carmel said with a bittersweet smile, "I was the one who always said I'm not marrying a poor boy. I've had enough with struggling to get by. And it never made a difference to you. The rich boy just fell into your lap anyway."

"I'm not marrying him because he's rich. I feel alive and excited when I'm with him."

"Well, you go, girl! Mom always said, 'Don't marry a guy who's tighter than a nun's knees. You'll never be happy.'"

I smiled at Carmel. "Thank you for being a great friend." I stood and we hugged. "I need to get going. I still have to buy a dress for tonight."

5:30 P.M., FRIDAY, JULY 26, 2024
THE NINES, 917 WASHINGTON AVENUE, DETROIT LAKES

I love this gem of a clothing boutique. The dresses are casual but classy. I found an ivory crochet backless dress. It ended right above my knees, which gave me the opportunity to show off my new black boots. *Perfect for tonight. Not revealing but pretty.* I stepped out of the dressing room to get some feedback.

"Wow." The thin, middle-aged clerk smiled at my appearance as she bent and straightened the hem on one side. "It blends into your skin tone and shows off your beautiful dark hair. It's a perfect match for your cocoa eyes and makes those doe-like peepers pop." She circled around me and said, "It fits perfectly."

"I agree."

"You are too gorgeous. What's the occasion?"

"Not sure." I couldn't hide my mischievous grin. Lorenzo and I have been in a committed relationship for almost a year, and I have a feeling that tonight will be the night. I told Lorenzo I wanted to be at the Arts on the Lake event on Sunday, so he offered to meet me here on Saturday and get a nice hotel room for us. My stomach churned in giddy elation. All I have to say is, "Yes."

After completing my purchase, I received a text from Lorenzo.

"Where are you?"

"Be there in 10," I texted back. Shopping had taken longer than anticipated.

I rushed out to the car. The cars parked on each side of mine were so close I was forced to shimmy into the driver's seat, careful to avoid getting my dress dirty. *Made it inside, unscathed.* I would have to back up straight for a bit before I could start turning. Fortunately, the stall in the row behind me was empty, so I could back partially into it before departing. My phone rang from an unknown caller. It was probably a telemarketer. But I immediately thought, *What if my son and the babysitter had an accident and the hospital was calling?* "Hello?"

"This is Donny. I was wondering if I could talk to you about having a visitation with my son."

"Are you kidding me? After two years of no contact, you think, 'Maybe I'll call her on a Friday night and see if she wants me back?'"

"I don't want you back," Donny clarified. "I want to speak to my son. I can swing over for just five minutes. It's an expensive visit when you consider all the child support I paid."

"I'm in Detroit Lakes. You seem to have forgotten you terminated your parental rights two years ago."

"I know—well, not legally. I was a dumb twenty-year-old kid who couldn't afford the child support. I'm not taking Luis from you. I just want to explain my side." When I didn't respond, he added, "The rumor is you're dating a mobster. I don't want that life for my son."

Neither do I, was my thought. His parents are mobsters, but Lorenzo isn't. I said, "That window has closed, Donny. I begged you to help me, and you didn't have time for us. Now that he's out of diapers and it's convenient for you, you want in. Luis is doing great. Do you really want to mess that up?"

"I guess that's that then."

"How did you get my number?"

"Carmel thought you'd softened on the visitation idea. Because you're a good person. You are a practicing Christian, right?"

I hung up. "Not tonight."

My phone buzzed again. I grabbed it out of the console and yelled, "Donny—leave me the hell alone!" Fortunately, no one heard me. Lorenzo had texted. "Can't wait to see you." I sighed and said to myself, "Calm down." Instead of responding, I quickly backed up.

"Crunch!" It sounded like a very large pop can being crushed. That can't be good. For a second, I heard a dog barking. My heart sank as I stepped out of the car. When I was looking at the text, a Jeep had pulled into the vacant spot behind my car. He had a bike rack mounted on the back, and I crushed the wheel of his bike between our vehicles. This couldn't be happening. Not today!

A young, fit man in his twenties stepped out and studied his mountain bike. He was a clean-cut Matt Damon-looking guy. I could tell he was upset, but he asked calmly, "Would you mind pulling ahead? You're crushing my bike."

"I didn't see you."

"I hope not," he remarked. "Do you have a bomb in your car? I could've sworn I heard ticking."

I listened. There was no ticking. "My car is a bit of a bomb, but no, I'm not transporting one. I did hear a dog."

"Fortunately, there's no dog."

I got back into my car and pulled back into the parking spot. When I returned to him, he said, "I'm going to need a new front wheel."

"How much?" I asked meekly.

"About eight hundred dollars."

"For a bike wheel? I can't afford that. I'm a single mother. I have school shopping." I paused and said, "What were you even doing here?"

He silently studied the damage as he pointed to the DL Bikes store across the street.

"This is just as much your fault as mine," I blurted. "I bet if we call the police, they're going to say your bike rack was sticking out too far."

"We can walk if you'd like." He pointed down the street. "The police station is right there." He took out his wallet and showed me his badge. "Or you can just talk to me. Can I see your insurance?"

I went back to my car and frantically dug through the glovebox, but couldn't find my newest insurance form. I was sure I paid it. Crap. Now what? I didn't want to cry, but I could feel my eyes welling up. I could be getting engaged. Instead, I'd probably spend the next couple of hours at the station.

"I'm Mike."

I didn't respond.

"Step out of the vehicle," he said.

I got out of the car and, in feigned contrition, reached out my arms and hung my head, daring him to cuff me.

"You shouldn't have to do more than a year in prison," he teased, "with good time."

With one open eye, I peeked up at his smile.

"I'm not at work. I won't report this if you agree to have a cup of coffee with me. With mountain biking off the table, my evening has suddenly opened up." Recognizing my reticence, he added, "You're not married, are you?"

"No."

"Engaged?"

"No."

"Mi Cartagena Café has great coffee," he suggested.

"Can we do 908 Coffee and Tea instead? I love their matcha." Mi Cartagena is on Detroit Lake, close to our hotel. I didn't want Lorenzo to walk in and see me with another man.

"Sure," he said. The boy had a cute smile.

"And if I agree to coffee, and just coffee, you'll forget about this?"

"Yes. No expectations. I'll even buy," he offered.

"Why would you do that?"

He crossed one leg over the other as he stood. "As soon as I saw what happened, I knew I was out eight hundred dollars. Minnesota's a no-fault insurance state, so as a young male, my insurance goes up automatically. I thought maybe if you had a great insurance policy, I could still be saved. But it doesn't appear that you even have insurance."

"I have insurance. But it's the cheapest. Money's tight." I looked back at the bike shop. "Aren't you going to pick up a new wheel?"

"No. I can't afford it right now. But I can afford to buy coffee." He smiled. Feeling a little guilty, I walked with him to the coffee shop.

6:08 P.M.
908 COFFEE + TEA, 908 WASHINGTON AVENUE,
DETROIT LAKES

I was nervous about making the big decision tonight. Now I'm nervous about not getting there. If Mike had a normal car, I would have turned before I hit it, but he had to have that damn bike rack sticking out. And now I'm having tea with him to avoid having to deal with my insurance company. There's only a small dent in the trunk of my car, and it's old enough that it's not worth fixing.

Mike was handsome, with short brown hair and blue eyes. He obviously worked out regularly and was plenty polite. He pulled my chair out for me as we sat with our beverages at a small table. He asked, "Are you familiar with the area? Amazing gymnasts. Detroit Lakes won the gymnastics state championship five years in a row."

I was sidetracked by a text from Lorenzo: "Where are you?"

After glancing at my phone, I rudely picked it up and texted back, "Be there in twenty minutes."

"Shopping better than me?" Lorenzo responded in his text.

Sometimes, but I didn't dare say that. "Want to look perfect!" I texted.

"Clothing unnecessary," Lorenzo responded.

I forced a smile and set my phone on the table, screen down. I took a sip of tea and asked, "So, Mike, what do you do?"

"I thought showing you my badge was a solid clue. I'm law enforcement, but it's not full-time for me yet. I'm picking up hours at departments all over the state until I have enough experience to get a full-time gig. Tell me a little about yourself. I don't even have your name."

9

"Hazel." I don't know why I lied. I was so nervous. I continued, "I'm twenty-two and have a six-year-old son."

"What do you do for a living?" Mike asked.

"I work as a cashier at a convenience store." Not wanting to talk about myself, I said, "Tell me about your most embarrassing date."

"I agreed to go on a blind date, and it turned out to be my first cousin."

"You didn't recognize her name?" I couldn't help but smile.

"I wasn't given her name." He shrugged his shoulders. "It actually didn't turn out that bad."

"Good kisser?" I teased.

"No," he blushed. "We abandoned the date. We went for a long walk, talked about loneliness, and became good friends. What was your most embarrassing date?"

"I don't know if I can narrow it down to one. I do remember my most mortifying moments. At sixteen, I told my guy I was pregnant. He said, 'I'm not paying for a child.' I told him, 'Fine, I don't want your money anyway.' A year later, after I realized how expensive a baby was, I took him to court for child support. That was humiliating. But I have a wonderful six-year-old son."

Larry, as in Larry-who-dated-and-tried-to-sexually-assault-my-friend, entered the coffee shop. He was the brother of one of Lorenzo's close friends. I squirmed in my seat and turned away as he approached. *Please don't see me.*

"Eliana!" he shouted as he came directly to our table. Larry was a hillbilly-looking guy who wore a tattered baseball cap. "Went fishin' with Lorenzo yesterday. Slayed the walleyes."

"I'm here for the craft fair. It's on the lake, so it's a beautiful venue." God must hate liars. My lie to Mike was spat back in my face so quickly.

"Four on the Floor played at the city park last night," Larry said. "Great show!"

Feeling sickened, I nodded and waited for him to leave.

Larry awkwardly waited for me to keep talking. When I turned away, he squinted and wrinkled up his nose at me as if I rendered a rancid odor. He finally went to the counter to order.

Mike said patiently, "So your name is Hazel, but they call you Eliana for short."

"I'm sorry." I felt a warm flush across my face. "My name is Eliana Castillo. I'm in a relationship. I can't afford to turn this accident into my insurance, and you insisted I have coffee. Why?"

"I was intrigued by the mysteriousness in your tawny brown eyes, and I wanted to know more." Mike smiled, "Just go. I have no desire to torment you. I thought you might be interesting to talk to."

When I hesitated, he said, "I'm starting out in my career, so I live in a small apartment. I don't have a lot of money or a great car. I'm honest, and I try to be nice to people. Treat people like you'd want someone to treat your family. I drive to St. Otto's Care Center and play cribbage with my grandma every Thursday. I'm not exciting. You're not missing out."

He was giving me reasons to walk away, but his honesty was kind of appealing. Time for me to be honest, too. "Mike—I'm not married or engaged, but I hope to be soon. Maybe even tonight. You are such a nice guy—" I started.

"Don't do that," he said. "It's how my relationships always end. Please just go. Enjoy your evening."

"I promise she's out there for you, Mike." I picked up my phone, and I could feel his eyes on me as I departed.

2

Our hotel room was perfectly clean. A bottle of champagne on ice was surrounded by chocolate hearts wrapped in red foil. The champagne glasses had *Lorenzo & Eliana* etched on the sides, and they will forever rest in a hutch to commemorate this moment. Our second-floor balcony had large wooden posts and overlooked the lake, and I planned to kiss her passionately in the moonlight. This was going to be a night to remember!

I texted Eliana again, "Where are you?"

I have made this entire weekend perfect—and Eliana can't put off shopping to be here? I checked the Find My iPhone app we shared. After I cheated on her, she insisted we share locations. Eliana's sitting at 908 Coffee. *What the hell?*

She responds to my text with, "Want to look perfect."

"Clothing unnecessary," I texted back. *Okay, then, what are you doing in a coffee shop?* Angry, I paced about the room. I was giving up everything for her. This ring cost a small fortune. Mom never wanted me to marry her, but I've been willing to step out of Mom's good graces—for my love of Eliana.

Screw it. I dug out my laptop and signed into OnlyFans. *If you're going to dis me, I'll find someone else to talk to.* My online girl, Londyn Lust, looks a lot like Eliana. At my command, Londyn does whatever I want on live chat. She does things I'd like Eliana to do, but out of respect for her, I don't demand. In a way, I'm being considerate. I've only actually met Londyn a couple of times, and the truth is, she was a bit of a disappointment in person. Even when I'm with her, my fantasies are always about Eliana, so it isn't really cheating. Hell, their names are almost the same. I took the laptop into the bathroom to give me time to close it when Eliana finally arrived.

I clicked into Londyn's website, and she responded immediately. *That's what I'm talkin' about.*

She came on screen in a white silk robe and said, "Hon, so nice to hear from you. I was worried when you said you were getting engaged and ending it with me." She opened the robe to reveal red lingerie on her petite frame. With a sensuous drawl, she added, "I would miss you terribly. I can be your pleasure during that stressful marriage planning process. You're going to need it. Our hot little secret. Or in this case, our sizzling big secret."

"Let's FaceTime. That way, I can be aroused by you, and you can be aroused by me."

"Sounds perfect," she purred.

I'm Londyn's "Findom," as she calls it—a man she can financially dominate by requesting presents and gift cards as a demonstration of my affection. This is in addition to the monthly fee I pay to talk to her. But the power dynamic has shifted since I told her I was going to quit. When she thought she'd lost me, Londyn even offered to meet me and pleasure me in my Hummer. It made me realize she's become dependent on my income. I'm not a dweeb. Londyn gets nothing without offering something in return. Tonight, I'll have her beg for me. I might hang on to her for the time being as a safety net.

I instruct her, "Strip nice and slow and lie back on the bed."

The bathroom door suddenly swung open. *Crap!* I was in

trouble. Surprised by my naked state, Eliana glared and asked, "What are you doing?"

"Thinking about you," I managed. "I didn't hear you come in." I mumbled, "Would—would you step out a minute? I'll be right out."

Her gaze fixated on my laptop. She lunged and grabbed hold of it.

I slammed it shut.

"I saw the naked woman!" Ellie sneered.

"It just popped up." I couldn't hide the panic in my tone. "You need to trust me." Now she was trying to open it. I never should've shared my password with her.

"Let me see!" Ellie yanked hard on it.

Angry at myself, I pushed the damn thing hard into her face. *Keep it!*

The edge of the laptop cracked her on the forehead, and Eliana fell backward onto the floor.

I hadn't intended to strike her that hard. I immediately knelt next to her and apologized. "I'm sorry. It slipped out of my hand. Are you okay?"

"Pornography?" she spat out. "You're back here watching porn?"

"OnlyFans. It's a chat site."

"OnlyFans is a porn site. You're paying for live porn."

I swallowed hard. "Ellie, if you can let go of this tonight, I promise it will never be an issue again." I sat back on my heels and begged for forgiveness. "Tonight will be the best night of your life. Please, let it go. I never cheated on you. I was just chatting." I needed a do-over. The night hadn't started as I had intended.

Eliana rolled to her feet and ran out the door.

Still naked, I leaned out the door and yelled, "Wait! I'm sorry. Please, come back. It's not what you think." I paced restlessly about the room. "Damn it!" *Why?* If she hadn't stopped at the coffee shop, this would never have happened. If Londyn hadn't immediately answered, the temptation would have just passed. I called Eliana's phone and heard it buzzing on the TV counter. It was resting next to her purse. *She has to return.*

I was told in my domestic violence program to let her go. I'd slapped her a couple of times after she provoked me. Nothing crazy. I agreed to do an anger management program, and there has been no knocking around between us since—until tonight. I'm supposed to give her time to calm down and then talk to her. I forced myself to sit on the bed for a minute. *Okay—I can't do it.* I quickly dressed. I needed to find her.

3

Alone in the elevator, I opened Lorenzo's laptop. He solicited a woman named Londyn Lust—probably not her birth name. Londyn was an online sex worker. Subscribers apparently pay to watch her engage in sexual acts. I'd be curious to know how much Lorenzo paid for this, though not so curious that I'd have another conversation about it. He's right. It wasn't as bad as I thought. It was worse. Our relationship will never recover from what he was asking her to do. I closed the laptop and carried it out of the hotel. Ugh! I hate starting over. I have feelings for Lorenzo, but I just can't do this. I was ready to commit to spending the rest of my life with him! Lorenzo could be so attentive and caring. My son had fun with him. Lorenzo had just bought him a trampoline. Ugh! The reality is that I've had doubts about Lorenzo—but my fantasy of what we could be kept overriding logic. I made excuses for him over and over. I assumed that when I didn't know what he was doing, it must be something kind because he was always so considerate around me. It was easier to pretend he was my knight in shining armor. I told myself Lorenzo kept his reasons for not being there for me to himself because he was humble, and he didn't want to brag about his honorable deeds. So stupid.

After leaving the hotel, I walked toward Lake Melissa. Mom and I used to visit the Shady Hollow Flea Market in this area. Even in the dark, I could spot the white "Candy Store" banner on the dark main building. I meandered over to it, felt the moistness of the cool grass with my hand, and then sat on the ground and leaned against the building. My life had just blown up. I opened the laptop. No internet connection. I'd seen enough anyway. I hunched over and cried. *Could this day get any worse? Why are men such dicks? Why am I so stupid?* Lorenzo had an affair last year. We'd just "worked through it." Now he's having online sex. What a catch! I wasn't sure how long I'd been sulking, but I finally concluded the best remedy would be to go home to my darling boy. Luis would never treat a girl like Lorenzo treated me. I'd make sure of it. It would be better to die an old spinster than go through this again. Wait until my bestie, Carmel, hears about this. She's told me a hundred times that Lorenzo would be the death of me. Now she gets to hear she was right. I reached for my phone to call her. *Crap! I left my phone in the room. Great!*

A voice from the shadows said, "Finally—I found you."

4

LORENZO TURRISI CARUSO
10:00 P.M. FRIDAY, JULY 26, 2024
THE LODGE ON LAKE DETROIT
1200 EAST SHORE DRIVE, DETROIT LAKES

I returned to the room wet from a combination of sweat and the warm mist in the air. Four hours ago, Eliana loved me and wanted to spend the rest of her life with me. Now, it was over. I seriously messed up tonight, and there was no way of undoing it. I paced for a moment and then picked up the champagne flutes and fired them into the wall. I grabbed the champagne bottle by the neck and smashed it against the floor. Glass shattered, shimmering in the candlelight like a diamond ring. I dumped the ice bucket over the candles and punched the wall. *What is wrong with me?*

It wasn't long before security was in the hall, knocking at my door. "I need to come in," the guard announced. I let him in, and he walked about the room. "What happened?"

"I lost my fiancée." I picked up my billfold. "I'm sorry. I'll pay for the damages." I leafed out hundred-dollar bills and handed them to him. "There won't be any more damage. I promise. I didn't hit her. I was frustrated—at myself."

"Where is she?" he asked.

"I don't know. She took off."

"Call her," he directed.

I dialed the number, and we both turned to see her phone ringing on the counter.

"I need to talk to my boss," The guard responded, eyebrows raised. "No more damage, all right?"

"Yeah. No more." I sat on the edge of the bed. "I'm sorry. I'll take care of this, okay? I'm a Turrisi. We don't leave debts unsettled."

The security guard nodded and left the room.

I was getting the hell out of here before the police arrived. *What was my best move?* I called Eliana's friend, Carmel, and explained Eliana had left.

"I haven't heard from her," Carmel said. "Any idea where she would go?"

"None."

Carmel paused and then said, "Sit tight. I'll come and help you look for her. I'd bet she's sitting someplace crying. I feel like if you drive me around town, I'll figure out where she'd go. I'll get there as fast as I can."

"Thanks, Carmel."

5

ELIANA CASTILLO
12:30 A.M., SATURDAY, JULY 27, 2024
DUNTON LOCKS COUNTY PARK
DUNTON LOCKS COUNTY ROAD (ONE MILE NORTH OF
SHADY HOLLOW), DETROIT LAKES

As I slowly came to consciousness, my first thought was, *Where am I?* It was dark, and I was lying on the ground outside. The rapid, high-pitched "er-er-er-er" chirp of crickets rubbing their front wings together to attract mates echoed in the night. There was an occasional rattle mixed in. I'm not sure if it emanated from a bug or a bird. I tried to move, but my body hurt—bad. When I raised my fingers, I could feel they'd been crushed. I had open wounds on my chest and abdomen. I needed help.

The wet dew beneath my body chilled my bare legs. I felt dirty and had stabbing pains in my abdomen. *I had been shot. That dirtball shot me with some sort of pipe. Who was he? It was someone I knew, but I couldn't remember who.* "Miércoles." I moaned. Miércoles was my family's acceptable swear word. It sounded a little like "oh, shit" in Spanish, but simply meant "Wednesday," which was kind of like White people saying "fudge." *Who the hell assaulted me? I think he liked me once. That much I remembered.* After he was done, he'd left me lying on the damp forest floor like a rag.

I heard a soft "moo." Too gentle to be a cow. *Where was I?* I could see the moon. It was cool, but the assault left my body feeling numb. I had to move, or I was going to die here. My body would be picked apart by scavengers. One of my eyes was swelling shut.

It hurt, but I gingerly made my way to my feet. It began misting. Not surprising. I swear it's rained every day this summer. A desperate sound, like a screaming woman in the distance, startled me. I tried to calm myself by saying, "Just a fox." I'd heard that sound once while camping with my son, and our guide told us it was the sound a red fox makes at night. Tonight, it could be a woman screaming. The heel of my right foot felt raw as it came in contact with the ground, but the cool, wet grass felt soothing. The last thing I remembered was walking toward Shady Hollow. Honestly, I didn't know where I was, other than deep in the woods. I don't recall ever being here before.

I heard barking. That was good. Dogs are often close to their homes. The pain in my groin was excruciating, and it was hard to walk. What happened to me was worse than rough sex. Flashbacks of my body convulsing on the ground, with every penetration, intrusively bolted through my head, but I chased the nightmare away. *How did I end up here?* It didn't make sense.

I limped and plodded along toward the barking. I yelled, "Keep barking, Trusty, I'll find you!" *What am I saying?* Trusty was my guardian from as early as I can remember until she died of old age when I was twelve—a decade ago. *I'm not going to make it. Okay, just ten more steps.* "One, two, three..." I repeated, "Just ten more steps. One, two, three..." I muttered this mantra over and over.

And then a large figure, at least forty feet tall, stood before me. I had initially thought it was the menacing shadow of a Norway pine, but as I approached, I realized it was a monster. "Miércoles," I dragged out the word. A gigantic troll stuck his tongue out at me. I stopped dead in my tracks and waited for him to grab me and crush me, but he remained motionless. It felt like I was in some weird Alice in Wonderland dream, but the pain was all too real. I cowered away from the monster and limped on. I had to keep moving or I was going to die. The troll silently observed as I hobbled on. The phrase, "Curiouser and curiouser," from the book came to mind. I remember my English teacher saying Lewis Carroll was a perv who took naked pictures of Alice's thirteen-year-old sister.

I could taste metal, and I was hallucinating. Both are precursors to death. Like a child, I spoke my thoughts out loud. "Keep moving."

The hound kept calling, and I followed.

Suddenly, I realized I wasn't alone. I could hear breathing. Someone was trudging through the woods. It wasn't a small animal, and it wasn't far away. The entity was lumbering along, parallel to me, just out of my sight.

I didn't have the energy to run. It was all I could do to stay upright. I was afraid that if I bent down and hid, I'd never get back up again. So, I kept moving.

Now he was in front of me. *Please just leave me alone. Had a predator circled me?* I raised my chin and forced both my eyes open. I needed to know if this was real.

An adult black bear stood about twenty-five feet away. I froze. I thought I was supposed to make noise or try to make myself look big, but simply being alive took all my energy. The bear dropped down on all fours and moseyed on its way.

Evidently, I wasn't that interesting.

And the crickets kept calling "er-er-er-er" to their potential mates. At least they weren't raping them. The hound continued its baying, and I followed her call in the wild. I'm not sure why I thought it was female. It seemed like I needed a woman to save me. I was in the kind of trouble you needed a mom for. I was nauseated, and I wanted to quit, but I stepped on. I was reduced to telling myself, "Just three more steps." Ten seemed impossible. And then I saw a glow from a porch light between the dark trees. *I've almost made it.* My legs felt weighted, and it was all I could do to keep them moving. *I've lost too much blood. Don't think, just walk. Thinking is too much energy.*

I was only twenty feet away from the door when I tripped and fell flat on my face. And there I lay. I couldn't get up. The dog barked again. *Where was that dog?* Why wasn't the owner tending to her? Trusty, help me! I felt her nudge and knew I had to crawl to the house. I dug my hands into the wet earth and made my way to the steps. I only had to make it up three steps. I crawled onto the porch and lay there, completely spent. I was done. As hard as I willed my body to move, there was nothing left. Please, God, help me. I raised my hand and weakly slapped the porch. My body was shutting down. I could give in to the darkness any second. My greatest regret was not being kinder to Mom. I know she loved me. She could be so damn overbearing.

The door opened, and an elderly woman stood in the doorway.

My last words were, "Please tell Mom I love her."

6

JON FREDERICK
2:00 A.M.
SUNDAY, JULY 28, 2024
PIERZ

I was pacing the kitchen floor in boxer shorts, holding baby Cami in my arms, when my phone buzzed. I loved this little peanut of a girl, but she didn't sleep for more than two hours at a time, and it was exhausting. I rocked our four-month-old as I listened to my boss and ultimately agreed to go to work.

By the time the call ended, Serena was awake and wearily standing in front of me in her pajamas, reaching for our girl. I had turned in my resignation for the Bureau of Criminal Apprehension shortly before Cami's birth. The agreement allowed me to burn up my vacation and paternity leave first so I could maintain my state benefits for as long as possible. By August, I had to either leave or rescind my resignation and return to work. I wanted to walk away after the way our last case ended, but Serena very much wanted me to stay with the BCA so we could keep our insurance. She handled our finances and knew the significance of the benefits package.

"Are you going to work?" she asked. Cami stopped fussing, as if she sensed the seriousness of the conversation. Depression had engulfed Serena after Cami's birth, and while she was present with all her heart for the kids, I took the brunt of it. And that's okay. I just wish it weren't there at all. There were some good days, and she was never cruel or mean. Serena was going through the motions of being a good mom, but the fire in her eyes had gone out. When my efforts weren't enough, she'd give me this heart-wrenching look of disappointment that cut right through me. And I was there every day, changing the baby, making meals, entertaining the kids, assembling baby products. I felt bad for Serena. She's the kindest person I've ever met, and even in her despondent state, she had moments of sincere contrition. We both knew it was coming since the melancholy and loss of pleasure occurred after every birth. She didn't want to take medication because she didn't want to stop breastfeeding.

"I'm going to work," I said, with some sense of relief.

"Good. You should think about getting a vasectomy."

"I love you too," I joked.

"I'm serious," she responded.

"Honey, I need to change and hit the road. There was an assault in Detroit Lakes. I'll be back as soon as I can. Warn Nora and Jackson that I probably won't see them at all tomorrow." After kissing Serena and the top of Cami's head, I rushed upstairs to change. I threw together a carry-on suitcase full of clothes and grooming items, as I had no idea what was in store for me. I miss my time with the kids when I start a new case. Nora is an insightful and loving nine-year-old who is closest in personality to me. She becomes fixated on a task until it's resolved. Jackson is a tender-hearted, compassionate boy who is kind to everybody. I snuck into Nora's and Jackson's rooms and kissed them before I left. My family was the force that helped me survive the life-threatening moments at work.

When I returned downstairs, I stopped in my tracks and, for a moment, watched Serena breastfeed Cami. It's such a heartwarming event. Our little tornado of a baby was so sweet and huggable at times. I kissed Serena one more time.

She responded with, "I'm serious about the vasectomy. Do you want me to make an appointment for you?"

"I'd like more than two minutes at two in the morning to think about getting sterilized."

"I've been on the pill forever, and it's not good for me." She hesitated, "I can't do this again. The depression gets worse with each baby."

"I promise to think about it."

She looked disappointed but nodded and softly reassured me, "I love you, John."

"I love you, too." I needed that. As I drove away, I felt a sense of loss at the thought of never having another child. I loved our kids, but there was a lot to think about. Serena has suffered miscarriages between children, and her depression was significantly worse every time. Our home life was unsustainable. We could survive for a while, like all new parents do, but could we do it again? I couldn't reconcile asking Serena to stay home with one more baby. I didn't have the right to expect her to do something I couldn't do myself. Right now, we don't need any more kids. We need more parents.

4:20 A.M.
DUNTON LOCKS COUNTY PARK, DUNTON LOCKS
COUNTY ROAD
(ONE MILE NORTH OF SHADY HOLLOW) DETROIT
LAKES

Detroit Lakes was initially called "Detroit." The name was changed to Detroit Lakes in 1927 to avoid confusion with the slightly more popular city in southern Michigan. Detroit Lakes was once a resting place on the Red River oxcart trail that ran from Winnipeg to St. Paul. The trail was used from 1820 for fifty years until it was replaced by railway. I appreciate cruising through this pouring rain in a warm car, on a tar road, as opposed to riding in a cart on wooden wheels on a muddy trail. The temperature had been in the eighties earlier in the day, and it was still in the seventies when I arrived at Dunton Lakes County Park. tonight. I met with Chief of Police Steve Lee and Becker County Sheriff

26

Todd Miller at the home of Candy Zapzalka-Ahles. Sheriff Miller asked, "How did the BCA get involved in this case so quickly?"

"You didn't ask for help?" I looked at the two officers.

They shook their heads. Chief Lee added, "We're not turning help from the BCA away. We've got officers canvassing the area for clues, but with this relentless rain, we have no footprints. We have a naked woman discovered on a porch who's been beaten and shot. Her last words were, 'Tell Mom I love her,' before she went unconscious."

Sheriff Miller added, "She could have come from any direction. She might have been dumped out of a car or assaulted in the nearby woods. We've got a search team implementing a plan. I'd prefer you didn't interfere. My team talks to each other as they canvass an area. If you walk in, they'll assume you're a suspect."

"No problem. If you don't mind, I'd like to talk to the woman who found her."

Sheriff Miller paused. "Who called you into the case?"

"Sean Reynolds, the BCA Superintendent. He didn't say who called him. I assumed it was law enforcement."

"Somebody knows something about this case that we don't have yet," the chief remarked.

"I'll call my supervisor." I stepped a few feet away from the duo and called, but Sean didn't answer. I returned and told them, "Looks like I won't have an answer until morning. If you don't mind, I'm going to head off on my own for a bit, and I'll get back to you if I discover something. I'd appreciate the same. I'm not interested in getting credit for this. I just want this perp behind bars."

We exchanged numbers, and I spent the next thirty minutes talking to the seventy-eight-year-old who found a young woman on her porch. Candy had pulled the victim inside and covered her with a blanket to comfort her. Candy held the young woman's head and spoke to her until the ambulance arrived. Candy was a reminder of the tremendous amount of good in the world. She was also one more person traumatized by the terrible person who committed this crime.

Six months ago, this case could have been solved relatively quickly. Google had a geofencing program we could use to go back and identify all the cell phones in an area at any point in history. The technology was so good you could zero in on a location the size of a house and watch the cell phone numbers enter and leave on a specific day. Over 35,000 geofence warrants were issued in 2023, which was overwhelming for Google. On May 15, 2024, just two months ago, Google announced they would no longer be cooperating with these warrants. Their statement was, "We don't want to be the repository for the world." Further, the American Civil Liberties Union pointed out that innocent people are swept into these searches. An appeal court is presently reviewing Google's refusal to comply with these warrants. As an investigator, I would like to see the warrants continue, but I anticipate that Google will win this case. Courts don't allow "blanket subpoenas." In other words, they don't allow investigators to go on a fishing expedition to find evidence without an identified suspect, and we didn't have one yet.

7:00 A.M.
CENTRACARE ST. CLOUD HOSPITAL, 1406 6TH
AVENUE NORTH, ST. CLOUD

As a result of her life-threatening injuries, the victim had been airlifted to CentraCare in St. Cloud. I needed to catch up to her, so I put the siren on and drove two hours south. She still had not been identified. Her prints weren't in the system. There was no missing person report on a young woman in the area. But someone had an idea of who she was, and that person had contacted my supervisor. I wanted to see who I'd find in the waiting room in St. Cloud.

After going through the metal detector, I found the large figure of a man slumped in a chair with his eyes closed in the emergency room. All six feet, six inches of the mob boss Roan Caruso sat right in front of me. Roan was the one who contacted Sean and requested my involvement in the case. I couldn't get away from this guy. Knowing the victim was in her twenties, I assumed his son, Lorenzo, had something to do with this. Lorenzo had a history of abusive behavior with women.

Standing directly in front of him, I asked, "Why me? I'm not cutting Lorenzo any slack on this. That was our agreement; no favors."

"Lorenzo didn't do this. I don't know for sure if it's Eliana, but if it is, I want to get in front of it." He wiped sleep from the corner of his eyes with his thumb and forefinger.

"You strongly suspect it is, or we wouldn't be here."

Roan sat up and gave the waiting room a once-over to make sure no one was nearby. The only others in the waiting room at the moment were two Somali women and a Somali teen sitting a dozen feet from us.

"Roan, I need to know the Genovese Mafia didn't have anything to do with this." The Genovese were the most powerful mob family in the United States. Roan had killed three members in the past.

"No. Not at all. But I need Lorenzo cleared of suspicion."

I sat down next to him and nudged him. "This is a no-win situation for me. You're going to kill me if you're wrong—just to save your son."

"I promise I won't."

I didn't know if I believed him, but I asked, "What happened?"

"Lorenzo bought an engagement ring for Eliana. They were staying at a lodge on the lake. Big romantic night planned. Eliana got a little jealous over someone he was talking to online and stormed out. Lorenzo did the domestic violence class crap and let her go, just like he'd been instructed. Let her come back on her own and all that bullshit. He gave her a call to see if she was okay and realized her phone was still in the room. He called Carmel Cano to see if she'd heard from her, but she hadn't. Carmel's her best friend. Eliana would have found a way to contact her. Carmel offered to come help search for her. When they were about to give up, they were told someone heard over the scanner that the body of a young woman was found near Highway 53 in Detroit Lakes. That's when Lorenzo called me."

"Why isn't Lorenzo here?"

"There's no point in showing his face until we know he can visit her." Roan nodded toward the parking lot.

"I need to talk to him. The victim's in bad shape, and I don't want her dying here alone. I need some identifying features."

"You know what she looks like," Roan said.

"She's badly beaten and shot. Her family deserves to be here, but I'm not calling anyone and suggesting their daughter might die until her identity is clear."

"All right." He tapped on his phone. "He's outside. I'll have him meet you at the entry."

When I exited the emergency room, Roan's handsome son was waiting. "I didn't do this," he blurted out. "Is she going to be okay?"

"I don't know."

"I need to see her," he pleaded.

"First, I need to verify it's her. Give me something to identify her."

"Dark hair, brown eyes, five feet four."

"More specific," I demanded.

"She was wearing a brand-new dress, light brown."

"This woman was naked. Any birthmarks or tattoos?"

The news bothered him, and he shut down for a second before he softly replied, "Yeah, she has a tattoo of hummingbird on her left ankle with the initials BS right below it. Her ancestors lived in the Mexican state of Baja California Sur, and BS is the abbreviation." Trying for some sad humor, he said, "I said you could go with BJS, but she went with BS—almost as bad."

Finding no humor in the situation, I told him, "Stick around. I'll see if I can verify it's her."

"Can you come out and tell me right away?" Lorenzo asked.

"No, probably not. Give me your cell number, and I'll text when I know. I need to talk to you, but not right now. And you won't be allowed to visit her until we have an idea of what happened." If Lorenzo wasn't the one who assaulted her, this had to be devastating for him.

When I returned to the emergency room, I flashed my badge at the security guard, and she took me to the room where the assault victim lay. A young woman in her early twenties of Hispanic ancestry lay in a baby blue hospital gown half-covered with a blanket. Her face was bruised, and strands of her dark hair were matted with blood. Her jaw had been wired shut. Her right hand was disfigured, as if it had been pounded with a large rock. She wasn't dying, and she wasn't living. She just *was*. Still, the doctor informed me this was progress from where she was a couple of hours ago. Eliana had stabilized but remained unconscious. I sat and watched her breathe. After seeing her, I was doubly committed to finding the predator who hurt her.

A doctor entered the room, and I told her, "I need to see her left ankle. We're trying to identify her."

She lifted the bottom of the blanket so I could look at Eliana's legs. The left ankle had a hummingbird with the initials "BS" below.

I nodded, and the doctor covered her back up. The victim was confirmed to be Eliana Maria Castillo. I asked, "Have they done a sexual assault evidence kit yet?

"Yes. It was just completed," the doctor replied.

I didn't want to leave Eliana alone. There were people out there who loved her. In addition, her assailant might try to finish the job if he heard she was still alive. I would request an armed guard and remain in her room until that officer came to relieve me.

After the doctor departed, I was immediately on the phone, contacting Eliana's family. When finished, I texted Lorenzo and told him it was Eliana. I instructed him to tell Roan I was done talking to them both for the time being, but Lorenzo needed to stay in touch. I then contacted the officers in Detroit Lakes and shared the information I had about the victim, including the fact that Lorenzo and Eliana had an argument at the lodge. I got on the phone and left a message for my supervisor. "I want Dr. Amaya Ho to come and look at Eliana..." Dr. Ho was the medical examiner the BCA used for most of our homicide cases. Even though Eliana wasn't dead, Dr. Ho specializes in identifying the types of weapons used to create wounds.

I made sure Eliana's tattooed ankle was comfortably covered.

The ancient Aztecs believed hummingbirds were warriors who journeyed between the physical world and the spiritual realm. According to legend, those brave enough to make the journey risked death at every turn.

Finally, an officer arrived to relieve me. As we shook hands, I said, "Jon Frederick. I need to get home, get some sleep, and hug my kids before I return. Call me if there's any change in her status. I didn't catch your name."

"Mike Haney."

7

JON FREDERICK
5:00 P.M.
SUNDAY, JULY 28, 2024
PIERZ

Serena had very kindly let me sleep in. I then spent some time entertaining Cami, Jackson and Nora before I had to leave again. We enjoyed the sunny 78-degree day as a family, and I was now dropping them off at Serena's parents' house for supper. My nine-year-old daughter was in the backseat, right behind Serena, and I was singing Taylor Swift's "Shake It Off" with her to make her laugh. A deer crept to the side of the road, so I stopped and waited for it to cross. I turned to Nora. "We question chickens crossing, but no other animals. What did the deer yell when she was about to cross the road?"

"What?" Nora asked with a smirk.

"Hang on for deer life!"

After a groan, Nora said, "Why *do* deer go on the road?"

"Typically, they are running from predators in the woods. Deer are not great fighters, but they can run. So, if they hear anything that seems like a threat, they run. Sometimes to the road."

Serena interjected, "The Lakota consider deer spirit animals and believe they are attracted to those with strong intuition. Deer trust their intuition and run. They represent gentleness and sensitivity in the Lakota culture."

Nora asked, "So, who in the Explorer has great intuition?"

I told her, "You, Jackson, and your mother. Cami and I are working on it."

My SUV was approaching an irrigation system that was spraying water on the road on Serena and Nora's side of the car. We were still one hundred feet away. As a joke, I hit the window buttons on their side to lower them.

The devastated look Serena gave me shocked me. I quickly put the windows back up, and she tearfully buried her head in her sleeve.

Unable to see her mother's response, Nora remarked, "Not funny, Dad."

"I promise I would have had them rolled up before the water hit."

"Well, that's as bad as your dad jokes," Nora laughed.

Not wanting the kids to pick up on Serena's response, I redirected the conversation. "That reminds me. Do you remember the show we watched on Dubai and Abu Dhabi?"

"Yeah," Nora responded.

"What's the difference between the two?"

"Abu Dhabi is the capital, and Dubai is where rich people vacation," Nora recited.

"Folks in Dubai don't like The Flintstones, but Abu Dhabi do."

Jackson chimed in, "Bad dad jokes."

I pulled into the Bell driveway. "Okay, Amigos, we're here. Nora, you walk Jackson in, and I'll carry in the baby. Mom and I need to talk a little before I go to work."

Serena's mother looked back at the car toward Serena as I handed Cami off. "Is she okay?"

"No. She isn't. But I need to get to work, and I want to talk to her before I leave."

I returned to the vehicle and told Serena, "I'm sorry."

"You don't love me anymore," she whispered. "I get it."

"I love you as much as ever. I was just trying to lighten the mood. I was being stupid. I thought you'd laugh and punch me in the arm or something."

"It's easy for you, with your six-foot plus strong build and intimate sky blue eyes. You have that warm voice with just the right hint of sarcasm at times. I can only imagine the attention you get. And now you've got this slug of a wife. You're sick of me."

"No, I'm not. The reality is that if anyone had to choose between being with your compassionate kindness, and my obsessiveness, I'd be left in the dust. Regardless, I'm going through this with you, and I want to help you. There are three things you can do to battle depression. Exercise, therapy, and medication." I didn't need to remind her she wasn't doing any of them.

"I don't have any energy," she replied. "I'm exhausted all the time."

"I need you to fight this. You've been through it before." Serena struggled with depression after each child.

"Not this bad," she mumbled.

"I know. You won't have to, ever again. I'll get a vasectomy. We'll talk more later, but I have to be at work now. We need the money. You'll be in my thoughts every free minute." I was trying to think of a solution. The odds of us connecting for a call when I had a free minute, and the kids were giving her a break were slim. "I'll write a letter, take a picture of it, and text it to you every day. So, you'll have something you can look at."

"You don't have to." She gave me a doleful look.

"I know. But I want to. I'd love to."

"That's sweet," she said. "You could just send an email."

"I'm a better writer. Emailing is for people you don't really want to talk to. I'll save the letters and give them to you." Serena has a hope chest where she's kept all my love notes since high school.

"I'd like that." Her emerald eyes were still glassy. "You have to get to work." She stepped out of the car, and I walked her to the house, kissing her before departing.

7:00 P.M.
BECKER COUNTY JAIL, 925 LAKE AVENUE, DETROIT LAKES

The Detroit Lakes police chief informed me, "There was a struggle in the room Lorenzo and Eliana were staying in. No blood, but a hole was punched in the wall, and there was broken glass on the floor."

"No blood?" I tried to visualize the fight.

"No. It looks like a fight occurred there, but the shooting didn't. Eliana's cell phone, purse, car keys, and suitcase were in the room. Her car was in the parking lot. The parking lot camera showed a guy entering her car and popping the trunk after the assault occurred. We can see the trunk slightly open, but we have no view of what's inside. As the man approached, a semitruck pulled between the camera and the car, blocking the view. It was dark and raining, so we didn't have a clear view of the guy. The entire clip of the man lasts less than five seconds. When the semi pulled away, the man was gone. I have no idea what he was looking for."

"What does Lorenzo say about it?"

"He's refusing to talk to us. Lorenzo said he'll speak to you."

"Alright. I'll see what he has to say."

"I'll be on the other side of the glass," the Chief said.

Lorenzo sat at a square table in the interview room, looking exhausted. He ran his hand through his thick, dark hair as he said, "I didn't hurt Eliana. I love her."

"What were you doing in Detroit Lakes?" I asked. "We'll be sifting through the details, so you might as well be honest with me."

"I was going to ask her to marry me. I rented the lodge, and we had a second-floor balcony overlooking the lake. Ellie wanted to go to the arts and crafts fair on Sunday since she knows a bunch of the vendors. I wanted to give her the chance to show off the rock I'd bought her."

"Did you drive together?"

"No, I had fished the lake with friends on Thursday for my last unattached hurrah, so Ellie drove here on her own. She wanted to stop at this dress shop on the way over. I think she had a pretty good idea of what was coming."

"What was the argument about? Be honest."

"I was frustrated that she was taking so long." He rubbed his forehead. "I checked our phone app and saw she was sitting at a coffee shop. I was pissed. She knew I was waiting. I was bored and decided to look at some porn. I think I do it sometimes just to get back at her. And, of course, as soon as I opened it up, she walked in and saw it. Just plain bad," he paused, "luck. She took my laptop and left. I let her go. Thought I'd give her time to calm down." He sighed, "I never saw her again. I need to see her, man. Is she going to make it?"

"I don't know. She's stabilized."

"Can you get me in to see her?" Lorenzo begged.

"Not yet. Right now, you're the prime suspect. I've seen some of the damage you've done to your ex-lovers." I worked with a witness in a previous case who had her nose broken by Lorenzo when she refused to have sex with him. Lorenzo's dad talked her out of bringing charges against him. "I would never hurt Ellie. I loved her. Wanted to marry her."

"If she grabbed the laptop and left, how did the room get trashed?"

"I did that after she was gone. I was so torqued I saw red. I had everything I've ever wanted, and I blew it. I drove around and searched the bars. When I got back to the room, I couldn't take it anymore. I destroyed the relationship. Might as well destroy all the fanfare, too."

I considered everything he'd said. "Where is your laptop?"

"Who the hell knows? Probably lying out there in the rain somewhere."

8

JON FREDERICK
10:00 A.M., MONDAY, JULY 29, 2024
CENTRACARE ST. CLOUD HOSPITAL
1406 6TH AVENUE NORTH, ST. CLOUD

Mike Haney called from the St. Cloud Hospital this morning and told me Eliana Castillo was regaining consciousness, which made my heart sing.

I stopped and spoke to the doctor briefly before entering the room.

"How is Eliana doing?" I asked.

"She'll survive, but it will be a long recovery. She's young. I have a feeling her body will heal before her mind does. She was hit on the head with some kind of object. Her hand was pummeled, probably with the same object. And then she was shot three times with a low-caliber gun, twice in the abdomen and once in the chest. Close to lethal, but it just missed. All the bullets have been removed."

"What did the Sexual Assault Nurse Examiner find?"

"Eliana was sexually assaulted." The doctor sighed and continued, "It appears she was assaulted with a smooth, hard object, probably in addition to a penis. We're waiting for the lab

38

to tell us if there was any DNA evidence."

Somebody wanted her to suffer and die.

When I entered the room, Mike greeted me in a whisper. "Eliana's sleeping." He'd obviously been up all night. "Her friend Carmel Cano visited briefly, along with Catania Turrisi. I wasn't sure whether to let them in. Eliana's parents approved, so I did. They said Carmel is Eliana's best friend."

"Let's not have Catania visit for now. Cat is Lorenzo's mom, and he's the prime suspect at the moment. I want to know exactly what happened first. Anything interesting come out of the visit?"

Mike looked bothered.

"What happened?" I asked.

"Eliana can't speak or write. Catania asked her if she knew who did this. Eliana was quiet for a long time and then circled her finger by her ear. Like people do when they signal 'crazy.' Carmel whispered something to her, but I couldn't hear it. Eliana fell back asleep. They waited for a bit and then departed."

"Go home and get some sleep. I'll stay with her."

"Call me when you need to go. I don't care if I'm getting paid. I don't want her to be left alone," Mike said.

I stood over Eliana, listening to her labored breathing. There was a straight-line bruise on her forehead. After I was done speaking to Eliana, I'd need to find Carmel and discover what Eliana meant by the gesture. *Was the argument between Lorenzo and Eliana related to the assault?* I have worked cases where someone left home after an argument and was assaulted by a stranger.

I sat and wrote a quick note to Serena.

I love you, Serena. I start missing you when I walk out the door and you're not with me. If I don't tell you I love you enough, it's simply because I'm so comforted in your presence that it feels like my life's goal has been met. When we're apart, I think about how I am often reminded of your beauty. Inconspicuous moments I seldom remark on, like watching you pull your hair into a ponytail or hang a picture. You are my desire, and I will always love you.

Jon

I took a picture of the letter and scanned it to her.

I scanned through a list of calls made to and from Eliana's phone on the day of the assault. There was a number that only appeared once and wasn't identified. When I called, a man answered, "Hello, who is this?"

"Bureau of Criminal Apprehension Investigator Jon Frederick. Your number was taken off the cell phone of a woman who's in the hospital fighting for her life. Please identify yourself."

"Donny Nyguen. What happened?"

"She was assaulted and left for dead."

"That's terrible. Was it her gangster boyfriend?"

"I don't know," I told him. "Why did you call her?"

"I wanted to see my son. I've paid her thousands of dollars in child support. I deserve to tell him my side of the story."

"Did Eliana allow you a visit?"

The phone fell silent. I'm the master at waiting out silence. Donny finally said, "What is she saying?"

"Eliana isn't talking." I didn't bother to tell him I might still be able to communicate with her.

"She said we'd work something out. She had to go. I think her and her thug boyfriend had something going."

"Can I pick up my son to support him? Imagine what that poor boy's going through."

"What's the custody arrangement?"

"I told her two years ago that if I could stop paying child support, I'd never talk to either of them again. But my rights weren't legally terminated. Ellie and I were going to work something out."

It bothered me that Donny was constantly feeling out exactly how much I knew during our conversation. Eliana's failure to bring resolution to Donny's parenting status meant that if she died, Donny would get custody of her son. People become spiteful and can get violent in custody cases. I needed to protect her son until Donny was cleared as a suspect. I said, "If Eliana wants to talk to you, she will."

"I thought she couldn't talk."

"Yeah, that's a tough break, isn't it?" The idea of Luis's father worming in for custody while she recovered annoyed me.

Eliana slowly awakened, and I introduced myself. "I'm Investigator Jon Frederick. I've been told you can't speak or write, so I'm going to ask you to blink hard once for *yes* and twice for *no*. Do you understand me?"

She blinked hard once, "Yes."

"Did Lorenzo hurt you?"

She hesitated and then blinked, "Yes."

Roan isn't going to be happy to hear this. I need to make sure I have this right. "Is Lorenzo the reason you're in the hospital?"

Eliana blinked once, "Yes," then twice, "No."

"Did Lorenzo rape you?"

"No."

"Do you know who raped you?"

"Yes," she blinked, then, "No."

"Donny called. Did you agree to let him see your son?'

"No," she blinked twice. Her vitals raised on the monitors.

Not wanting to send her into crisis, I assured Eliana, "No worries. He's not taking Luis on my watch." Changing gears, I asked, "Who is crazy?" Okay, bad question. "Is 'crazy' someone you know through work?"

Her heart rate escalated further, and her breathing became heavy. Eliana was moving her thumb up and down and gesturing toward her foot.

I moved toward the foot of the bed and lifted the sheet. Her heel was black and cut up from her barefoot adventure in the woods.

A nurse hurried into the room and directed me, "You need to leave her alone. She's healing." I raised my hands in retreat and backed away.

"Can I stay if I sit in the chair and stop asking questions?"

Eliana blinked, "Yes."

I shut up and let the nurse do her work.

Eliana fell back to sleep.

I called the Detroit Lakes police chief and shared what I had learned from my conversation with Eliana.

"I was looking at the recording of your interview with Lorenzo. When did he and Eliana have sex?"

"They didn't have sex that night. The argument started when she entered the room. Why do you ask?"

"The ultraviolet light we scanned his room with suggested Lorenzo had sex with somebody in the bed. We have her on the hotel video running out of the room. He's lying. I'm thinking he raped her, and she ran out of the room. He found her, dragged her out to the woods, and shot her. Lorenzo's lying, and we're hauling him in."

After I hung up, I called Lorenzo. He immediately asked, "Can I visit her yet? C'mon man, I've got to see her."

"No. Eliana's saying you hurt her."

"Well, no. I mean, we were wrestling for my laptop, and it slipped out of my hands and hit her in the forehead."

That explains the straight-line bruise on her forehead.

Lorenzo continued, "Unless she means I hurt her by being on OnlyFans."

"You need to be straight with me. You told me you were looking at porn. You were talking to a woman on OnlyFans?"

"Yeah. It's basically Pornhub live. I was talking to this woman who calls herself Londyn Lust. I'm not proud of it, but I imagine I'm her biggest benefactor. I wanted to quit, but she begged me to stay. I wasn't just another guy to her. I was tryin' to help a young woman out."

"Was she at the hotel?"

"No," Lorenzo responded adamantly. "Londyn was at home, in bed."

"Who did you have sex with in the hotel room?"

The line went quiet.

"Law enforcement knows you had sex with someone in the room. I can't help you if you can't be honest with me. Everything will come to the surface. They'll do DNA testing on the sheets."

"Shiiiit." He dragged out the word. "It was a stupid mistake. It must have been about two or three in the morning when Carmel and I got back to the room. She was going to sleep in her car, and I told her she could just sleep in the other half of the king-size bed. We planned on continuing the search as soon as we woke up. During the night, I got upset, and she hugged me. One thing led to another. You can't tell Ellie. It meant nothing. We were both messed up. I think I'm a sex addict."

I looked over at Eliana. She was resting peacefully. I think I'll restrict her visitors to immediate family. Someone brutally assaulted her, and now her closest two friends have betrayed her.

Lorenzo continued, "I was torn up over losing Eliana, and it just happened. It's hard for me to turn my back when it's right there. I think it's got to be easier for guys who aren't attractive."

"What a burden you carry," I remarked.

"Now you're just pulling my chain. I meant it would be easier if it weren't always so easy."

"This isn't about you, Lorenzo." Getting back to task, I asked, "When did you arrive in Detroit Lakes?"

"I came up with friends on Thursday and fished for walleyes. We limited out."

"Any of your friends dislike Eliana?"

"No, they all think she's too good for me."

"Who did you fish with?"

"Dante, Ross, and Ross's brother Larry."

"Tell me about your friends."

"Dante and Ross are studs." Lorenzo confidently bragged, "Almost in as good as shape as I am. Larry's a bit out there, but the man knows boats and the lakes. "

"Did they all stick around Detroit Lakes?"

"Dante and Ross said they were headed back to the Twin Cities. I don't know what Larry did. If Ross isn't around, I don't spend any time with that nutbar Larry."

"What's Larry's last name?" "Nutbar" piqued my curiosity.

"McBride."

"Do you ever refer to him as Crazy Larry?" I questioned.

"We had to call him Crazy Larry because there's a racer named Larry 'Spiderman' McBride. Different guy."

"What does Crazy Larry think about Eliana?"

"Hates her. Even took me to a strip club to get over her. Nothin' against Ellie. He's like that about all women."

"You said your friends loved her."

"I don't really consider Crazy Larry a friend. He's an incel guy."

That's not good. Incel stands for involuntary celibate. It's essentially a hate group of misogynistic men who feel that feminist women rule the world and are to blame for incels' lack of romantic and sexual success.

Lorenzo continued, "I've never been wild about Larry, but Ross is a great guy, and he's trying to get his brother out of his crazy online conspiracy theories, so we invited him along. If that peckerwood assaulted Eliana, I'll take care of him myself."

"Let us handle it. Where are you staying?"

"Residence Inn in Waite Park. I thought I'd stay close in case I get a chance to see Eliana."

"Okay."

After ending the call, I contacted the Detroit Lakes police chief and gave him Lorenzo's location. I needed to find Crazy Larry.

9

JON FREDERICK
8:00 A.M., TUESDAY, JULY 30, 2024
THE MARSH
15000 MINNETONKA BOULEVARD, MINNETONKA

Unable to track down Crazy Larry McBride, I got up early and drove to Minnetonka to speak to his brother. Ross worked at a seven-acre fitness center operated by the city of Minnetonka called The Marsh, which features a multistory baby blue meditation tower tucked into the northeast corner of the facility. We met in the weight room, which was unoccupied.

Ross was a bodybuilder who stood about five feet eight inches tall and had short, dark hair. He wore clean royal blue sweats and pristine white tennis shoes. I couldn't help thinking his clientele fared better financially than those who frequented the weight rooms I'd worked out at in the past. I explained that I was an investigator gathering information on Eliana Castillo's assault.

Ross said, "I'm so sorry to hear what happened to her. Eliana was a sweetheart. She was good for Lorenzo."

"How so?" I wondered.

"Lorenzo is just Lorenzo." He shrugged. "Ladies' man. Spoiled rich kid. But not a terrible guy. He liked hook-ups, and for the most part, nobody got hurt. A couple of lonely people together for a night. It's harmless."

"Not when you claim to be in a committed relationship."

"I'm not saying I approved of everything he did, but nobody's perfect. Lorenzo was a good friend, but he was also a piece of work. He implemented 'the Lorenzo plan,' as he called it."

"And what was that?"

"Never confirm a date." Ross paced as he spoke. "If it's important to her, she'll remember. The date has to be at least two days away to heighten her anticipation. Never text a chick three times in a row without a response. At some point, request a nude picture, but back off if she isn't comfortable. She will send one in the future, trying to make up during an argument. Save it in a file, but delete it from your phone so you can show her that you were respectful and deleted it. Never send one of yourself. And it's not lying if you don't actually say it. For example, if his girl asks if he was with another woman last night, he'll respond, 'I was at the Wolves game with Ross,' which may all be true, but he didn't answer the question. He had all these rules, and sadly, they seemed to work."

"And you don't mind having a friend that lies all the time?"

"We're all works in progress. It was entertaining to watch Lorenzo work his scheme. And in the last year, he's changed. He used to scan every environment for attractive women. He still does sometimes, but it's not automatic anymore. And Eliana's one of those people who is just fun. I used to tease him that he should send her my way if he ever dumps her."

"Were you ever with Eliana?"

"No." He gave me a pointed look. "Not my type."

"What is your type?"

"She's kind and caring. I like that a lot. But my type is male."

"Were you ever with Lorenzo?"

"No. He's not my type, either. Too thirsty. I'd be worried about ending up with a disease."

I could understand why Lorenzo liked Ross as a friend. Ross was fit, but offered no competition for women.

"What do you need from me?" he asked.

"Right now, I'm collecting alibis to rule out everyone who was in Detroit Lakes on the night Eliana was assaulted."

"I wasn't in Detroit Lakes that night. Dante and I were at Boom Days listening to music at Boom Island Brewing. They'll have us on camera. We headed back to the metro early Friday morning. Dante and I have been together for a year."

"Okay. Back to your brother. Why did Larry hang around Detroit Lakes?"

"He talked about seeing some band. I wouldn't have minded staying for the music, but I can only tolerate Larry in small doses. I haven't spoken to him since fishing."

"Tell me more about your brother."

"Do you think he had something to do with this?" Ross asked with sincere concern.

"I don't know. I'm gathering information." I could see the uncertainty in his eyes. He believed his brother could have done this.

"Larry's into all that far-right conspiracy bullshit. But I don't see him doing this. I hope to God not. Our dad was the voice of reason in our family. When Dad died, the house became a loony bin. Mom's the one who filled Larry's head with thoughts that women are just out to trap him. Maybe because she trapped Dad. I got the hell out of town. Larry assumes I'm gay because I've given up on women. The truth of the matter is, I'm gay because I'm attracted to men. I don't dislike women; I have great female friends. Logic doesn't work on Larry." Ross glanced out the window at the well-kept landscaping. "When we were kids, it was funny to have this redneck little brother. As I got older, I realized how damaged he was. All that online militant crap feeds the craziness."

I believed Ross. He didn't assault Eliana. He didn't fit the profile. He didn't have the kind of anger and jealousy that was acted out in the assault. I said, "I would greatly appreciate it if you'd talk to Larry and your mom and get an idea of what he was doing and who he was talking to. I don't want to see anyone else get hurt."

"I can tell Larry you want to talk to him if he calls."

"I'd prefer you didn't. But please call me if you hear from him. If he didn't do it, I could clear his name. Where does Larry live?"

"In Aurora with Mom."

After I recorded the address and Ross's phone number, I headed north to St. Cloud to meet with Eliana and forensic pathologist Dr. Amaya Ho.

10:30 A.M.
CENTRACARE ST. CLOUD HOSPITAL, 1406, 6TH AVENUE NORTH, ST. CLOUD

I met Dr. Amaya Ho at the St. Cloud Hospital. I waited outside the room as Amaya carefully studied Eliana's body.

Amaya finally called me back in and shared her findings. "There are a variety of injuries that appear to have been made by a round instrument. My guess is a hammer. The internal damage suggests the handle was smooth. Likely wood, not rubber."

"A framing hammer," I suggested. "The wood-handled hammers are generally cheaper." This implied that the person who used it wasn't employed in construction. Home builders don't buy cheap hammers.

We both looked to Eliana for a response, but she shook her head slightly as if she didn't remember.

Amaya continued, "I'm not sure how those injuries fit with the straight-line bruise across her forehead."

I held a small mirror in front of Eliana so she could see the bruise and asked, "Did the bruise on your forehead come from the laptop?"

Eliana blinked once. "Yes."

"Eliana and Lorenzo fought over his laptop before she left the hotel. In the struggle, it apparently struck her in the forehead."

Amaya asked, "Did that have anything to do with the rape?"

Eliana hesitated and then blinked, "No."

"Okay. That's helpful," Amaya kindly assured Eliana. "Do you remember how your hand was injured?"

Eliana blinked, "No."

"Do you remember who assaulted you?" I asked Eliana.

48

She didn't blink. Instead, she shrugged her shoulders.

Amaya said, "Give her another day or two. Her memory may be coming back." She turned to Eliana, "I'm going to make a mold of your hand. I'll use alginate, which is made from seaweed. It's safe to use on your skin. Once the mold hardens, I'll fill it with soft silicone rubber and use the rubber hand to examine devices that could have created your injuries. This way, I won't have to mess with you and ask you so many questions."

Eliana nodded.

10

JON FREDERICK
8:00 A.M. THURSDAY, AUGUST 1, 2024
ST. CLOUD SURGICAL CENTER
1526 NORTHWAY DRIVE, ST. CLOUD

I called Donny Nguyen's wife, Eve Fang, from the waiting room. She'd kept her clan name, which is common for Hmong couples. I was curious about what she had to say about Donny.

"I'm Jon Frederick, Bureau of Criminal Apprehension Investigator. I have a couple of questions about Donny if you have a minute. You can call me Jon."

"Donny had nothing to do with the assault. Was she even assaulted?" Eve demanded. "And you can call me Mrs. Fang."

"Eliana was brutally assaulted."

"Donny told you he was home with our family all night. You checked his phone. What did you discover?" Eve questioned aggressively.

I had checked the phone. "The phone never left your home all night." I wanted to know if she would say he accidentally left it at home.

"Okay, you have your evidence. Why are you calling?"

"He didn't make any calls," I pointed out.

"Of course, he didn't. He didn't have to. Donny was home. He's a medical technician. Donny could take calls all night if he wanted to. When we first dated, he was coming and going at all hours, so I drew the line. I told him, 'If you want to be with me, you can't take any work calls after your shift ends. You take one call, and I'm leaving.' I'm an RN, so I'm the breadwinner, and I need to know he will be home with the kids if I have to go in. He was worried about losing his job," she crowed. "I told him, 'They'll never fire you. Everybody's short of medical help. They can't afford to.' And guess what? He shuts his phone off when he gets home, and he's still employed. And we're all happier."

"Were you home that night?"

"Yes. Donny already told you that."

"I noticed he doesn't have a lot of calls from anyone but you. What's the story with his family?"

"They shun him for fathering a child outside of wedlock. We moved on. He has his family now."

"Donny was the one who asked for contact."

"You're kidding."

"I am not."

"We'll see about that," Mrs. Fang hissed. "Leave us alone. Any further calls can be addressed to our attorney." She hung up. Donny claims he was home all night, and I couldn't disprove it. So, for the moment, that was a dead end.

The last couple of days have not been great. Crazy Larry McBride was nowhere to be found. Larry lived with his mother, Molly. She was distressed over not seeing Larry for several days and was convinced someone had kidnapped her poor son. Molly admitted that Larry had a history of spending a couple of weeks in the Twin Cities and returning without telling her. I told her that if she allowed our electronic crimes unit to search the home computer, I could see if there was any evidence of kidnapping. I asked them to check if Larry had posted anything on the assault. Incel is categorized as a terrorist group in the United States due to the ties a couple of mass shooters have with the organization.

I did manage to eliminate Ross McBride and Dante Peterson

as suspects. Video footage from Boom Island Brewing provided alibis for both at the time of the assault.

Serena responded to my love letter by sending me the following message: "I chipped a tooth, so now I look like an old hag. I feel fat and ugly and not deserving of your kindness."

I texted: "You're beautiful. You need to destroy this note and send me another. If my letters elicit this type of response, I will not send another. 'Thank you' would suffice."

In turn, I received the message, "Thank you."

I didn't want to be part of fostering her misery. I wanted her to feel loved and not dismiss my honest feelings for her.

11:15 A.M.

There was a cancellation, so they managed to get me in today for my vasectomy. I was at the surgical center in the recovery room. Serena left briefly to pick up some groceries and then was going to take me home. I drifted in and out of sleep for a while. Eventually, I felt coherent enough to leave.

The door opened, and I was about to tell Serena I was good to go when I saw Roan Caruso's hulking figure enter. "You had my son arrested," he spat out.

"I'm doing my job. It includes working closely with law enforcement agencies."

"They're going to nail him for Eliana's assault. It would be different if he had anything to do with it. He's an innocent man sitting in the Becker County jail."

Serena burst into the room and yelled at Roan, "Get the hell out of here! Go now, or I'll scream."

Roan glared at me and left.

"I am so sorry," Serena said. "Was he going to kill you?"

"No. That was a message that he can get to me when I'm vulnerable."

"I'm sorry," Serena said. "I'm going to call your dad and have him watch the house tonight."

My dad was a veteran who never hesitated to show up as an armed guard upon request. He didn't enter the house and was never in sight, so his armed presence wouldn't scare the children. It was probably not necessary, but I wasn't going to argue.

11

ELIANA CASTILLO
10:00 A.M., FRIDAY, AUGUST 2, 2024
CENTRACARE
ST. CLOUD HOSPITAL, ST. CLOUD

That damn Donny had an attorney, and he was trying to arrange a visit with my son. Even though I could have Lorenzo's Mafia family on my side, the contingency would be returning to Lorenzo. Pieces of what happened that night are slowly coming back to me, but it's mixed into this weird hallucination. I honestly don't believe I'll ever be able to offer an accurate account of the assault. I remember feeling so hurt by Lorenzo, and I remember his laptop flying into my head. At some point that night, I think I saw Crazy Larry. I also saw a forty-foot troll and a bear and heard a mellow cow, a frantic bloodhound, and crickets, lots of crickets.

I glanced over at the man sitting in the chair by my bed. He kind of reminded me of Jason Bourne. Was Bourne a good guy or a bad guy? I only caught the last one, and I think my date and I started making out about ten minutes into it. The man in my room was wearing a gun. My heart started racing. I knew him. I saw him that night.

A nurse rushed into the room and studied the monitors with concern. She turned to the man and asked, "What happened?"

"Nothing," he responded.

The nurse asked me, "Is this man bothering you?"

"Yes," I blinked.

She addressed the man. "Sir, you need to leave."

The man turned to me. "I'm Mike. Do you remember me?"

"No," I blinked. But I knew his name was Mike. *How did I know that?*

"Leave right now," the nurse directed.

"She needs protection," he argued.

"It's not going to be you."

I cried as he left. The man who assaulted me could have been sitting right next to me, and I never would have known it.

Mom was soon back in the room. She lay next to me in bed and said, "It's going to be okay. Luis is safe. He's with Destiny. I'll be here with you. No worries." I snuggled my injured body into hers as best I could.

12

JON FREDERICK
JON FREDERICK
10:00 A.M., MONDAY, AUGUST 5, 2024
PIERZ

I was recovering from surgery. The lift restrictions were easier to abide by at work. At home, my kids expected me to pick them up and play.

Mike Haney agreed to meet me at the Morrison County Sheriff's office in Little Falls to answer some questions about what had occurred at the hospital last week.

Mike was a clean-cut man, twenty-three years of age. He wore a maroon polo shirt and blue jeans to the interview.

After introductions, I asked, "Where did you first meet Eliana Castillo?"

"She smashed into my bike just outside the DL Bike Shop."

"Were you hurt?" I asked.

"No. It was mounted onto the back of my Jeep. After we shared our information, I told her that if she had coffee with me, I'd forget about it."

"Wow. That was a kind gesture." Mike seemed a little embarrassed. He clearly had an attraction to Eliana.

Trying to downplay his feelings, he said, "Well, you know what it's like as a guy paying for insurance. If you make a claim, your rates triple. I've always said car insurance is a fine for being male."

"Do you belong to any organizations in the manosphere?"

"Manosphere?"

"It refers to a variety of online resources that oppose feminism."

"No—no." he shook his head. "Never. I didn't mean to—It's probably the same for women paying for insurance. I'm just sharing my experience."

"How do you go from Eliana smashing your bike to buying her coffee?"

"Honestly, she was pretty, but there was a sadness in her eyes that drew me in—an anxious discontent. I have an inquiring mind. I had to investigate."

That was an interesting observation, considering that she was expecting a marriage proposal at the time. Did Eliana know she was building a house of cards? "How did your coffeehouse date end?"

"Disappointingly," he said with a smile. "She told me she was about to be engaged, and I told her to go. I didn't see her again until she was in the hospital. When I heard there had been an attack, I offered to help the police search through the woods for evidence that night. I never even considered that Eliana was the victim. When she was identified, I volunteered to provide security."

"What did you do after you left the coffee shop?"

"My intention was to do the Young Life Triathlon in Detroit Lakes. I had planned to try a dry run of the course. The one-mile swim is the killer. But after my bike wheel was smashed, I realized I would never have the extra money to replace it in time for the event, so I was down in the dumps. I went to the Long Bridge Bar and had a Busch Light, then decided to drive to Hillman and look over the area I deer hunt in the fall."

"Was anyone with you?"

"No. I tried calling my dad from the hunting shack, but then I remembered it's rural Hillman—no phone reception. I did stop at Porky's on the way back."

Porky's is a bar located in an area referred to as "Bullshit Junction" near Hillman.

"Do you mind if I take your picture and text it to the bartender to verify?"

"No, not at all."

"I'd also like to confiscate your phone for the day to verify the towers it was bouncing off."

"Aww, come on. It is really a pain not to have a phone." He grimaced. "I'm on call for work. I'm trying to get a foot in the door with a department so I can land some steady employment."

"I'm dealing with a rape and an attempted murder. You're one of the last people to see the victim prior to the assault."

"I get it." Mike reluctantly handed over his phone. "Is there any possible way you could get this back to me soon? I really need the work and the money right now."

"I'll drive it to the BCA office today and put a rush on it. You could have it back tomorrow if you're willing to drive to the BCA headquarters in St. Paul to pick it up."

"I will."

After I took his picture, Michael Haney was on his way. He was respectful and seemed genuinely concerned about Eliana, but even psychopaths can make a good first impression, which is why I always check alibis.

I needed to get Mike's phone to our diagnostics lab at the BCA office in St. Paul. On my way south, I called Porky's and got a phone number I could text Mike's picture to.

The bartender called back and said, "I'm sorry, but I don't remember him. It was a week ago, and we have our walleye fish fry on Fridays. It's crazy busy…"

Mike doesn't have an alibi, but maybe his phone will provide one. After the call ended, I received a call from Molly McBride. "Larry's home, but he locked himself in his room, and he won't come out. Something's happened to my Larry, and I'm worried."

"Give me your address, and I'll be on my way."

"Railroad Avenue West. We're across the lake from St. James

Pit."

"Okay." Trivia related to the mining town of Aurora ran through my brain. Aurora is the poorest city in Minnesota. On the north edge of town is St. James Lake, a former mine pit stocked with trout that's about 380 feet deep. The water can be sixty degrees at the top and thirty-nine degrees a hundred feet down. Luigina "Jeno" Paulucci, inventor of Jeno's Pizza and Chun King Chow Mein, was born in Aurora. 1960s B-movie fans know the tall, buxom blond actress Francine York was born there. She went from being a Hamline graduate to a sweater model and a Bimbo's showgirl in LA. Francine appeared on the hottest shows of the era, including Perry Mason, Bewitched, Green Acres, and Batman. She never married, and her response to being asked why was, "They don't make Cinderella slippers in a size ten." Though, as a hopeless romantic, I believe Cinderella slippers come in all sizes. Aurora is one of the host sites of the Northern Lights Music Festival, which features professional opera, chamber music, and symphonic concerts. You can view the fluorescent northern lights from the venue on clear nights. It's a truly awe-inspiring event.

After I got Mike's phone to St. Paul, I needed to drive three and a half hours in the other direction to Aurora. I made a couple of calls, and it was agreed that I'd leave the phone at the Wright County Sheriff's Department in Monticello and then head north. The BCA would send an agent from St. Paul to retrieve it.

3:30 P.M.
WEST RAILROAD AVENUE, AURORA

I drove into the dirt driveway of a trailer house that sat on the edge of the St. James Mine Pit. The grass hadn't been mown in the recent past, and overgrown brush flanked each side of the trailer, keeping it out of view from the distant neighbors. A matte black, mud-covered truck with rusted hubcaps sat in the driveway. A bumper sticker on the tailgate read, *Wheels—own a home with, and a car without.* The sky was gray, and I could smell smoke from the Canadian wildfires when I got out of my vehicle. As I approached the trailer, I could see the outline of a noose hanging inside. I called the East Range Police Department, which serves the city of Aurora.

"I'm at the home of Molly and Larry McBride. I'm here to speak to Larry, and I can see a noose hanging in the house." I kept the officer on the line as I approached the front door. It was an old trailer. The light was off, and it was difficult to see what was occurring inside against the dark brown paneling. When I knocked, I heard a chair tip over. I yelled, "Are you okay?" but no one answered. The door was locked. I stepped back and kicked the door open. Pain radiated through my groin. I hoped to hell I hadn't torn open my stitches.

A wiry critter of a man hung by a noose in the living room. He was pulling hard on the noose, apparently now reconsidering suicide. I stood the chair beside him, lifted him by the legs, and guided him to it. While he stood on the chair, I went to the kitchen to retrieve a knife to cut him down. There was a basket of laundry on the kitchen table. I couldn't help noticing an ivory crochet dress that fit the description of the dress Eliana was wearing when she was assaulted. It seemed a little small for Eliana, but I was bothered that the dress was never found. I quickly looked at the tag—Tenné brand, size four. I grabbed a knife, ran back to Larry, carefully cut the rope that tightened his airway, and walked him outside. A squad car pulled up, and the officers ran to us.

Larry hunched over, gasped, and spit.

I told one of the officers of the East Range Department to call an ambulance and stay with Larry.

I recognized the second officer and pulled her aside. I was familiar with Rhonda from the time she worked at the Crow Wing County Jail while completing her law enforcement degree at Central Lakes College. I told her, "Larry McBride is a suspect in an attempted murder in Detroit Lakes. The victim's dress might be sitting on the kitchen table. I want this home secured until I can get a warrant."

"I will do everything I can to assist. I've told folks since I first arrived here that boy is going to kill someone."

Larry broke from the male officer and said, "I'm okay." He started walking toward the house.

I stepped in front of him. "Attempted suicide is a crime in Minnesota. We are securing the home as a crime scene." This wasn't entirely true since the crime was actually *aiding* an attempted suicide, but I was betting Larry wasn't intimately familiar with state statutes, and I needed to buy time to collect the dress as evidence.

"That's the stupidest thing I've ever heard," he argued. "How are you going to punish me—death?"

"I don't write the laws. I just enforce them. And you need to get to a hospital and make sure you didn't do permanent damage to your neck."

Rhonda stood solid with me, adding, "You're staying in a hospital tonight. We can't simply walk away from an attempted suicide and leave you here. We're securing the house until further notice."

"Bitch." Larry spat at her. "Just another Becky."

Rhonda appeared to be considering arresting him for assault.

"Feminist bullshit rules the world," Larry grumbled. "Men have no rights."

Rhonda told the male officer, "Get him out of here."

"Mom's gonna be pissed," Larry muttered as he was escorted away.

Rhonda furrowed her brow and shrugged her shoulders. "Nice guy," she said, her voice dripping with sarcasm.

"You could have had him arrested," I suggested.

"And put the burden of the suicide watch on the jail staff? No, if he's suicidal, he belongs in the hospital. Just another day of dealing with the McBrides. Who's Becky?"

"Incels divide women into 'Beckys' and 'Stacys.' Stacys are attractive, hostile, and unattainable for 80% of men. The majority of women are Beckys, and incels feel Beckys owe men attention and sex because even though they think they are better than men, they are inferior."

"Charming."

Molly McBride pulled into the driveway as the ambulance drove away. "Is he alright?"

"Yes," I answered. "But they'll hold him overnight in the

hospital. I had to kick in the door to get in and cut him down. We have secured the home as a crime scene, so you'll need to stay somewhere else tonight. Where did Larry get the dress?"

"I don't know what you're talking about," Molly said. Appearing concerned about her son, Molly asked Rhonda, "Essentia Health in Aurora?"

"Yes."

Molly turned to me. "Thank you," she said and departed.

I called The Nines clothing store in Detroit Lakes and confirmed that Eliana Castillo had purchased a dress that matched the description in a size four. I then drove to the courthouse to pick up a search warrant.

When I returned to the trailer, Rhonda told me, "Molly McBride's been inside. She must have gone straight to an attorney, who contacted us and ordered us to let her into her home. Molly left with a suitcase."

That was disappointing. "I imagine the evidence is gone now. I have a search warrant, so if she returns, I'll ask you to keep Molly outside until I'm done." I put on latex gloves and turned to Rhonda. "Please put your camera on and join me in the search for now."

I stepped into the kitchen and noticed the ivory dress was gone. Molly was quick to cover her son's tracks. Larry's cell phone and computer were gone. He had taken neither when he left. I wondered how much Molly knew about the assault. *Was Molly involved or just protecting her son?*

Larry's bedroom reminded me of the worst parts of my childhood. The dirty gray carpet was worn thin, and the walls were calf-shit brown. A similar gray carpet had covered my bedroom as a child. It had a stain where my older sister had thrown up. The combination of rug cleaner and whatever she had eaten stained the carpet, and it remained faded pink long after the mess was cleaned up, adorning my room from age eleven until I left home. I asked my dad about cutting away that spot. He responded, "You shouldn't be wasting your life in the house anyway." They did replace the carpet after I left home because "guests would be staying there." In the carpet world, dye rubbing off due to inadequate washing after dyeing is called "crocking."

Moving farther into the room as my brain went off on a carpet tangent, a small safe in the corner caught my attention, and I couldn't help wondering what was inside. Larry was unlikely to cooperate with sharing the combination, so I asked Rhonda, "Could you have someone sent here with tools to remove it and a two-wheeled cart to transport it? I don't trust that it will be here when we return if we leave without it."

"I'll take care of it." Rhonda looked at the floor around the safe and got on the phone.

I opened the dresser drawers to find old underwear and ratty T-shirts. I was glad to be wearing gloves. I showed Rhonda T-shirts that read, *We broke up, but we will always be cousins; I got pegged at Cracker Barrel; Camel Towing—when it's wedged in tight—call me; Trashy like your mom*, and *Hick with a Stick*. This last was the most concerning. I remarked, "Hard to believe he couldn't get a date." In the bottom drawer, I removed flannel shirts and discovered a homemade gun made from a pipe. *Unbelievable. Why was this gun still here?* My first thought was *Larry hadn't told his mom that he had shot Eliana.* They used to be called "zip guns." Now, criminals refer to them as "ghost guns." This was a crude gun that would fire .22 caliber cartridges—the same make Eliana was shot with. The zip gun explained why he hadn't killed her. They have terrible aim.

I called Rhonda over to ensure my bagging of the evidence was all on film. There was a circular metal cookie cutter with a metal *M* wired across the middle. It was charred, indicating it had been heated by a flame. A rancid smell hit me when I picked up the homemade branding iron. It smelled like death. I placed it in an evidence bag. At the very bottom of the drawer, I found a shirt in a clear Ziploc bag. I didn't open the bag but could see it was a baseball T-shirt, white with gold sleeves in a woman's size small. I showed it to Rhonda. "Are those small droplets of blood?"

"He has a previous victim," she surmised.

"I'll get it to the lab."

"I'll stay here until help comes to remove the safe," Rhonda said.

When I stepped outside, Molly McBride came running at me. "I talked to an attorney, and he told me you can't keep me out of my home."

I held up the search warrant. "Where's the dress?"

"What dress?" Molly scowled.

"Where's Larry's computer and cell phone?"

"How the hell would I know? Do I look like someone who spends a lot of time online?"

"Where did you go?"

Molly pointed to the warrant. "That warrant's for the house, not for me. Talk to my attorney."

8:30 P.M.
EAST RANGE POLICE DEPARTMENT
16 WEST 2ND AVENUE NORTH, AURORA

The main office for the East Range police is in Hoyt Lakes, but there is a satellite office in Aurora. I sat at the Aurora office, completing my paperwork for the day. When I was finally finished, the sun was starting to set. I wrote Serena a quick note:

Dearest Serena,

I'm looking at a crescent moon in the setting sun. The surrounding sky is pink, fading to orange, with the black silhouette of aspen trees on the horizon. It reminds me of you. I only need to see a little of you to know your beauty and how much you mean to me. You take my breath away. Thank you for being exactly who you are.

Love, Jon

13

JON FREDERICK
7:00 A.M. WEDNESDAY, AUGUST 7, 2024
PIERZ

The kids were still asleep, so Serena and I had a moment at the kitchen table to discuss the case. It seemed better now that we weren't hiding Serena's depression from her family anymore. Serena didn't want to worry her family but I think sometimes families should worry. Her sister, Andi, now spoke to Serena every day.

Serena was wearing her white pajamas and was savoring a large cup of green matcha as she ate her toast. I was already dressed since I had to see the doctor this morning to make sure I hadn't ripped open any stitches when I lifted Larry onto the chair. My breakfast was a little more complicated than Serena's. I had a bowl of raspberries, strawberries, blueberries, and blackberries drizzled with jalapeño honey and three boiled egg whites sprinkled with pepper and covered with salsa verde.

Serena wrapped her hand around her hot mug of tea and then placed her warm hand on my wrist. "I'm sorry. I know it's not fun crawling into bed with someone who's sad and exhausted every night. Not exactly what you signed up for."

"When the priest said for better or for worse, I said, 'I'll take the better,' but he said it was an all-or-nothing thing. So, it *is* what I signed up for." I held her hand and kissed it. "Kidding. I want you any way I can have you."

"I'm having more days that I can slip out from the weighted blanket I've been under. It's still a chore to brush my teeth and wash my face some days." Her eyes welled up. "I have the husband I want; I love my children and our house. I get to stay home with the kids. I know it's stupid. I appreciate that you never tell me I shouldn't be depressed."

"It's not relevant. You are, and we can only go from where we're at." I leaned into her and kissed her.

Serena patted her eyes dry with a napkin. "Okay, tell me about the investigation."

"The tech team managed to find a message on an incel site generated from a computer traced to Larry McBride's house. Crazy Larry claimed to have committed untraceable attacks against women in revenge for feminism."

"Women—plural?" Serena asked.

"Yes."

"Do you think they'll ever find the dress you saw in the laundry?"

"I don't know. I'm hoping I can eventually get a search warrant for Molly's car. We could use the data recorder from her vehicle to find out exactly where she drove." A vehicle has a black box, similar to an airplane's, that can be used to trace its travels. "My guess is that the dress is buried in the woods somewhere. Burning the dress could have drawn attention to it. But even if we find it, I'm not sure we can prove it was Eliana's dress. It did seem a little small."

"Didn't you say it was a crochet knit dress?" Serena asked.

"Yes."

"Then it shrank. Eliana could wear a size four dress." Serena postulated, "Either Larry washed it, not knowing it would shrink, or Molly saw the bloody dress on the floor and decided she better wash it, regardless."

"I'm guessing the latter." I ate a strawberry. "Larry's suicide attempt doesn't make sense to me. One day, he's bragging about committing the perfect crime, and a couple of days later, he's trying to kill himself."

"Maybe he has bipolar disorder," Serena suggested. "Anything else you're struggling with?"

"I need to talk to Eliana again. There are a number of things I can't make sense of. The scene was cleaned. Her dress was gone. Her boots were gone. The laptop was never found. Strangers don't clean up crime scenes. People close to the victim clean up scenes, and Larry wasn't close to Eliana. I can see Larry keeping a souvenir, but what happened to the rest of it? Another piece is the damage to her right hand. That seemed personal. Eliana has little movement with her hand, but moved her thumb up and down as if she was trying to tell me something."

Serena slowly sipped her tea as she pondered what I'd shared. She moved her thumb up and down and finally said, "He burned her. She was signaling a lighter."

"That's good." I stood up and kissed her.

"You're just trying to make me feel better."

"I'm not. Well, I am, but I'm not being supercilious. At the hospital, Eliana pointed to her foot. Her heel was black and cut up. I assumed it was from her trek through the woods. I need to get Dr. Amaya Ho to examine this carefully."

11:30 P.M.

The urologist determined I hadn't damaged the surgical area. My pain was from straining an area that had recently been operated on. I had played with the kids for a couple of hours, and now I needed to shower and begin my workday. Serena was taking our three kids to her parents, so I helped them pack up and kissed them all goodbye.

I slipped under the spray from the showerhead and considered the case. The piece I struggle with is how Larry got Eliana to go with him. I think Larry kept the ghost gun because he thought it was untraceable. After all, that's the message delivered in the media over and over. But it's not true. Ghost guns are not traceable in the traditional sense. Some states, like California, microstamp new guns, allowing for ballistic identification. Minnesota doesn't have a similar system. A ghost gun, or any gun made at home, doesn't go through the process, so it can't be traced in the system. However, every barrel that fires a bullet leaves distinct markings. These markings are produced by the breech face itself, the firing pin, extractor, and ejector. Firearms examiners are able to examine bullets and cartridge casings to determine whether they were expelled from the same firearm. The Integrated Ballistic Identification System, or IBIS, is a computerized system capable of comparing types of ballistic evidence found at crime scenes. The Bureau of Alcohol, Tobacco, Firearms and Explosives, the ATF, is examining the ghost gun I removed from Larry's home and comparing it to the bullets removed from Eliana's torso. I will know if Larry's homemade gun fired those bullets soon enough.

I relaxed as the warm water ran over my body. The shower door opened, and Serena joined me. She is so incredibly beautiful.

After a long, passionate kiss, Serena said, "I think the kids can do without me for a bit. What did the doctor say about making love?"

"He was for it."

"He said that?" Serena smiled coyly.

"Not in so many words." Not in any words, actually. The warmth of her body and her kiss ignited a fire within me. "A gentle massage would be nice."

"Is there a body part in particular that needs work?" she whispered seductively into my ear.

"As a matter of fact, there is."

"Let the treatment begin."

5:00 P.M. THURSDAY, AUGUST 8, 2024
WEST RAILROAD AVENUE, AURORA

Mike Haney's cell phone was bouncing off towers in the Hillman area on the evening of Eliana's assault, supporting his story. The ATF contacted me and told me the zip gun taken from

Larry McBride's house had fired the bullets into Eliana Castillo. Larry had been picked up by a sheriff's deputy and was headed one hour due south to the St. Louis County Jail in Duluth. I had a search warrant for Molly McBride's car and had just arrived in Aurora. Auto electronics expert James Weber met me at Molly's house. James was a former Gulf War veteran who stood about five feet, eight inches tall. He was balding and sported a scraggly beard. He had specialized training in the new field of digital vehicle forensics.

Molly hurried out of the trailer and met us in the driveway. "Haven't you harassed my boy enough? Why can't you leave us alone and arrest some of those homeless drug fiends in Duluth?"

Despite dire poverty, the crime rates in Aurora are lower than in the rest of the state. I showed her the search warrant. "We're going to borrow your car for a bit. Unless you want to tell us what you did with the dress and the suitcase."

"The suitcase is still in my car," Molly said with a wry smile. "Take it if that gets you your jollies."

Molly went to the house to retrieve the keys to her white 2017 Chevy Malibu.

I smiled at her use of "get your jollies." It was a British phrase used to describe enjoyment from doing something disreputable. I asked James, "Does this car have a black box?"

"Yeah. I can trace where it's been from the data recorder."

Molly returned and unlocked the car. With a grin, she opened the suitcase. It was empty.

I took the keys from her. She studied us. "I don't know what you think you're going to find."

"We'll be back."

James used the vehicle's computer system to trace Molly's routes and stops. We drove to the Aurora grocery store and to the hospital. Eventually, we were driving an uninhabited path along the St. James Mine Pit.

"She stopped right here," James announced.

"Look for disturbed earth."

When I exited the car, I slipped on my latex gloves and crouched as I studied the brush for bent grass. There appeared to be a path through foot-long grass, so I followed it for thirty feet until the trail ended. *Okay, now what?* I searched twenty feet in all directions and was coming to the end of my circle when I stopped in my tracks. I couldn't believe it. There, on a thimbleberry bush, hung the missing dress. Molly had walked thirty feet into the brush and thrown the dress.

"Got it!" I yelled and, with a grin, bagged the dress. I would have Molly charged with obstructing the legal process when we returned. It would be difficult to make it stick because Larry hadn't been charged when she got rid of the evidence, but I might be able to use it as leverage to get Larry to talk. It would be hard for Molly to deny discarding the dress since we used the data recorder from her car to find it.

We searched further for Larry's cell phone and laptop without success. I imagined they were resting beneath the water at the bottom of the 380-foot-deep mine pit. At least we'd found the dress. I suspected Molly hadn't thrown the dress in the lake with the other items out of fear it would float.

8:00 P.M.
ST. LOUIS COUNTY JAIL, 4334 HAINES ROAD,
DULUTH

Larry McBride sat across from me in an interview room at the St. Louis County jail dressed in an orange jumpsuit. His eyes darted about the room as he rambled, "There's a reason they always look at the boyfriend when a woman's murdered. Men have a good reason to beat women. If I saw Lorenzo beating the hell out of that bitch, I wouldn't step in. You know damn well she did something to deserve it."

This interview was unlikely to yield anything productive. Larry was in classic narcissistic injury mode and was on the attack. He wanted an argument. I calmly asked, "What exactly did Eliana do? She was in the park grieving the loss of her relationship."

"She's not the only one who lost a relationship. Carmel was interested in me. Look on my computer. We were setting up dates.

But before I got a chance, Eliana came along and trashed me out, and that was the end of that. Snowball's chance in hell. That's what I had. Women decide who men go out with. What choices do men have?"

"Eliana's single-parenting a child because a man wouldn't take responsibility for the child."

"Yeah, and that's another thing. It's a woman's choice. He didn't want the baby, but she gets to decide. And then he has to pay child support for the next eighteen years for a kid he never wanted in the first place. It's bullshit. You want the kid; you pay for it."

"If you want to dance, you got to pay the band." It was my dad's classic way of saying men should take responsibility for their children. Larry didn't seem to pick up on it. I leaned back. "Let me get this straight. You raped her because she kept her child?"

"No evidence!" He slapped the table. "I'm going to sue the county for false arrest."

The safe had been opened and the only items inside were blasting caps for dynamite and wires. There was no dynamite in the safe. The sheriff's department told me Larry had a permit to possess dynamite. It was used to break up beaver dams when they blocked streams to the degree that fields became flooded. No work permit is required to do this in Minnesota, provided you have a permit for the explosives. "We opened the safe. Where's the dynamite?"

"I'm out." Larry shrugged. "Even if I had it, I wouldn't store them with the caps. Don't want no legal troubles."

"What do you need dynamite for?"

"Breaking up dams." Larry grinned, "You already know that. I had to explain when I got the permit. I can give you the names of farmers I've worked for."

"That would be helpful," I said.

"But I won't," Larry continued. "Don't need to."

When the electronic crimes unit went through the McBrides' home computer, they discovered searches on how to tap into a vehicle's electronics without being noticed. I had no evidence that

Larry was creating a car bomb, but since he was a member of a terrorist organization, I had to consider it. For the time being, I'd store this information but keep it in mind if additional evidence emerged.

"What were you doing in Eliana's car?"

"What are you talking about?" His sly grin suggested he knew exactly what I was talking about.

"After the assault, you returned to the hotel and took something out of Eliana's trunk."

"Prove it," he laughed.

"We found the dress."

Larry stopped for a moment. He was rattled but, feigning confidence, said, "What dress?"

"The dress Eliana was wearing on the night you raped her. I know you raped and shot her. I want to know why."

"That's bullshit."

"The ATF was able to match the ballistics from the bullets removed from Eliana to the zip gun removed from your dresser."

"You're a liar. I know for a fact you can't trace ghost guns." Larry clicked his thumb and forefinger at me like he was firing a gun. "Nice try, po-po."

"You can't trace ghost guns to a manufacturer, but once we have the firearm in our possession, we can match the tool marks on the bullets to the firing mechanism. The Zodiac Killer in New York City was convicted by tool markings on the zip guns he made from pipes, too. Zodiac, like you, didn't realize they could be matched to the crime scene bullets. Big mistake, Larry. I'm not expecting you to believe me. Talk to your lawyer about it."

"There is no way in hell you have that dress," Larry exclaimed.

I exited the room and returned with the dress, now in a plastic bag. I showed it to Larry, and he recognized it. He argued, "That can't be Eliana's dress. It's too small for her."

"You know as well as I do it shrank in the wash. I'm not going to waste any more time arguing with you tonight. But you should know that your mom's been charged for obstructing the legal process. Let the guards know when you're ready to talk to me again." Before leaving, I added, "You may have your little clique of friends who support what you did, but even most incel guys would kick your ass for ramming that stick into her."

"I'm not the one who shoved that hammer in her. I'm the victim here," Larry argued.

I never said hammer. Aloud, I said, "Tell me about the women's baseball T-shirt in the bottom drawer of your dresser. Who wore that shirt?"

"For me to know and you to find out," Larry smirked.

"We'll have DNA soon enough."

Quickly shifting to explosive anger, Larry screamed, "I've been so victimized I'm black-pilled! You're so damn blue-pilled you can't even see it!"

Incel members have created a code inspired by *The Matrix*. They claim that most people are stuck in an illusion, which in the film was the result of taking the blue pill. Incels claim they've taken the red pill, which enables them to see reality. Black-pilled members are the ones who've become extremely cynical as a result of over-exposure to reality. If you are black-pilled, there is no hope that a woman will ever be attracted to you. "So, your reality is based on a science fiction movie?" When he didn't respond, I asked, "If you didn't take the hammer to her, who did?"

"Don't for a moment think that she didn't deserve it." Larry pointed directly at me and yelled, "Wake the fuck up, Frederick! Women rule the world. Men like me are trying to put it in balance again. It's so lopsided right now that a man can't get justice. This is a war!" Larry stood up and undid his orange jumpsuit. He turned his back to me and let it drop to the floor. He dropped his underwear to reveal his bare backside. From the top of his back to his ankles was a tattoo of a naked woman. Her head seductively peeked up at the top of his back. Her private area was in his buttocks. The fronts of her legs were tattooed on the back of his. It was obviously fresh and done by a skilled artisan. Probably a couple of talented tattoo artists.

"Why in God's name did you do that?" I asked. The model-like woman tattooed on his back would make him a rape target in prison.

"I didn't do that. It's why I tried to hang myself. I'd like to kill that filthy bitch."

"Who?"

"I'll talk when my charges are dropped."

"Your charges aren't getting dropped, Larry. You can charge the person who tattooed you with assault. You're getting charged with attempted murder and criminal sexual conduct."

"That's bullshit. No, I'm not." He pulled his jumpsuit back on. "Fucking bitches."

Someone, apparently a woman, had purposely made Larry a prison rape magnet. I thought about Mike's comment that Eliana had made the "crazy" gesture in front of Carmel Cano and Catania Turrisi. Cat was the only one in this case who had the resources to punish Larry in this manner, and I could definitely see Cat setting him up to receive what he had dished out.

9:00 P.M. North Pier, Canal Park, Duluth

After leaving the jail, I drove to Canal Park and sat on the shore of Lake Superior to write Serena a quick letter before returning home. Everyone would be sleeping by the time I arrived. The lighthouse at the end of the boardwalk reflected gold light onto the midnight blue lake. Like Serena, the lake brought me a moment of peace.

Dearest Serena,

I appreciate the loving manner in which you have woven your way into my heart. You have a way of reflecting my thoughts and supporting my efforts that makes me a better man. The best moments of my life are when I'm lying next to you, spooning against your smooth back, feeling your warmth, and drinking in your love. When you hug me, you set the world right again. I appreciate your talents and the special skill that enables you to create tender synchrony with our children of nine, five, and five months. I love the way you love me, and I am forever indebted to you for this blessing. The allure of your love is why this letter is short. I can't wait to be home with you.

Jon

14

ELIANA CASTILLO
10:00 A.M., THURSDAY, AUGUST 8, 2024
CENTRACARE ST. CLOUD HOSPITAL
1406, 6TH AVENUE NORTH, ST. CLOUD

I've been in the hospital for two weeks now. I can't wait to talk again. Every conversation ends without being heard. My memory is clearer about some of the things that happened, but I struggle with remembering what occurred when I left the park. There were so many weird things. Was there even a dog? Nobody's mentioned a dog. I did get to hug Candy, the woman who saved me, in person. She was so sweet. I wish I could have told her so.

Today, Investigator Jon Frederick and Dr. Amaya Ho are here to meet with me. I feel like people have been trying to protect me from the truth regarding the investigation, but I need people to be honest and up-front with me. It will be easier for me to clarify what happened once I have some facts I can lean on. I have a laptop in front of me now that I peck on with my left hand so I can communicate more than "yes" and "no."

Jon wore his usual untucked button-down shirt and black jeans. There's always something like "Faith" or "Compassion" embroidered on the front tails. He stood over and asked, "Did Larry McBride shoot you?"

I typed on the keyboard, "I think so. I remember Larry standing over me with a pipe."

"We found the pipe gun in his home that fired the bullets into your body."

My heart rate increased on the monitor as I typed, "Ok."

"Did Larry rape you?"

"I think so," I typed. "I kind of remember him standing over me."

Amaya asked, "Could there have been two people?"

"Maybe," I typed. I hadn't really thought about it.

"Do you have any idea why Larry targeted you?" Jon questioned.

"No," I typed. "Larry's an ass."

"I agree," he responded. "It sounds like you had an opinion about him before that night. What led you to that belief?"

"He dated Carmel," I typed. "Disrespected her. Larry's an old-school chauvinist. I told her to dump him."

"And she did?" John asked.

I nodded.

"Motive," Jon remarked.

"Rape DNA?" I typed.

Amaya shook her head. "No. The rapist was a non-secreter. About twenty percent of men are non-secreters, which makes it more challenging to get a DNA profile. Traditional serological testing relied on detecting blood group antigens. Non-secreters do not secrete these antigens. Now we can use polymerase chain reaction to enhance amplification of DNA to overcome this."

"So, what does that mean?" I typed.

Amaya reassured me, "The testing will take longer, but we will identify the man who assaulted you."

Jon quickly added, "Larry McBride had the gun you were shot with. He had your dress. We'll get him."

I could feel my heart racing.

"What happened to your boots?" Jon asked.

"In the lake," I typed. I suddenly remembered hearing them

splash. This was the first time I had that memory, and it seemed solid. That had to be a good sign.

"And the computer?" Jon wondered.

I shrugged. I hadn't thought about it. "I don't know," I typed.

"Do you mind if I ask you about the assault?" Amaya removed a rubber hand from her bag.

I did mind, but shook my head. I wanted answers, too.

"The bruises on your head, face, and hands appear to have been made with a hammer. Do you recall getting hit by a hammer?"

My body instinctively jerked. I typed, "I remember being hit, but I can't see who hit me." I closed my eyes and tried to visualize the moment.

Amaya told me, "Show us your wrists."

I held them out and slowly rotated my arms.

Amaya pointed to matching black-and-blue marks on each wrist. "Do you remember how these bruises happened?"

"No," I blinked twice.

Amaya held the rubber hand as if she was shaking hands and then slid her fingers forward to the wrist of the rubber hand, pressing her thumb down. Amaya then walked to the head of my bed, pulled my hands over my head, and held them as if someone was behind me, holding my arms back.

When she let go, I typed, "Two people."

Amaya nodded in agreement. "I think someone was holding your arms back."

"Does Donny have an alibi?" I typed. "Maybe he thought it would give him sole custody of Luis."

"Donny's married," Jon said. "His wife said he was home all night."

"Phone?" I typed.

"Donny's phone was home all night, too," Jon responded.

"Any video of Donny at home?" I typed.

"None," Jon responded. "We have nothing on Donny at this point beyond that he called you for the first time in two years that night." He asked, "Was it Lorenzo?"

"I don't know. I remember seeing Crazy Larry standing over

me. I don't remember another person. Why do you think it's Lorenzo?"

"Lorenzo left the hotel shortly after you did and disappeared for a couple of hours. He claims he was searching nearby bars for you. We have him on camera in two bars. The other establishments didn't have working cameras, leaving enough of a gap that he could have been involved. I'm not saying he was. I'm simply saying he doesn't have an alibi."

"Why would he think I'd go to a bar?" I typed.

"Because that's what he would do," Jon responded. He asked, "Was it Mike?"

"I don't know." I shrugged. "I don't remember."

Jon continued, "Mike appears to have an alibi. He reported he went to Hillman to check out his hunting land, and his phone was pinging off towers in the area that night."

I felt relieved. I liked Mike. I typed, "Can Mike be my guard again?"

Jon responded, "If you're okay with it."

"I am," I typed.

"I'll check into it," Jon said. "Have you ever met Larry's mother, Molly?"

I shook my head.

He showed me a picture of her. "You don't remember seeing her that night?"

"No. Why do you ask?"

"Molly was aware that Larry had your dress."

"Redneck mama?" I typed.

"Yes," Jon said.

"There's something you're not telling me," I typed.

Amaya looked at Jon as if it was his call, confirming my suspicion.

Jon blew out a long breath and said, "Larry McBride is an incel guy. He feels justified in attacking women because he thinks feminists rule the world."

I held my hands out to suggest, "Take a look at me."

Jon shared, "Larry has claimed on an incel chatline that he's attacked women, and there is no way to trace the crimes back to him. It makes me wonder if he had a prior rape, and they were unable to connect it to him because he is a non-secreter. I know he didn't think the zip guns could be traced to him, but he was wrong. Did Larry mention any other victims when he assaulted you?"

I thought hard and finally shook my head.

"Did he burn you?" Jon asked. "You were trying to signal something to me the other day, but I wasn't getting it. When I mentioned it to my wife, Serena, she suggested you were mimicking a lighter."

I nodded with excitement. I typed, "On the bottom of my right heel."

Dr. Amaya Ho pulled the blankets off my foot and carefully examined it. "I'm going to take a picture of it with a couple of different cameras. I'm also going to place some amido black on your foot. Amido black reacts with the protein from blood and can identify if a dried bloody mark was left on your body."

Jon picked up the hand mirror by my bed and held it below my foot so I could see what Amaya was doing. It was difficult to see exactly, but a dotted circle appeared on my right heel.

Jon asked, "Is that an *M* in the middle?"

"It appears so," Amaya answered. With consternation, she continued to study the burn.

I frantically typed, "What does that mean?"

"Incels are a terrorist group that's been linked to a number of mass shootings and other acts of violence against women. Larry's part of the incel community," Jon responded.

"Why the letter *M*?

"Moonshot is an organization that fights incel terrorism," Jon said. "The idea of the moonshot is to 'think bigger.' I like the symbolism." He paused, considering. "I have a feeling an incel put the *M* here as an insult to the organization. How did he get it on your foot?"

I typed, "He heated a metal ring with a lighter and pressed it into my heel."

"He branded you," Amaya muttered.

"Is this bad news?" I typed.

"No," Jon said. "It's actually good news. It means that if there is another victim, she might have the same brand. We probably missed it on the first victim, too. You have really helped us here, Eliana."

"Did you ever tell Carmel or Catania that Larry assaulted you?" Jon queried.

"I don't know," I typed. "I had a lot running through my head the first few days, and I don't remember what I said."

"That's enough for now," Amaya interjected. She nodded toward the machines tracking Eliana's vitals. "They have continued to rise since we've arrived. We need to let her relax again."

A female officer stepped in when Jon and Amaya departed, and I realized I had forgotten to ask why they thought I had mentioned Larry to Carmel and Cat. My guard was nice enough, but I wanted to see Mike again.

15

JON FREDERICK
10:00 A.M., FRIDAY, AUGUST 9, 2024
BECKER COUNTY COURT HOUSE
913 LAKE AVENUE, DETROIT LAKES

I sent an email to every city police department and county sheriff's department in the state today, asking if Larry McBride had ever been a suspect in a murder case. I was hoping someone would recognize his name, as there wasn't a great way to look it up. I was back in Detroit Lakes for an arraignment hearing for McBride. Larry stood in a dark brown suit next to his attorney.

The Honorable Greta Olson stated, "Larry McBride, you have been charged with attempted first-degree murder and two counts of criminal sexual conduct in the first degree. How do you plead?"

"Not guilty, Your Honor," Larry replied. He obviously had the capacity to be respectful to a woman if the situation warranted it.

Larry's attorney spoke. "We have not been presented with a statement by the victim that she has accused Larry of this offense. In addition, we will prove that the ballistic evidence the prosecution claims to have is inaccurate. We all know there is a history of false positive reports in ballistic reports. It's far from a perfect science."

Ballistics used to be problematic, but is now very good. Ballistics tests today are accurate more than 99% of the time.

The prosecutor responded, "The victim hasn't made a statement because her jaw was injured so severely, she is unable to speak."

The defense attorney interjected, "There was no DNA evidence linking Larry to this crime. The victim's lover, Lorenzo Caruso, fought with her that night. Lorenzo was also arrested for this crime."

"Not true," the prosecutor responded. "Lorenzo was brought in for questioning and released."

The judge asked, "Is there no DNA evidence?"

"No," the prosecutor replied reluctantly. "Not yet."

"Larry McBride has no prior felony charges," the defense attorney added. "He doesn't represent a flight risk. He's barely ever left the county."

Larry appeared insulted by the remark.

The judge hit the gavel and ruled, "Bail is set at $250,000."

Molly McBride stood in the galley and yelled at the judge, "Greedy shitbird!"

Security quickly escorted her out of the courtroom.

My perspective of bail was different from Molly's. Larry only had to come up with ten percent, and I had a feeling his friends would cover it. I needed to find more evidence.

I asked to speak to Larry in a side room before he was returned to jail.

Larry didn't bother to sit. He grinned at me. "You know as well as I do that I'm walking out of here. Maybe not today, but eventually."

"We all go through periods of loneliness. It's not a conspiracy. It's life." I would continue to present a healthier perspective to Larry with the understanding that we were playing a long game. He'll blow me off today, but two months from now, he'll give up the name of his accomplice. He still hadn't accepted the reality that he was going to be locked up for a long time. That would change.

"Eliana's a Becky. And that mob bitch gave me a tattoo of a naked whore I will have for the rest of my life. Thank you, Cat! Likin' it more and more. She thinks I'll get mine in prison, but I'm not goin' to prison."

"Where did you and Catania Turrisi cross paths?"

Larry opened the door to leave. "I'll talk when all my charges are dropped."

"Not happening."

3:00 P.M.

BLUE LINE SPORTS BAR, 1101 2nd Street South, Sartell

My hope of obtaining a warrant to have Google identify all the cell phones in the Detroit Lakes City Park at the time of Eliana's assault ended today. The U.S. Court of Appeals for the Fifth Circuit ruled in *United States v. Jamarr Smith* that geofence warrants are unconstitutional under the Fourth Amendment. Jamaar had been identified as a suspect in an armed robbery by a Google search of cell phones in the area. The court ruled that the broad scope of geofence warrants, which require searching a vast database, is a violation of the Fourth Amendment and is legally unjustifiable. The Fourth Amendment states that warrants must describe the place, the items, and the people to be investigated. Geofencing does not identify the people. It is a fishing expedition, and "general warrants" are illegal. I understood the purpose of the ruling. We don't want police to randomly search innocent people's houses. But I think if a violent crime happens in a person's home, the owner should have the right to see whose phones entered their house that day. With this finding, it's not allowed. The ruling was disappointing but expected.

3:30 P.M.

Roan Caruso met me for a late lunch at the Blue Line. He smiled as he sipped on a glass of Summit's Slugfest IPA. "I'm not confirming that Cat had the peckerwood tattooed, but you gotta admit, it's pretty damn funny. Good ol' Crazy Larry is going to

83

have second thoughts about raping that poor girl after he's on the receiving end a couple of times in prison."

"First, I need enough evidence to convict him. I'm praying Eliana can heal enough to make a clear statement. Every time I ask, Eliana indicates she isn't ready." I took a sip of my root beer. It was too early in the day, and the week for that matter, for me to relax with a beer. "Once Larry realizes he's going to prison, he could charge Cat with assault."

"But did she *assault* him? She paid for his tattoo. Is that a crime?" Roan took a bite of his Redline Burger and said with his mouth half full, "Why did you tell the police where Lorenzo was staying? It pissed me off. I told you he didn't do it."

"I'm working for the BCA," I reminded him. "I work closely with investigative teams throughout the state. You have to be patient and let the process run its course. Law enforcement was looking for Lorenzo, and I knew where he was, so I told them. If I had let you or Lorenzo know ahead of time, he would have run and would now have multiple charges. Instead, he's been released, and Larry McBride's been charged with attempted murder."

"It's hard seeing your kid locked up for something he didn't do."

"I get it. That boy needs to get his sexuality under control. He was accessing porn right before he planned on proposing, and then he screwed Eliana's best friend while he was grieving her loss." I shook my head.

"I didn't mind Eliana, but Cat was never wild about her."

"Cat must have had to dish out some serious cash for the tattooing."

"You don't rape someone who's dating a Turrisi," Roan stated matter-of-factly. "It was a given that there would be consequences. Intense consequences. You know, so learning occurs."

"Speaking of learning," I warned Roan, "don't come after me again."

"I don't know what you're talking about."

"Walking in after my surgery was not only a threat to me, it was a threat to my family. If it wasn't for the work I've done on this case, Lorenzo would still be in jail. I'll find the truth if you stay out of my way."

"Message received," Roan said.

My phone buzzed with a call from Dr. Amaya Ho, and I stepped outside to take it. Knowing Amaya doesn't call me for social reasons, I asked, "What do you have?"

"I was able to pull DNA off the shirt from Larry McBride's trailer. The blood belongs to a woman named Cheri Wilde, who was hammered to death in Inver Grove Heights. I had her body delivered to the Hennepin County Medical Examiner's office. If you can be here before five, I can speak to you briefly about our findings."

I headed back into the Blue Line and said, "I'm on my way. Thank you, Amaya."

Roan caught the end of my conversation and asked wryly, "You have someone more important to talk to than me?"

"I do."

5:00 P.M.
HENNEPIN COUNTY MEDICAL EXAMINER'S OFFICE
14250 COUNTY ROAD 62, MINNETONKA

The medical examiner's office sits outside of the city of Minnetonka, surrounded by trees. I sat next to Dr. Amaya Ho, who was sporting her white lab coat in the conference room. She said, "I have good news regarding the polymerase chain reaction testing we performed on Eliana Castillo's SANE kit. Remember how the initial report said no DNA? That wasn't accurate. The perpetrator was a nonsecreter, in which case there isn't enough DNA to extract through traditional means. We have a new technique that creates a chain reaction which replicates enough DNA to create a read. The PCR proved that the DNA from the sexual assault on Eliana was from Larry McBride."

"Okay. That should thwart his release."

Amaya leafed through pictures in a folder, finally stopping at a photo taken from the foot of the cadaver table of a dead woman lying supine. "This is the body of Cheri Wilde. Look at the bottom of her left heel."

There was a familiar circle, but it could have been made by stepping on a round object. It was hard to read. Disappointed, I said, "I don't know. I don't think I can use this."

"The skin pattern on the bottom of her foot makes it hard to see." With a coy grin, she added, "But we might have a computer program that can eliminate the skin pattern and show the remaining image." Amaya slid out another picture. It was a circle with a clear, small *m* in the middle.

"This is perfect." Amaya showed me a photo of Cheri's right hand, desecrated like Eliana's. She slid me a third picture — Cheri's face. I asked, "Were her teeth hammered out?"

"Yes. And there's a brutal twist. All of her organs burst." Amaya wasn't generally an expressive woman, but I could see pain in her eyes.

"As a result of the severe beating?"

"The only way this can happen is to jump up and down on her body."

That was disturbing. I let her sit with her feelings for a moment to give her the opportunity to talk more if she wished. This killer had a lot of anger. I broke the silence by saying, "I have an incel guy as a suspect, but this seems very personal, doesn't it?"

"That's your call." Amaya scratched her neck, almost as if it served as a distraction. With mild irritation, she remarked, "I'm just telling you what we have. That symbol was burned into the bottom of Cheri's foot. This is an unsolved homicide. She was raped by a non-secreter. By the time her body was discovered, there was no usable DNA from her attacker. That's all we have." Her voice was terse.

I thought about the women's shirt I had confiscated from Larry's trailer that I had turned over to her lab. Amaya was having a tough day, but I still had questions to ask, so I gave her a moment before I continued. I pulled up a picture I had of the shirt on my phone and asked, "Was Cheri wearing the shirt?"

"It wasn't McBride's blood. But I could test for Cheri's if you'd like." Her head remained down as she answered.

"Please do. Where did Cheri work?"

Her tone softened. "King of Diamonds in Inver Grove Heights."

I understood her frustration. Sometimes, in this line of work, a particular case gets under your skin and itches until it blisters. I offered, "Thank you for addressing this so quickly."

"There's a lot of tension in the office these days. All of our work is under so much scrutiny now that one of our examiners messed up. People used to assume our reports were facts. Now they assume we're lying. And people" —she pointed to the file— "can be so cruel."

"No worries, Amaya. I get it. You're good with me. It's why I always ask for you."

"My reports remain facts." Amaya stood, put her hand on my shoulder for a moment, and then departed. This was her way of apologizing for being short with me.

I called the Becker County Sheriff's office and informed the deputy, "The DNA testing is completed on Eliana Castillo's assault, and it verifies that Larry McBride is the man who assaulted her. Larry is also going to be charged with the murder of Cheri Wilde. She was an exotic dancer from Inver Grove Heights." I felt bad reducing Cheri to this one aspect of her life, but it was likely the reason she was murdered. I could envision an angry incel guy like Larry being upset that she didn't give him the attention he felt was warranted.

"Larry bailed out two hours ago," the deputy informed me.

"Could you please pick him back up?"

"I'd love to. One less thing to worry about in Aurora. I'll call the sheriff, and we'll have him picked up," she responded.

When I was walking to my car, my phone buzzed with a text from Eliana Castillo. "Guard is gone. Cousin left. Home alone. Can you contact Mike Haney? I'd feel better if someone was here with me tonight."

I didn't realize Eliana had been released from the hospital.

She sent a follow-up text, "Jaw still wired shut."

"I'll be right there," I responded. "Text me your address."

I called Serena on the way to Eliana's house and told her I

wouldn't be coming home tonight. It wasn't what she wanted to hear, but she understood.

6:00 P.M.
CESAR CHAVEZ STREET
DISTRICT DEL SOL
WEST SIDE, ST. PAUL

Eliana Castillo answered the door in a mauve long-sleeved cotton shirt and distressed jeans. The bruises were fading, and her pretty brown eyes had lost the red veins that had encapsulated them when she was hospitalized. She had a cast on her right hand with fingers protruding out the end. Her jaw remained wired shut, so I would be the only one speaking.

"I didn't realize you'd been released from the hospital. I had requested to be contacted, but I imagine one of their HIPAA enforcers determined it was a violation of your rights."

Eliana locked the door behind me and escorted me to the kitchen table. She sat by her laptop and gingerly typed with two hands, "Sorry for calling. I know you have a family. I may not need you if Carmel shows up. She promised she'd be here last night, but didn't show. My cousin came over and stayed. He can't tonight. I can't be here alone. Sorry."

My first reaction was to type in a response, but remembering she could hear, I said, "No worries. I want someone here with you. Where's your son?"

Returning to the laptop, she typed, "He has baseball tonight. Then he's staying with my parents. I won't have him with me at night until I know I'm not being hunted. I want my parents protecting him. They're a bit of a story themselves, but that's not related to this case. Are you hungry? I already ate, but I can make you something."

"I'm good." I was hungry but didn't want to put her out. I was curious about her parents, but I wasn't going to push it. We had a long night ahead. I could always come back to it. Hearing a car, I stood and looked out the window. A neighbor was pulling out of his driveway. On the counter near the window, I noticed a bag of

Moonstruck Dreamy Dark Hot Chocolate Mix.

Eliana stood up and pointed to the bag and then to me, raising her eyebrows.

"I am a fan of hot chocolate. I'd be forever indebted if you could make a mocha with that."

She nodded in approval. Eliana opened the cupboard and, with the dramatics of a ringmaster, waved through her different-sized cups.

"The largest possible."

Eliana raised her finger as if she had a thought. She went back to her laptop and typed, "Pick something good for us to watch. I'm not much for conversation. Please pick a crime show with a mature rating. People have insisted I watch chick flicks or reality shows so I don't get upset. Do you ever watch chick flicks? *Steel Magnolias, My Sister's Keeper, The Notebook, Beaches*? They all involve dying a slow death. I hate that shit! Please..."

I smiled, and she returned to making my mocha. Even though protecting her was part of my job, I felt a little guilty about watching a show with her since it was something I usually did with Serena, but the truth was that I'd be paying much more attention to what was happening outside.

Eliana pulled down a "World's Greatest Mom" mug from the cupboard and filled hers with hot chocolate. She poured a cold brew from the fridge into the remaining hot chocolate and stirred it in. After filling my mug, she pointed to the brew left in the pan and then to me, suggesting I could have more if I so desired.

"Have you watched *Case Histories*? It's based on a series written by Kate Atkinson."

She shook her head.

"I've watched the first one, so while you start watching it, I'll walk through the house to make sure it's secure." We didn't have DNA connecting Larry McBride to the assault. The evidence we desperately needed to get a conviction was a statement from Eliana. She's been too traumatized to give a decent account of her assault, and we've used her wired jaw to postpone an official statement. My job now was to keep her alive and get that statement.

16

LORENZO TURRISI CARUSO
7:00 P.M., FRIDAY, AUGUST 9, 2024
PIERCE STREET NORTHEAST
BELTRAMI, MINNEAPOLIS

Eliana still wasn't talking to me. She had filed an order for protection, and I wasn't allowed within three hundred feet of her. I was pissed, but I was respecting it. I knew damn well it wasn't her idea. Those damn investigators still haven't let me off the hook, even though they have a man in custody.

It didn't help my mood that Mom was following me about the house, ranting, "Eliana could have that order for protection removed if she wanted. It wouldn't be in place without her signature. That should be a pretty solid message of where you stand. If you had just listened to me and dumped her, you wouldn't be in this mess."

I wanted to scream, *shut the hell up!* Instead, I politely told her, "I'm sorry, Mom, but I need to make a call." Feeling restless, I called Carmel. "Hey, what are you up to?"

"I promised Ellie I'd stay with her tonight."

"Would you rather spend the night with Ellie or me?"

"I feel like I shouldn't bail on her." She paused. "That poor girl's been through hell."

"When she needs protection, she'll call me. Ellie obviously doesn't need it too badly yet." When Carmel didn't reply, I added, "I'm thinking we hit Euphoria for a margarita and maybe head back to your place for some lovin'." She hesitated, so I pleaded, "Come on, Carmel. I know you want to. I miss your warm body against mine. You deserve to be cared for, too. Ellie will be okay."

"I need to be honest with you about something first. I was the one who lured McBride to my house so your mom could have him tattooed. You know how insistent Catania can be."

I do know that. "So, how did you get him to lie still?"

"Roofied him. Cat took it from there. I don't know if it was right or not. I was so angry at the time."

"I wish you would have beaten that bastard to death. Thanks for helping. Please, you gotta stay with me tonight. You got me all fired up. I absolutely have to be with you."

"All right," Carmel conceded. "I have strawberry shortcake and fresh strawberries."

"Let's go to your place." I would get Eliana to talk to me, even if it meant hijacking her best friend to make it happen. One nice thing about getting it on with Carmel is that she is one person who would never tell Eliana. It would be too shameful for her to admit she betrayed her best friend.

17

JON FREDERICK
7:30 P.M., FRIDAY, AUGUST 9, 2024
CESAR CHAVEZ STREET, DISTRICT DEL SOL
WEST SIDE, ST. PAUL

After securing the safety of the house, I finally sat on the opposite end of the couch from Eliana. Her laptop rested between us so she could communicate. She gave me a thumbs up, indicating she was enjoying the show. Her phone buzzed. She picked it up, looked at the text, and set it back down.

"Is that something I should know about?" I asked.

She showed me a text from Carmel, which read, "Running late. Don't wait up."

I was glad I stayed. "You hinted earlier that you confronted Larry McBride. What happened?"

Eliana hesitated and then typed, "I paid Lorenzo a surprise visit one night, and Carmel was there. It"—she hesitated briefly as she searched for the right word before typing—"bewildered me. I was dating Lorenzo. I didn't know my bestie even knew him. I hadn't introduced them yet. I asked Carmel what she was doing there. She said she had gone out with Lorenzo's friend,

Crazy Larry, and he tried to assault her. She felt Lorenzo should know what his friend was really like. If Carmel had asked me, I would have told her he's psycho. The next weekend, Larry was with his brother at Lorenzo's, and I confronted Larry in front of everybody. I wanted all of his friends to know what a dirtball he was. I directed him to stay away from my friends."

My phone buzzed, so I stepped into the next room to take it.

The Becker County Deputy said, "We can't find Larry McBride. We have an APB out for him."

"Okay. Let me know if this changes."

"I will."

"I will stay at Eliana Castillo's home tonight."

"She's been released from the hospital? They should have told us."

"I agree. Fortunately, Eliana reached out."

"Okay. Sounds good. I'll let you know immediately if we find Larry."

"Thank you."

Eliana studied me when I returned from the call. She picked up the laptop and typed, "What happened?"

"Larry McBride bailed out of jail, and now they can't find him."

"No sleep for me tonight." She replied.

"Where would you hide if I spotted someone in the yard?"

Eliana shrugged and then typed, "Maybe in the closet."

"Do you have an attic?"

"You need a ladder to enter it, and the ladder's in the garage," she typed. She quickly added, "Please stay in the house with me."

McBride could be waiting outside the house to pick us off one at a time. I nodded in agreement. "Where is the entry?"

"In the closet in Luis's bedroom," she typed.

I went to the bedroom and opened the closet. When I turned, Eliana was right behind me, holding her laptop. I told her, "I'll get a kitchen chair and set it here. If we decide you have to hide up here, I'm going to kneel down." I knelt down in front of her. "You put your legs on my shoulders, and I'll stand up. I'll step up on the chair and you crawl into the attic, all right?"

She nodded.

The darkened curtains in the bedroom indicated the sun was starting to set. I said, "I'd like to shut off all of the unnecessary lights in this house. We want to make it as difficult as possible for someone to see in."

Eliana typed, "Leave a bathroom light on dim. It has a dimmer switch. Shut the rest off."

As I turned off the lights, I called Mike Haney. After greetings, I asked, "Are you interested in some work?"

"What days? Benton County might have some work for me."

"I need someone to stay with Eliana Castillo in St. Paul at night. At least until Larry McBride's back in custody."

"Did he escape?"

"No, made bail and has since disappeared."

"Bail? How the hell did he get bail?" Mike wondered.

"No DNA. His attorney brought up the old ballistic flaws."

"I'll take every shift you have. If you need me tonight, I'm good to go. I worked a graveyard shift last night, so I slept today. I'm headed home from the gym now."

"Get cleaned up, and you can replace me when you're ready. No hurry. If you arrive in the middle of the night, call first to warn me."

"Alright. If you don't mind, I'll take my time and get things in order at home so I can be prepared to work several long days in a row. I'll call first."

"Perfect."

MIDNIGHT

It was Friday night, and there were kids biking up and down the street until ten o'clock. Teenagers cruised up and down the streets, and millennials jogged by with their dogs. After eleven, it was eerily quiet. It should have been peaceful, but instead, I feared I was missing something. Sometimes I get a sense that something dire is about to go down. I'm not always right, but I am more often than not. Tonight, the feeling was stronger than ever. I don't believe I sat for more than fifteen minutes at a stretch since I'd arrived. Now I was on my feet more often than not.

After finishing the fifth episode of *Case Histories*, Eliana typed, "I'm going to try sleeping. Thank you! I'll get ready for bed. I want you armed with a gun in my bedroom, or I won't be able to sleep."

"I appreciate that you're not afraid to ask for what you need. When you're ready, let me know, and I will bring a chair in." I walked through the house and peered out every window. All quiet on the western front. Well, in every direction at the moment.

12:15 A.M.

I brought a chair into the bedroom and sat next to Eliana while she snuggled beneath her blankets. I forced myself to remain sitting while she fell asleep. She badly needed rest. When she closed her eyes, I quietly stood and carefully glanced out the window. Something about tonight didn't feel right. *Where the hell is Larry McBride? I think he's here, waiting—planning.* I glanced back at Eliana, who twitched as she slept. I could only imagine the horrible thoughts tormenting that poor woman. I remained by the window for a good thirty minutes when a shadow of a person crept across the yard. The person was out of sight, but his shadow from the streetlight gave him away. Someone was out there. Then there was nothing. Either I imagined it, or he was so close that the shadow of the eaves now covered him. I unbuttoned my shoulder holster.

I nudged Eliana, and she immediately jerked to a sitting position. Terror haunted her eyes.

"I need you to go to the attic."

She didn't question. Instead, she leaned into me as we went to her son's bedroom.

"I think I saw someone outside. Don't come down until I yell 'Taurus.'" I knelt. "Taurus will be our code word."

Eliana swung her legs over my shoulders, and I stood. I stepped up onto the chair. She lifted the attic door and crawled inside. Once inside, she gently put the cover back in place. I wasn't going to say *it's probably nothing* because I wasn't sure. One thing I've learned from working with victims is that honesty is essential.

I grabbed the chair and moved it to another room.

Once she was secure, I immediately called law enforcement. I told the dispatcher, "We have a 10-25 at 133 Cesar Chavez Street on the west side of St. Paul." This was code for a suspected break-in. Report in person.

I slid partially into the hall by the bedroom door, planning to use the doorframe as a shield. It would be a death wish to step outside looking for the killer. Larry likely had an infrared scope that could give him a clear outline of me at night. I waited in eager anticipation of sirens.

Instead, I heard the quiet clicking of the front door. The intruder had a key. I needed to be careful to make certain it wasn't Carmel or one of Eliana's parents coming to check on her. I didn't want to hurt an innocent person. At the same time, I didn't want to give up my location and draw a volley of shots from an automatic weapon. I silently waited. A friend of Eliana's would have texted or yelled out before entering. *God help me.* Footsteps padded softly about the house. I swear I could hear my heart pounding. This was a horrible situation. If I shot an unarmed person, I'd end up in prison. Even if the intruder was armed, I'd have to prove he intended to use his weapon.

Finally, the intruder stepped through the hall into Eliana's bedroom. I could make out the outline of someone who was about five feet, eight inches tall. This is the height of Larry McBride, Carmel, and Eliana's mother, so it wasn't all that helpful. When the figure stepped into the hall, I said, "Identify yourself."

At that moment, there was a thump overhead. Eliana must have slipped on something in the attic. The intruder raised his gun to fire as I aimed mine.

"BANG!" A shot rocketed through the night.

The intruder fell to the floor.

Confused, I looked at my gun. I never pulled the trigger.

I clicked the hall light on to see Larry McBride slumped on the floor—his blood and brain matter splattered on the wall. I stepped toward him and kicked his gun away. The entry wound was always smaller than the exit wound. The bullet displaced more matter as it flattened out. Larry was shot in the side of his head, about two inches below the top of his skull. I shouted, "Hello!" as I stepped forward. No one stood to his left, where the shot had come from. However, there was a bullet hole high in the living room window. Someone had shot him from outside.

Sirens now approached the house. *God's not given up on me tonight.*

I waited until law enforcement entered and then yelled, "Taurus!"

I asked the officers at the scene, "Who shot him?"

No one responded. I could understand why an officer would be reluctant to admit it. Every shooting is a potential criminal charge. My question drew a line between me and the police officers. The BCA investigates officer shootings.

 "Okay, don't call any more officers to this scene. Everybody here needs to be tested for gun residue," I directed. "Before we do that, I need a laser pointer." Again, there was no response, so I said, "Eliana's in the attic. Someone to go to the bedroom and help her down." I ran out to my car and retrieved a laser pointer.

Eliana came out of the room, clinging to an officer. I told the officer, "Stay with her."

I walked over to Larry, careful not to interfere with the body. I held the laser five feet six inches high, the height at which the bullet entered his body. I pointed the laser at the hole in the window. "Somebody go outside and tell me where that laser's headed."

An officer stepped out and returned. "It points to the roof of St. Paul Tattoo. It's a flat roof about a block from here."

Okay, let's have an officer stay here with Eliana, and everyone else come with me. We need to secure that building, and we'll work our way to the roof. Bring the battering ram."

The sergeant on the scene got on his radio and ordered, "We're establishing a perimeter in a four-block area surrounding 133 Cesar Chavez Street in Paul. I want every car coming out of the area pulled over and all passengers ID'd. If they don't have IDs, they remain on the perimeter with their car until someone can ID them."

A half dozen officers and I rushed to St. Paul Tattoo. I couldn't help thinking that Catania Turrisi had friends in the tattoo world. The metal door was locked and had to be rammed open. We cleared the main business quickly and headed upstairs, where two officers stayed to cover the hallway leading to the second-floor apartments in the building. The rest of us raced up the ladder toward the roof. An officer looked down for the go-ahead before carefully opening the roof door. We all knew that he was risking his life by opening that door.

Once opened, he crawled on the roof, and we followed him, but no one was there. With bright Maglites, we walked the perimeter of the old gray tar roof. There was no indication anyone had been up here.

I received a text from Mike Haney stating, "I'm here."

I immediately called him. "Larry McBride's dead." I asked Mike, "Did you shoot him?"

"No. Is Eliana okay?"

"Yes." I took the laser back out and pointed it toward Eliana Castillo's house. "Enter Eliana's home. I'm pointing the laser back toward you. I need you to guide me until I have the laser pointed through the hole in the window and shining on the wall where Larry was shot. You'll be able to see the laser on the glass until I have it in the hole."

Mike gave me directions, and I moved back and forth on the roof until I was in the exact spot. I told the officer next to me, "I am standing precisely where the shot was fired. Not maybe. This is the trajectory from the hole in the window to the bullet in the wall. I'm going back to ground level. Point the laser straight down from here."

I ran down the steps and outside of the building. When I located the red dot on the ground, I searched the parking lot. About ten feet away was the casing for an M118 long-range bullet. The casing had discharged over the side of the building and rolled a few feet. When I picked it up, it was still warm. I smiled for the first time. This was a break.

2:00 A.M.

When I returned to Eliana's, she had typed out a statement for the Ramsey County Investigator. I had a night of paperwork to do, which included calling Becker County and telling them their suspect was dead.

Eliana was sitting on the couch, rocking.

Mike sat next to her, took her hand, and said, "Take a deep breath."

I approached them and asked Eliana, "Do you want to go to your parents' place?"

She shook her head. She picked up the laptop and typed, "Can I stay with Mike?"

Surprised by the message, Mike looked at me and said, "Okay, but I live in Sauk Rapids."

I looked down at the two and said, "Get a hotel room. If she wants two rooms, get two."

Eliana shook her head and typed in, "Same as you."

I explained to Mike. "Get a room. The BCA will cover it. Eliana will want you to sit awake in a chair in the room all night, armed for her protection."

Eliana tiredly nodded in agreement.

"Okay," Mike said.

I turned to Eliana. "Pack clothes for tomorrow. Your home is now a crime scene. I'll see what we can do to find you a place to live until you can return."

She glanced toward the blood-spattered wall and typed, "Return?"

"Mike will bring you back tomorrow, and you'll pack everything you and your son need for the next month. Mike needs to be with you to make sure you don't interfere with the crime scene. I'll find a place for you to stay for the time being."

9:30 A.M SATURDAY, AUGUST 10, 2024
PIERZ

I had now been up for twenty-seven hours and was ready to crash. When I arrived home, Serena looked tired, and the kids were ready to play. I apologized to all and went to bed.

5:00 P.M.

The house was quiet when I woke. I dressed and went downstairs to see Serena sitting at the kitchen table. Her hair was uncombed, and she wore loose gray sweats. She commented despondently, "Do you ever think you'd be better off without me?"

"No, I don't." I approached her, leaned down, and kissed her. Serena's sadness weighed heavily in the room.

"You have so much energy, and here I sit. There's got to be someone out there like you who can go full bore all day and still have energy in the evening."

"I love you, and I have no desire to be with someone like me." I retrieved some raspberries and blueberries from the fridge and rinsed them off before adding them to some dry cereal.

"I swear I'm losing my hair, and I'm flabby where I used to have muscle. My face—"

"Stop. You're beautiful, and I love you—just as you are. Your emerald green eyes still capture me, and there's nothing better on earth than lying next to you. Don't tell me what I should want. I know. When you tell me I should want someone else, I feel like you don't know me. I feel damn lucky to be with you. I want you."

"It has to be tempting to consider someone else when I'm so—yuck." Serena continued to test me, looking for a crack of doubt to amplify her misery. "Has Eliana ever hit on you?"

"No. This isn't one of those cop shows where they always sleep with the woman they're protecting." I sat at the table next to her. "There is no temptation. Everyone who knows me knows I love you. You're my lover. Through thick and thin."

"We're at the thick part." She held her forehead in her hands as she spoke. "I'm sorry. I trust you. I'm tormented by these crazy, depressing thoughts."

I took her hand and held it. "I appreciate the way you've been battling the depression. I know it hangs over you like an overcast day, but you get up every day and take care of our kids."

"I think I liked the way you handled it last time better."

"But it almost killed me." I released her hand. "Remember when the depression hit after you had Nora?"

"Yeah. You didn't talk to me."

"I know. That was my mistake. You told me that you needed to sort things out by yourself."

"But I didn't mean total silence," she argued.

"I was raised with the motto, 'Say what you mean and mean what you say.' And instead of contacting me, you began talking to another guy."

"I'm sorry." She put her hand on mine.

"It's okay. We've been through this. So, with Jackson, I fought off every negative comment you made with loving, caring feedback. I never expressed my frustration because I didn't want to bring you down further. Pretended I was okay and worried about you night and day. And I almost got killed at work because I was distracted."

"Now it's tough love time," she commented as she turned away.

"No." I got out of my chair and knelt before her, forcing her to face me once again. "Just love. I can't save you on my own. I need you to brush away those negative thoughts. I love you. We have three amazing kids who love you. I didn't expect enough from you last time, and it exhausted me. So, this time, I'm being honest with you and letting you know when I'm having a bad day. Because I need you, too. You're tougher than I gave you credit for. This time, I'm respecting your ability to battle it."

"I love you, Jon." She finally relented and hugged me.

"Where are the kids?" I asked as I returned to the chair next to hers.

"At my parents'. We've got thirty minutes. Unfortunately for you, I want to hear about your work. Rough night?"

"You could say that." I explained everything that had transpired. I ended with, "I have concerns about Lorenzo."

"Why?"

"Larry McBride bails out of jail and heads to Eliana Castillo's house. How did he know she was out of the hospital? We didn't even know she had been released. How did he know where she lived?"

"And you think Lorenzo knew she had been released?"

"I do. Roan has access to a lot of information. Even though Lorenzo hasn't violated the no-contact order, I think he knows everything that's going on with Eliana."

"Larry was friends with Lorenzo. They fished together the day before the assault, right?"

"Yes. Larry never busted in the door. He entered with a key."

Serena looked concerned. "Larry had an inside partner."

"And now he's dead. He can't give him up anymore."

"But it sounds like the shooter saved Eliana's life. Maybe yours, too." She gently squeezed my hand. "The story on the news this morning was that the police had killed a man during the course of a burglary in St. Paul."

"The St. Paul police handled the situation perfectly. Law enforcement didn't kill him. I had every officer at the scene tested for gun residue. He was killed with a sniper rifle." I took a baggie out of my pocket and set it on the table.

Serena glanced at the shell casing inside. "Why didn't you enter it as evidence?"

"I did enter the shell into evidence."

"So, what are you doing with that casing?"

"Remember how our last case ended?"

She gasped, "I'll never forget."

"I kept a shell casing from one of the long-range bullets in Roan's sniper rifle. I have a gut feeling that it could be a match."

"You never should have kept that casing. We promised we'd never use anything from that scene."

"I can't use it as evidence. But I could use it to know with certainty."

Serena's brow furrowed. "How do you perform a ballistics comparison without revealing where the shell casing came from?"

"That is the million-dollar question. I'm thinking of going to Sean and telling him I obtained the casing illegally, but I have it, and it could be useful. Sean's the one who will be catching the heat over another police shooting." Sean Reynolds is the Superintendent of the Bureau of Criminal Apprehension and my supervisor. The BCA has the task of investigating police shootings, which is why I had all the officers tested for gun residue. Anytime police are accused of a shooting, and it's dismissed, the BCA is accused of a cover-up. I wondered if Mike Haney was tested for gun residue. He had shown up after the announcement was made.

"I thought you said Roan seems to have something on Sean."

"I think he does. But Sean was also the one who made me an investigator. And he assigned me this task. We've got some major players involved in this case—incel, the Minneapolis Combination. This is bigger than me. I need to put faith in someone besides you."

"If you're wrong, and Sean's sold out to the Mafia, Roan Caruso will come after you—us." Serena whispered.

"I'm in trouble either way. If I'm right that Lorenzo did this, and Sean will support me over what he owes Roan, I have an ally with resources. If Sean doesn't support me, my work may lead to the same place, but I'll be on my own."

"I'm going to talk to your dad about guarding our house."

"I'll talk to Dad. I have something else I need to ask him about anyway."

"I wish I had never talked you into going back to work. I should have known Sean would give you the worst possible case. Don't let him bury you. I need you, Jon. More than you'll ever know. The kids need you."

"I need you, Serena—always."

18

JON FREDERICK
5:00 P.M., SATURDAY, AUGUST 10, 2024
PIERZ

My phone buzzed, and seeing it was Ross McBride, I quickly answered it. "Jon Frederick."

"This is Ross. I need to know. Did you kill Larry?"

"No, I didn't. I was in the home to protect Eliana. Larry broke in and was shot by someone outside. I plan on finding out who killed him."

"Damn it, Larry. What the hell were you thinking?" Ross paused. "I'm going to tell you what I know to make it clear I'm not a part of Larry and Ma's craziness. I was visiting with Ma in Aurora. Words can't describe how much I hate talking to her. She told me Larry made a bomb and sold it to somebody. She didn't know who it was."

"It wasn't for a beaver dam?"

"She didn't know for sure, but it didn't seem like it. Larry was quiet about it, which worried her. She told him, 'I don't want to see any innocent kids being killed.' It makes me nervous with his incel connections."

"Do you know where he had to drive to deliver it?" I asked.

"No. All I have is that he made a bomb with dynamite and wires and sold it. She said that Larry had told her it would be triggered by a cell phone call. I wondered if a telemarketer call could set it off, and she said she hadn't thought about asking. Ma's not going to cooperate. She was madder than a puffed toad. She's having a fit because she believes you killed Larry and you're covering it up."

"I didn't. I appreciate the call. Thank you."

7:30 P.M., KING'S POINT ROAD ON HALSTED BAY, MINNETRISTA

Sean Reynolds asked me to meet him at Jada Anderson's house on Lake Minnetonka. Sean and Jada had a five-year-old son, Isaiah, together and have had an on-and-off relationship throughout Isaiah's life. For the boy's sake, I was glad to see they were together again. I had dated Jada for four years before I dated Serena, and before Jada got together with Sean. Still, Sean always seemed to have some resentment toward me for this.

Jada answered the door and welcomed me into her beautiful home. She grinned. "Always good seeing you, Jon."

"You look good, Jada." I smiled and complied with her quick hug. She was always beautiful, but she looked happy. She knew what I meant. We could have stayed friends, but we didn't. It would be hurtful to Serena for me to maintain a friendship with a former lover, and I wouldn't do that to her—no point in unnecessary worry. Relationships are complicated enough.

Jada brought me to Sean, who was sitting at the dining table. The room had a floor-to-ceiling window overlooking the lake. I told Jada, "Impressive." It didn't surprise me that she had done well for herself. She was a successful news reporter.

She grinned and said, "I'll leave you boys to your business," and departed.

"What's the emergency? You wouldn't be here on a Saturday if it wasn't serious."

"I need to know why you asked me to back off from investigating Roan."

"I told you; the request was made by another agency." Sean leaned forward aggressively and thrust his index finger uncomfortably close to my face. "I don't report to you." He leaned back. "Health and Human Services Inspector General Christi Grimm said they were running a major fraud investigation."

"They fined Precision Lens and its owner $485 million, but settled for $12 million."

"I know." Sean nodded. "And Roan walked away with nothing. I should clarify—no fine. I imagine he walked away with at least a couple mil. The man's Teflon—he's poison, but nothing sticks."

Prior to 2013, Teflon used the "forever chemical" perfluorooctanoic acid in its cookware coating, which was linked to a variety of health concerns, including infertility and testicular cancer. The chemical was banned in 2014. Chemours, a 2015 DuPont spinoff company that owned Teflon, initially skirted the lawsuits in 2020 based on procedural issues, but in 2023, they agreed to a $4 billion settlement. Teflon is still used to coat air fryer baskets, but the new chemical coating has been determined safe.

"Larry McBride's brother called me and told me Larry made and sold a dynamite bomb to somebody."

"Any idea of who he sold it to?"

"None."

"He had a permit for dynamite. It could have been for a dam. Could have been for a Fourth of July party. I've seen videos of these hillbillies blowing a dryer fifty feet up into the air with dynamite," Sean said.

"It bothers me when I think of the video of McBride going through Eliana's car after the assault."

"You're thinking the original plan was to blow her up."

"Yes. When Eliana ran from the hotel and sat alone in the park, she made it easy for them. They didn't need the bomb."

"We still don't have great evidence that it was two people. Just Dr. Ho's theory."

Sean wasn't interested in my opinion. He needed evidence, and I didn't have it. I took the baggie out of my pocket, which contained an M118LR bullet, and set it on the table.

"You broke the chain of evidence by removing this," Sean remarked.

"This isn't the shell we found at the scene. This is a shell I confiscated from Roan Caruso illegally. During the last case, I noticed Roan had an MRAD with a scope." An MRAD is a Multi-Role Adaptive Design bolt-action rifle. It's the best sniper rifle for a long-range shot. "I picked up a casing sitting by it, thinking the rifle would eventually be used in a crime. I knew we'd never be able to use the casing as evidence, but it could let us know if we were headed in the right direction."

"You never should have picked it up," Sean said. He took the baggie and looked at the bullet. "Do you think Roan killed Larry?"

"It could have been Roan, Catania, or Lorenzo. Cat had a naked woman tatted onto Larry's back after she found out he was the one who raped Eliana."

Sean laughed. "You have to admit that's pretty damn good. One way to guarantee he gets raped in prison for what he did."

"There's lots of motive. Larry could have charged Cat for assault. And they don't tolerate crimes against the family. Roan killed a kid for jacking his car in the past. I don't think he'd hesitate to kill someone who raped his son's fiancée."

"We can't use it," Sean reiterated.

"The St. Paul police are taking a lot of heat for this shooting. If this casing matches the one taken from the scene, you could honestly announce we have evidence the shooter wasn't a member of law enforcement." I reminded him, "You're the boss. I can't have this bullet tested without identifying where it came from. But you could."

Sean set the baggie in front of him. "Okay. Better to know, one way or another. It's best you don't say a word about this to anyone."

"I want to hide Eliana Castillo out for a couple of weeks until I've identified the second person involved in her assault. Can the BCA help with this?"

"The man who assaulted her is dead. Even if Larry had an

accomplice, Larry can't testify against the accomplice now. Eliana should be safe. Roan Caruso offered to protect her when she was first identified. You can check with him."

"I don't want her staying in Caruso housing. Not while his son is still a suspect."

"I can't justify it," Sean replied matter-of-factly. "Try victim services if you're worried."

"It could take months to get the funding. I need a place now."

"Sorry, I can't help you there."

After I left, I contacted my dad, who has lived as a bachelor since Mom died. He was ex-military and loved being called on to protect people. It's what he lived for. Bill had a couple of empty bedrooms in his house and was more than happy to help. I still wasn't entirely sure if I could trust Sean. Roan had something he was holding over Sean, and I wasn't sure if Sean was strong enough to stand up against it.

I called Eliana and told her, "I found a place for you, but it's in northern Minnesota."

"How northern?"

"That's a great question." You can drive almost six hours north from St. Paul and still be in Minnesota. "Only a couple hours north. You and your son will be staying at a farmhouse near Pierz. My dad is ex-military, and I can guarantee you will be safe with him. The Pierz school district is one of the best in the state. Pioneer Elementary received a national blue-ribbon award for its academics. Only six schools in the state received that recognition."

"Would it be okay if Mike also stayed for a day or two? He helped me pack."

"Sure. You can have him stay as long as you wish."

"Okay."

I pulled into the Holiday station at Maple Grove to fill up with gas and decided to send Serena a quick note before I returned home.

Serena,

I think of you every now and then. When my mind is sojourning to places I'd rather be, it's always with you. And I'm thankful for you—

now and then. I love you, Serena.

Jon

19

ELIANA CASTILLO
9:30 P.M., SUNDAY, AUGUST 11, 2024
PIERZ

L ast night, my six-year-old son Luis and I slept in the same bed in this old farmhouse, for my sake as much as his. Tonight, he was tucked into his own bedroom and sound asleep after adventuring through the woods and to the river with Mike and me. Mike was my voice. I texted him, and he shared my thoughts with my son. Mike showed Luis where a deer had nested. They slipped off their socks and shoes and waded into the river. It was hard not to talk to my son, but he understood and hugged me over and over. Today, Serena Frederick stopped by with her son, Jackson, who will be starting kindergarten this year with Luis—if I'm still here. Luis felt better about being here now that he had a friend.

Jon's dad, who asked me to call him Billy, barbecued chicken and boiled sweet corn for us. It was essential to Billy that we knew it was Janson sweet corn, grown a couple of miles down the road in Buckman. It was the sweetest corn I've ever eaten. The fact that it dripped in butter didn't hurt either.

After dinner, Mike went upstairs to settle into his own

bedroom, and I was left downstairs with Billy. I sat on the couch and typed into my laptop, "Thank you for your kindness and generosity. I promise to pay you back someday." I turned the screen so Billy could see it.

Billy was sitting on a recliner in the living room. He smiled. "You pay me back just by being here. I've always wanted a do-over as a father, so it's nice having your son here."

"Jon turned out fine," I typed.

"True," Billy said. "When Jon was a kid, we worked all the time. His older sister, Theresa, rebelled against her mom's intense religion. So, I'd take Theresa with me if we needed something in town. We'd stop at the bar, and I'd have a drink or two while we talked. Jon was left at home to do chores and take care of his mentally ill brother, Vic. Jon doesn't realize it, but he came out the winner in all of it. Jon's a worker. I thought my time with Theresa would get her on track. Instead, she learned to go to the bar to relax. And Jon rebelled by partying like he had a death wish the first year he left home. Camille prayed for our kids every night. I knew I seriously messed up. Then one day, Jon just quit the party scene. When that boy makes up his mind, that's it. He went to college, worked night and day, and played baseball on Sundays. Theresa settled down, they found the right meds for Vic, and my family was good. But the only time we saw Jon was after baseball games."

"Jon trusts you. That's why I'm here," I typed. I wasn't sure if this was the end of the story.

"After college, Jon met that reporter, Jada Anderson. They were both all about their careers. They'd leave holiday gatherings so they could get back to work."

"Jada Anderson from the TV news?" I typed.

"Yeah. Jon played baseball one more year, and then we didn't see him at all, except for holidays. One day, he told us he was going to propose. She accepted, with the stipulation that there would be no kids. That ended that. Jon didn't go out with her again. Like I said, once he makes up his mind, that's it. I told him to give her a few years. He said, 'I'm not going into a marriage hoping she changes. There's no point in dating.' Well, a couple of years later, she had a kid anyway, with Jon's boss."

"Do you think Jada went after his boss?"

"Nah. Other direction. I do wonder if Jon got invited to investigative work as fast as he did because his boss liked having Jada around."

The remark was insulting to Jon, implying he hadn't truly earned his position. I wasn't sure how I felt about that. "Do you think Jon regrets losing Jada?"

"Not for a moment. They're still friends. Jon got assigned the Murder Book case in this area, and Camille talked Jon into attending Christmas mass with us. And that's when we got our miracle." He turned the volume up on the TV as if that was the end of the story.

I took the remote from him and muted it. I typed, "TELL ME!"

He laughed at my assertiveness. "Serena happened to be in town that day. They were friends in high school, but not much more than that. Serena talked to Jon after mass, and as far as I know, every day since. Serena's all about family. Within a year, they had Nora, and she was tight with her Grandma Camille. Serena visits with the kids all the time, with or without Jon. Before Camille died, we had the perfect family."

"Thanks for sharing all that." I turned the volume back up again and handed him the remote. I typed, "Serena was a godsend."

"Yeah." Bill turned the volume back down again. "But Jon has good reason to resent me. My discipline was hard. I couldn't hit Theresa. You don't hit girls. And I couldn't hit Vic. He's mentally ill. It's not his fault." He tapped the remote against the armrest for a moment as he silently reflected.

I had a feeling there was much more to the story I would never know.

Bill finally added, "I don't hit anyone anymore. I grew up in a different time. When I was your son's age, my family was sitting at the dinner table when my older brother Bernie told Mom he'd been bullied at school. Dad was still working in the field that night. Ma told Bernie that he should punch the kid the next time that happened. Ma made Bernie stand in front of us, and she started jabbing at him like a boxer. She taunted, 'Hit me.' Bernie kept saying, 'I'm not hitting my mom.' But Ma danced around and jabbed at him progressively harder, telling him, 'Find an opportunity and land a punch.' Well, Dad came walking into the house, and when Ma turned, Bernie blasted her, dropping her to the floor. Dad yelled, 'What is wrong with you, boy?' A little groggy, Ma got to her feet and told Dad, 'Don't you punish that boy. He did exactly what he was supposed to do. He found an opening and took it.'"

I typed, "Did Bernie get kicked out of school?" I smiled.

"Not in that era. He did end the bullying."

"Well, after that heart-warming bedtime story, I'm heading upstairs. Good night, Billy."

"Good night," he said. "And you're welcome."

I hesitated, then typed, "Would you mind if I asked Mike to stay in my room? No funny business," I reassured him. "I would just feel safer."

"You do what you need to do, girl." He nodded his approval, and I headed upstairs.

Mike was settled in and sitting on the edge of his bed when I entered his room. "What can I do for you?" he asked.

I took his hand and escorted him into my room. I patted the bed, and he sat next to me.

I typed into my laptop, "Thank you for today. I want you to sleep in here tonight—for my sake."

"Okay. I'll grab a chair."

I shook my head. I typed, "Can you sleep in the same bed as me without wanting sex? It would help me if I could reach and feel your presence." I couldn't believe I said that. The truth is that if I would have had to say it out loud, I wouldn't have.

"Yes. I can even snore if it makes you more comfortable," Mike teased.

I squeezed his hand in thanks. Honestly, it wouldn't bother me if he snored. I needed to know he was there. I wanted to hug and be held, but that wasn't in the cards for me at the moment. It would be unfair to Mike. I knew he was attracted to me, and I had no idea what I was doing. I was being silently shuffled from one place to the next while people waited for me to get my act together.

My parents were great, but moving in with them would be a recipe for disaster. I sort of have two moms. Dad announced a decade ago that he was transgender and changed his name to Destiny. *She* doesn't want me to call her "Dad" because she has always felt she was a woman, even though she married Mom in an attempt to "be a man" and comply with social conventions. Still, I only feel right calling my birth mother "Mom," so I introduce them as my mom and my Destiny. They divorced, and both dated other women since Destiny defines herself as a lesbian woman. As the saying goes, *If you've met one trans person, you've met one trans person.* Three years ago, Destiny moved back in with Mom. They are best friends and have a better relationship than I've ever had with a romantic partner. Destiny never had confirmation surgery, and I believe they sometimes sleep together—TMI. I try not to think about it. My point is that if McBride and his accomplice will rape and kill me because I'm a woman, imagine what would happen if I moved in with my transgender parent. I can't do that. I love my parents.

Both Jon and Dr. Amaya are convinced that two people were involved in the assault. I only remember Crazy Larry, standing over me, shooting me. Pieces do come back sometimes. Painful, horrible pieces, like Larry on top of me, breathing on my neck. I remember squeezing my eyes tight as an object was thrust into me. I shook my head. That was enough.

"Are you okay?" Mike was studying me with concern.

I leaned into Mike's shoulder and hugged his arm. The phantoms had disappeared into wisps of air—for the moment.

He wrapped his arm around me and whispered, "You're safe now. I promise I won't let anything bad happen to you."

I needed to get to a happy place or, at the very least, get my thoughts out of hell. I rested my head against his shoulder and said, "Tell me about the most beautiful place you've ever been."

"The Boundary Waters, about two years ago. I woke up early and took a walk in the crisp summer morning air. The sun was rising, and there was a mist over the beautiful blue lake. No signs that humans had ever been there. The earth was clean and full of possibilities. It could have been heaven. I loved it, and then I was sad."

I glanced up at his face and drew a question mark in the air.

"I had no one to share it with."

For a moment, I imagined being with Mike at the Boundary Waters. The two of us snuggled together by a fire, enjoying something warm in the cool morning air. I snuggled my head into the crook of his neck, and my rosy cheek was comforted by the warmth of his chest.

In my mind's eye, the morning sun slowly ascended in a blaze of scarlet, orange, and magenta, promising a new day, free from the constraints of the world. *Was I the woman he wanted to share the sunrise with?*

My body and brain were constantly at odds when I was with Mike. My brain was telling me to get my act together before pursuing another guy. My body felt like Mike was an open door for me; it wanted to squeeze him in so close we'd be one entity. Maybe if he knew how damaged I was, he'd distance himself. I pulled away and typed, "I can't have babies now."

"It's kind of late in the evening to give birth anyway," Mike remarked. I bumped his shoulder, and he said, "I know what you meant. My thought is that you develop a great friendship with a partner and head out on an adventure. True love stays on that path through good and bad. Being with you is the dream. Everything that comes with it is icing on the cake. And fortunately, you already have a baby."

"We're approaching cuffing season," I teased.

"Cuffing?"

"You need to get out of your small town. Cuffing is partnering up to get through the cold months together. It begins in the fall and ends after Valentine's Day."

"Cuffing—like rolling up your cuffs and digging in, or like handcuffs?" Mike wondered.

"It's taken from handcuffs, but it's intended to be cute and unrestrained."

"More like having a trusting, cozy companion," Mike

suggested.

"Yes." His manner and tone warmed my heart. I said, "I'll go to the bathroom and get ready for bed. Get comfortable. Not 'naked' comfortable. 'Having-to-share-a-bed-with-your-sister' comfortable. That's all I'm ready for right now."

20

T he Jazz Authority was playing Karla Bonoff's "Personally" softly in the background. *"I've got something to give you that the mailman can't deliver…so I'm bringing it to you personally…"* Roan and Catania Caruso sat with me at a table in the warm night overlooking the moonlit bay. The two of them sipped on wine while I chose ice water. This was a serious conversation. Sean had contacted me and told me the ballistics report matched the bullet from Roan's sniper rifle to the one used to kill Larry McBride. He also told me that Roan was on camera playing poker at Mystic Lake Casino at the time of the shooting.

Roan snapped, "We had an agreement. Nothing would be used from the past."

"Nothing that was collected prior to this case is being used to prosecute anyone." That was true. I had no idea how much Sean had shared with him. I needed to be careful, as saying the wrong thing could put my life and my family's lives in jeopardy. Roan and Cat were barbaric when it came to protecting Lorenzo.

Roan raised his finger to eye level as if he was about to say something, and then stopped himself. He pointed his finger directly at me. "How do you know Larry McBride was shot with my rifle? Huh? Tell me that, wise guy."

"Can you think of a family that might have a connection to a tattoo parlor?" I turned to Catania. "You put the tattoo on Larry. He could have filed assault charges."

Cat smiled. "Do you really think I wanted him dead? I would have just killed him. I wanted him to take it up the ass over and over in prison as a reminder of what he did to poor Eliana. He ruined her."

Roan started to rock back and forth slightly as he silently seethed.

Catania didn't shoot Larry. I'd been working so hard on this case, while trying to keep everyone happy at home, that I hadn't given this situation the thought it warranted. I disliked her suggestion that Eliana was ruined and said, "Eliana's tough. She'll fight her way back."

"It's over." Cat dismissed me with a wave of her hand. "I know how your do-good brain works, but it isn't reality. Do you think Lorenzo's the kind of guy who's going to sit by her bed and hold her hand through her nightmares? I raised Lorenzo. He's high-maintenance. Lorenzo needs a woman doting on him twenty-four hours a day." She shrugged and challenged me, "You can try to put Eliana back with him, but he'll be in his Hummer with one dolly after another hummin' away while she's suffering. Is that the life you want for her?"

"No, it's not. You're right."

"Don't patronize us!" Roan shouted at me.

I didn't particularly like Lorenzo, so I hoped Eliana would move on. I wasn't convinced she was ready, though. Eliana had been planning to marry him.

Roan continued, "You need to back off of Lorenzo. Promise me you're going to do that."

"I can't promise you anything. I didn't want this damn case from the very beginning. You were the one who insisted I work it. You used whatever you have on Sean to put me on this case."

"Lorenzo didn't rape Eliana. That's all you have to prove." Roan squeezed his fist repeatedly as he spoke. He was itching for a fight.

"Then let me do my job. I needed to let law enforcement interview him. I traced the attempted murder to Larry McBride and got Lorenzo released. That's pretty damn good when you consider our victim still hasn't been able to make a statement we can use in court." I stood up. "My work here is done. I'm going to let you enjoy your night."

As I walked away, Roan shouted, "Back off of Lorenzo. That's not a suggestion."

His insistence convinced me further that Lorenzo had shot Larry McBride. The family was hiding Lorenzo out, and I needed to find him. The unanswered question was whether Lorenzo was involved with Larry in Eliana's assault after she rejected him. *Was Larry's murder a way of shutting him up?*

21

ELIANA CASTILLO
10:30 P.M., THURSDAY, AUGUST 15, 2024
PIERZ

The wires had been removed from my jaw, so I could talk again. I finally had the chance to tell Luis I loved him when I tucked him into bed. I missed that terribly. I had been touching my heart and his, but I wished I could say it out loud. Now I'm doing both.

Billy, Mike, and I watched another episode of *Case Histories*. We were getting to the end of the series. I hate finding a good show and then learning there are no more seasons.

Mike stood in the bedroom, waiting for me to go to the bathroom and put my nightshirt on.

Instead, I turned my back to him and undressed. I slipped on a nightshirt and, now braless, was ready for bed. I turned to Mike, picked up the laptop, and laughed at my foolishness. I set it back down and said, "I guess I can talk now." He smiled as I asked, "What do you usually sleep in?"

"When I'm alone, just my boxers."

"Are you hot in sweatpants and a T-shirt?"

"Yeah, but it's okay. It's worth it to be with you."

"Are you getting paid for this?"

"No. I want to make sure you're safe."

"Then strip down to your boxers and crawl into bed. I promise I won't make any moves. I like having you here. Even if you fall asleep with me sometimes."

"I'm awake at the slightest sound," he assured me.

I crawled into bed and watched Mike remove his outer layers, shut off the light, and join me. He was in great shape. "Thank you for staying with me, Mike."

"You tell me that every night."

"I mean it every night." I turned toward him. "Would you mind scratching my back?"

"I would not."

It was dark, with a slight hint of moonlight slipping through the edge of the closed curtain to illuminate our forms.

I turned onto my stomach and lifted my shirt. "Scratch away."

After a few minutes, I said, "That's good," and pulled my shirt back down. The darkness made it easier to talk. I couldn't see him, and he couldn't see me, so there would be no visible judgment. "I've been thinking about incels. I remember for a moment, at fifteen, feeling like I had power. Guys wanted to do things for me. But it was creepy, too, because they wanted to do things to me. Things I wasn't ready for."

"In some ways, that had to feel good. I mean, I've never felt I had that power over women," Mike shared. "I imagine it was scary, too."

"But that's the thing, Mike, guys have power. Think about what it's like for girls. For me, I was always dating someone stronger and a couple of years older. And I regret it. The boys in my class acted goofy, and the older guys had cars and places of their own. I thought I was so lucky that they wanted me. For a moment, I was a celebrity. And then I got knocked up, and I was a joke."

"The irony is that the goofy guys in your grade probably wouldn't have walked away from parenting your son."

"That's true." I reminisced about the male friends I had in my grade. It was absolutely true. I wish I would have spent more time with my class. Lorenzo had put me on a pedestal again. The fact that I had a child was neither a curse nor a blessing. He wanted me any way he could have me, but it's hard to imagine a future with a man you can't trust. Shifting my attention back to power over women, I said, "Incels are wrong. They don't know what it's like to rush to your car and immediately lock it. Or have to worry when you're driving alone that some creep's following you or some guy's going to run you off the road and rape you. How you can never dare to show you're angry at a guy if you're alone with him. I had to go through the cost/benefit of having you here. You're bigger, stronger, and you've got a gun. I finally concluded that the odds are better that I'd be assaulted if you *weren't* here. And it's not just theory. It happened to me."

Even though his outline was dark, I could sense him turning toward me as he said softly, "I'm sorry. I can promise you I will never hurt you. Is there anything I can do? Get you a warm blanket—anything. If you need a hug or my hand on your shoulder, you need to say, because I'm not going to touch you unless you ask."

I kind of wanted a hug, but then again, I didn't want to make this weird. *Weirder.* I felt a tear on my cheek and turned away. "I'm good. I think you might be my best friend, Mike."

"Thank you. I think you're mine, too."

"Why are you single?"

"I'm one of those safe types. Let's say you wanted to hike on our first date. I'd check out the trail ahead of time, and if I noticed part of it had collapsed, I'd suggest we take another way. The guy who gets the girl is the one who shows up late, takes the bad trail, and lets the girl fall over the side, but he grabs her hand and rescues her at the last minute."

"I need safe, Mike."

"I know." It was silent for a moment before he finally said, "Do you know what limerence is?"

"I've seen it online. Isn't it like being infatuated with someone even when they don't feel the same way?" Where was he going with this?

"I worry about it. My relationships always end with people

saying, 'You're too nice.' What they really mean is, 'I don't feel connected to you.' When you love someone, their kindness feels good." He groaned. "I've been less than successful." He chuckled, "I guess 'failure' is the word I'm avoiding."

"Do you feel like a failure with me?" I debated hugging him and turned to face him again. I couldn't really see him. I needed to reach my arm over without slapping him.

"No." Mike whispered, "Good night, Eliana," and turned his back to me.

Well, so much for that. I blew out a long breath. I might have just dodged a bullet. *What am I doing?* I couldn't make love to him. It was bad enough that I invited my guard into my bed.

2:30 A.M., FRIDAY, AUGUST 18, 2024
PIERZ

I woke up and realized Mike was lying on his back, and I was sleeping with my head on his chest. I slowly looked up at him and asked, "You awake?"

"Sound asleep," he responded.

"Sorry about that."

"It's not the first night it's happened. Sometimes, after you have a nightmare, you come to me. It's all good. You can stay there if you want to."

"What are you thinking, Mike?"

"I think I'm falling in love with you."

I pulled away and turned my back to him. I wished he hadn't said that. The truth is, I want to give him my life and have him take it over for me. *Please tell me what to do. I will submit unconditionally.* But I know myself. Little by little, I'll start resenting him until I completely hate him for it. I'm unraveling at the seams. Why can't he see it? People are caring for me like I'm a child just to keep me functioning. I'm a long way from well. I feel like a Greek tragedy in the making. We might be sailing now, but I'm crashing this ship into the rocks. I always do. I'll destroy him, and he's so incredibly kind. *Please don't fall in love with me.*

22

JON FREDERICK
9:00 P.M., FRIDAY, AUGUST 16, 2024
ROUNDHOUSE BREWERY
23836 SMILEY ROAD, NISSWA

Serena pulled into the dirt parking lot behind Roundhouse Brewery to drop me off. She planned to stop at a friend's house to prepare for our mystery date. She loves to walk into a bar and pretend we just met. Tonight, like many "chance meeting" nights, she apparently needed to dress in a manner for which I would not be prepared. I admired the courage it took to do this in her depressed state. Her beautiful emerald eyes met mine. "I don't know if I should even try this."

Serena had been rereading Jane Eyre by Charlotte Brontë, so I anticipated she would be greeting me in Bridgerton style and discourse. Serena gets completely into the role and can be incredibly entertaining. We both like the challenge of adjusting to an impromptu dialogue. I told her, "Let's give it a shot. I've had a rough week of work. Even if we completely bomb, it will be the best thing that's happened to me."

"I didn't know Brothers Tone was playing tonight. The place is packed." She gazed over at the outdoor stage.

"Even better. It's a great band." I smiled. Both Serena and I loved to listen to Karla Jensen sing. "Everybody's outside listening to the band. Meet me in the bar."

"The only reason I'm not backing out is that I have a couple of friends in town, waiting to help me get ready." She considered her options and said, "Okay. Give me thirty minutes. If I haven't entered the bar by then, I've chickened out. I'll pick you up here."

I leaned over and kissed her. "I love you, Serena."

"If I don't do this, it's because I love you and don't want to embarrass you."

"I'm not easily embarrassed." I stepped out and watched her drive away.

I sat at the horseshoe bar and ordered a red lager called Der Zug. I nursed my Festbier to give Serena every opportunity to walk in. Festbiers are smooth and clean with a moderately strong malty flavor and are typically brewed as Oktoberfest beers. The name Der Zug, which means "the train," is perfect for Roundhouse Brewery. A roundhouse is a locomotive maintenance shed built around a turntable. The outdoor seating was packed, but only a few couples were standing by the bar. I sat quietly and ran case scenarios through my head. Roan didn't shoot Larry, and I don't think Catania did either. I finally finished my last swallow and stood.

The door opened, and all heads turned. Serena wore a pastel blue, high-waisted Regency dress with subtle embroidery and glistening brocade. The neckline was bare from one puffy short sleeve to the other. There was graceful beauty in her smooth shoulders. A row of powder blue forget-me-nots had been expertly French braided into her hair, which hung over her right shoulder to her breast. Her magical elegance took my breath away, and I silently watched her approach. I sat back down and turned to the bartender, "I think I'll have me an Angel."

Serena immediately interjected, "I am no angel, and I don't plan on being one 'til I die. I will be myself."

"I'm ordering an amber beer. It's called Angel Seat." Her "I'm no angel" quote was one of my favorites from Brontë's book. Prepared for a barrage of references from *Jane Eyre*, I asked, "Are you here alone?"

She twirled in a pirouette, hands out front, gracefully guiding her. Her dress billowed out as she turned. Serena swept her hand through the empty space around her and asked, "Are you having visions? I see no one. No net ensnares me. I am a free human being with an independent will."

"When I asked the last woman I dated if she was still free, she said, 'No, I charge now.'"

The comment earned a smile from two of the couples at the bar, but Serena didn't flinch. "I do not sell my soul to buy bliss if that's what you're implying."

"I wouldn't sully your purity by such an implication." Honestly, my brain was fried from worry about work and home. I tried again. "Can I buy you a beverage? They don't have mead, but they do have a wild rice ale."

Serena turned to the bartender. "Do you have any virgin cocktails?"

"Mocktails? We have kombucha."

"Thank you, my lady." Serena handed the bartender a twenty-dollar bill and curtsied, then returned her attention to me. "I will have you know, I care for myself. The more solitary, the more friendless, and the more unfunded I am, the more I respect myself. Do you think, because I am plain and little, I am soulless and heartless? You think wrong!"

"You are far from plain, and I feel at any moment I could burst into flames from the fire in your soul and the warmth of your heart." My mind suddenly went blank. I met her eyes and told her exactly what I was thinking. "I am sorry I'm so incompetent. You're amazing."

"Flirting is a woman's trade," Serena said, covering for me. "One must keep in practice. If there were only one simple phrase a man could speak in my language, they would capture a permanent place in my heart's very hearthstone."

When I failed to respond immediately, she sighed and glanced down. I searched my brain for the phrase Mr. Rochester had said to Jane Eyre. I had memorized it once in anticipation of this very moment, but it wasn't coming back to me. Realizing I was bombing, I decided to paraphrase as best I could. "Women who please me only by their faces bedevil me when I find their souls have no character and their hearts no compassion. But give me a woman with an eloquent tongue, a soul made of fire, and a character that bends but does not break, and I will always be tender and true."

She stepped into me, wrapped her arms around my neck, and kissed me, long and hard. It's been a tough couple of months for us, and I treasured the moment. We were met with cheers. Her embrace pulsated warm, soothing love through my veins.

"I fear hell for what I'm about to ask of an angel such as yourself. I want to know your love, sorrow, fear, elation, and flesh—unveiled. And not for a moment. For the rest of my existence," I proclaimed.

"That sounds heavenly. How do you envision hell?" she stepped back and asked.

"Eternal fire and brimstone."

"If your intentions are salacious, how do you plan to avoid the inferno?"

"By keeping in good health and not dying."

It was all Serena could do to hold back her laughter. "I'd rather be happy than dignified. It's in vain to say human beings ought to be satisfied with tranquility: they must have action, and they will make it if they cannot find it. If you feel you can handle me, I'm yours."

"I would love to handle you." I took her hand and drove her home.

23

JON FREDERICK
5:30 A.M., SUNDAY, AUGUST 18, 2024
PIERZ

My phone buzzed, and I quickly grabbed it off the nightstand. It was my dad. "Is Eliana okay?"

"Yeah, but you're not," Bill replied. "Check out the cameras in the woods behind your house."

I rushed downstairs to my office computer. The infrared night vision cameras I'd installed revealed a man walking up the hill toward my house carrying a rifle. I directed the camera to focus on the man. He had moved behind a tree, so I couldn't see his face. I couldn't believe he'd noticed the camera, which is difficult to see, especially at night. He finally stepped forward, and I had his face on camera—Lorenzo Turrisi Caruso. I told Dad, "He's finding a spot to set up so he can shoot me through the window when I get up in the morning. What are you doing out there?"

"I've been here every night since Serena called me. Mike can protect Eliana at night. Do you want me to kill him?"

"No."

"I kind of want to. Since your mom died, I feel like I don't have a lot to lose anymore." "BANG!" A shot rang out in the night. I watched bark come flying off a tree close to Lorenzo's head. He quickly turned and looked around.

He stopped in his tracks and waited for two minutes. Finally, Lorenzo took one more step forward.

"BANG!" A second shot ricocheted off a rock in front of Lorenzo. He slowly began backing up. After a few steps, he turned and ran away from my house as fast as he could.

"Next time, they'll be burying that son of a bitch," Dad said.

Serena walked into the office. "I heard gunshots. They sounded close."

I explained to her what had happened. I ended by telling her, "You can go back to bed. I'll stay up and watch the cameras."

"Thank God for your dad. Are you calling the police?"

"I am. I want a record that Lorenzo was here. Even if he gets out of any charges."

She hugged me and said, "I'll try to sleep."

I needed to find a way out of this. I called Roan Caruso. He didn't answer the phone, but I left him a message. "Lorenzo was outside my house at 5:30 a.m. with a rifle. I could have killed him, but I didn't. It's been reported to law enforcement. The video has been forwarded to law enforcement. If he's not guilty, why is he coming to kill the man who's trying to solve the case?"

24

ELIANA CASTILLO
1:00 P.M., SUNDAY, AUGUST 18, 2024
PIERZ

I was standing in the kitchen looking out at the green fields surrounding the farm. I could hear Mike on the phone, turning down the opportunity to work today. My heart sank. His care and compassion were so intense they were almost tangible. Mike would be a great cop. But here he was, babysitting me.

I called Carmel and found myself intensely rubbing my forehead as I told her, "Remember the law enforcement guy I've been telling you about? I'm thinking of asking him to leave."

"Why?" she asked. "You're always so excited when you talk about him. You were telling me yesterday he's perfect."

"It's too fast. He's sleeping in my bed now. Luis is confused. I'm confused. I want him here, and then I wonder if I'm just afraid to be alone. There are nights I want to make love to him. But I feel like maybe it's because I haven't let anyone else in. I mean, I didn't seek him out. He just walked into my life. I worry that I might have accepted anybody in."

"Ellie, you're thinking too much about it. Relax and enjoy the ride. From what you've told me, he seems so right for you. I know you. You're going to regret letting go. I think you're afraid to be happy again..."

Carmel had me thinking, but I wasn't going to be distracted from my plan. I needed to have a heart-to-heart with Mike.

2:00 p.m.

Later, Mike and I walked a dirt ATV path bordering a cornfield. The stalks of corn towered eight feet high and were so thick that it would be impossible to run through the field. There were no rows to be chased through, like I'd seen in horror movies. I began, "I want to thank you for staying here with me. I don't know how I can ever repay you." I loved having Mike here, but I had to let him move on with his life. We'd been together day and night. I needed to step back and make certain this was exactly what I needed before I dove in again with all my heart.

"I can stay until the nightmares go away. I don't mind helping you. I enjoy it. And Luis is a great kid."

"That's part of the problem," I said. "First, there was Lorenzo, and now you. What am I doing to my kid?" He looked disheartened, so I quickly added, "You're great with Luis. I love the way you listen to him and have him excited about biking and exploring. But it's confusing for him. He asked me if you're going to be his next dad."

"What did you say?" Mike glanced at me as he spoke.

I wasn't prepared to answer that question. I looked straight ahead and said, "I don't think so." Even as I said it, I wasn't sure I meant it. I felt so incredibly sad.

"Okay." He replied, clearly pained.

"I should never have asked you to get so personal with me. You need to get back to work. How do you even survive?"

"I've worked here and there when Billy's around. Don't worry about me."

"I'm asking you to stop spending time with me. I have to fix things with Lorenzo."

"You're kidding." He stopped in his tracks. "If you don't want me around, I get it. But don't go back to that dirtball."

I wasn't sure that I was necessarily going back to Lorenzo, but I needed resolution. I turned to face Mike and, seeing the tears in his eyes, said, "I need to end one relationship before I can start another. It's too messy." After a few silent steps, I summoned my courage and said, "I've made up my mind." Mike was so hurt, and he was such a good friend. I was struggling to explain myself. I wasn't abandoning him forever. I wanted to clean my slate and start over. "What are you thinking? Please talk to me."

"I'm frustrated." He stared at the ground as he walked. "I get up every morning and try to be the best person I can be. I try to be kind and respectful. Guys like Lorenzo don't have to do anything. He can disrespect you, cheat on you, even hit you, and you take him back. Because he's handsome and rich."

"If that's what you think of me, why would you even want to be with me?" It hurt to be seen as so incredibly small and shallow.

"Because I see something better in you. After you had Luis, you felt unattractive. You were still the intelligent and funny woman you'd always been, but I think it bothered you not to get second glances. And then Lorenzo came along, and he only cared about how you looked. It was flattering because it reawakened that power you had back at fifteen. But that's just polishing the shine on the outside. When you talk about Lorenzo, you talk about the new dresses and vacations. When you talk to me, you're excited about something you're considering or something you've learned. If all you need is new dresses, you don't need me. Lorenzo's your man. Lorenzo's a shiny new toy guy, and for the moment, you're it."

I turned away to hold back my tears. I was too hurt to say another word. I started walking back to the house without him. I felt shaky and weak, but I needed to do this. I couldn't let him see me falling apart.

"I'm sorry," Mike apologized as he hurried to catch up. "I'm being a jerk. You don't want to be with me, and that's your right. I will respect that." Without another word, he jogged ahead of me toward the house. I stayed outside and watched as he carried out his duffel bags, tossed them in his Jeep, and tore out of the driveway. I could feel his pain, and I felt terrible for him. It's a punishing world for tender-hearted people. I know. I used to be one.

My phone buzzed, and seeing it was Roan Caruso, I took it. He said, "You okay? I heard you can talk again."

"Not really. Healing."

"Yeah, I was sorry to hear it. You're a good woman, Eliana. I just wanted to tell you we miss you."

"I always felt like Cat hated me."

"Cat doesn't think anyone's good enough for Lorenzo. If Lorenzo loves you, she'll come around to loving you, too. Remember how crappy Cat treated my daughter Halle when she first met her?"

"She still isn't very nice to her." I was with the Turrisi Caruso family for Easter, and I don't recall Cat saying a word to Halle or her fiancé.

"Shunning is progress from directly insulting her," Roan observed. "It's a process. From my perspective, you're Lorenzo's only shot at being with a normal person. You should see the clowns that he's traipsed through this house—in full clown makeup. He misses you. I know he messed up, but that's how relationships are. We learn and grow together. I think if you could give him another chance, you'd never regret it."

"I promise to think about it." I didn't bother telling him Lorenzo had already had another chance. Too many, in fact.

"Did Jon Frederick talk to you about last night yet?" Roan asked.

"No. What happened?" My anxiety skyrocketed.

"Lorenzo was wandering outside Jon's house last night with a rifle. He was trying to intimidate Jon into backing off. You know as well as I do that Lorenzo never assaulted you. For him to be accused of this while still loving you so intensely tears him apart. It would be a lifesaver if you could give him another chance. At least until he's back on the rails again."

I didn't respond. *Should I be responsible for fixing him?* I certainly didn't want to be responsible for any harm coming to Jon and Serena. Dating Lorenzo has made it clear that his combination of money and Mafia connections will buffer him from experiencing consequences for anything short of killing someone.

"The truth is, Lorenzo's never loved anyone like he loves you. The lack of contact is tearing him apart," Roan said. Not being one to beg, he quickly toughened up and added, "Do whatever you need to do. If you need anything, call me."

"Thank you, Roan. I promise to think about it." I knew I could calm down Lorenzo. I'd done so a hundred times in the past. Lorenzo would listen to me and leave the Fredericks alone. If he was off the rails, as Roan had suggested, he was dangerous. Lorenzo was a sharpshooter, and Ross had shared stories of Lorenzo picking off a deer at three hundred yards, which is insane when you think about it—almost the height of the Empire State Building away. I could really use Mike back. He would return if I called, but I couldn't call. I wouldn't call. A realization began to germinate inside me. I should have thought of this the night McBride was executed in my home.

Jon and Serena had done so much for me, and I had put their family at risk. I needed to resolve this. Billy agreed to take Luis to see his father, Donny. I was hoping to avoid a court case by allowing him a couple of visits.

6:00 P.M., WCCO 90 SOUTH 11TH STREET, MINNEAPOLIS

If I were going to save Jon's family, I needed to go big. I contacted news reporter Jada Anderson and sat down with her for a recorded interview. Jada and I were spotlighted in the center of the room while half a dozen station employees were in the dark perimeter running sound and filming. Jada's smooth chocolate skin seemed poreless. Her confident demeanor was intimidating. My makeup was touched up, and we were ready to start filming.

She reassured me, "This will be a piece of cake. I'll ask questions, and you simply need to answer them as best you can. I'll fill in if you're struggling. No worries. You've got this, girl!" She briefly glanced over my head, turned back, and yelled at the film crew, "Shut your damn phones off! I'm getting a flicker of a reflection in the background off someone's phone." Jada turned back to me and calmly began the interview. "I'm sitting here with Eliana Castillo, the victim of a brutal attack in Detroit Lakes less than a month ago. On August 9, the man who assaulted her broke in and was killed by a shooter from outside her home. There has been a great deal of speculation that law enforcement killed Larry McBride. Eliana is here to tell us that this isn't the case."

I swallowed hard. I was still struggling with speaking and couldn't get words out.

Jada intervened, "Do you mind if I start by explaining in more detail what you've been through?"

"No," I rattled out hoarsely.

"Eliana had purchased a new dress and was set to meet her boyfriend at a beautiful lodge on Detroit Lake. She knew he had planned to propose to her. They had a misunderstanding, and Eliana went to a park to seriously consider this major decision. Eliana was abducted from the park by Larry McBride, who proceeded to rape her and beat her so severely that her jaw had to be wired shut. She has only recently started talking again. Eliana was assaulted with a hammer and shot before she was left for dead in the woods. She managed to drag herself to her feet and walk through the woods for almost a mile before she found help. This is a remarkable young woman."

"Thank you."

Jada's tone became even more serious as she shared, "Larry McBride was arrested, and the weapon used to shoot Eliana was taken from his home. But Larry managed to make bail and sought out Eliana to kill the one witness who could testify against him. He broke into your house, correct?"

"Yes," I nodded. "Investigator Jon Frederick hid me in the attic. But my attic is all blown insulation, so the boards are all covered like a big snowbank. I slipped off a two-by-six, and when I tried to catch myself, my hand banged on the ceiling below. McBride knew exactly where I was and raised his gun to murder me."

"That must have been terrifying," Jada interrupted to build the tension. "What happened next?"

"My fiancé had been watching over me because he was afraid McBride might come after me. Law enforcement had asked Lorenzo to stay three hundred feet away from me, and he was respecting their directive. I had been with him before the attack, so when I was unconscious, he was the first suspect, and a no-contact order was put in place. Lorenzo had a rifle with a scope so he could observe my home from the required distance. That night, when Lorenzo saw that McBride was about to kill me, he shot him to save my life. I am asking that Lorenzo not be charged for saving my life. I would hope anyone's fiancé would do the same."

"How can you be so certain Lorenzo Caruso fired that shot?" Jada questioned.

"I just spoke to him, and he admitted it."

Jada stood and said to the crew, "That is a take. Let's get this out to news stations." She smiled at me. "Great work!"

On the way home, I called Billy to see how the visit with Luis and his dad had gone. Billy told me, "Donny didn't show. But Luis and I went to the science museum. We did experiments, melted marshmallows, and ate supper at Minnesota Nice Cream."

Luis yelled from the back seat, "I had the Happy Camper cone. Marshmallows. Sprinkles. It was awesome!"

"Thank you, Billy," I said with heartfelt appreciation.

When the call was over, I was ready to pitch a hissy fit. I immediately called Donny, scream-yelling into the phone, "What the fuck, Donny? You set him up just to break his heart."

A woman responded coolly, "Luis will never be part of our family. Donny forgot to have this conversation with me. You appall me, using your son as bait to get Donny back. You're no different than you were at sixteen."

"I hope I never see Donny again," I shot back.

"Good. Then we're on the same page." She hung up.

25

JON FREDERICK
7:30 A.M., MONDAY, AUGUST 19, 2024
ST. JOSEPH'S CHURCH
68 MAIN STREET NORTH, PIERZ

I filled my vehicle with gas and started south on Main Street when I saw a despondent Mike Haney plodding down the sidewalk in front of the church. I pulled over, got out of my car, and approached him. "You okay?"

"Yeah."

We stood by a stone retaining wall as we spoke.

Mike studied me briefly before saying, "You've heard."

"Eliana talks to Serena," I said as I nodded.

"It's the second time she's told me she doesn't want me around anymore." He sighed, "I miss her like childhood—a good time I can't go back to." We watched a large John Deere tractor with dual tires pulling a combine that was more than a lane wide. Mike continued, "I don't know why Eliana's rejection floored me. Everyone has heartbreak, but this was rock bottom. It's hard to find someone who's so easy to talk to."

I continued to watch the tractor and harvester rumble down the road.

Finally, Mike asked, "You listening?"

"We just watched a million dollars of farm equipment roll by in a minute's time. Those two machines are worth more than we ever made on the farm and more than it was worth when we lost it." I wasn't sure what to say. I didn't want to give him false hope, but I honestly didn't feel Eliana and Mike were over. I turned back to him. "All we have are intersections of time with people, so make the most of them. Serena and I weren't born at the same time, and with any luck, we won't die at the same time, so I try to make the most of the intersection we have right now."

"Why is it lucky to die at different times?"

"Think about it. If we die at the same time, it will either be the result of an accident or homicide. It would be my preference for us both to live into old age."

Mike leaned back against the wall. "What did I do wrong?"

"As Eliana's bodyguard, you did everything right. You kept her alive." I had a feeling deep inside that hadn't worked its way to the surface yet, suggesting someone may still want her dead. That thought was better left unsaid until I worked it out. I told him, "Eliana's dealing with a lot right now. Serena would say you did everything right."

"But you wouldn't."

"Serena's nicer than I am. You skipped opportunities to develop your career so you could stay with Eliana."

"She needed protection."

"True. But that's why she's living with Bill. You put Eliana in the position of worrying not only about her safety but also about you because you stopped pursuing your career."

"I made her safety a priority," Mike said.

"I love Serena, and I love my kids. But she understands I have to work. You need to be a little more selfish. You get satisfaction from helping Eliana, right?"

"Yeah."

"You deny her that satisfaction by not allowing her to do things for you. Eventually, she's going to feel you don't need her, and the only way she can get that satisfaction is to help somebody else."

"But Lorenzo?" He glanced away and then back again. "I guess this is the moment when I shouldn't say anything at all about him. He belongs in orange, and I don't mean hunting orange."

"Eliana's looking for answers. Sometimes, you need to talk to people you'd prefer not to in order to get 'em. You're a cop, you understand."

"So, what should I do?" Mike wondered.

"Fulfill your own destiny. Relationships are about compromise, not abandoning your goals. Get back to your career. Keep being a decent guy. Work out to burn off the frustration. Learn from this and go into your next relationship a little wiser. The hits keep coming. Life's a bumpy road."

"I hate that she pushed me away, but I get it. It was too much too soon." Mike nodded. "I've never shared that kind of intimacy with anyone."

"Do you regret that time?"

"No," he said sadly.

I felt that was as much emotion as two guys could handle at 7:30 in the morning. Time to move on. "With all the time you've spent with Eliana, do you have any suspicions of who her second attacker might be?"

"Lorenzo. Whenever she'd mention McBride, she'd start talking about Lorenzo's infidelity. His unfaithfulness was the reason Eliana left that hotel room."

"God bless you, Mike. You've been helpful. I think I'm headed in the right direction. I appreciate you stepping up to help Eliana." I got up and shook his hand. "I've got to get to work."

10:00 A.M.
BUREAU OF CRIMINAL APPREHENSION
1430 MARYLAND AVENUE, ST. PAUL

Sean Reynolds called me into his office to discuss the case. I sat in front of his desk and told him, "You could have given me a heads-up on Jada's interview."

"Do you think Jada consults with me about her reporting?" He took a sip from his white mug of coffee, which had "100 Black Men" printed in bold letters on the side. It was a Twin Cities organization he belonged to that mentored African American youth. "I was thinking *you* should have told me Eliana was going to make a statement."

"She hadn't told me about it." Eliana managed to pull me out of the Caruso family's crosshairs by garnering sympathy for Lorenzo. I had to give her credit for stepping up for us.

"Lorenzo independently came to the Ramsey County Sheriff's office and made a statement that he was the one who shot Larry McBride." Sean tapped his desk. "Lorenzo's story is trending online, and he's on his way to being an internet star. I don't see him walking away with any charges. All this attention is going to make it difficult to prove he killed McBride to shut him up."

"I made a statement on the night of McBride's death that the shooter saved Eliana's life."

"This was back when you were trying to protect law enforcement," Sean suggested.

"I was telling the truth. Regardless of the reason, Lorenzo saved her life. I was about to shoot McBride, but you know how handgun shootouts go. It could have ended with either of us dead."

"Close the case so we can finally be done with the Carusos."

"I need to speak to a couple more people first."

"Wrap it up. I want it done. Is something going on with you and Eliana?"

I paused. "Why would you even suggest that?"

"Lorenzo complained to me about your boundaries with Eliana."

"You know me better than that. Lorenzo is the classic cheating partner who's assuming Eliana is like him. What does Roan have on you?"

"Nothing." Sean stood up and looked out the window.

"I don't believe you. I'm investigating the Minnesota Mafia at your request. I need to know that I can trust you."

Sean sighed. "Roan had videos of me in a hotel room with Lauren Herald back when Jada and I were engaged." Sean turned back to me. "He insisted I put you on this case, or he would put them online. I wanted you on the case anyway, so I went along. Jada and I are finally working it out. Lauren is engaged to Zave. There was no need to stir up all this old drama. The videos are destroyed now, and I never compromised my work to protect the Carusos. I wouldn't do that." Sean glanced back at me. "You have two weeks, then shut it down."

10:45 A.M.

Not long after my conversation with Sean ended, a call was forwarded to my BCA office from Roan Caruso.

"Mr. Jon Frederick. I have to give you credit for the Eliana Castillo interview. I couldn't see a way of clearing Lorenzo on this charge, but you got that girl to do it."

"So, are we good?" I didn't have anything to do with it, but if it got Roan to leave my family alone, I wouldn't bother to explain.

"All good. Sorry for the intrusion. No charges are coming down on Lorenzo for the other night. He explained that he was having some car trouble. He was looking for help and got lost. He had his rifle with him because of the stories he's heard about wolves in northern Minnesota."

"We both know that's not true."

"Look, he just wanted to scare you off—stupid kid. I've drilled it into his head that if anything happens to you or your family now, he's toast. You have him on video. It won't happen again. I promise. Are you done with my son?"

"Provided he doesn't have other crimes."

"Okay. You're done."

3:00 P.M.
KING OF DIAMONDS GENTLEMAN'S CLUB
6600 RIVER ROAD
INVER GROVE HEIGHTS

I met with friends of Cheri Wilde about an hour before the Gentleman's Club opened. The scent of *Eau de Strip Club* that permeated the air was equal parts sweat, perfume, cologne, and sanitizer. I think it's hard not to look at women walking around naked in these places, but it's not about arousal for me. It's more like, "You're in a public place. Put some clothes on." It's a glance and then back to business. Honestly, I'd rather it wasn't around me. I wonder if it would be the same for Serena around naked men. I've never had the guts to ask her.

The need to prove a connection between Cheri and Larry McBride became less urgent after his death. Still, I wanted to bring resolution to Cheri's murder. I sat with Zig, the bartender, and exotic dancers Ivory and Capri at the bar, sharing some pictures.

Zig pointed to a picture of McBride and said in his gravelly voice, "I recognize that asshole. He paid for a private dance and started pushing Cheri around because she refused to have sex with him."

Ivory's long, painted nails ran over the picture. "That's the guy. I didn't see him, but I heard about it. Cheri said he kept referring to her as Stacy. What is that about?"

"McBride was an incel. In incel lingo, a Stacy is a woman who is narcissistic and feels she is far too good for the average guy." I set out a picture of McBride with Lorenzo and the crew on their fishing trip.

"What a creep," Capri added. She glanced over the group picture and said, "I liked this guy." She pointed to Lorenzo.

"How did you know him?"

"He's been here. Cheri was starting to have feelings for him. I told her, 'Girl, be careful. It's just a job. You both have a different life outside of here.' Cheri said, 'I've been with him outside of here.'"

"How long ago was this?" I asked.

"It must have been—" She tapped her long, glittery nails on her lips. "Early summer. A couple weeks before she was murdered."

No matter how badly I wanted to close this, Lorenzo kept drawing me back into it. I was curious about what Lorenzo's OnlyFans lover, Londyn Lust, had to say about Lorenzo.

26

ELIANA CASTILLO
10:00 A.M., WEDNESDAY, AUGUST 21, 2024
CESAR CHAVEZ STREET, DISTRICT DEL SOL
WEST SIDE, ST. PAUL

My house was no longer a protected crime scene, so I returned to clean up. I love this house, and I have so many good memories with Luis. But I couldn't get the image of McBride's brain matter on my wall out of my head. The hallway was a monster that I tiptoed through as if afraid to wake it up.

I called Roan for protection while I gathered my things. He sent Lorenzo to help me. In a polo shirt that clung to his muscular chest, Lorenzo walked about my home like he owned the place. He seemed even a little more arrogant now that he'd gotten away with a justified shooting.

Picking up on my trepidation, he said, "Why don't you stay with your parents for a bit? I'll get this cleaned up, plastered, and painted over. When you come back, it'll be like nothing ever happened."

"I left Luis in Pierz for now." I took a deep breath and tamped down my old feelings. "Lorenzo, where are we at?"

"I liked your referring to me as your fiancé in the interview."

"I had to speak on your behalf after I realized you killed McBride for me." I paused and looked at him. "You had moments when you were my knight in shining armor."

"I always will be." He grinned.

"McBride deserved to die for what he put me through. I didn't want you to have any charges for shooting him." I peeked up at Lorenzo. "We can never be the same again. I'm not the same."

"Of course we can." Lorenzo gave me that perfect smile as he approached. His coffee brown eyes shimmered with hope. "I love you, Ellie. I've never stopped loving you."

My bullshit meter for Lorenzo had kicked into full gear since the assault. When Lorenzo said, "I love you," it really meant, "I want sex." I responded, "We're not engaged. You never proposed to me, and I never said *yes*."

"That can be arranged." He stepped close and motioned with his hands for me to come to him.

"Slow down, Romeo." I stepped back. "Where are you at with the cheating and the porn?"

"It's over. There's been no porn since that night. Believe me, I've learned my lesson." He took another step toward me and pulled me into an embrace.

I stiffly accepted the hug. When I gazed into his eyes, all I could see was the empty shell of a man. What I heard him saying was, "There is nothing you can prove." I dropped my eyes and said, "I'm still healing. I don't know when I'll be able to have intercourse again."

Lorenzo remarked nonchalantly as he stepped away, "The wires are off your mouth now. There are other ways you can pleasure me."

Was that supposed to be a joke? *I don't think so.* It grated on me. "I won't be able to have any more children."

I looked back up at him, trying to read his thoughts. Lorenzo turned away and said nothing. It was disheartening. My translation: "If I can't sire a child with you, you're worthless to me." I walked over to the door and glanced back at Lorenzo. For the first time, I saw him in a different light. He reminded me of a home from the 1970s. At one time, it was the coolest place in town. But no matter how well it's kept up, it's still a home designed in the 1970s—a place to sneak a look at but no longer a place to live. Even visiting would get old. Out the window, I watched Carmel pull up in her Soul Red Crystal Mazda MX-5 Miata Sport. When I reached to open the door, I realized it wasn't damaged. "How did McBride get into my house?"

"Did you leave the door open?" Lorenzo asked.

"No. Absolutely not."

"He must have got a key somehow." Lorenzo walked over to the bullet hole in the wall. "Gotta admit, that was a hell of a shot." Oblivious to my trauma, he took out his phone and took a picture of his work. "I'll get a hold of a contractor and get this all cleaned up."

Translation: "I'm so amazing. If my parents pay to fix this up, maybe you'll sleep with me again." His mood had cooled. I was now relegated to a side piece for Lorenzo. It angered me, but I wasn't sure why because I felt nothing for him at that moment. This house didn't feel like home anymore.

Curious as to why Carmel hadn't come in, I stepped outside and rushed to greet her. "I miss you, girl!" We hugged briefly, and then she pushed me back. I didn't know what to think about that. It wasn't like I hadn't showered.

Carmel leaned against her red Mazda and lit a cigarette. "I watched your interview. You looked good."

"Thanks. It's amazing what they can do with makeup."

"Is Lorenzo in there?" she asked.

"Yeah. If you need to talk to him, go on in. Would you mind making sure the door's locked when you leave?" I stopped and looked at her face more closely. "What's going on?" I know that look from Carmel. It's the snarky, hurtful expression she gives me when she's done something shitty. Like sharing online that I was pregnant at sixteen and then flirting with Donny when he wasn't talking to me.

Carmel raised an eyebrow and glanced at the ground. "I'm going to make this quick. I have somethin' to tell you that ain't easy."

"Nothing's easy for me anymore. Spit it out."

She put out her cigarette with her foot. "On the night you disappeared, Lorenzo slept with me. We searched until we were exhausted, and then I needed a place to rest. I had planned on sleeping in my car, but he talked me into sharing his bed. Lorenzo said he had feelings for me he could no longer contain, and" — she turned her palms up — "one thing led to another."

"Are you kidding me?" It felt like a punch in the stomach. I paced back and forth in front of her. "You knew I was going to accept his proposal. You're my best friend." I felt so empty and alone.

"Don't be a hypocrite," Carmel snapped defensively. "You're sleeping with a cop."

"In the same bed. Not sexual. Have you and Lorenzo been together since?"

"You want honesty, girl—here it is. You turned your back on Lorenzo." She dug another cigarette out of her pocket and lit it. After blowing out a stream of smoke, Carmel studied me carefully as she muttered, "I don't like having to tell you this, but here it is. On the night I promised to stay with you, I was with Lorenzo. He said if I wanted a chance with him, I needed to stay with him. You know how charming he can be."

I thought back. "Do you remember that night when I went to surprise Lorenzo and found you there?"

She nodded.

"You told me you were talking with Lorenzo because Larry McBride tried to assault you. Were you ever assaulted by Larry McBride?"

She slowly shook her head and looked at me slyly. "Honestly, when you stopped over, Lorenzo and I had just finished. We wined and dined and 69'd."

A fury burned through me that was difficult to contain. "Miércoles," is what I said. *You filthy bitch* is what I thought. "Do you realize I ripped McBride a new one because I thought he assaulted you?" I wanted to kill her. Carmel was so incredibly candid; it was as if she were saying something as unemotional as

"I took the garbage out." Lorenzo had told me he was golfing with friends. I took a deep breath, restrained myself, and simply said, "You knew we were dating."

"*I* was with Lorenzo before you two were ever an item."

"I didn't know that."

"You're a liar. I try to be your friend, but I get so frustrated over how blind you are. You met Lorenzo at a party at *my* house."

"The two of you weren't even talking."

"I was hosting. I had asked him to check and see if people were having a good time. It's what Lorenzo's good at. And then I discovered he'd left with you."

I was speechless. *Why didn't she ever say anything to me? Why didn't Lorenzo ever mention it?*

Carmel continued, "I know you're pissed that I kept talking to Donny even though he didn't want your baby. He still loved you, and he was only eighteen, back when everyone thinks they might be a rock star or the next president. After a few years, Donny started to consider what his life would have been like if he had raised his son. I gave him your number, hoping you could show him some compassion. He just wanted to see his son." Carmel glanced over at the window of my house as if she didn't want Lorenzo to see her talking to me.

I couldn't read her expression. *Was it fear or anger?* "Has Lorenzo been abusive to you?"

After an uncomfortable silence, she said, "No."

Her tone wasn't believable, but I wasn't in the mood to rescue her. She'd slept with my boyfriend and had no remorse over it. I didn't know Carmel or Lorenzo anymore. The hell with them both. They could have each other. I got in my car and drove back to Pierz. Carmel didn't get it. I had confronted McBride for no reason and paid one hell of a price for it.

2:00 P.M. PIERZ

I stopped at Jon and Serena's house to pick up Luis. He always had so much fun with Jackson. I pulled into their long driveway thinking, *I can't believe I'm living in a town that has Hillbilly Haven as its motel name.*

Serena was holding her baby, Cami, when she welcomed me in. After giving me a once-over, she asked, "Rough day?" It was then that I realized I had been crying, and the tears streaked my makeup. Serena called her nine-year-old daughter over and told her, "Nora, could you play with Cami for a bit? Eliana and I need to talk."

"I need to peek in on the boys quick. For my own sake. Where can I find Luis and Jackson?"

Nora grinned and said, "Mom just gave them a snack. You can follow the crumbs."

"I'm sorry. I know Luis can be messy."

"He's no worse than Jackson," Serena said gently.

While Serena got Cami and Nora set to play in the living room, I went to check on Luis. Jackson and Luis were busy building a Hogwarts Castle Lego set. Luis was ignoring me out of fear I'd ask him to leave. The Fredericks had a music room next to the play area, and noticing the door was partially open, I peeked in.

My picture was on the wall, with strings running to Lorenzo, Donny, Mike, Carmel, and McBride. I realized these were the suspects in my assault. Lorenzo was connected to all but Donny and Mike. The only connection Donny and Mike had was to me. Carmel was connected to all but Mike. There was a triangle of strings connecting Lorenzo, McBride, and Carmel. They all knew each other. A picture of Londyn Lust was off to the side, only connected to Lorenzo.

I shuddered and tried to shake away the creepy feeling that had come over me. I refocused and said, "Hi, Jackson."

"Hi, Ms. Castillo," he responded.

I bent down and kissed Luis on the head. "I love you, Luis."

Luis smiled and nodded.

I walked past Nora, who was playing attentively with her sister in the living room. She was trying to teach Cami to drop a ball into a plastic whale. The whale blew the ball out through the blowhole, and they giggled. I wanted a family like this, but it was no longer an option for me. I felt so angry at McBride. His death didn't bother me—well, other than the fact that it happened in my house.

Serena made me a mug of hot chocolate covered with whipped cream while I filled her in on my day. She took her tea and joined me at the kitchen table. She asked, "What was Lorenzo's relationship like with Larry McBride? They fished together."

"Lorenzo tolerated McBride. He was friends with Larry's brother, Ross, and Ross is a great guy who came from a dirtbag family. Ross sent me a very nice card apologizing for his brother's behavior. It's not his fault, but still, I don't want to ever see him again."

"That's okay. I understand. Seeing Larry's brother triggers trauma."

"I heard a dog barking when I backed into Mike's Jeep, just for a second, and then it stopped immediately."

"Did you recognize the dog?"

"There was no dog. Why would you ask that?"

"In the Lakota culture, dogs were considered sacred beings that provided protection and assistance in difficult times."

I was proud of my Mexican culture, which for me is Guaycura and Spanish. The Guaycuras were nomads of the Baja Peninsula and spoke a language unrelated to any other Indigenous language. According to historians, we no longer exist due to being almost entirely wiped out by communicable diseases, but Destiny tells me Guaycura blood runs through my veins as strongly as the Spanish Jesuit who contributed to my heritage. The Jesuits were eventually run out of Baja because Spain perceived them as dangerous due to their education and faith in the teachings of Jesus. This forced mestizo families like mine to integrate into the Mexican culture at large. I told Serena, "It's not unique to the Lakota. In my culture, each person is believed to have a personal animal spirit that protects them and wards off evil spirits. It is referred to as 'the Nahual.' I may have always had spiritual influence, but I've truly felt it since my dog died. I had a bloodhound named Trusty, after *Lady and the Tramp*. She was part of my life for the first twelve years, and it was devastating to put her down. Trusty was my bodyguard. The barking sounded like Trusty." I decided not to go into the story of Trusty guiding me out of the woods. Instead, I said, "Isn't it weird that Donny called me for the first time in two years that day?"

"It is. What are you thinking?"

"Did Donny think killing me would give him custody of Luis?"

"What's the connection between Donny and McBride?" she asked.

"I can't think of any. It doesn't seem like Donny would be into any of that incel stuff, but honestly, I don't really know him anymore."

"What was Donny's family like? Any criminals?"

"No. Businesspeople. High achievers. Always talking about investments. Dating Donny brought my grades up, so my parents were happy with it until I got pregnant."

"Why did his family abandon him?"

"That was my fault. His parents and brother warned us that if I got pregnant, they'd disown both of us. I shouldn't have let it happen."

"I think the abandonment is his parents' fault. Half of teens have sex. Some get pregnant. That doesn't mean you turn your back on your kids."

"I couldn't give the baby up." I had been through this so many times that it no longer bothered me to talk about it. I have Luis now, and he's amazing.

"Understandable." She pressed on, "What was Lorenzo's family like?"

"Well, you've met Cat. 'Witch' is the first word that comes to mind." I made claws with my hands and snarled as I said in my creepiest witch tone, "Midnight black hair. Eyes that flicker like candles in the darkness. Weaving spells of tales from the crypts."

"That's good," Serena laughed. "I've met her. I can't argue with you."

Toning it back down, I shared, "I've always felt threatened by Cat. She was nice to me when Lorenzo was around, but would snipe at me when he wasn't. I was polite to her, for Lorenzo's sake. Roan liked me. But you know they're both up to those rich people scams all the time. I was trying to get Lorenzo closer to my family." I stopped. "But Lorenzo's sister Halle—I loved her. She had no issue standing up to Cat. Always defended me." I should take Halle up on her offer for coffee sometime.

"And Carmel was your best friend, at least until today?" Serena wondered.

"Carmel's dad overdosed on fentanyl when she was thirteen. It was when the whole fentanyl thing was just taking off. Carmel felt guilty because she was being an oppositional teen at the time. Her dad seemed so chill. Looking back, 'detached' would probably be a better word. Her mom was always at work." I paused, thinking back on our friendship. "Carmel can be a tiger. She defended me through everything. So, it was out of character for her when she got involved with an abusive guy right after high school. I couldn't believe it. I guess her mom liked the guy because he had money. Carmel finally ended it after a few years, but she's struggled with relationships since." I blew out a hard breath. "I hate her. I shouldn't. She's right. I know how charming Lorenzo can be. When I'm with Lorenzo, it's like I'm the only one in the world for him. But then I imagine he's the same with Carmel, too."

"Chameleon," Serena said.

5:00 P.M.

Luis talked me into allowing him to spend the night at the Fredericks' house. I typically didn't allow him to spend a weeknight, but I felt so dysregulated. I sat silently at the farmhouse's kitchen table, feeling lost and alone, as if I had just spun off the earth and was now floating away in my own solitary orbit.

Jon's dad had stopped at Thielen Meats and made us pastrami and sauerkraut sandwiches for dinner. Billy had Jon's strong and lanky build with well-earned wrinkles around his eyes. He carried himself with confidence yet still shared a kindness that I enjoyed being around. I finally realized Billy had asked me a question.

He said, "So you'd prefer not to render an opinion on our homemade sauerkraut. I've always felt that a life without sauerkraut is possible but pointless."

"Sorry, I can't focus." I smiled at his effort to cheer me up.

He studied me for a moment and said, "Let's go for a drive."

I followed him to his truck, and we headed south. My misery poured out. "My entire life was a lie. My best friend was sleeping with my boyfriend. I feel like I'm falling apart." *Disintegrating into nothingness.* I asked, "Where are we going?

"Existentially or literally," Billy said. "We're going to find some answers,"

"Answers to what?"

"To whatever's spinning around in that head of yours. I never got answers by sitting around the house stewing over something. Give me a question. I don't care what it is."

"Okay—is Lorenzo in love with Carmel? I would like to see the two of them together."

"And that will help you how?" Billy asked.

"It will bring closure." Maybe. Maybe it's just morbid curiosity.

"Let's find Lorenzo and see what he's up to. Where does he go on Wednesday nights?"

I took out my phone. "I can tell you exactly where he is. We have the Find My Phone app."

"You were both given your phones back?"

"Yeah. The detectives went through them, gleaned what they needed, and gave them back."

"Jon has told me they have a program called Cellibrite. It downloads everything on your phone. They can go back to what they've downloaded at any time to reinvestigate. Did you tell Jon they gave you your phone?"

"No. The Detroit Lakes police department returned it. Why would Jon care?"

"It's a problem," Billy said. "It means Lorenzo's known exactly where you're at all along."

"But he hasn't been to our house, has he?" I questioned.

"No, he hasn't." Billy looked puzzled.

"Maybe he forgot about the app. That would be like him." I set my phone on the console between us so we both could see

Lorenzo's location. "He's leaving the restaurant and is headed north on Highway 169."

"We can cut him off and catch up to him." Billy turned west in Buckman. "Let's see where he ends up. Time for us to do some spy work. Do you want to be Starsky or Hutch?"

"I was thinking Miss Scarlet and the Duke," I teased.

"Who's Duke? Her dog?"

"No—let's see. Who's an investigator you'd know?" I offered, "I'll be Clarice Starling. I've always been a fan of Jodie Foster."

"From *Silence of the Lambs*? Who does that make me?"

"Being Billy is plenty. You're kind of a hero to people around here."

"You obviously haven't heard from everybody."

"What was Camille like?" I asked.

"Camille was amazing. Beautiful. Kindhearted but disciplined. Unrelenting in her faith. Didn't hesitate to call me out. She was also damn funny. I got to see a side of her that only those closest to her witnessed." A grin crept across his face. "I have a story, but I would appreciate you not repeating it."

"My lips are sealed. Well, they *were* sealed. You don't talk about me, and I won't talk about you."

"Camille and I were together since we were teens. After we made love the first time, I asked, 'Was I the first?' Without missing a beat, she said, 'Do you mean today?'"

"That is damn funny!" I burst out laughing. "So, were you her first?"

"Well, I feel like that's personal." Billy smiled. "Okay, but not answering is worse. Yes, I was her first." A tear formed in his eye. "Camille made jokes with me no one would ever believe she'd say. I joked with her, too, but I wasn't as funny. I loved her."

"How long ago did Camille die?"

"Four years now," Billy sighed.

"I admire how hard you loved her. She was a lucky woman."

"Not as lucky as me."

Billy could live another twenty years. I said, "Spending time with someone else wouldn't mean you loved her any less."

He glanced at me as if I wasn't capable of understanding, but said nothing.

7:00 P.M.
Sunken Ship Brewing 32273 124th Street, Princeton

We followed the tracking app to a taproom in Princeton. We pulled into the parking lot, where Lorenzo's Mercedes GT 63 was parked. I told Billy, "Do you want to know why we're here?"

"Sure," he responded.

"Carmel works Wednesday nights, and this is far enough away from the Twin Cities where he isn't going to run into anyone who knows Carmel."

We stepped into the taproom, and I remained at Billy's side so nobody at the bar could see me. I snuck over to look at the clothing on the far side of the taproom while Billy went to the bar and ordered a beer.

Billy soon joined me at the rack and said, "The Old Crown is a damn good ale."

I used his body to shield me.

Lorenzo leaned back with his elbows on the bar, confidently studying the crowd with his *here I am, ladies, come and get me* demeanor. It wasn't long before he was approached by a woman about a decade older than he was. My heart sank as I watched him express the same charming mannerisms he used with me. I even knew what he was saying. She leaned into him and flirted. I thought he was so into me, but it was just a routine he does—rather effectively, I might add. I turned to Billy. "I needed to see this. Now I've seen it." I couldn't get out of there fast enough.

"I've still got three-quarters of my beer left."

"Can I have a sip?" I asked.

"Sure." Billy handed it to me.

I gulped until I couldn't swallow anymore. I handed the glass back, leaving about an inch of liquid at the bottom.

Billy finished it off and remarked, "I guess I'm ready to go, too." He smiled at my assertiveness. We had respect for each other that didn't require explanations.

27

JON FREDERICK
8:00 A.M., FRIDAY, AUGUST 23, 2024
PIERZ

Serena suggested I stop over at Dad's to talk to Eliana. Before leaving, I left her a note on her pillow that read:

Dearest Serena,

Some people say you need to love yourself before you can love someone else. I don't spend any energy thinking about that. I love you, and being with you makes me love you more. I love you and our kids more every day. I am happier, kinder, and more at peace when I'm with you. You are my life. Plus, I must admit, you're a damn good investigator.

Love, Jon

When I arrived at Dad's, I was surprised to see Heather Hilton answer the door. Heather was a petite pixie of a woman who had graduated from high school with Serena and me. She put her glasses on and cocked her head as she asked, "Jon? What are you doing here?"

"Are you Eliana's attorney?" I suddenly realized she was wearing my father's flannel shirt.

"No." She smirked. "I should have put it together. You have

to be Billy's cousin—same last name and all. So, how old is he? Billy said the only reason he's with me is that he's in a midlife crisis."

"If that's the case, he must plan on living to be a hundred and thirty," I said. Unbelievable—Heather slept with my dad.

"Shit." The realization finally hit Heather. "Billy's your dad?"

"He is."

Embarrassed, Heather ran back to Dad's bedroom.

I went inside and found Eliana and Luis eating breakfast at the kitchen table.

"I was hoping I'd find you here."

Eliana said, "Billy offered us the chance to stay, but I think we should go." She said softly, "He brought someone home last night. I don't want to intrude. You have to be so happy that he's not alone."

"I don't know that I've completely let go of Mom."

"Wasn't that years ago?" she asked.

"Yes. That's not why I'm here, though. I need to get your official statement."

I heard the door slam, and out the window, I could see Heather tearing out of the

driveway. Unabashed, Dad entered the kitchen, sat next to Luis, and said, "What are we having for breakfast?"

"Dad, would you mind hanging out with Luis while Eliana steps outside for a minute?"

"Not at all." Dad grinned. "Got a bit of an appetite."

Choosing to ignore him, I headed for the front porch, and Eliana followed. I asked, "Do you like it here?"

"Yeah, your dad's been amazing with Luis."

He was a better grandfather than a father, but I kept that thought to myself. I needed to give him credit for the man he was now. "We need to talk about the assault."

"I had auditory and visual hallucinations that night—monsters, weird animal noises. I followed a baying bloodhound to that kind woman's house. She never heard a dog. There was no dog. My memory of that night isn't going to be helpful."

"But you remember Larry McBride being there."

"I do. I remember Larry standing over me and shooting me." She seemed embarrassed when she added, "With a pipe."

"He *did* shoot you with a pipe."

"Yeah, I guess I did hear that. It just didn't seem real."

"Do you remember a second person?"

Eliana swallowed hard. "Maybe. I don't have a visual of the second guy, but I can see McBride looking at me upside down when some jerk was ramming something hard into me. I heard what Dr. Amaya said. Maybe McBride was the one who was holding my wrists."

Larry McBride had told me, "I never shoved that hammer into her." I said to Eliana, "And you have no memory of anyone else?"

"Not assaulting me. What do you have? You know something, don't you?"

"That brand Larry McBride burned into you. We found that same brand burned into the foot of a dead stripper. People at the club where she worked connect McBride to her. They also connect Lorenzo to her. He'd spent time with her outside of the club."

"While we were together?" Eliana asked with disappointment.

"It appears so."

"I must be brain-dead. How was I so stupid?"

"You trusted him. That's not an insult to you. I'm telling you this because I'd prefer you stay with Dad for a bit longer until I know you're safe."

"If your dad's okay with it, I don't really have a better place to be."

"He loves having you here." I gazed out at the fields of corn. "Maybe you're not as crazy as you think. I'd like to drive you to Detroit Lakes and walk you through that night."

"Today?"

"Yes."

"Okay," Eliana anxiously responded. "I need to talk to Luis first."

"Go ahead, finish breakfast, and let me know when you're ready."

Shortly after Eliana entered the house, Dad came out to speak to me. He shrugged and said, "I will always love your mom and only your mom. Camille was everything to me. I miss her. I don't know what to do with myself. I drank a little too much at Frosty's last night, and Heather was into me. We ended the night here."

I didn't respond.

"I don't expect you to understand. I was a bad father. I was raised to believe that a good man provides for his family, and after three generations, I lost the farm. And then, worse than that, I took it all out on you. Your mom made me realize that."

"You used to take Theresa hunting. You never took me." Theresa was a daddy's girl.

He scratched his head and gazed out at the cornfield as I had done moments earlier. Dad said, "You know how Vic struggled with his schizophrenia. You were the only one who could handle him. I needed you at home." Dad turned back to me. "I know you think I love Theresa more, but I don't. I love all three of you in different ways. Your sister was out of control and at war with your mom, so I needed to spend time with her. You didn't need guidance. Especially from some jerk who was beating the crap out of you. I'm sorry, Jon."

I still felt a little burn from his explanation. I wanted to say, "I was the youngest child in the family, and *I* was the only one who could handle my mentally ill brother?" The trick no one else understood was that you couldn't be trying to accomplish something else when you were with Vic. But it was water under the bridge. I said, "I appreciate the apology. We're good."

"All right." Dad squeezed my shoulder and headed back into the house.

28

LORENZO TURRISI CARUSO
9:15 A.M., FRIDAY, AUGUST 23, 2024
PIERCE STREET NORTHEAST
BELTRAMI, MINNEAPOLIS

Dad was pissed that I had gone to Jon Frederick's house. Roan said he could handle the investigators. *But Dad, no, you can't.* Jon Frederick wasn't a guy you "handle." He's one of those folks who was more likely to burn you because you implied you could control him. They wouldn't allow me to visit Eliana in the hospital, and now they've turned her against me. If only I could talk to her. I needed to call her.

Eliana answered abrasively, "What do you want?"

"I love you, too. Hon, can we get together and talk this through? Where are you staying?"

"They have me protected on a military base."

I knew that wasn't true, but I didn't argue with her. "Why did you take off without saying goodbye? I've tried to call you a dozen times, and you haven't answered."

"Carmel told me you've been sleeping with her."

"That's not true," I protested. Then I remembered the DNA that had been collected from the hotel sheets.

"Stop lying to me," Eliana responded. "You lied when I asked about cheating, and you're lying again."

The truth is, we all lie to each other. That's why we end up falling in love with the image of a person no one can live up to. I replied honestly, "I told you I hadn't been looking at porn, and I'm not. As for Carmel, I slept with her on the night you disappeared. I was torn up and worn out from searching for you. I wasn't thinking clearly. You broke my heart. She crawled into bed with me and did everything. I was just lying there."

"Have you hit her?"

"No. What the hell is she telling you?"

"You made her choose between being your hookup or my friend, and she chose you."

"Carmel is infatuated with me, but I want *you*. If she's telling you she's sleeping with me, it's only to get you to walk away. Please, meet with me. Stay with me. I will prove my love to you. I've already demonstrated I'm the only one who can protect you."

"Jon Frederick's here to take my official statement."

"Are you having an affair with him?" It would explain why Frederick's trying to railroad me.

"Are you kidding?" Ellie responded. "I need to go." She hung up.

Londyn Lust, you might be getting a call before the night's over.

10:00 A.M.
CESAR CHAVEZ STREET, DISTRICT DEL SOL
WEST SIDE, ST. PAUL

Furious, I drove over to Carmel's. She came slinking to the door in tight jeans and a sleeveless T-shirt.

"Why aren't you working?"

"I could ask the same of you," she said.

"My work is mostly nights." On paper, I work at my mom's restaurant. I do a lot of deliveries for my parents.

Carmel waved me in. "I am working." I followed her into the living room as she continued, "I don't know if you've watched the news recently, but people work from home."

"What exactly do you do?" I realized I'd never considered how she spends her days.

"I score tests for Pearson Assessments. I don't tell people because as soon as professionals hear it, they start bitching, 'Pearson is such a rip-off.' I think they're just smart. They infiltrate the minds of people on boards of psychology and education, and those people make every licensed psychologist and special ed teacher pay for our newest tests—no worries about quality. If you have to use that test to keep your license, you use that test. It's legalized extortion."

"Whatever. Why did you tell Eliana we're sleeping together?" *I can't trust anybody.*

"You made me choose. The wheel spins both ways," she remarked coyly.

"I did choose. I bought Eliana a rock."

Carmel slapped me.

I turned as if I was about to leave, but instead reared back a punch and knocked her to the floor. "Stupid bitch. Now look what you made me do." I bent down and tried to help her up, but she swept my hands away.

"Get the fuck out of my house!" she ordered.

"Please, don't call the police," I pleaded. "An assault will be enough to convince them I was the second guy in Ellie's rape. I swear, I wasn't. They'll lock me up for life. If you ever want a shot with me again, you can't call the police." I raised my hands in submission as I retreated from the house. *Dammit, Carmel!*

29

ELIANA CASTILLO
1:00 P.M., FRIDAY, AUGUST 23, 2024
WASHINGTON PARK
1355 WASHINGTON AVENUE, DETROIT LAKES

J on Frederick walked me to a bench in Detroit Lakes City Park. He handed me the laptop, hoping it would trigger some memories. Jon told me, "On the night of the assault, you made it a good mile along the lake from the hotel in a dress and boots, holding a laptop. Your feet had to hurt."

"I didn't feel my feet. I ran until I couldn't breathe. I remember thinking my whole world had ended."

"Who approached you?"

I couldn't stop thinking about the rose petals lying out on the hotel bed. I imagined Carmel and Lorenzo making mad, passionate love on top of them over and over. I rubbed my forehead. "I am so sorry. I don't remember. Honestly, all I can think of at the moment is Lorenzo sleeping with my best friend. He called me just before we left."

"What did you tell him?" I asked.

"I hung up on him. Part of me feels like Lorenzo is somehow connected to this. I know that's not fair." It was a gut instinct I couldn't shake. I stood up. "I don't think I was here. I might have walked the other way around the lake." I stood up and started walking through the park.

Jon followed me with his laptop. I glanced to my right and was overcome with a vision of a twenty-foot troll, like the one I'd seen on the night I was assaulted. *I swear I have gone full-blown batshit crazy.* It was so real. The troll was holding a large wooden spoon over her head and appeared to have a mixing bowl at her side. Jon quickly approached me, and I grabbed his arm, squeezed it tight, and whispered, "Do you see that?"

"Yes. That's Alexa, mixing an elixir. There are half a dozen of those statues throughout the woods here."

I dropped to my knees and breathed a tremendous sigh of relief. *Maybe I'm not crazy.* Jon helped me back to my feet. "I swear to God I saw a forty-foot troll sticking its tongue out at me — taunting. I've been afraid to admit it. I didn't want to end up in a psych ward."

Jon smiled. "That troll is called Ronny Funny Face. It's the closest troll to where you were found that night. Ronny is a couple miles from here in Dunton Locks County Park. Somehow, your abductor got you in a car and drove you to a forest on the edge of Muskrat Lake."

"I wasn't here." I looked around the park. "I went the other way around Detroit Lake, to Shady Hollow."

"Muskrat Lake is south of here, and Shady Hollow is even further south. If your attackers found you in Shady Hollow, Dunton Locks would be the first uninhabited park they'd encounter. It was convenient."

"I remember going to Shady Hollow, sitting on the ground and leaning against a shed, but I don't remember leaving. It's so weird. I know about roofies, but there wasn't any Rohypnol in my blood test. I asked." Jon helped me to my feet.

"There was ketamine." He seemed surprised they hadn't told me. "It's a fast-acting drug used by veterinarians to sedate cats. It's also used to treat excited delirium."

"What is that?" I asked.

"It's a life-threatening state of excitement or a high level of agitation. Ketamine is used a lot more in rural emergency rooms than metro."

"Why?" That doesn't make sense.

"That's a great question," Jon remarked. "It shouldn't be the first sedative of choice, but it's used because it works fast. EMTs have told me cops have learned to say, 'This guy's suffering from excited delirium,' because it's more likely to get the guy sedated. Ketamine is preferred because in five minutes, you're sedated and your memory is gone. It impacts the hippocampus, preventing the process of new memories. Close to a hundred individuals have died in custody after administration of ketamine. Most of them Black."

"The doctor asked me if I was on medication for depression, which confused me. I told her 'Yes' because I had taken Zoloft to treat postpartum depression after I had Luis, but after she left the room, I wondered if she meant *now*. I wasn't taking any meds when I was assaulted—other than birth control."

"Okay." Jon looked frustrated. "There's been a recent movement to use ketamine to treat depression. I don't like it, but I'm not a psychiatrist. Ketamine is an anesthetic that creates hallucinogenic effects."

"How would that treat depression?"

"I think it's kind of like shock treatment. It's an eraser, but it's not a selective eraser. The research I've conducted suggests that its success isn't significantly better than the placebo effect. If you give a depressed person an M&M, but they think it's an antidepressant, sixty percent of people report feeling better. Ketamine is about sixty-five percent effective. I don't like the fact that ketamine is so easily available now because of its use as a date rape drug. Rapists prefer Rohypnol because it lasts longer. Ketamine lasts about half an hour. If the rapist wanted to erase your memory while you were hauled away, but then have you fully experience the assault, ketamine would be the drug of choice. The advantage of ketamine for rapists is that it also often erases the memory of what happened right before you took it." Jon reluctantly added, "I think the person who attacked you wanted you to feel the pain."

"I don't know of anyone who hates me that much. Maybe Crazy Larry." I shuddered at the thought of someone wanting to torture me and added, "Maybe Lorenzo hates me now. Maybe he did that night, too. I ruined his plans."

DUNTON LOCKS COUNTY PARK
DUNTON LOCKS COUNTY ROAD
(ONE MILE NORTH OF SHADY HOLLOW), DETROIT LAKES

Once we were in Jon's vehicle, he asked, "Does this trigger any memories of being in a car that night?"

"I'm not sure if it's real. I recall being in a dark car, talking and looking straight ahead at the road, but it's all very blurry. I felt nauseated. I have no memory of anyone else in the car. And then I got tired, and I must have passed out." For a moment, I remembered the first time I drank alcohol at a party. Carmel drove me home, and I told her I thought I was going to be sick. She jacked me up and yelled at me not to puke in her car because she'd just cleaned it. The stuff I worried about as a teen seems so minor today.

Jon suggested, "You must have been slipped the ketamine in the park before you left."

"I don't remember."

"That's why rapists use it. The victim doesn't remember what happened right before it was administered. You don't remember who or how. And ketamine has no odor. But it's bitter and turns your stomach, which is where your nausea came from." After driving a little over a mile, he pulled over, and we began walking along a trail into the woods. He said, "I'm not going to say a word as I don't want to interfere with your thoughts. Please tell me when memories occur."

After one-third of a mile walking in silence, I saw the troll standing forty feet over me, sticking his tongue out. "I was here." My heart raced a little. "I saw a bear that night, too."

"What did the bear do?"

"Looked at me and moseyed on."

165

"There are a lot of bears around this summer. The Canadian wildfires moved the bruins south." His casual demeanor was comforting. He didn't seem surprised at all.

"I think I heard a cow."

"Was it loud?"

"No." I bellered a soft, "Mooo." Then, I shook my head at the absurdity of it. "I'm pretty sure there aren't any cows around here."

He knelt on one knee, opened up his laptop, and played the exact sound.

I glanced at the screen. "That's the sound a doe makes?"

"It is. And there are deer here."

As we walked further into the woods, I told him, "I heard what sounded like a woman screaming, but I knew that it could have been a fox. I remember McBride raping me. And then everything went black. When I came to, McBride's face was upside down, looking directly into mine. He was the one holding my hands down. It went black again, and McBride was standing over me with a cocky smirk. He shot me with a pipe."

We walked further, but the woods all looked the same to me. Finally, I told Jon, "I don't know where it happened. Would it help if I lay on the ground?"

"If you're okay trying, it might trigger a memory."

I carefully lay on my back on the ground. The flashbacks started immediately. My body convulsed as I felt the hammer handle rammed into me.

Jon pulled me back to my feet, and feeling weak, I leaned into him for support. He whispered, "I'm sorry. This was a bad idea. Let me know when you're ready, and we'll head home." He held me until I stopped trembling.

30

LORENZO TURRISI CARUSO
1:00 P.M., FRIDAY, SEPTEMBER 13, 2024
TARGET FIELD
TWINS WAY, MINNEAPOLIS

I was sitting alone in the right field bleachers at Target Field. It was seventy-three degrees, the sun was shining, and there was no wind. I was enjoying a cold beer and a soft pretzel. Despite the perfect weather, there were only a dozen people out here, and no one within five seats of me. The Twins collapsed at the end of the season, and their once-certain playoff spot was slipping away. We were losing to the Cincinnati Reds, who were in fifth place out of six teams in the National League Central. It was hard to watch. I called Jon Frederick and told him I was ready to talk. *It was as good a place to get interrogated as any.*

When Jon approached me, I took a sip from my large glass of beer and said, "Carl Pohlad claims this team has everything they need."

"In a sense, that's true," Jon remarked. "They have a great stadium, faithful fans, and new uniforms." He sat next to me.

"Dad says I need to be honest with you. So, *honestly*, I was pissed when you came after me for shooting that piece of shit

McBride. I thought you set me up."

"Well, imagine how angry I was when I saw you with a rifle outside my house. I didn't want to, but I almost ended your life for the preservation of my family."

"I was just going to fire a warning shot." I could see Jon didn't believe me, but he chose not to respond. I never liked that about Frederick. He was hard to read. "I left a clue—by accident, but Dad said you couldn't use it. I was in a hurry to get off the roof, and I looked for the shell. When I couldn't find it, I thought I'd already pocketed it. I didn't even consider that it discharged over the edge of the building."

"I didn't need you to leave a clue to know it was someone in your family. The tattoo shop wasn't broken into. It was entered with a key. Catania demonstrated that your family had a connection to tattoo artists when she had McBride expertly tattooed. And I know Cat didn't shoot him. She would have killed him instead of tattooing him if she wanted McBride dead. She wanted him to suffer, and I don't believe Cat cared enough about Eliana to protect her. Roan was at a poker game at the time. That left you. And I had another reason to suspect you. We locked down the neighborhood immediately after the shooting. I thought that ruled you out since you lived in Minneapolis, but then I remembered you've been sleeping with Carmel. She's just down the block from Eliana. Carmel hid you out."

I couldn't hide my grin. "I didn't anticipate all the love I'd get for killing McBride. Hell, I would have admitted it sooner."

"How well did you know McBride?"

"I never liked that yokel piece of shit." His mood quickly shifted to anger. "I only allowed him around 'cause his brother's a decent man. I feel guilty that Larry raped Ellie. McBride knew Ellie through me."

"Some of the investigators think you killed McBride so that he couldn't identify you as his accomplice in the rape."

"Do you honestly think I would get involved with a hick hillbilly like McBride? What's my motive? I love Ellie."

"You get angry when you don't get your way."

"I wanted Ellie back. I still do."

The Cincinnati Reds had the bases loaded. Elly De Le Cruz was at the plate. Elly leads the Reds in home runs this year, but he has no career grand slams. The first pitch to him was a waist-high fastball. De Le Cruz turned on it and sent the pitch flying into the bleachers in front of us. Elly had just hit his first career grand slam, and the Twins' playoff hopes were gone. We watched a ten-year-old boy race to grab the ball with his father in tow.

"Well, at least one Elly's knocking it out of the park," I remarked. I thought out loud, "Do you need to tell Ellie everything? That might be a dealbreaker for me."

Jon responded, "I want to find out who assisted McBride with assaulting Eliana. I have no desire to gossip. Tell me about your relationship with Cheri Wilde."

What the hell does she have to do with this? "We're talkin' man to man? You're not runnin' to Ellie with this?"

"No. I already know you've been with Cheri. I talked to her friends at the club."

"All right. The shit I have to tell you. Okay. Ever heard of the Mile High Club?"

"I have. People who've had sex on planes."

"Well, I wanted to be a member. Never had a date who'd do it. I offered Cheri a thousand dollars to take a night flight with me to Vegas. She gave me a hand job under a blanket on the way there. Head on the way back. It was dark. Everybody was sleeping. No harm, no foul—right? I know Cheri, like every other stripper, was hoping I'd rescue her from the snake pit she was in, but that wasn't gonna happen. I'm not runnin' away with a stripper." I stopped myself. "But I'm not hurtin' her either. She did her job; I paid her and sent her on her way. I heard she was murdered. It didn't really surprise me. She got me to think about strip clubs differently. Never been to one since."

"Please explain," Jon said.

"Cheri was raped at the place she worked before Inver Grove. She told me a wealthy businessman gave her an ecstasy pill and then asked for a private dance. He took her to a room and raped her. The guy paid off a security guard to stand outside the room and make sure no one entered. Cheri said every stripper gets raped eventually. If you have drugs in your system, you're not a reliable witness against a respected businessman."

"Every strip club has drugs running through it," Jon stated flatly. "Merck Pharmaceuticals developed ecstasy over a hundred years ago as an appetite suppressant. Once they realized it was a combination of meth and a hallucinogen, it was removed from the market." He finished his rant and asked me, "Did you ever tell Larry McBride about your night with Cheri?"

"Of course." I laughed. "What's the point of being in the Mile High Club if you don't tell anyone? Larry asked, 'Do you think she'd do the same for me?' I told him, 'No harm in asking.'" I sighed. "I should have just told him she wouldn't do it, but I didn't want to insult the guy. I mean, look at Larry. I don't know if he showered this year. No chance in hell, even if he paid her. Do you think Crazy Larry killed Cheri?"

"Cheri had the same brand burned into her foot that Eliana has."

"I didn't know he branded Ellie." My heart sank. I felt terrible for her. "You think Larry did both?"

"I do. Isn't it odd that you knew both intimately?"

"Do you think Crazy Larry set me up? I always had the sense that he resented me."

"Incels believe that twenty percent of the men get eighty percent of the women. I'd imagine he'd put you in that twenty percent."

"That might be true." I get more than my share. "I had nothing to do with the assaults on either. I probably shouldn't answer any more questions about Cheri without a lawyer present."

Jon took a deep breath as he studied me and then changed the topic. "Have you heard from Londyn Lust lately?"

"Only because Ellie won't talk to me. A man has needs. I talked to her a couple of weeks ago before she went batshit crazy."

"What do you mean?"

"Londyn keyed my Mercedes-Benz. It's a six-figure car. She threatened to destroy me if I didn't commit to her. *Pazza cagna.* Look at these texts." I pulled out my phone and read them out loud as Jon looked on. "'You need to step up your game. I need more of your time. I'm not someone you can just ignore for weeks at a time.' When I didn't respond, she sent me this text two days later: 'I saw you with that blond slut. There will be consequences for ignoring me.' And then my car was keyed."

"*Pazza cagna?*"

"Crazy bitch," I interpreted.

"Who's the blonde?"

"Carmel." I grinned. "An affair of convenience." I felt like I could have Carmel whenever I wanted. In fact, I should call her. "You know, Londyn could have been the second person in the assault on Eliana. She might have witnessed the fight between Ellie and me. I was FaceTiming with Londyn when Ellie barged in."

John responded, "She might be upset with you, but it's unlikely she was involved in the assault on Eliana. I haven't been able to find a connection between Londyn and Larry McBride. For your theory to work, Londyn would have needed to drive to Detroit Lakes, meet and befriend McBride, agree to and then plan out a murder with him, all within two hours. I don't see it."

"Just because you haven't found a connection doesn't mean there wasn't one."

11:30 P.M.
PIERCE STREET NORTHEAST
BELTRAMI, MINNEAPOLIS

I opened the door and let Carmel into my house. Well, my parents' house. Carmel had been out for drinks with friends and looked hot in her sleeveless crop top and jeans. Dad was at poker night, but Mom was in her room watching TV. Carmel giggled as I snuck her into my bedroom.

"For God's sake, we're in our twenties," she told me.

"Why create any drama when you don't have to?" I kissed her and asked, "Have you heard anything from that *schifo cagna* Londyn Lust? I wish I had never said a word to her. She keyed my Mercedes."

"She threatened to hurt me for being with you." Carmel pulled

171

away.

"Do you think we should stay away from each other? I don't want to see anyone else hurt." I meant it.

"No. I think it's too late. I'm afraid she's coming after me."

"Do you want me to send her a message?" I stood strong.

"I'm afraid that will only make it worse." She stepped into me and hugged me. "I don't want you to be in any more trouble. I'd rather you took care of me."

"I will tonight. Let me know if she escalates."

Carmel showed me her phone. The text message read, "I'll burn you, slut."

I could feel my blood boiling. Carmel undid the button on my jeans.

31

LORENZO TURRISI CARUSO
3:20 A.M., WEDNESDAY, SEPTEMBER 25, 2024
PIERCE STREET NORTHEAST
BELTRAMI, MINNEAPOLIS

The phone buzzed, and I grabbed it off the stand next to my bed. I hoped Eliana was okay. "Hello?"

"It's Carmel." She was crying. "Londyn did it."

"What are you talking about?"

"She burned my house down. Please come over."

3:45 A.M.
CESAR CHAVEZ STREET, DISTRICT DEL SOL
WEST SIDE, ST. PAUL

When I arrived, the house was engulfed in flames. Carmel was in a robe, standing on the street next to a squad car. She ran to me, and we embraced.

"She burned my house down. Do you have any idea of how close I was to paying it off?"

"Are you hurt?" Her arm was bandaged.

"No. I cut my arm on the window when I crawled out."

Carmel leaned against me and said, "I thought I was going to die. My bedroom window was the only way out. I had an overnight suitcase by my bed, and I threw it through the window to break the glass. Lorenzo, what am I going to do?" She buried her head in my chest and sobbed.

"I'm going to kill that bitch," I assured her as I held her close. "It's okay. What were you able to salvage?"

The firefighters had gotten the blaze under control, and Carmel led me to the side of the house, pointing to a surprisingly large "overnight" bag on the ground.

"Okay, talk to the sergeant in charge and find out what you need to do so you can leave. I'll load your bag in the back of my Hummer. You'll stay with me tonight."

3:20 P.M., WEDNESDAY, SEPTEMBER 25, 2024
NICOLLET MALL, MINNEAPOLIS

I left Carmel in bed and went to Mom's restaurant to help her through the noon rush. September 25 was World Dense Breast Day, so I thought I'd wear a pink polo shirt and tight white pants for the ladies, even though wearing white was a bit of a risk in an Italian restaurant. One of Catania's best customers, Francesca Gallo, an elegant woman in her seventies, called me over to meet her granddaughter. Francesca likes to introduce me to a new woman about once a month. Francesca remained seated as she spoke. "This is Isabella Rossi. She's attending St. Thomas and is a finance major."

"I could use a finance major," I joked as I bent down and kissed Francesca's cheek. When Isabella stood, I was stunned by her beauty. Her beach brown eyes and sun-streaked hair had me thinking about the best moments of my vacations.

She stood, swept a strand of hair out of her face, and said, "You can call me Bella."

I shook her hand. "I promise to. And you can call me Lorenzo."

Francesca suggested, "Maybe you could sit with us for a minute and answer questions about the menu."

"I'd love to." Francesca knew our menu better than I did, but I couldn't resist the invitation.

I headed back toward the kitchen with Bella's phone number tucked into my pocket. As I passed Mom at the hostess station, she teased, "It's so kind of you to keep our customers happy."

A text buzzed in my pocket, and I pulled out my phone to read it. "I can see you. Pink shirt. White pants. Talking to another one of your whores. I'll kill every last one."

Picking up on my worry, Mom asked, "What?"

I showed her the text. She looked about the restaurant. "Who sent this?"

"Londyn Lust. The psycho who burned down Carmel's house."

Mom took my arm. "We need to get you out of the dining area. Go back to the office and look at the cameras. Text me if you see her. I'll call your dad, and he'll have this place secure in minutes."

8:30 P.M.
PIERCE STREET NORTHEAST
BELTRAMI, MINNEAPOLIS

Dad, Mom, and I were sitting at the kitchen table while Carmel headed to the bathroom to shower. Mom turned to Dad. "Roan, do you want to start with him?"

"We're not a hotel," Dad said. "What the hell is going on?"

"An ex-girlfriend of mine burned down Carmel's house last night. I'd like to let Carmel stay here a couple of weeks until she can figure out what to do."

"Who's the arsonist?" Mom asked.

"Londyn Lust."

Catania laughed satirically. "Of course it is. One hooker goin' after another."

"Carmel isn't a sex worker. She does assessments."

"I guess I do, too. I just gave you one of Carmel. I want her out. I don't trust her. She walks around like she's casing the place."

"Mom, I can't just put her out on the street. My crazy ex burned her place to the ground." I looked to Dad for support, but he sat silent.

Mom continued, "I heard they used to call Carmel and Eliana 'double trouble.'"

"We got the short end of that stick as far as houseguests go," Dad interjected.

Carmel had returned from the bathroom and suddenly materialized behind my parents, obviously hearing the entire conversation.

Mom sighed when she realized Carmel was behind her. She turned and casually told her, "Okay, if you're going to stay here, I want you to stop bleaching your hair. And tone down the makeup. People are going to think we're bringing in a hooker to help our boy deal with the loss of Eliana."

"Okay. I can do that." Carmel meekly asked, "Is it okay if I use the shampoo in the shower stall?"

"Of course," Mom responded.

Carmel returned to the bathroom.

"Where can I find this Lust broad?" Dad asked.

"I don't know. I talked to her on OnlyFans."

"What the hell is OnlyFans?" Dad asked. "Be honest."

I blew out a long breath before revealing, "It's a website where you tell people to do sexual things. Live porn, basically."

"And the psycho was stalking you at the restaurant today?" Dad questioned.

"Yeah," I admitted. "And she's damn good at it. I studied the cameras, and I couldn't find her anywhere."

"I had the boys search the neighborhood for anyone sitting in a car watching the restaurant, but there wasn't anybody suspicious around. Give me some pictures of her."

"Clothes on," Mom suggested. "And don't let Carmel get too comfortable. She's not staying for more than a week — two weeks maximum. I get the feeling she'd like to make this permanent."

"We're going to have to pull Jon Frederick back into this," Dad muttered.

"That's a mistake," I warned. "I don't think that guy's going to help me stay out of jail. Especially after he caught me with a rifle in his backyard."

"Let me handle him," Dad said.

"Can you handle him?" I immediately regretted challenging Dad.

He glared at me and explained, "You shot and killed a man in a house you were directed to stay away from, and you didn't serve one day for it. Don't question our ability to handle it."

Catania ruled, "Roan will talk to Sean, Jon Frederick's boss. The BCA has resources we don't have. It's not like we can find this woman by looking up 'Lust' in the Yellow Pages."

"What are yellow pages?" I wondered.

32

JON FREDERICK
2:40 P.M., FRIDAY, SEPTEMBER 27, 2024
RED'S AUTO
104 MAIN STREET NORTH, PIERZ

I t's been three weeks since Eliana and I walked through the park. Sean had reassigned me to other cases while local investigators continued looking into Eliana's. The challenge this case presented to Detroit Lakes law enforcement was that none of the players were local. The city police had interrogated the usual suspects in the area, but nothing materialized. It was time for me to circle back.

Finding Londyn Lust wasn't particularly difficult. Her birth name was Londyn Larson, and she lived in Battle Lake, forty-seven miles south of Detroit Lakes. In northern Minnesota, any community less than an hour's drive is considered a hop, skip, and a jump away.

Eliana had taken a job in the deli at Red's Auto in Pierz. Luis was in kindergarten with our son Jackson. Nora was already in fourth grade. Cami was six months old and had begun to tone down her intensity—slightly. She is far more demanding than our older two were at the same age. Fortunately, she was in a new environment today and snuggled into my chest as she looked around.

Eliana said it was time for her break, so she'd talk to Serena and me in a booth. While we waited, Heather Hilton entered the store and bought a coffee. After seeing us, she turned her back. Heather was obviously embarrassed about sleeping with my dad. When she slipped out, Serena followed her and caught up to her. Serena and Heather were friends. I watched out the window as they exchanged words and then hugged. Heather relaxed as their conversation continued.

In her red polo work shirt, Eliana sat across from me in the booth.

Still holding Cami, I asked Eliana, "Did Londyn Lust ever contact you?"

"No. Why would she?"

"Apparently, she burned down Carmel's house."

"Is Carmel okay?"

"Yes. Londyn had threatened her prior. The two are arguing over Lorenzo."

"That seems so weird, doesn't it? I'm not fighting for Lorenzo. If he can't choose me over someone—" she cut herself off. "I'm such a hypocrite."

"Live and learn."

Eliana smiled at Cami, and Cami buried her head in my shoulder.

"Hey," Eliana said, squeezing my arm, "You didn't tell me Mike Haney was from Pierz."

"I didn't know it mattered."

"There was a tall woman with sandy blond hair in here the other day, talking about him. Sounds like he's moved on."

I knew Eliana liked Mike, but I teased, "Moved on from what?"

"I don't know. That was the problem. I think about him. I miss our conversations." She paused, glanced out the window, and nodded toward Heather. "Did you know she's been back since that night?"

"No, I didn't." I wasn't sure what to think about it. I guess it wasn't my business.

"Not often. About once every couple of weeks. But getting back to Mike, what's his family like?"

"Very kind. His dad imbibes alcohol to the degree a lot of folks from the area do, which is heavy compared to the rest of the world, but I like him. He's a good guy. He would help anyone. His mom and sister are sweethearts. The kind of people you'd love to have for friends."

"I miss Mike." Eliana's thoughts drifted, and after a brief contemplation, she shared, "Mike was easy. I put no effort into our friendship. He was always there. When things come easy, you don't appreciate their value."

"That's true."

"I think it would be good for me to be alone for a bit."

She had me thinking about her friendships. "Tell me a little about Carmel."

"She could burp the alphabet when we were young."

"Quite impressive. Could you?"

"No, we never had enough soda in the house to hone the skill." Eliana relaxed. "Carmel's funny, smart, and very competitive. When we lost a softball game, she'd be mad all night. But if you were on her good side, she'd part the sea for you. Carmel never tolerated anyone saying anything bad about me. We used to laugh until we cried. She'd say, 'Call me Elizabeth or Latifah, cause someday I'm gonna be queen.' I told her, 'You ain't the first lady of hip-hop.' I called her Lilibet instead. That was Queen Elizabeth's childhood nickname because she couldn't pronounce her name. Carmel would say, 'Dana will suffice. Until I'm officially queen.'" Dana Owens was Queen Latifah's birth name.

After sharing a couple of pleasant childhood stories, Eliana had to get back to work, and Serena and I needed to pick up our kids from school. Because of the safety concerns my work created, we always dropped the kids off and picked them up after school. Cami had started to get comfortable with the new environment and was returning to her natural state—crabby. I loved Cami, but she was a challenge. It must be frustrating for her to have parents who didn't always understand her needs. When I stepped outside, Serena and Heather were heading back to their respective vehicles.

As Heather was about to enter her car, Serena shouted, "Heather! Is it too early to start calling you Mom?"

Heather's face brightened with embarrassment. With a smile, she flipped Serena off and departed.

9:10 P.M.
PIERZ

Serena and I were at home, and all three kids were in their beds, asleep. We felt like we'd just won the World Series of parenting. We each found a beverage to sip on as we relaxed in front of the fireplace. I had a cold glass of Harvest AAA Amber from a crowler that a friend had picked up for me from ABC Brewing in Battle Lake. Serena had a glass of Liberty School Reserve Cabernet.

In her sleepwear, an oversized tee, Serena sat by me and considered her wine. "I can't wait until the 2023 cabs are released. The wineries are saying 2023 was the perfect weather. They finally had the rain they needed in California. The wines are barreled for a year, so they should start becoming available in 2025." She sat back and lay her bare legs across my lap.

I had warmed some lotion and began rubbing it onto her feet and legs.

"Mmmm," Serena purred. "Tell me about the Castillo case. What are you struggling with?"

"The hammer. Why did the rapist smash Eliana's right hand?" I thought about Cheri's hand and mouth being hammered after her Vegas night with Lorenzo.

"Hammers are convenient," Serena suggested. "Everybody has one. She was sexually assaulted with the handle, right?"

"Yes."

"Any other hammer cases?"

"Not open. There were a couple of Minnesota serial killers who used hammers. The most notorious was Harvey 'the Hammer' Carignan. Harvey died in maximum security in Oak Park Heights last year."

"Tell me about Harvey the Hammer," Serena coaxed.

"Harvey was first arrested when he was enlisted in the army and stationed in Alaska. He raped and murdered a woman. During the interrogation, Harvey admitted he had difficulty maintaining an erection and brutally assaulted the woman with a hammer. He was given the death penalty, but the Supreme Court ruled his confession was improperly obtained since he was told he could avoid the death penalty if he confessed. The murder charge was dismissed. He served eight years at Alcatraz for assault before being paroled. He committed a burglary in Minneapolis with his brother, Clinton, who was released from Alcatraz at the same time. Harvey was sent to prison in Leavenworth and then Walla Walla in Washington after his next burglary. After he was let out, Harvey raped a nineteen-year-old girl and a fifteen-year-old girl in Washington. Both had responded to ads he'd posted for help at his gas station. Harvey beat both to death with a hammer. One of the girls was pulled off a reservation."

"Why is that significant?" Serena asked.

"It's not important to this case, but it's relevant to Paula's project." A colleague of mine, Paula Fineday, is investigating the significant number of Indigenous women who have disappeared. "She's finding that it's less likely there's a serial killer targeting Native women specifically, and more probable that killers are targeting vulnerable girls and women in general. Reservations and low-income housing areas are fertile hunting grounds for predators." I paused for a moment before continuing, "Harvey returned to Minnesota and assaulted a thirteen-year-old girl with a hammer. She talked him into releasing her, but didn't report the assault until months later. A naive churchgoing woman, Eileen Hunley, moved in with Harvey in an effort to help him change. After she broke up with him, her body was found in Zimmerman. He then picked up a seventeen-year-old girl and a sixteen-year-old girl in Minneapolis. He beat the seventeen-year-old to death with a hammer during a rape and left her body along the road forty miles north of Minneapolis. The sixteen-year-old escaped."

"Does this keep going?" Serena asked.

"Yes."

"In Minnesota?"

"Yes."

"Continue," she sighed.

"Harvey picked up Gwen Burton from a Sears parking lot. He ripped her clothing, choked her into semi-consciousness, and sexually assaulted her with the handle of a hammer. He dumped her body in a field. She survived and was able to crawl to the roadside for help. Four days later, he picked up two more young women and assaulted them. Both girls escaped when Carignan stopped for fuel. Two days later, eighteen-year-old Kathy Schultz of Minneapolis did not show up for her college classes. Her body was found the next day by hunters in a cornfield near Cambridge. Statements from his surviving victims led to his arrest. I know a guard who worked with Harvey at Oak Park Heights. Harvey was a beast. He weighed two-seventy but did one-arm pull-ups regularly."

"What a horrifying monster. Can you summarize the second guy?"

"Joseph Ture Jr. killed the Huling family in Clearwater. He later told a cellmate he killed Alice, the mom, because she wouldn't let him be with her sixteen-year-old daughter. He killed her children to cover up Alice's murder. One child hid and escaped. That boy ran through the snow on a cold December night in his pajamas to get help. But the child never saw Ture. A year later, Ture raped eighteen-year-old Marlys Wohlenhaus in her Afton home and murdered her with a hammer. The next year, he raped and murdered nineteen-year-old Diane Edwards. She was a University of Minnesota student and was abducted after her shift ended at a Perkins in West St. Paul. Diane's body was found in a field by Elk River. He's also suspected of killing twenty-year-old Joan Bierschbach from St. Cloud. She left her apartment to play volleyball in Waite Park. Her car was found in the St. Cloud Perkins parking lot. Her remains were discovered five years later in Monticello. Ture told a cellmate he forced her into his vehicle in the Perkins lot."

"Is he dead?"

"No, he's doing life in prison. He's been involved in a number of fights at the correctional facility in Stillwater. I'm not sure where he's headed when that prison closes, but for the time being he's still rotting away in Stillwater."

"Please, no more examples." Serena furrowed her brow and pulled her legs away from me. She turned the television on and asked, "Why do you think Eliana's assailant hammered her hand?"

"That's a great question. Maybe something she wrote or did with her hand. She could have flipped off the wrong guy. That piece seems very personal."

"What does Eliana say about it?" Serena wondered.

"No clue. Eliana doesn't recall giving anyone the finger, and she described letter-writing as archaic. She doesn't do that."

Serena closed her eyes, and I knew any chance at intimacy was gone. I understood. I can casually talk about horrible things because of my job, but Serena needed time to process it. I sat back and sipped my ale.

After ten minutes of quietly watching TV, Serena muted the show and asked, "What were the families like for the hammer guys?"

"Dysfunctional. Harvey was sexually abused by a babysitter. Wet himself throughout school. Finished his childhood in reform school. Ture was raised in an orphanage and also ended up in reform school. Both had failed efforts as young adults in the military and received less-than-honorable discharges."

She put the show back on.

I had ruined what could have been a great night by overwhelming her with my obsessive details about the killers. She was shutting down for the night, and I didn't blame her. I asked, "Is there anything you'd like to talk about?"

Serena silently leaned into the corner of the couch and closed her eyes.

I sighed. Live and learn.

She finally opened her eyes and appeared to have experienced an "aha" moment. "Pseudologia fantastica. Pathological lying.

What if someone lied and *told* the killer Eliana did something with her hand that was insulting? You can question Eliana all you want, and she'll never have the answer."

33

JON FREDERICK
10:00 A.M., MONDAY, SEPTEMBER 30, 2024
WATER STATION APARTMENTS
402 WEST HOLDT STREET, BATTLE LAKE

Londyn Larson lived in an affordable apartment in Battle Lake. She clearly did not live a glamorous life, and most likely survived paycheck to paycheck. Londyn didn't return my calls, but I was able to contact her mother, Lexi, and we met at Londyn's apartment. Lexi was in her late forties, stood about five feet, five inches tall, weighed approximately one hundred seventy pounds, and had short, brown, pixie-cut hair. She wore an oversized sweater, jeans, and hiking boots. Lexi said as she led me in the door, "You're the second guy who's come looking for her in the last couple of weeks." Once inside, she explained, "If you know what Londyn does, you understand that guys are always looking for her. They typically don't show up in person."

"I'm familiar with her Londyn Lust persona and her OnlyFans account. Who was the other guy?"

"He didn't give me his name. Big Italian guy. Told me to warn Londyn to stay away from Lorenzo Caruso. I tried calling her, but her phone went immediately to voicemail."

I hope Roan Caruso didn't get to her first. Londyn's apartment was unremarkable and clean. It hadn't been ransacked. An iconic black-and-white reprint of the 1950 photo "Kiss by the Hôtel De Ville" by Robert Doisneau hung on the wall. The photo featured a man kissing a woman goodbye at a Paris train station. It struck me that a woman who was so overtly sexual online had a G-rated romantic picture in the living room.

After observing me studying the picture, Lexi said, "I decorated all of the rooms but the bedroom." She walked me down the hall. "It's insane. Londyn's always been anxious. She quietly hungered for the attention all the other girls were getting, but she didn't date. They used to call her 'Emo' in school because she was so nervous and quiet. Then she got swept away by social networking and realized she could stay in her bedroom and get the boys' love right here in bed. It's sick. She's an embarrassment. Attention is her drug of choice. But honestly, I think it's a stage she's going through."

"Are you worried something might have happened to Londyn?" I asked. "She's not answering my calls."

"Londyn doesn't answer calls unless she recognizes the caller. She worried that one of those online pervs would eventually get her number."

"I know at least one guy she shared her number with," I remarked.

"Only findoms," Lexi said. "Do you know what findoms are?"

"Yes, men she financially dominates or takes advantage of." I didn't bother to explain that Lorenzo wasn't technically a "findom," since he wasn't submissive to her. He was a "sugar daddy" who gave her money in excess of her typical fees for special favors. "Where do you think she is?"

"I have no idea." With concerned eyes, Lexi nervously studied me before adding, "She does this. Londyn will disappear for a couple weeks at a time with one of her findom guys. I've tried to tell her 'If this is such a great gig, why am I always bailing you out with your bills?' These guys pay to use her on vacation, and that's it. She tells me, 'I'll get to see the world.' See the world all right. I said, 'Yeah, you're a regular Nellie Bly.' Londyn can tell me what the ceiling of a Super 8 Motel looks like in Milwaukee, Crookston, and Minot."

"If she's anxious and introverted, how does vacationing with strangers work?" I wondered.

"There are only a couple of guys in this category, and she talks to them for months before she goes."

I was looking at a bed covered with a white satin comforter and matching pillowcases. Translucent ivory curtains hung over the headboard with LED white lights in the material, mimicking stars. "Do you know their names?"

"No."

"And she doesn't tell you ahead of time when she leaves?"

"No. She knows I'd try to talk her out of it."

"Has something stressful happened in Londyn's life recently? People have reported receiving threatening messages from her."

"Not that I'm aware of." Lexi pondered for a moment and then shared, "Londyn's biggest thing was trying to make everyone happy. She loved attention. I wasn't happy about what she was doing, so we weren't on good terms. If her 'business,' or whatever you call it, was failing, I think she would lose it. It was her whole identity. She was an OnlyFans sensation!" Lexi said sarcastically.

"Living in a low-rent apartment," I added. The camera in the bedroom was positioned to make the room look much larger than it was. This room was Londyn's studio, and from the camera, it looked classy. Standing in the bedroom, you could see the wall behind the camera covered floor-to-ceiling with hooks and easy-to-access midriff shirts, miniskirts, and lingerie. It reminded me of a Hot Topic store. "Any idea where I'd find Londyn?"

"None," Lexi responded. "If I knew, I'd give her a talking to. This is what my girl does. Takes off with a guy and leaves everyone worrying about her. Talk about disappointment. My daughter masturbates for a living. She doesn't maintain relationships because they interfere with her online work. It's all, 'Look at me!' And they pay her for it. What the hell is wrong with people?"

My conversation with Serena about the hammer killers had my

profiler's brain working. I invited Lexi to sit with me at the kitchen table. I asked, "What was Londyn like as a child?"

"She was the third of my four kids, and to be honest with you, she didn't get a lot of attention. Her dad and I had heated arguments throughout the first three years she was with us. We finally divorced when Londyn was thirteen. Believe me, I have my regrets about how that was handled. Her dad interrogated her for information to use against me in the custody battle. It was a shit show. Londyn got lost in it all. She was powerless. My oldest was the boss when we weren't around. I should clarify that my oldest and youngest daughters are my biological kids. The middle two were adopted."

"Where was Londyn before she was with you?"

Lexi hesitated. "Is this going to be public information?"

"No. I'm trying to solve a rape and attempted murder case."

"We rescued her and her older brother from a home by Wolf Lake."

"How did she do in school?"

"Passing. No real problems. Well, she was suspended once, but it was nothing."

"What did she do?"

"A girl was making fun of her, and she told her, 'I will fuck you up.' I still can't believe it. Not just once. Every time the girl opened her mouth, Londyn said it again. It was especially creepy because Londyn was typically so quiet. The threat completely freaked out the girl. But if you ask me, she deserved it. You can only make fun of a girl so long before she's gonna respond. Honestly, it didn't bother me. I thought about fucking the girl up myself."

"What was the fallout?"

"Nothing." Lexi shrugged. "Londyn was suspended for three days. When she returned to school, the girl never spoke to her again."

"Was Londyn in band, drama, sports, a youth group?"

"No, money was tight, and we moved too often."

"Tell me about Londyn's trauma?" I asked. Repeating a threat the way she had was reflective of a past trauma."

"We took her out of a terrible situation. Londyn's parents were combat veterans. Her dad died of cancer when she was five. Her mom had PTSD from being deployed and raped in Afghanistan. She was a hardcore alcoholic. Child Protective Services was called to the home after a teacher reported that Londyn smelled and hadn't changed her clothes for days. They found the mom naked and dead in bed. There were empty wine boxes throughout the bedroom, an empty gallon of vodka by her bed, and buckets full of urine. She hadn't left the room for weeks."

The manner in which people recreate their past trauma is fascinating to me and is the basis of my profiling work. Like her mother, Londyn lives primarily in her bedroom. "How long was she dead?"

"They're not sure. Two or three days." Lexi sighed. Londyn was ten, and she'd been sleeping with her fifteen-year-old brother, Luger, on a mattress on the floor. On his deathbed, their dad told Luger he had to take care of Londyn when he was gone. Luger made sure she went to school every day so she could get a semi-healthy meal."

"Was Londyn sexually abused?"

"Yeah." She hesitated. "No intercourse. They touched each other."

"Like she does to herself now."

"Yeah, I guess so." Lexi considered. "All they had was each other, and then we had to separate them. Luger was just a kid, raising another kid. Later there was the porn thing."

"The porn thing?"

"I thought my husband was accessing a lot of porn. He blamed Londyn. I still think it was him. I don't see girls doing that."

"Porn sites claim one-third of their users are female, so it's possible. Could Londyn be staying with your ex?"

"No. He doesn't talk to Londyn anymore. He's pissed about the OnlyFans crap. Left me to deal with it. He and Luger moved to Alaska. My daughters disowned her. But I can't walk away. What Londyn's been through was so unfair. I still have hope that someday, she'll turn it around."

"Do you think she could have participated in a sexual assault against somebody?"

"No." Lexi swallowed hard. "I don't think so. She never hurt anybody. I don't know. Maybe? A guy could talk her into it. I don't see her planning to hurt anybody. Isolation was her thing. She only went with findoms to maintain an income."

I felt it was important to tell Lexi what I *didn't* see. "Londyn's phone, laptop, purse, and car were all gone. Please call me as soon as you hear from her." I paused, "Call, even if you just hear about her somewhere." I left her my card.

34

JON FREDERICK
10:00 A.M., FRIDAY, OCTOBER 4, 2024
PIERCE STREET NORTHEAST
BELTRAMI, MINNEAPOLIS

I drove to Roan Caruso's house to meet with his son. Obviously proud of his muscular physique and tight abs, Lorenzo answered the door shirtless. His only attire was a pair of spandex shorts.

"Get dressed. We need to talk."

When Lorenzo returned, he had added only a yellow T-shirt. Carmel came walking out in a pair of Lorenzo's boxers. She was braless and wore an oversized shirt. They invited me into the living room, where they snuggled together on the couch.

I couldn't help but notice Carmel had fresh rope indentations on her wrists and ankles. I asked Lorenzo, "Do you need to tie her up?"

Carmel rescued him. "It's the submissive who experiences all of the pleasure."

I said, "Roan shared that Londyn called you at work."

"Londyn's stalking me," Lorenzo said. "She described exactly what I was wearing and knew I was talking to a woman. Dad had people in the area, but they couldn't find her. Londyn's like a world-class spy."

I needed to think about that.

"I've been thinking about Londyn. On the night Eliana caught me talking to her online, we were FaceTiming. Londyn may have witnessed the fight between Ellie and me. Ellie was pissed that I was talking to Londyn."

"Can I see your phone?" I asked. "I'd like to get to work on this immediately. I want to see where Londyn's calling from."

"Can't do that." Lorenzo gripped his phone. "Everything I've shared with law enforcement has come back to bite me in the ass. Dad might trust you, but I sure as hell don't. Why would you help me?"

"I want to see the person who assaulted Eliana behind bars."

"He's dead." Lorenzo sat back confidently. "I shot him."

"There was a second person involved," I explained. "If Londyn's harassing you, I need your phone to trace her location. Stalkers don't just suddenly stop."

When Lorenzo didn't respond, I added, "I can't do anything without your help."

"Then earn my trust," Lorenzo said.

"What are you suggesting I do?" It was an annoying comment from someone who was in my yard in the middle of the night with a rifle. I resented that Roan called my boss, and Sean sent me over to help Lorenzo.

"Well, you could stop banging Ellie, for one. You're the one who turned her against me."

The accusation was so absurd, I wasn't sure it warranted a response. It reflected Lorenzo's strong feelings for Eliana, and this seemed to bother Carmel. I said, "I have not crossed any boundaries with Eliana. I simply want to find the second person involved in her assault." I turned to Carmel. "I was told Londyn called you before your house burned down. Had she threatened you before?"

"Yes, Lorenzo's witnessed the threats," she said. "Crazy jealous puta. Something's wrong with a freak who spends her day paddling the pink canoe."

"Lorenzo, were you with Carmel when the threats came in on her phone?" I questioned. This would suggest they both had an alibi.

"Well, no," he responded. "I wasn't sittin' there starin' at her phone. But she showed them to me right after she got them."

I reached my hand out to Carmel. "If you want my help, I'll need your phone."

She started to hand it to me and then pulled it back. "I don't think so. Not yet." Carmel snuggled closer to Lorenzo. "If my man can't trust you, why should I? The Turrisis and Carusos are taking care of me. I'm not doin' nothin' Lorenzo doesn't want."

"Londyn burned your house down," I reminded her.

"So, find the bitch," she sneered.

10:45 A.M., HIGHWAY 94 WEST, MINNEAPOLIS

I left the house and called Roan Caruso. After I told him neither Lorenzo nor Carmel were cooperating, he muttered, "Ma che cazzo."

"Means?" I asked.

"What the fuck? Don't be ignorant. Learn some Italian."

"Yes, those are important words to know."

"Damn kids," Roan continued. "They think they have all the answers. I'll talk to them. We're out of town, but I promise to deal with them when I get back."

"Lorenzo looked pretty comfortable with Carmel," I shared.

"What is that supposed to mean?"

"It's just an observation." I wanted Roan to consider the possibility that Lorenzo set all of this up. "Call me when they're ready to cooperate. There's nothing I can do until then."

2:30 P.M.
PIERZ

I returned to Pierz, and Serena asked if I would take our five-year-old to the doctor. Both Serena and baby Cami needed a nap. Jackson was running a fever. While walking into the doctor's office, Jackson told me, "I'm really having a tough time."

"I know." I put my hand on his shoulder. Serena has said a hundred times to Jackson, "You're really having a tough time, aren't you?" I felt bad for our little guy. Jackson was a momma's boy, and his tender heart suffered with her sadness. "You're not feeling good. Mom's not feeling good, and Cami hangs on her like a baby koala bear."

Jackson smiled at the comparison.

"But the doctor's going to help us out here. And Mom's going to feel better, and in a couple of months, Cami will be less clingy. We're all going to be okay. Maybe we can do something fun with Nora when she gets home from school." At age nine, Nora was already more like me in her ability to compartmentalize and focus on other tasks.

"Maybe we could cook something for Mom."

"Yes. I've made some chicken soup for today, but we can cook something for tomorrow. Plus, we might need to have some ice cream tonight to help bring your fever down."

As we sat in the waiting room, I felt his forehead, and Jackson's fever appeared to be already fading.

Jackson picked up a pamphlet and recited, "You have to wash your hands, or you'll get sick."

The woman sitting next to me said, "That boy can read. He's pretty little for that."

I handed her the pamphlet. It was on mammograms. I smiled. "He can't read, but he's very good at faking it."

We were called in to meet with the doctor, who proceeded to tell us Jackson had a virus, but he was getting over it. Jackson was in a good mood after hearing there would be no shots and no medication. I put him in his car seat, and we headed home.

"Mom usually plays a game in the car," Jackson said.

"Like what?"

"I Spy or Simon Says."

"Okay, let's play Simon Says and start with, 'Dad tells the best jokes.'"

Jackson smiled and sat silent.

"Simon says, make fish lips."

Jackson made fish lips.

I had pulled up to the four-way stop on Edward Street. No one was coming in any direction, so I rolled through. Suddenly, squad car lights lit up from around the corner. In the rearview mirror, Jackson was still in game mode. I told him, "You can stop. I need to talk to this guy."

I rolled down the window, and the officer smiled and asked, "Didn't you see the stop sign?"

"Sick kid, trying to get him home."

Jackson put his head down and remained silent.

"Next time, stop, all right?" The officer tapped the roof of my car.

"I will."

The officer left, and I turned to look at Jackson. "You don't have to be afraid of him."

"I'm not. He fingerprinted my whole class yesterday," Jackson said casually.

"Why didn't you say 'Hi?'"

"I was still making fish lips," he argued.

"I told you you could stop."

"You never said 'Simon says.'"

3:30

Cami and Serena were still sleeping. Serena was having fewer bad days and had started therapy. After Jackson and I picked Nora up from school, I brought them to the kitchen.

I set up a chair for Jackson to stand on while Nora stood next to me. I instructed, "We're going to make cornbread dressing. We'll start it now and eat it tomorrow."

"How do you make cornbread?" Nora asked.

"Next summer, we'll make it from scratch. But today, we're using a box mix."

"Scratch?" Jackson asked.

"It means to cook by creating everything we pour out of this box instead of using someone else's mixture."

Nora interjected, "We should use that good Buckman corn."

"That's a great idea." I handed Nora a bowl, a carton of milk, and eggs. "Okay, read the recipe and mix it all together."

Nora looked at Jackson, "Should he be touching the food? Isn't he sick?"

"He won't be touching the food, but he will help."

I took out our biggest cookie pan and set it on the counter. "Jackson, you're going to pour some olive oil on this. Then I'm going to cut some peppers and onions into pieces and have you press them through the handheld chopper." I knew he'd need help, as they never press as smoothly as advertised.

Nora asked, "Why aren't we using a cake pan?"

"Great question. Because the best part of cornbread is the top, so we're going to make it less than an inch deep, with lots of top."

"Are we going to put honey on it?" she asked.

"Not this time. We're going to bake it, cut it into about one-inch squares, and leave it out to dry. Tomorrow, we'll add the chicken broth, sausage, and vegetables."

I helped Jackson press red and green peppers into squares.

"Why is Mom so sad?" Nora asked.

Jackson added, "She wasn't like that before Cami."

"It happens sometimes after a woman has a baby." You hope the kids don't pick up on it, but of course, they do. "Imagine the chemical changes that have to take place so another person could grow in her. When the baby is born, the body has to fix itself again, and that process creates depression for a bit. Your mom was like that after both of you were born. You were babies, so you don't remember."

"She isn't sad every day," Nora optimistically pointed out.

"No, she isn't. And she'll keep having more and more good days until the sadness is gone." I hugged each of them. "We're a family. We help each other out when anyone struggles."

7:20 P.M.

Serena's parents had us over for supper and agreed to keep the kids for a couple of hours, so Serena and I could have some alone time. After three kids, you become less embarrassed about what

197

your parents think you might be doing. You realize they are hoping you're making good use of the time and not cleaning or doing chores.

We were lying in bed, at peace after making love. Serena's head rested on my chest as she whispered, "This moment never lasts long enough."

"True."

With a curious smile, she prodded, "Time for me to hear about the case."

I went through everything I could remember, ending with my frustration over Lorenzo's and Carmel's reluctance to share their phones.

Serena suggested, "Talk to Lorenzo's sister. It would be interesting to see what she has to say about Lorenzo and Carmel. Halle is the one sane person in Roan's family."

"Great idea." Roan Caruso had a daughter, Halle Day, who is now a therapist in the wealthy Kenwood area of Minneapolis. Halle is Lorenzo's half sister.

"Where do you think Londyn's hiding?"

"She hasn't used a credit card since she disappeared, and there's been no action on her OnlyFans site."

"Do you think she's dead?" Serena raised her head, and her beautiful green eyes looked into mine.

"I don't know. Maybe. Here's the piece I struggle with. It doesn't seem like Lorenzo, and it doesn't seem like Londyn. I can't find anything that connects Londyn to McBride. So, Londyn sees Eliana on the laptop in their hotel room. She drives to Detroit Lakes. Meets Larry McBride, and within two hours, they rape Eliana together."

"Yeah, not likely. Personally, I like Lorenzo for it. If Londyn's off with a findom, he's paying all Londyn's expenses, so she doesn't need her credit card." She wrinkled her nose, as she does when she's having a counterthought. "Londyn is socially introverted off-screen, right?"

"Yes."

"And you said Lorenzo's her findom."

"Technically, he's her sugar daddy."

"He might be the only guy she would have agreed to meet with."

"They didn't speak face-to-face much, according to Lorenzo. They primarily communicated online."

"If you can believe Lorenzo," Serena added. "Did you ever find his laptop?"

"No. I need to find Londyn, and the easiest way might be to locate her car. I sent a BOLO out to law enforcement. I've asked Bruce, Schmitty, and Dad to let hunters know we're looking for a black Toyota Camry Extreme Sports Edition."

"Those three could get it out to a lot of people." Serena smiled knowingly. "BOLO?"

"Be on the lookout."

"Doesn't Schmitty work in a lumberyard?"

"He does." I kissed her and reluctantly got out of bed. "I'll go pick up the three musketeers."

"I miss them already," Serena said.

"So do I." I wanted to be with the kids. I wanted to be alone with Serena. And I wanted to be an investigator. I was constantly juggling the three, always trying to maintain a balance. The alone time with Serena suffered the most, but we both knew it was the stage of parenting we were in. It's been better since we turned to Serena's parents and asked for their help.

35

ELIANA CASTILLO
12:00 P.M., FRIDAY, OCTOBER 11, 2024
REDS AUTO
104 MAIN STREET NORTH, PIERZ

People wouldn't believe how busy this store is on a daily basis. We go through four hundred mini pizzas every lunch shift. Not occasionally—every day, we're rolling out dough as fast as we can until the rush is over.

My phone buzzed, and I pulled it out of my pocket to make sure nothing had happened to Luis at school. The text read: "We're done sharing Lorenzo. Looks like you lost. Your trailer-trash BS tattoo didn't work."

I didn't recognize the number. I quickly texted, "Who are you, and how did you get my number?" It wasn't worth explaining that BS stood for Baja Sol, the home of my ancestors.

"Lust :)" she responded. "Londyn style."

"You won?" I texted back. "I hope you wear your participation medal proudly."

"Yeah, I know about you. He told me all the disgusting things you did for him. Did he tell you he fantasizes about me when you're having sex?"

"That is curious, because when I'm having sex, he's not there. Get a life." I put my phone away and got back to work.

1:00 P.M.

The rush was over. I was offered the opportunity for a break and took it.

Londyn responded to my text with: "I'll kiss him goodnight for you. Anywhere in particular?"

"Ass seems appropriate," I responded and shut my phone off.

Mia Malasheski was in the store eating a walleye sandwich by herself in a booth, so I decided to join her. It was time for my break, and the other booths were full, so it felt natural to ask, "Do you mind if I share her booth?" My inquiring mind had to know how she and Mike were doing.

Mia set down her sandwich and gestured for me to sit. "I'm Mia."

"I'm Eliana."

Mia smiled. "I know who you are. This is Pierz. When you see somebody new, you ask and get the story. I heard you and your son are living at the old Frederick farm."

"Isn't it just the Frederick farm? Billy's been there for decades."

"Billy lost the farm in the nineties, but the bankruptcy court allowed him to keep the house. So, it's the Frederick house, but the old Frederick farm."

"I thought he just rented the land out." I quickly added, "It doesn't make any difference; he's been a savior to me."

"I didn't mean anything disparaging." Mia smiled again. "I was just clarifying so you know what people are talking about. I like Billy Frederick. Great guy. He'd give you the shirt off his back."

A young man in his thirties walked in, and Mia's face lit up. "Hey, Noah."

"Mia," he said, with a twinkle in his eye. "Be right back."

Mia turned to me and asked, "Do you mind?" suggesting I depart.

"Aren't you with Mike Haney?" I asked.

"Yeah." She blushed. "But what he doesn't know can't hurt him, right? I mean, it's not like we're married or anything."

I was bothered, but quietly went back to work. *Why can't people be honest with their partners? Is it too much to ask?* That poor boy was going to get his heart broken again. I still consider Mike a friend, and I didn't want him to be hurt, but the thought that he might be available again energized me. Now, how do I let Mike know without being the bearer of bad news? I don't want to appear petty and gossipy, but I do want another chance.

Noah returned from the restroom and sat in the booth with Mia. He leaned into her, and she took his hands.

Before returning to work, I turned my phone back on and stepped outside the store. There were no additional texts. I called Jon and said, "Londyn Lust texted me. Apparently, she and Lorenzo are a 'thing' again."

"That was her first mistake." Jon explained, "I couldn't get Carmel or Lorenzo to give me phone access, but if you'll allow me to track the call, I'll find out where she's at."

"Come and get it."

36

JON FREDERICK
2:00 P.M., WEDNESDAY, OCTOBER 15, 2024
165 WESTERN AVENUE NORTH (SELBY AVENUE)
ST. PAUL

L ondyn's call was traced to Nina's Coffee Café in St. Paul. Nina's is a historic deep red stone building with large pillars at the entry. There is a myth that Nina's was built on the grounds of a former brothel. It wasn't, but it was named after former brothel owner Nina Clifford, whose given name had been Hannah Steinbrecher. Nina was born in Canada and started building a brothel in St. Paul in 1887, the same time they were building our church in Pierz. The former brothel is now the Science Museum of Minnesota. In the early 1900s, it was lavish with elegant rooms, three maids, a cook, a housekeeper, a porter, and a musician. A chandelier taken from the building hangs in the office of the Saint Paul Mayor today. Nina's was located half a block away from the police station. The madams were arrested monthly, but were friendly with the police, and they knew the police would protect them if customers got out of hand. One of the challenges with old ornate buildings is that there are lots of nooks and crannies not covered by cameras. When I glanced around, I noticed a diverse mix of people enjoying hot and cold brews in the coffee shop. For a moment, I believed Londyn Lust might be hanging out somewhere in St. Paul.

The shop owner, June Berkowitz, greeted me in a do-rag and sunglasses with small, round lenses. June was creative and intelligent, and she was a business owner who made her community better. I had informed her of my need to find a killer, and she allowed me to look at video footage from October 11. We knew someone was texting Eliana at noon on that day from this location.

I sat at a computer in the office while June stood behind me, watching the screen over my shoulder. She named one customer after another, until we came to a woman in a black sweatshirt with the hood pulled up.

"She has no face," June commented.

In the video, there was a bright ball of light where her face should be. I explained, "She's wearing a camera-shy hoodie. It's a hooded sweatshirt with infrared LED lights directed outward. The lights are imperceptible to the human eye. When they're pointed toward surveillance cameras, they make the person's face indistinguishable."

"That's insane."

I watched the woman go through the line while June observed the beverage that was being made for her. "I can tell you what she ordered," June said. "A Madame Nina. It's espresso, milk, honey, and cinnamon."

"She's not a regular," I remarked.

"How do you know?"

"Nobody's greeted her." I shared what little I could conclude. "She's somewhere between five-two and five-six, as are half of all women in the U.S."

The woman sat at a table by herself and spent time on her phone before departing.

I sighed. "Well, we know it's a woman."

"Sorry, I couldn't be of more help."

"Thank you. I will have to buy one of your mochas before I leave." My guess was that this woman covered her tracks well. I didn't anticipate getting anything better from other cameras in the area.

After I stepped outside, mocha in hand, my phone buzzed with a call from Scott Schmidt. Schmitty was a man of many stories, but didn't mince words when there was work to be done. "I've got your car here."

"Where are you at?"

"North of New York Mills. I got a call from a hunter and drove there to check it out. You've got a dead woman lying in the woods outside of her car. I'll stay here until you get here. The crows were pecking at her eyes. Looks like a horror movie, man."

"A murder of crows."

"No, it looks like she was shot in the chest."

"A flock of crows is called a 'murder.'"

"I know what a murder of crows is," Schmitty remarked. "Just cutting to the chase."

"How did you find her?" I was already on my way to my car.

"I got the word out. A couple of Eagles found her."

"Eagles? Do you mean circling above?" I questioned.

"No. New York Mills Eagles. Seniors at the high school—out here hunting. Get with the program, Jon. I know my bird groups, too."

"Okay. I can be there by 5:30. I'll call the Otter Tail County Sheriff's Department. I need to make sure we get spotlights out there. Sunset's at 6:30."

5:30 P.M. MINNESOTA STREET, NEW YORK MILLS

Following Schmitty's directions, I took Highway 10 to County Road 137 and headed north for three miles. I then drove down a gravel road called Minnesota Street, west for half a mile, and took a field road north. Sheriff's cars lit up the area, so it was easy to find the woods' entry.

It was a cool forty-two degrees. The woods were all shade, and I appreciated that the deputies had spotlighted the scene. Londyn Lust must have selected the meeting site. Wolf Lake, where she was raised, was only twenty miles from here. Londyn's body lay on its side a few feet from her car. She appeared to be running back to it when she was shot. My immediate thought was it looked like a mob hit, but it wasn't. Their calling card is two shots—pop, pop, and depart. But Roan would have shot her in the head and not taken a chance on Londyn running. I glanced at the scene in its entirety. The driver's side door was closed, but the passenger door was open.

A thin male deputy asked, "Do you think she had a passenger?"

"Pop the trunk. She should have a laptop and a cell phone. If she doesn't, I'd bet the person who shot her took it."

The Ottertail County sheriff was a husky man with a thick mustache. He approached and pointed out, "This is a hell of a place to leave a body. You're only an hour from both North Dakota and Canada."

Crossing state lines and national boundaries complicates investigations. If a killer wanted to buy time, crossing one of these lines would force the investigators to pause and get permission to investigate in a new area. But I'm inclined to believe the victim picked this area, not the killer.

"Who is the medical examiner you use?" I asked. "I'd like to get Hennepin County Medical Examiner Dr. Amaya Ho involved. She's already helping with this case."

"Aren't they overturning a bunch of Hennepin County cases because of the examiner?"

"Only with one examiner," I clarified. "Hennepin County has multiple examiners, and Dr. Ho's cases are all solid.

"Then it shouldn't be a problem. We use Dr. Rebecca Ash-Kendrick, who drives here from Ramsey. She'll either work with Dr. Ho or save herself the three-hour drive and hand over the case."

One of the deputies shouted, "We have a tire print from a second vehicle!"

We were fortunate that it hadn't rained for a month. I walked over and crouched down to study the tire track. "Good work. It's a little worn from the weather, so we won't be able to make an exact match, but we could likely identify the tire type. This isn't a typical tire, is it?"

"It looks like an off-road vehicle," the deputy responded. He then left to retrieve plaster to pour a mold.

After studying the track, I went back and looked at the tire prints left by Londyn's Camry. The second vehicle was considerably heavier.

"Anybody notice any footprints?" Londyn was barefoot.

"No," the deputy said.

The sheriff announced, "No laptop in the vehicle. There is a wallet with Londyn Larson's driver's license in it, but no cell phone."

With gloved hands, I felt through the pockets of her thin, full-length coat. I discovered two unwrapped condoms. I carefully unbuttoned the coat to find that Londyn had been wearing only lingerie beneath. "No cell here, either."

I stepped away from the scene to call Dr. Ho.

Schmitty had been standing off to one side, observing. He commented, "I saw the tracks. I was thinking it's a heavy-duty four-wheel drive mudding truck."

"Any possibility it could have been a Hummer?"

"Damn straight." Schmitty smiled. "It would explain why the tracks are still there. The electric Hummers weigh four and a half tons. It's one of the heaviest consumer vehicles sold. You put five guys in a Hummer EV, and you're at max capacity for crossing rural bridges."

"I just happen to know someone who owns one." *Lorenzo Turrisi Caruso.*

9:00 P.M., EVERLASTING DRIVE, PARK RAPIDS

I had a dreadful visit to make. I had to drive to Lexi Larson's and tell her Londyn was dead. My plan was to be honest and straightforward.

Lexi Larson lived in a rambler-style house on Everlasting Drive, which is, ironically, less than half a mile long. Her eyes were glassy by the time she unlocked the door. She knew why I had come.

"Can I come in?"

"Yeah." She waved me in the door and led me to the couch.

"We found a body in the woods north of New York Mills. Londyn is dead."

"I was afraid of this." Lex bit her bottom lip. "So afraid I couldn't even voice my worries out loud."

"I'm sorry."

"Was she raped?"

"I don't think so. She was shot twice. It looks like she was meeting someone, and they killed her before anything happened."

"Why?"

"I don't know, but I intend to find out."

She bowed her head and cried, holding both hands over her face.

"Is there someone you can call to stay with you tonight?"

"My oldest daughter, but she isn't going to be helpful. I need to call my ex. He's just going to say, 'I told you so.'"

"I'm sorry."

Lexi retrieved her phone from the cupboard and made a call. "Ryan, call me when you get a chance. It's Londyn. She's dead." Lexi hung up. "I might as well get it over with. Get my lecture on why we should never have taken those kids in. Ryan thinks that's why we divorced."

Her phone buzzed. Lexi put it on speaker and said, "Here it is."

"What happened?" Ryan asked.

"They found Londyn in the woods. She's been murdered."

"Why?" he asked.

"I don't have the details yet. The cop's here to ask me to ID the body, I suppose."

"I'm so sorry," Ryan said with genuine compassion. "You dedicated your life to helping those kids."

I hadn't planned on taking Lexi to identify the body, but if she wanted to get it over with, I'd take her.

"Go ahead and say it," Lexi challenged Ryan.

"I just did," Ryan responded. "I'm sorry. What happened to

those kids wasn't your fault or mine. You did everything you could to help. Something got locked into that girl's head that nobody could get back out. You gave her normalcy, and she did okay for a while. I love you for that…"

I appreciated Ryan's reaction and whispered to Lexi, "I'll wait for you outside."

37

JON FREDERICK
8:00 A.M., THURSDAY, OCTOBER 16, 2024
PIERZ

Nora and Jackson were at school, and I had gotten home late, so I slept in. When I strolled down the steps, Serena immediately shushed me and whispered, "Cami's still sleeping." She hugged me and said, "Made you a mocha. Your eggs are on the table."

I kissed her, and we sat at the kitchen table.

Serena said, "Tell me about Londyn Larson."

I had shared some brief details when I finally arrived home last night. "We found her body north of New York Mills yesterday. She was shot twice. Londyn was wearing lingerie covered by a full-length coat, so she was obviously meeting someone for sex."

"Was the coat still buttoned?"

"Yes. My guess is she never made it to the second vehicle. I don't imagine we're going to get any DNA from the killer. The CSI crew is going through Londyn's vehicle. Her laptop and cell phone were gone. We found deep tire tracks from the killer's vehicle."

Serena's eyes glistened as she studied mine. She had the advantage of being driven to investigate a case without having to stand over the victims. She probed further. "I can see you have a theory. And deep tracks mean…?"

"Lorenzo Turrisi Caruso's Hummer weighs four and a half tons."

"We can never get rid of that family, can we?"

"It's electric, and you can't drive it from St. Paul to where Londyn's body was ditched and back without recharging it. BCA staff have agreed to help me out by checking the charging stations between St. Paul and New York Mills. You can't pay cash at a charging station, so there should be an electronic footprint."

"That's good. So, Lorenzo got tired of Londyn harassing him and killed her. He is a bit of a narcissist. He's a Turrisi. Nobody threatens a Turrisi."

"I've got Dr. Amaya Ho looking at the body. I am very interested in her determination of Londyn's time of death."

"Hmm. The plot thickens." Serena stopped and considered the gravity of our discussion. "I'd like to say a quick prayer for Londyn. She was a young woman who thought her value came from her sexual availability. She didn't get the chance to learn the foolishness of that venture, and it's sad. All these online fans cheering the demise of her virtue took her right to her grave. All alone, in the middle of nowhere."

When the prayer was finished, I stepped behind Serena's chair and began rubbing her shoulders. She leaned forward and pulled up the back of her shirt, prompting me to rub her entire back. Serena then took my hand and said seductively, "If you want some of this, I'd suggest you follow me upstairs."

She quickly stripped and crawled under the covers. As I removed my clothes, I couldn't help smiling.

"What?" she asked.

"I never thought you were much of a morning person."

"The concept of time has pretty much gone out the window since Cami was born."

As I slid my boxers down, Serena asked coyly, "Is this a debriefing?" As I reached for the covers, she said, "Stop. Just stand there for a moment."

Pleased to see her so happy, I slowly turned in a circle.

"Join me," she simpered. "I'm going to straighten you out, boy." She giggled, "I promise no more puns."

I appreciated her ability to change gears so quickly. It was something I'd gotten used to in order to enjoy time with my family. We both knew either Cami would wake up, or something would come up at work, and I'd get called in soon. William Penn once said, "Time is what we want most, but what we use the worst." When I felt her naked warmth against mine, I knew that wouldn't be the case for Serena and me.

38

ELIANA CASTILLO
7:15 P.M., THURSDAY, OCTOBER 16, 2024
ST. OTTO'S CARE CENTER
920 4TH STREET SOUTHEAST, LITTLE FALLS

Am I a terrible person? My curiosity was killing me. I needed to find out if Mike had been honest with me. *Why? He has no interest in me.* I guess it would help me get over him. The very first time we met, Mike told me he played cribbage with his grandmother on Thursday nights. If he had lied to me, it would be much easier to get over him. It would make him like every other guy I've dated, rather than this new brand of partner I fantasize about. I want to say I'm sorry. God, I want to say I'm sorry. I love Mike. But I messed it up. I didn't know what I had.

A healthcare worker in maroon scrubs stopped and asked, "Can I help you?"

"I'm looking for Mrs. Delores Haney." Fortunately, my work at Red's Deli had allowed me to discover the name of Mike's paternal grandmother.

She escorted me to the elevator and said, "Second floor. Last door at the end of the hall. Delores will enjoy a visitor. It's been a quiet night."

It seemed my suspicions were dead on, but I needed to see for myself. I tapped my foot impatiently as I rode the elevator to the second floor. In the last room down the hall, an elderly woman sat, trying to get her television to work. It was so sad. It bothered me for her sake and mine. I wanted to believe in somebody, even if I couldn't have Mike. I couldn't walk away and leave the octogenarian struggling. I stepped into the room and said, "Ma'am, can I help you?"

"Deary, it would be so kind of you."

I picked up the remote and, after messing with it a bit, managed to turn the television on. "There. What channel do you want it on?"

"Hallmark. What is your name, Deary?"

"Eliana. My son and I live in Pierz with Billy Frederick."

"I didn't know Bill well, but that Camille was a saint. She helped me when I moved here from Browerville. Did you know Tom Brady's mom, Galynn Johnson, was from Browerville? Galynn was our homecoming queen back in 1961."

"I didn't know that."

"Galynn was a sweetheart. Tommy and his sisters spent their summers in town when they were young. I still see that little boy in him when I watch him announcing games."

While I worked on the TV, the woman rambled on. "I moved in with my sister after Harvey died. Stella's house was haunted. Stella was supposed to have her leg amputated, but refused. Died at home the next day. After her funeral, I moved into her room because it was a little bigger than mine." She tugged at my arm to make sure I was paying attention.

"I'm listening. You moved into Stella's room."

"Okay. This is important," she insisted. "During the middle of the night, I was approached by her ghost. Socked me right in the boob. The tender one."

Surprised by the sudden turn in the conversation, I looked up and asked, "What did you do?"

"I moved my bed to the other side of the room, and she never bothered me again."

I'm not sure that moving her bed several feet over would elude a ghost who managed to find her and punch her in her tender breast, but I opted not to respond.

"But that's not the weird part," she added.

"I think I have it fixed." I turned the channel to Hallmark. I had to admit, I wanted to hear the weird part.

"I set up a camera to capture the ghost on film, and guess what?"

"What?" I asked with increasing curiosity.

"The battery was dead the next morning." She smiled and nodded her head as if she'd just proved her point.

"I'm not sure what that means." It was everything I could do not to burst out laughing. It was absurd to think there would be a logical conclusion.

"Well, everyone knows ghosts drain batteries."

"Okay." I handed her the remote. "Tell me a little about Mike. Your grandson Mike was a good friend of mine."

"You must be talking about Marne. I don't have a grandson, Mike. Marne's a little shy. Maybe it's why he's still single. You should look him up."

"No, I'm looking for Mike. Are you Delores Haney?"

"No." She smiled. Delores is across the hall.

"Oh." I deliberated. "Is there anything else I could get you?" I stood up.

"No. But say hi to Mike."

I stepped into the hall and saw Mike inside the room next door, playing cribbage with his grandmother. His back was to me. His grandmother smiled at me, but I quickly turned on my heel and headed down the hall. *What was I thinking?* He was still in a relationship, and I was now a stalker. I had to be at work in less than twelve hours. I needed to get home.

7:15 A.M., FRIDAY, OCTOBER 17, 2024
RED'S AUTO, 104 MAIN STREET NORTH, PIERZ

A scraggly old curmudgeon of a man approached the deli to order breakfast. Alex, one of my coworkers, said, "You get to wait on Railroad."

"Why do they call him Railroad?" I asked.

"His name is Ivan, and he works for Burlington Northern."

"Why don't they just call him Ivan?"

Alex smiled as he quietly sang, "Ivan working on the railroad, all the livelong day."

I shook my head and stepped to the counter to take Railroad's order.

"I'll have some of that Thielen's bacon, eggs, and hashbrowns with a cuppa joe."

"You can choose your coffee here." I pointed to the selections on the counter and the disposable coffee cups.

"It's my anniversary today," Railroad announced. "I married a Fertile woman. We fell in love at Climax."

When I looked confused, Alex muttered, "Both are Minnesota towns. Just wait; it gets worse."

I opted to ignore Railroad, but as he filled his coffee, he went on, "After I wet a line at Big Dick Lake, I brought her to Embarrass. Things went south from there. I got to Remer, but after a bit, I got to Aitkin." He laughed at his own humor. "Now we're in Golden Valley." When he realized I remained straight-faced, he said, "Ah, come on. Where are you from?"

"Based on my history of relationships, you'd think Burnsville."

"Ha! You know, my wife had a wild sister who moved to Pardeeville, Wisconsin. Straight east of Random Lake," Railroad continued to speak as I returned to the deli. Realizing he'd lost his audience, he finally left to find a booth.

Enough with the small-town craziness.

Mike Haney walked into the store wearing camouflage hunting gear. My stomach churned nervously, and I tried to avoid eye contact out of fear that he'd heard I was at St. Otto's last night. When I realized he wasn't paying any particular attention to me, my motivation shifted to, *Please notice me.* Still behind the counter, I stopped what I was doing and watched him help himself to a dark roast coffee. Suddenly, he turned toward me and looked directly into my eyes.

My face flushed. It was a little more notice than I had anticipated. I swallowed hard.

"I think I'll have a Denver breakfast sandwich," he said.

"You think you will, or you will?" I teased, my stomach in my throat. "I mean, the difference is, either I'll make it for you, or I'll think about making it for you. It's tasty. Ham, onion, and green pepper omelet on a fresh croissant."

"Sold!" He smiled. "I'll grab a booth while there is still one open."

"I'll deliver it personally," I promised. Mike looked more handsome than ever, and even though I'd only been at work for fifteen minutes, I asked if I could take my break after I delivered his sandwich.

I joined Mike in the booth and, embarrassed, asked, "On your way to bow hunting?" I felt like such a fool after I said it. *Duh! He's wearing hunting gear.*

"Not a lot of options in Pierz at this time of day. It's either that or church. I'm thinking of hunting this morning." He glanced out the window at St. Joseph's church. It was a large Catholic church built on a hill, so it towered over the community. It was visible in every direction as you approached town.

"Are you Catholic?" I wondered. It wasn't essential, but some type of religious belief was important to me. I believed a higher power used my spirit animal to guide me out of the woods. I don't think God interferes with life on earth a lot. You'd have to give people free will to show their true colors. But sometimes we're thrown a bone.

"I am." Mike softly explained, "I believe in a loving and compassionate God, and I admire tender hearts. But the world has its share of terrible people, so I've taken on the task of helping those in need. That's why I'm a cop."

"I grew up attending Our Lady of Guadalupe Church in St Paul, and I find some comfort in the large Catholic presence in this town. The feast day of Our Lady of Guadalupe commemorates the day that the Virgin Mary is believed to have appeared to a poor widower named Juan Diego. This religious holiday is important to my family in Mexico because it brought a message of self-worth and love at a time when they were enslaved by the Spaniards." I tried to tell myself to stop, but I kept blabbering. "People dress up more in my community for church than they do here." I smiled. "But I doubt Jesus cares. It's all good. No judgment."

"How are you and Luis doing?" Mike asked.

"Luis is great!" I paused and looked down at the table. "I'm okay." The next few words slipped out of my mouth, unfiltered. "I miss you."

"That's kind." Mike avoided eye contact as he said, "I miss our conversations too, but I'm in a committed relationship now."

"Are you still with Mia?" I wanted to share what I knew about Mia so badly it was torture to keep it in, but I didn't want to be a petty gossip.

"Yes." He studied me curiously. "How do you know her?"

I waved my arm toward the counter. "I work at Red's. Everybody in town comes here eventually. I—" I stopped myself.

"I guess that's true." Mike studied me. "Was there something you wanted to tell me?"

"No," I sighed. "I want you to be happy, Mike." I reached across the table and gently held his arm for a moment. "Thank you for being so good to me. I—" I stopped myself again. *What is wrong with me?* I think I was going to say, "I love you." *Tone it down. It's seven in the morning.* I pulled my hand back. "I better get back to work."

"Okay. It was nice seeing you."

I was hoping he'd stand up and hug me, but he went back to eating his sandwich. It is seven in the morning at Red's Auto, and Mike is dating someone else. I need to have better boundaries. This is how my relationship with Lorenzo started. Of course, I didn't know Lorenzo was in a relationship at the time. At least Mike is honest with me. Good men do exist. I think I'm ready to date again.

39

I called the Otter Tail County Sheriff's Department and asked, "Any luck with the tire match?"

"The tires are unique to the Hummer EV. The electric Hummer is so heavy it needs special tires."

It was all I needed to hear. I said goodbye and called my supervisor, Sean Reynolds. After brief introductions, I got to the point. "What do you have for me on the bullets that killed Londyn?"

"Nine by nineteen Parabellum. Fired by a Sig Sauer P365."

The most popular handgun sold in the U.S. I blew out a breath. "Does Lorenzo Caruso own one?"

"Already looked into it. As a matter of fact, he does."

"The tire prints are from a Hummer EV. Can you get me a search warrant for the Caruso home and to confiscate his vehicle?"

"I'll have it for you by the time you arrive at the BCA office."

10:00 A.M., PIERCE STREET NORTHEAST

BELTRAMI, MINNEAPOLIS

When I pulled up in front of the Caruso home, Roan was sitting on the porch sipping on a glass of iced tea. The Hummer was in the driveway. My first thought was that Sean had asked Roan to make sure his son was home. *This was good.*

I stepped onto the porch and handed Roan the search warrant. I asked him, "Did you kill Londyn Lust?" to see what he'd say.

"Killing is a business expense," he said with no emotional reaction. "We don't kill over heartache. That's a sign of weakness and is reflective of an unstable organization."

Having worked with Roan and Catania in the past, I knew it was exactly how they operated. They never killed over emotions such as love or jealousy. After entering the home, I realized Lorenzo and Carmel had bolted. Angry, I returned to the porch and confronted Roan. "Where is Lorenzo?"

"The lovebirds are off on vacation. Don't ask me where." He sat back, "Aren't you being a little ridiculous? Isn't it possible that a crime could have been committed by someone else with a similar vehicle?"

"There were only 2500 Hummer EVs produced in 2023. Eleven were sold in Minnesota. Of those eleven people, I would bet that Lorenzo was the only one who was a findom of Londyn's. That's how I got the search warrant and why I need to speak to your son."

"Lorenzo didn't kill Londyn. I know that for a fact. I don't know who did, but Lorenzo wouldn't drive three hours to kill a hooker. We can barely get him to drive five miles to a workplace where he spends the day flirting. You got the Hummer. Let's start with that. If it turns out not to be Lorenzo's Hummer, you won't need him."

The search of Lorenzo's room in the Caruso house indicated that Carmel had settled in. As I was going through his dresser, I found a picture of Lorenzo and his previous partner, Aurora, who had been killed in a drive-by shooting. She was pregnant with Lorenzo's son at the time. The loss of Aurora and her child reminded me that this boy had been through his share of trauma.

It also made me realize there were no pictures of Eliana. Her former presence had been wiped clean. Roan had obliged me and showed me his cache of legal weapons. I was sure any illegal weapons were removed before my arrival. There was no Sig Sauer handgun to be found.

I called my auto expert, James Weber, again. "I need you to go through the black box of another vehicle."

"It's called a data recorder in an automobile. What do you got?"

"2023 Hummer EV."

"That's what I'm talking about. Do I get to drive it?"

"To your heart's content. I need to know if it was anywhere near New York Mills, and if so, on what day?"

"I'll get to it this afternoon."

9:00 P.M., PIERZ

I was finally home, exhausted and disgusted from work. My efforts yielded nothing usable today. I discovered no electronics that allowed me to track Lorenzo or Carmel's whereabouts. The Hummer had not been recharged at any charging stations between St. Paul and New York Mills. It didn't make any sense. As my brother Vic says when he's discombobulated, "I can feel all the vertebrain jangling around in my head." It doesn't make any sense, but it's easy to visualize. I needed a moment of reflection with Serena.

The two of us rested on the couch in front of our fireplace, in T-shirts and underwear. I rubbed lotion on her feet while sipping a cold glass of Muggsy's Coffee Lager that I had picked up at Beaver Island. My glass became more translucent with each lotion-handed sip. Serena enjoyed a Juggernaut Cabernet. After venting my frustration with the investigation, I concluded, "If Lorenzo didn't murder Londyn, the killer must have had Lorenzo's laptop. Either Lorenzo murdered Londyn, or the killer impersonated Lorenzo to get her to the woods." I scratched my forehead. "I am not convinced Lorenzo killed Londyn. Roan's right. Lorenzo is inherently lazy. Plus, he's a sex addict. He wouldn't make the long trip to see Londyn without having sex with her. I can't get a grasp on the motivation for this murder, so I'm stuck."

"Maybe there's another way to get the motive." Serena closed her eyes and sat back as she asked, "The assaults were planned, not random, right?"

"Yes."

"Walk me through the sequence of the crimes."

I started, "The first murder involved a stripper named Cheri Wilde. She was hammered to death in her home. Larry McBride had an argument with her in the strip club that night. It's suspected the killer followed her home from the strip club after work. Cheri's killer stomped on her body after she was dead." I blew out a breath and said, "But I don't think McBride acted alone. The murders continued after McBride's death. And there is no connection between Londyn and Cheri. The only connection I have to all three murders is Lorenzo."

Serena pursed her lips. "How is Lorenzo connected to Cheri?"

"Lorenzo also had a brief affair with her."

"So, Cheri's murder ended her relationship with Lorenzo."

"True. Then Eliana was brutally assaulted and almost killed. Larry McBride was tattooed and then killed by Lorenzo Caruso."

"And Eliana's assault ended her relationship with Lorenzo," Serena added.

"Londyn was murdered while meeting someone in a Hummer for a sexual encounter."

"And Londyn's murder ended her relationship with Lorenzo," Serena repeated.

I leaned into Serena and kissed her. "You're a genius." She was exactly right. Who benefited from the outcome?

40

JON FREDERICK
8:00 A.M., MONDAY, OCTOBER 21, 2024
2442 WEST LAKE OF THE ISLES PARKWAY
KENWOOD, MINNEAPOLIS

Lorenzo and Carmel had absconded. They abandoned their personal cars and were almost certainly paying in cash, so I was having no luck running them down. I imagined Lorenzo rented a couple of cars, off paper, that could take weeks to find. I put a tail on Roan, knowing it would absolutely infuriate him to have law enforcement follow him all day. Eventually, he'd get his son to come to me.

I called the Detroit Lakes Chief of Police and asked, "Do you have an electric car charging station in Detroit Lakes?"

"Yes. In the Detroit Lakes City Liquor Store parking lot."

"I'm going to give you a couple of names, and I need you to find out if either charged a

car in Detroit Lakes since September."

"All right."

A clever killer might have considered that investigators would look to see if Lorenzo charged his Hummer between St. Paul and New York Mills. The killer could have avoided the net by charging in Detroit Lakes. It's just north of New York Mills, but still close enough to charge a car and drive it back to Minneapolis.

After the call ended, I stepped into Hope, Halle Day's counseling clinic. I needed to confirm Serena's theory. Halle was a therapist with an office in the wealthiest neighborhood in Minneapolis. She sat in her high-back cherry red leather chair, while I sat in a tan leather side chair across from her. Halle wore a dark burgundy velvet suit, and her long blond hair hung down in smooth, classy form. After summarizing the information we released to the public about our investigation, I asked Halle, "Do you believe Lorenzo had anything to do with the assault on Eliana Castillo?"

"No." Halle smiled. "Believe me, Lorenzo and I have our disagreements, but he wouldn't sexually assault Eliana. Lorenzo loved Eliana as much as he was capable of loving anyone."

"Are you aware that Lorenzo hit Eliana? At least a couple of times."

Halle blew out a long breath. "Lorenzo told me about it. He exhibits flash episodes of anger and then feels guilty afterward. Lorenzo is very immediate-gratification-oriented. He isn't angry about anything long enough to plan an assault against anybody. His anger is always an impulsive reaction."

"Tell me what you know about Carmel."

"Carmel's been Lorenzo's fallback girl when he's between relationships. Eliana told me she never knew Carmel had dated Lorenzo when she agreed to go out with him. I believe Eliana. I do know Carmel wasn't happy about the way she and Lorenzo ended. But I guess that's water under the bridge now that they're back together."

"How did he break up with her?"

Halle shrugged. "Carmel wouldn't say."

41

LORENZO TURRISI CARUSO
10:00 A.M., MONDAY, OCTOBER 21, 2024
GLACIAL RIDGE TRAIL
GREEN LAKE, NEW LONDON

I recognized Mom's number coming in on my burner phone. I answered, "Yeah?"

"You need to treat me with more respect. You didn't talk this way to me before you started running around with that skank Carmel."

Maybe, but I sure as hell thought it. Catania's comment made me wonder if she was killing off the whores I've dated.

Mom directed, "Value is what you accumulate from being selective. Respect is what you get based on your value. It's time for you to stop shopping at the Dollar Store. Call Jon Frederick. He's got some business for your new gal, El Cheapo, or whatever the hell her name is."

"Mom, I'm still on the fence about Carmel. Let me sort it out. She's been the one person who has been there for me through everything." She was about to blurt out another insult when I interrupted, "Out of respect for you, I'll call Frederick, but I'm not promising anything. Alright? Text me the number."

I gave Jon Frederick a call. "What do you want?"

"You need to come in and make a statement, Lorenzo. For your own safety."

"I'm feeling pretty good where I'm at."

"You're Hummer was at the site of Londyn's murder at the time she was murdered."

"That's ridiculous. Why would I kill Londyn?"

"Londyn was threatening you. You don't threaten a Turrisi."

A chill ran up my spine. I'd heard my mom say that a hundred times. Mom never liked Eliana, and she has nothing but hatred for strippers. "When was Londyn murdered?"

"My guess would be a couple of weeks ago. We're in the process of verifying the exact day."

"It's not me. That's all that matters. I'm not snitching anybody out."

Jon rambled on, "Has it occurred to you that Londyn might not have been the one stalking you?"

"She knew exactly what I was wearing," I pointed out.

"Maybe the woman stalking you knew what you were wearing because she was living with you."

"And she knew I was talking to a woman," I thought out loud

"Is there ever a day when you don't talk to a woman at work?" Jon questioned.

I didn't respond.

Jon continued, "Did Carmel ever ask for the passcode to your computer?"

"I gave it to her on the night of Eliana's assault. I didn't have my name on the computer, so she'd have to open it up to confirm it was mine." Jon was way off track.

"Tell me about your past break-up with Carmel. I spoke to Halle, and she said it was pretty dramatic."

"Ghosted her. Arrivederci, babe. Carmel called and wondered why. She knew there was somebody else. I was falling hard for Eliana, and there was no hiding it anymore. I tried letting Carmel down easy. Told her she was fine. I had fun with her. It was nothing she had done. You know, all the usual stuff you tell someone you don't hate when you've found someone better. The first time I saw Eliana with her dark skin in a white lace dress, it was like seeing a vision of an angel. Carmel couldn't compete with that. Nobody could."

"So, how did you end it with Carmel?"

"Carmel wouldn't let up. She was begging for another chance, and I didn't have the heart to tell her I was in love, so I made up this story." It was stupid. "Is it really relevant?"

"Yes. What was the lie you told Carmel?"

"She asked why I ignored her heartfelt plea when she called. I told her Eliana was giving me a hand job when I was on the phone with her, so I couldn't think clearly. It wasn't true. I was just trying to get Carmel to back off. If I wanted to keep tappin' the two of them, I needed to break up that friendship. And it worked. Carmel stopped talking to Ellie, and then she was available on demand."

"It didn't occur to you to tell me about that lie when you heard that Eliana's hand was hammered into a bloody pulp?"

"Whatever. Sayonara, Frederick." I hung up. I was done talking to that idiot. Carmel would never assault Eliana. "Dumbass." A delivery truck had pulled into the hotel parking lot, and the driver quickly maneuvered a two-wheel cart of goods inside. I walked over to the truck and tossed the burner phone into the open back. *Track that one down, bitches.* The implication that Carmel had anything to do with Eliana's assault was ridiculous. I know women.

When I returned to the room, Carmel looked incredibly hot in her seafoam green sundress. She said nervously, "I have something to tell you." She searched my eyes for clues, as if she was concerned about who I had been talking to.

"For God's sake, now what?" I said.

Meekly looking up through her long eyelashes, she said, "I need you to give me the same love people gave you when you killed Larry McBride." Carmel swallowed hard. "I'm the one who shot Londyn. She burned my house down. And when I confronted her, she told me this wasn't going to be finished until you were dead. She said she'd catch you when you least expected it. I couldn't let her harm you. I love you."

"Why? Why would Londyn kill me?" I wasn't sure what to do with this. Was it any different than me killing McBride? Carmel was protecting me. It still pisses me off that Londyn keyed my 911 Porsche ST. It's a $200,000 car with a three-year waiting list to purchase. I could have killed her myself.

"Don't you get it? She was obsessed with you," Carmel explained.

"Do you think Londyn might be the one who assaulted Eliana with McBride?"

"Of course." Carmel stepped into me and embraced me. They're both from northern Minnesota. Londyn couldn't accept that you were going to marry Eliana. You were funding her life."

I was so angry at myself for developing that stupid OnlyFans account. It almost got Ellie killed. I shouldn't have been surprised that a woman who allowed me to degrade her for money was crazy. Honestly, I was proud of Carmel for defending me.

"I hid you out when you shot McBride. I need you to help me out now," Carmel pleaded softly. "Please. I'd do anything for you." With a coy smile, she added, "There's got to be something I could do to persuade you." She stepped in front of the floor-to-ceiling window by the patio. I could see her naked body through her thin dress.

She had me, and she knew it.

42

ELIANA CASTILLO
11:00 A.M., MONDAY, OCTOBER 21, 2024
REDS AUTO
104 MAIN STREET NORTH, PIERZ

Mike Haney was in the store today. He was having some work done on his Jeep and was talking to our head mechanic outside the big garage doors. I was sitting in a booth, taking my pre-lunch-rush break. I watched tall and slender Mia Malasheski stroll from the pumps over to Mike. Her long, sandy hair had a smooth wave and a vibrant luster. Mia looked flawless in her full-length peacoat, with a red scarf perfectly wrapped around her neck. The mechanic stepped back into the garage. The conversation between Mike and Mia looked tense. Without giving it a second thought, I slipped out of the booth and through the inside of the store into the garage. I could stand on the other side of that garage door and hear the conversation.

I stepped behind the door and put my ear close to it. The mechanics glanced at me curiously and then went back to work.

"Have you reconsidered our conversation?" Mia asked.

"I did, but it hasn't changed the way I feel," Mike responded.

Had she come clean with him? I wondered. *Was he forgiving her?* I leaned even closer to the door.

"Mike, I don't understand," Mia said. I envisioned her pleading with her baby blue eyes.

"It doesn't feel right." Mike paused. "There's a distance between us I can't seem to traverse. I've been down this road too many times. I spend all my energy trying to make it work, and, in the end, I get dumped. I smell smoke. This time, I'm walking away before I get burned."

"What did Eliana tell you?" Mia questioned. "Mike, you have to tell me what she said."

"Eliana didn't tell me anything. What would Eliana have to tell me?"

"Never mind. It doesn't matter. Look, Mike, I admit I didn't feel the same at first, but you're starting to grow on me. My parents love you."

"Yeah, I get a lot of that," Mike laughed. "Right before it ends."

"It feels like you shouldn't be walking away from me," Mia remarked arrogantly.

There was a pause. *Please, don't give her another chance, Mike.*

"And still, I am," Mike said.

To my horror, the garage door suddenly rose. And there I stood, embarrassed.

Mike and Mia appeared confused. I could hear the mechanics laughing. Mia glared at me and marched away. Mike laughed. I rushed out of the area back to the deli.

2:30 P.M.

The lunch rush was a badly needed distraction. There was no time to think about anything other than making food as fast as possible. When I finally got a second, I pulled off my gloves, grabbed a napkin, and wiped my brow. My humiliation at being caught behind door number three wasn't my immediate thought. I had to laugh at myself for getting busted snooping. Then I suddenly realized the strings on the wall at the Frederick home were wrong.

After the lunch rush, I was able to leave work to speak to Serena. I was over my embarrassment and was now fixated on finding out who helped assault me. Serena let me in the house and immediately shushed me, signaling that the baby was napping. The rest of the kids were at school, so we had the chance to talk.

"A string is missing," I said in a hushed voice.

"What are you talking about?" Serena asked.

I led her to the music room. "Carmel was the one who encouraged Donny to call me. There should be a string from Carmel to Donny."

"Hmm. That's interesting. And there's a string from Carmel to McBride," Serena pointed out.

"But that isn't real. Carmel told me she lied about being assaulted by McBride. She was covering up for being romantically involved with Lorenzo."

"Carmel *was* talking to McBride at that time. Jon was able to verify it by looking at messages on McBride's home computer. There were notes from McBride to Carmel about getting together."

43

James Weber called first thing in the morning and revealed, "I've finished checking out the data recorder in the Hummer. It took me to the woods north of New York Mills and then led me to a taped-off crime scene in the middle of nowhere."

"Can you tell the day it was there?"

"September 13, 2024."

"That was before the threatening calls were made to Lorenzo and Carmel. This means Londyn didn't burn down Carmel's house. Thank you!"

I drove to Dad's house to speak to Eliana. She had Tuesdays off from work, and I hoped to catch her at home. This case was on the verge of busting open. I had people checking on leads in a hundred different directions who were supposed to be getting back to me by the end of the day.

Eliana was wiping down the kitchen cabinets when I entered the house. "Your dad has agreed that I can clean to cover my rent. Honestly, it was driving me crazy anyway. Your dad keeps it picked up. I keep it *clean*."

"We need to talk."

She slipped off her blue rubber gloves and joined me at the kitchen table. "What's going on?"

"When I took you back to Shady Hollow, I asked what you remembered, and you said all you could think of was Carmel being with Lorenzo. Is there any possibility that Carmel was the second person involved in your assault?"

"No." She shook her head as she dismissed the thought and then, in a softer tone, repeated, "No, that's crazy."

"Is it? Why was Carmel the first person you thought of?"

"It triggered a memory of seeing Carmel in the hollow looking for me."

"When would you have seen Carmel in the hollow? The only time you could have seen her in the park was right before the assault."

"Carmel? No." Eliana looked troubled.

"What are you thinking?"

"I had a memory when you and I were driving toward the site of my assault. I was in a car with Carmel. I was nauseated, and I assumed the memory was from the first time I drank alcohol at a party and Carmel drove me home. But I just realized that in the memory I'm wearing the dress I'd bought at The Nines on the day I was assaulted."

"Lorenzo told Carmel that you were giving him a hand job when she was pleading with him on the phone to stay with her. Your rapist pummeled your hand. Cheri's rapist pummeled her hand, too. Lorenzo said Cheri gave him a hand job on a flight to Vegas."

"But I didn't. That's not true. It doesn't make any sense. I've never done anything to hurt Carmel."

"People act on what they believe to be true, not necessarily what is true. I think Lorenzo's Hummer was at the site of Londyn's body, but I don't think Lorenzo was driving."

"Why not?" Eliana was struggling with accepting this new revelation. Her friendship with Carmel was stronger than her love for Lorenzo. She may have accepted that Lorenzo seduced Carmel, but she never questioned Carmel's fondness for her.

"Because I think sex is more important to Lorenzo than anything else in the world. And the person who killed Londyn didn't have sex with her. Even if Lorenzo were going to kill Londyn, he would have had sex with her first."

"Maybe he didn't want to leave DNA," Eliana suggested.

"No, Lorenzo would have known there would be no usable DNA by the time the body

was discovered. Roan has educated his son on usable evidence to prepare him for interrogations. Vaginal DNA is gone after five days, anal is unusable after three days, and oral is gone after one day. Londyn's clothing was undisturbed, and she had two unused condoms in her pocket."

"But Carmel? She wouldn't kill all those people just for Lorenzo."

"Maybe she was thinking bigger."

10:00 A.M.
THE MARSH
15000 MINNETONKA BOULEVARD, MINNETONKA

I met with Dr. Amaya Ho at the Hennepin County Medical Examiner's office. Amaya had Londyn Larson's body taken to her main office so she could use her best equipment.

Amaya sat in the conference room in her white lab coat. This is where she typically briefed me before we looked at a body. Amaya said, "Before we start talking about Londyn, I have something to share about the shirt you removed from Larry McBride's home. The specks of blood on that shirt were from Cheri White." Amaya wrinkled her forehead, "But Cheri wasn't wearing the shirt. The epidermis, the outer layer of skin, has dead skin cells that are constantly being shed. They're scraped off our bodies and end up in our sweat. And sweat accumulates on the inside of our clothing. Somebody else's DNA was on the inside of the shirt."

"Whose?"

"No idea," Amaya shrugged. "There wasn't a DNA match in the system."

"We know McBride was involved in the assault. Do you think it's possible that Larry sprinkled blood on somebody's shirt to set them up? He hated women. Why would he keep the shirt if it wasn't from a victim?"

"Intriguing." She tapped her lips with her forefinger. "Let me do some testing. Theory is your playground. Let's get to Londyn Larson." Amaya pointed to a picture. "Londyn was shot initially in the abdomen, but it wasn't lethal. It appears she turned to run and was shot in the back. The second shot went right through her heart and killed her."

"How long has she been dead?"

"Based on the level of decomposition, I'd say it's been over a month. If you want me to go into the significance of the types of insect larvae on the body, I can."

"Please don't. You can save the details for court. I do need your exact guess. I need guidance here, and the day makes a difference."

"If I were asked to bet on a date, I'd say five weeks ago."

I looked at my calendar. "That would put her death on September 13. She was still sending text messages after."

"She wasn't," Amaya corrected. "Maybe her phone was." She showed another picture of Londyn. Her eyes had been pecked out. "This damage was done after the murder. Most likely done by forest critters. Crows are the most likely culprit. They attack the soft tissue first. There was no bleeding with that injury, so she'd been dead for a while."

"Any DNA?"

"Only enough to verify it was Londyn Larson. No DNA from anyone else." Amaya scratched her head and said, "I do have something else, but it's not usable evidence. Follow me."

I followed her into her office and watched Amaya put on a full-length coat made of the same material as Londyn's. After buttoning it, she pointed just below the groin area. "There was a scrape against the material right here." Amaya proceeded to lie on the floor of her office while I curiously observed. She raised her knees and said, "Do you see the way the coat rises up? Step between my feet as if you were going to kick me in the groin."

I did as she suggested and thought out loud, "The killer kicked Londyn in the groin as she lay on the ground dying."

"Yes." Amaya stood back up. "But not with boots or leather shoes. The killer was wearing tennis shoes. The abrasion on the coat was made by soft rubber. It's not something that I can testify to beyond a reasonable doubt in court, but I thought you might find it interesting."

"Thank you. It is helpful." I had never seen either Roan, Cat, or Lorenzo in tennis shoes.

11:00 A.M.

The cards were starting to turn right side up for me. I received a call from the Ramsey County Fire Inspector. I answered, "Jon Frederick."

"This is Matt Kohner, Ramsey County Fire Chief. I have some information about the fire at Carmel Cano's you might be interested in. We knew from day one it was arson. If you recall, Carmel stated that the arsonists entered the home by breaking a living room window, and she escaped through her bedroom window. But we were able to reassemble the living room window, and there's a pattern of smoke staining the length of the window, suggesting the window was intact when the fire started. The window was broken after the fire was burning."

"You're suggesting Carmel started the fire, left through her bedroom window, and once outside, busted the window to make it look like someone broke in."

"It would appear that way," Matt said. "My guess is she didn't want to break the window first, since the noise could draw attention to the house. Carmel was significantly behind in her house payments."

"The fire may have served more than one purpose."

After a drought of proof, evidence was pouring in today.

The Detroit Lakes Chief of Police called. "Jon Frederick, have I got some news for you. The Hummer was charged in Detroit Lakes on Carmel's credit card. The charging station is in the parking lot of the Detroit Lakes City Liquor Store. We have video of Carmel in the liquor store."

"What kind of shoes was she wearing?"

"That's an odd question. Let me pull up the video. Do you have a footprint?"

"Sort of."

"Okay, she's wearing tennis shoes. They look like Converse All Stars."

"With the rubber toe?" I asked.

"Yes."

That was all I needed to hear.

1:30 P.M.
PIERCE STREET NORTHEAST
BELTRAMI, MINNEAPOLIS

I pulled up in front of the Caruso-Turrisi home. Both Roan and Catania were waiting for me on the porch. As I approached the house, I said, "We need to find Lorenzo and Carmel. We have evidence now that Carmel killed Londyn Lust, and she burned her own house down. Lorenzo's life might be in danger."

Catania was bothered but stayed silent. Roan told me, "I have a friend who told me he spotted Lorenzo. I'll take you to him, and I'll get him to talk to you."

Catania yelled, "I never liked that skank! You can't trust anyone who dyes their hair to hide their heritage. Own it. She burned down her own house. I've never left a home without some regret of losing the memories I made there. I sure as hell wouldn't torch a place I once called home. That's a pretty good indication of the kind of woman she is. Nothing is ever good enough for that puttana."

Realizing Cat's rant wasn't close to ending, Roan walked me outside to the driveway, where their Cadillac Escalade was parked. Once inside the SUV, he told me, "I'll get you to him. We were supposed to attend the Venice Debutante Grand Ball tonight. It's the coming-out party for Catania's niece. But we're going to rescue Lorenzo instead." Roan scratched his neck and grumbled, "Damn kid. He'll be the death of me."

44

"All of these were mere terrors in the night,
Phantoms of the mind that walk in darkness.
Though he had seen many specters in his time,
and been more than once beset by Satan, in diverse shapes, in his lonely pre-ambulation,
daylight put an end to these evils, and he would have had a pleasant life,
despite of the devil and all his works, if his path had not been crossed
by a being that causes more perplexity to mortal man than ghosts, goblins,
and the whole race of witches put together, and that was—a woman."

Washington Irving, The Legend of Sleepy Hollow

LORENZO TURRISI CARUSO
2:00 P.M., TUESDAY, OCTOBER 22, 2024
GLACIAL RIDGE TRAIL
GREEN LAKE, NEW LONDON

I watched Carmel dress and exit the bedroom. Green Lake is a beautiful destination, and I loved this quaint cabin adorned with a fireplace at the end of the bed. I've never had a woman who physically exhausted me before—long, thin legs and an ass that isn't as nice as Ellie's, but it would do. I could do worse. The question is, *Can I do better?* I reached over to the nightstand and dug Isabella Rossi's phone number out of my billfold. I hesitated for a moment and then called her.

"Hello," she answered.

"Bella, this is the fella with the mozzarella. Your nanna introduced us at the restaurant." I lay back in bed as I spoke.

"I recall," she said. "Lorenzo, right?"

"You are correct."

"I need to head off to a study group, but I have a couple of minutes," Bella said.

"*Some Like it Hot* is at the Orpheum if you're interested." There's nothing like a good old Mafia musical.

"I think it just ended. But *All the Devils Are Here: How Shakespeare Invented the Villain* is at the Guthrie."

I hate Shakespeare, but I could suffer through it to get to know Bella. I asked, "What do you think about raisins?"

"Okay," she paused and then added, "I like them in cookies."

"What would you say about a date?"

"Wow," she laughed. "It is the only fruit found on a calendar. Saturday nights work for me. Is this a dinner date?"

"Of course." I grinned.

"Sorry, but—gotta run. Call me when you have the tickets."

"I shall."

"Thank you, Lorenzo. I'm sorry for being in such a hurry, but I promise we'll talk again when I have more time."

"All good."

When she hung up, I noticed the shadow of Carmel's feet outside the bedroom door. I wondered how much she'd heard of the conversation.

Carmel entered the bedroom and sat beside me on the bed. "I think I'll stick around for a little bit." She ran her hand down my chest. She grinned slyly. "Want a wake-up call?"

"Sure."

"You've tied me and pleasured me. I think it's time I return the favor."

Had she heard me flirting with Bella?

"Imagine me pleasuring your body," she whispered and licked her upper red lip.

"Okay." In quick order, I was naked and secured in four-point restraints to the frame of the bed. Carmel was being more aggressive than was typical, and it made me nervous. She took an extra-long time securing my extremities to the bed. "I have to meet Dad to return his hunting cabin keys," I said.

"It won't be an issue."

"Okay." I guess we're good to go.

I watched as Carmel made a show of flinging her clothing into the air, like veils flying off an exotic dancer. She gripped my penis painfully hard. When I became erect, she laughed in giddy elation and announced, "I hold the scepter to the throne!" She crawled over my manacled body and said, "We'll start with you pleasuring me."

2:45 P.M.

Carmel got up and put her shirt back on. I felt used. It had been all about her. Regardless, I was fine with getting unchained and going about my day. She sat on the edge of the bed beside me. "Do you realize how powerful we can be together? I am the only woman you have ever been with who could run the family with the power of Catania. Tell me of another woman who would kill for you."

"I can't think of anyone else who would." She was right, but I didn't need anyone to kill for me.

She untied one of my hands and said, "I need you to make a phone call before I finish untying you." Carmel was holding a phone in a Kleenex. "I'll explain when you're done." She handed the phone to me and said, "Here's the number: 353-860-7730."

I had to admit, it was all a little odd. I studied her curiously and punched in the number. "Okay, now what?"

Carmel took the phone back from me, placed it in a baggie, and then in her purse. As she did, she showed me a separate cell phone displaying a video of my parents in their Cadillac Escalade.

"What are you doing?" When the call from the first phone went through, there was a flash on the screen, and then it went black. "What did you just do?"

In her most charming voice, Carmel said, "You are now the

head of the Turrisi family."

"Are you crazy? Did you just blow up my parents? Are you fucking crazy?" I tried to jerk my body free from my restraints. I worked hard at the knot on my left wrist, but I couldn't undo it.

"Pull yourself together." Carmel strolled to the fireplace and placed the poker in the fire.

"Untie me!" I demanded.

"Not yet. You have a decision to make. Are you with me or not?" Carmel paused before pointing out, "We are now millionaires! The world is wide open for us. We can do whatever we want. I saw your dad closing the safe in your house. There has to be over a million in cash in there."

The tip of the poker was now flaming orange. Carmel removed the poker, stared at my genital area, and walked over to me. She was going to castrate me.

Shit! I quickly covered my genitals with my free hand and exclaimed, "Don't do this." I couldn't let her do this. My life would be over. I had to come up with something, damn fast. I pleaded, "You're not in any trouble. What you did was genius." Carmel looked skeptical.

"Stop! Think!" I could see in her eyes that she didn't believe me. Dad taught me that when your life is on the line, you're better off doubling down on a lie than admitting it. "You set me up, and Dad knew I was going down for it. Dad had blackmail on the BCA director, and he got them to blame all the murders on Crazy Larry. Even Dad wasn't convinced of my innocence. You're free. We both are."

Carmel laughed as she struck the bed with the red-hot poker. The poker burned into the sheets and then the mattress between my legs. With a wicked grin, she turned away from me and lifted her bare leg onto the bed, exposing the left side of her buttocks to me. She pressed the hot poker against the side of her ass. The smell of her burning flesh was disgusting.

She winced in pain and then limped as she walked the poker back to the fireplace. "I'd like to hear you explain why you burned me, Lorenzo. Didn't you and McBride burn Eliana, too?"

"Why are you framing me?"

Carmel returned to sitting by me and ran her hand through my hair. "I have no desire to frame you. This is an insurance policy. We are now the head of the most powerful crime family in Minnesota. You need me, so don't dis me."

"Okay." I needed to win her over. If she felt I was walking away, she'd kill me, too. I knew she was untamed. I loved that about her. I just never realized she was this unhinged.

"Don't placate me. I know you're reeling over the losses. Roan loved Eliana. Catania hated me. Removing the obstacles is the only way we can be together. And you have something bigger to think about. Do you think it's a coincidence I've been available for sex on demand, with no time off, in every way you desire? I'm pregnant," she crowed and pulled up her shirt, revealing a small baby bump. I had seen it but attributed it to her eating habits. "How bad do you want this child?"

She knew having an heir was my greatest desire.

"Nothing can happen to me," Carmel gloated.

I couldn't lose this child. Resigned, I said, "I'll protect you. What do you need?"

Finally accepting that my contrition was genuine, she said, "Okay. "But you can't keep disrespecting me, Lorenzo. There will be a consequence every time. Who should take a hit this time? Bella or Eliana?"

"Bella? I was telling her—"

Carmel cut me off. "Before you finish that sentence, understand that if you lie to me, I'll kill her. I heard your entire conversation."

Still reeling from the death of my parents, I shut up. Bella was innocent—unscathed.

"I can't believe the way you protect Ellie," Carmel taunted. "She was with McBride at the coffee shop while you were waiting to propose. I watched her walk out to the woods with McBride that night. She screwed him to spite you. Do you want to share a woman with Larry McBride? Knowing every time you're with her, that dirty old peckerwood's had her? And Ellie's been bouncing on Jon Frederick like a flamenco dancer on a pogo stick."

"How do you know that?"

Carmel preened. "Ellie told me she's been sleeping with him at his father's place."

The thought of McBride with Ellie was disgusting, but Ellie getting her needs met by Jon Frederick was worse. Thoughts that Frederick could have taken advantage of my Ellie, in her vulnerable state, tormented me. *But could I trust Carmel?* Carmel wants someone dead. Eliana may never heal, and she can't have kids anymore, so she seemed to be the better choice. "Take Eliana." *I'm sorry, Ellie. So sorry.*

Carmel smiled. "Okay. I'll take care of business. You'll eventually get yourself free. Stop pulling so hard, and the knots will loosen up. If you ever want to see your baby, you won't say a word about this. Just sit back and wait to hear from me. If you can't follow directions, you will never see me again, and for damn sure will never meet your baby."

45

ELIANA CASTILLO
6:00 P.M., TUESDAY, OCTOBER 22, 2024
PIERZ

I had settled into a life of work and taking care of Luis. I was about to spend my first night alone at Billy's house. I wasn't sure I was ready, but Billy insisted it would be good for me. It's been one of the warmest falls in history, and it was a balmy seventy degrees. Billy and I sat on the porch, facing the barn, enjoying the warm sun. We had dropped Luis off at the Fredericks' for the night and Billy would be leaving soon to meet up with Heather. I told him, "I really miss Mike. I had a great friend for a moment and kicked him out the door. I should have known it wouldn't be long before he caught someone else's eye. I swear, my heart breaks every time I see him in the store. How do I get over it?"

"I'm the wrong guy to ask. I miss Camille every day. I think of everything I wish I had done. And we had thousands of great days. How am I getting over it? I'm going to have a few beers and sleep with someone else. Is that a great plan? Not really, but nothing works."

"Yeah, I guess my loss pales in comparison to yours. Your wife was lucky to have a man who loved her so intensely."

"I was lucky, too." He sighed. "Loss sucks—for everybody. Sometimes, I feel like my whole world died, and they just forgot to take me along. Ken and Jan Dahmen ran the grocery store. Leon and Betty Flicker had the bar. Hartmann's and Loyd Boeder had the hardware store. I guess the Kurtzes still have the furniture store. And above all the businesses towered St. Joseph's church. Catholicism scared the hell out of us, but beneath the terror, it still offered hope rather than being the punchline of a conversation about abuse. And if I had a bad day, I had Camille. We were always good by night's end."

"But you have a lot of great young couples running businesses here. Theilen's Meats remains a rock in this community. And your Christian youth group is amazing." Billy missed his great love, and I knew what that felt like. I was sad myself. Finally, I said, "Sorry, that's all I got."

"That's good enough." Billy's sly grin crept back. "What would Mike have to do to have another shot with you?"

"Smile at me." I laughed. "Maybe even just glance in my direction. Pretty pathetic, huh?"

"Mike asked if I thought you'd consider going on a date with him. I told him, 'You better come up with something good because Eliana's amazing and she deserves nothing but the best.'"

"Calling me would be fine. I don't want it to be difficult for him." Maybe I'd take a drive after Billy leaves and see if I can see Mike's Jeep around town. If fate's on my side, maybe we could casually run into each other and have a chat.

Suddenly, the hayloft door swung open, briefly banging against the side of the barn. Inside the door, on the upper deck of the barn, Mike stood holding a bottle of champagne and two glasses.

I turned to Billy, who was grinning widely. "It looks like your date's waiting. I will see you tomorrow. If you need anything, call me, but I don't anticipate being needed. And by the way, I'd never leave you here alone unless you requested it."

I assured Billy it was just fine to leave me alone here, and I ran to the barn, and scampered up into the hayloft. Mike took my hand and pulled me up the last step. "I can't tell you how badly I wanted to see you again. I am so sorry."

Mike had blankets laid out, giving us soft cushions to sit on. There was a charcuterie board with meat, cheese, and chocolate-dipped strawberries. In a metal pail was a bottle of champagne on ice and sweating bottles of Busch Light beer. As we sat, Mike said apologetically, "I'm not a big champagne guy."

"I'll have one of those beers with you before the night's over," I said with giddy elation.

"You don't need to apologize." Mike took my hand. "You had a lot to sort out, and that's okay. I'm happy to just have this moment with you right now ."

"Kiss me." I lay back. I needed him to hold me, and he was quick to oblige. Beautiful hues of pink and orange colored the sky as we lay in each other's arms in front of the hayloft door. My body hungered for his warmth. I've never enjoyed the isolated country more.

9:00 P.M.

A couple of empty beer bottles and a half-empty bottle of champagne rested next to our blanket. Half a dozen strawberry stems lay at their base. Mike had been working rotating shifts, so despite a valiant attempt to fight sleep, he had finally succumbed. He looked so peaceful.

I wrapped a blanket around my naked body, walked to the hayloft door, and gazed out at the stars. I would like to say we made "mad, passionate" love, but it was sort of the opposite — "happy, soothing" love. Unpressured fervor. Snuggling under a warm blanket on a cool night was delightfully sensuous. I took a deep, satisfied breath. This was the most romantic night of my life.

I turned back to Mike and realized he was watching me. I flashed open my cover, which brought a large, small-town-boy grin to his face. I strolled back to him and snuggled with him in the blanket.

"Do you want to head inside?" Mike asked softly.

"I want to stay right here. I swore I'd never feel safe under the stars again, but here I am. Do you mind sleeping here a little longer?"

"Not at all." He grabbed a handful of grapes and held them over me as I nibbled a couple off the vine.

When I looked up, I noticed a rooster weather vane hanging on a rusted metal nail above us. I remarked, "Shouldn't that be on top of the barn?"

"It fell down after Camille died, and Bill hasn't got around to putting it back up."

We covered up with blankets and snuggled skin to skin. Knowing how badly Billy would love to have another minute with Camille, I vowed to squeeze every drop of pleasure out of this moment.

10:45 P.M.

I woke up to the sound of Trusty barking. My anxiety skyrocketed. At first, I thought I was having a nightmare—but I wasn't. Mike was sound asleep next to me. The dog continued to bark in my head. I slid away from Mike and quickly dressed. When I told Serena I was saved by a mythical barking hound on the night of the assault, she taught me that the Lakota believe dogs are sacred beings that protect us. I carefully stepped to the hayloft opening. I looked at the blood moon, sometimes known as a hunter's moon. It was brighter this time of year because its orbit was closer to the earth.

Wickedness had crept in and vanquished the lighthearted nature of the night. My breathing became labored, and I swallowed hard. God closed her eyes, and the world became dark. *What is out there?* And then I saw someone in the farmyard walking toward the house. I snuck over to Mike and whispered, "There's someone in the yard."

Mike was dressed in a flash. He reached between a couple of haybales and pulled out his gun. Together, we moved toward the loft opening. Mike whispered, "Stay in the shadows. You can't be seen in the darkness."

We watched the figure approach the house. I recognized the athletic strut. "I think that's Carmel."

"What is she doing here?"

"Serena seems to think she was the second person involved in my assault."

Mike stepped closer to the hayloft opening.

I grabbed his arm. "Please, don't leave me."

"I should confront her." He studied my eyes and said, "But I won't. I will stay with you. But let's step back and see what she does."

Carmel slowly made her way around the house, attempting to see in at every turn. The house was completely dark, and there was no activity. She suddenly turned and walked toward the barn. Mike and I watched her look up into the loft.

"She can't see us. We're okay," he murmured.

Carmel hesitated for a second, and then I realized the champagne bottle was partially in the light. Carmel stopped and stared. She aimed her gun at the bottle.

I began to panic, deathly afraid I'd shriek at the sound of gunfire and give us away. The blasts would make the memories of my body being rocked with bullets impossible to contain. I started to feel pain in those areas. I closed my eyes in anticipation.

"BANG, BANG, BANG, BANG, BANG!" Carmel fired away.

Mike pulled me to the wooden floor and lay on top of me. "Stay down," he whispered. "Bullets might ricochet off the metal eave struts in the roof."

"BANG, BANG, BANG, BANG, BANG!"

On the tenth shot, I finally heard the champagne bottle shatter. Carmel emitted a maniacal laugh and continued to fire.

"BANG, BANG, BANG, BANG!"

I heard a thump on the floor, and my eyes popped open to see splintered wood only a foot away from my head. My body trembled, and I could feel my muscles tighten painfully.

"BANG, BANG!" Silence. I heard Carmel yell, "Hell, yeah!" Her laughter trailed off as if she'd turned her back to us and was walking away.

The onslaught of lead finally ended. As my breathing slowed

and my tension dissipated, I could feel the weight of Mike's body. He had relaxed, too. "We should get up," I suggested, "in case she comes up here." There was no response. And then I felt his warm blood running down my neck. I quickly rolled him off me, his body thudding onto its back. There was blood on his face and shoulder, and Mike was out cold. *Was he dead?* My throat constricted. "Qué diablos?"

I placed my hand on his bloody neck. He had a pulse. The rooster weather vane arrow was stuck into the wood next to Mike's head.

I dug my phone out of my pocket and called for help.

"911, what is your emergency?"

"Mike Haney's been shot. We're at the old Frederick farm by Pierz, just south of Genola. We need an ambulance—right away. We're in the hayloft."

"Is he breathing?"

"Yes." I felt again. "Shallow."

"Where was he shot?"

"I don't know. There's blood all over."

"What's your name?"

"Eliana. Please, I need help."

"How did it happen?"

"Some crazy bitch was shooting at us."

"Is she still there?"

"No—I don't know. Maybe."

"Eliana, I need you to see if you can slow the bleeding."

She was right. I set the phone down and noticed swelling on Mike's head and blood accumulating on his shoulder. I grabbed the thinnest blanket and wound it tightly around his bloody shoulder.

I could hear the dispatcher continue to say, "Eliana? Eliana?" but I left the phone and attended to Mike. Once I had his upper torso tightly wrapped, I noticed his gun had fallen from his hand. I'm not sure where I got the strength, but I dragged Mike's body to a post and propped him up to elevate the injury. I retrieved the gun and then squeezed between Mike and the post. I slid down to a sitting position, held Mike up between my legs, and rested his head back against mine. I sat with the gun facing the hayloft opening, silently daring Carmel to pop her head up. I yelled toward the phone, "Hurry!"

Sirens swelled in the distance, becoming progressively louder until I heard a car slide to a stop in the driveway. The door closed, and a man yelled, "This is the police. Are you still in the loft?"

"Yes!" I screamed.

The officer was soon in the loft next to me, checking Mike's vitals. "I'm Eric. Set down the gun." He took the gun out of my hand and slid it to the side. "He's still breathing, and it looks like you did a great job wrapping the wound. Do you want me to move him off you?"

"No." I wrapped my arms around Mike and continued to hold him sitting upright in front of me.

"Okay. Sit tight; the ambulance is entering the yard."

The ambulance crew entered the hayloft with Jon Frederick at their heels. As they prepared to take Mike out, I shared as much as I knew with Eric and Jon.

I ended with, "I think it was Carmel. I didn't see her clearly, but I know how she stands and walks. She didn't see us. We were up here and left a champagne bottle sitting by the opening of the loft. Carmel opened fire on the bottle. She fired sixteen shots. I counted." I glanced over at the opening and saw the shattered bottle.

I followed the crew outside with Mike's body.

"Do you know what she was driving?" Eric questioned.

"No. She owns a sporty red Mazda."

"It's sitting at the Caruso house," Jon said. Carmel borrowed someone's car. Any idea who?"

"No." I shook my head, "She doesn't have a lot of friends."

Serena Frederick was at the scene now, and even though I was covered with blood, she didn't hesitate to hug me as she asked, "Are you okay?"

"I'm not hurt, but I need to go with Mike."

Serena said, "I'll drive you. Ever since COVID, they haven't let people ride along in ambulances. Let's go into the house and get some different clothes on. They might not let you in the hospital wearing—"

The amount of blood on my clothes was concerning. "I need to call his family. I don't even know where to begin."

"I can help," Serena offered.

I heard Jon telling the officers on the scene, "We're not going to broadcast this search. If Carmel hears she shot a police officer, she'll go into hiding. She ran away with Lorenzo Caruso, and he has access to a lot of money and resources. Let's not broadcast this search to the media. For now, this BOLO stays within law enforcement."

Be on the lookout for my former best friend. I felt a sense of deep hatred, far beyond any resentment I've had for anyone. I hated McBride, but he was an idiot. Carmel was someone I once loved.

46

JON FREDERICK
11:30 P.M., TUESDAY, OCTOBER 22, 2024
HIGHWAY 25, BUCKMAN

The overcast night pulled the shade on the stars. The sheriff's department and local police officers were pulling over cars in search of Carmel Cano. I received a call from a Morrison County deputy. "I've got an electric Hummer headed south from Buckman on Highway 25. The plate reads TURRISI."

"Put the sirens on, but don't approach. This could be a Bonnie and Clyde situation. Lorenzo Turrisi and Carmel Cano are on the run together. I have reason to believe Carmel's been involved in three homicides."

"He's not pulling over. He's not speeding away, either."

"I'll be there in short order."

My phone buzzed again. "Jon, this is Lorenzo. I had nothing to do with the shooting at your folks' place."

"Pull over. I'll be right there. Is Carmel with you?"

"No. I followed her. I wasn't going to let her kill anyone else."

"Pull over. You're pulling in a net of police officers from every direction by trying to run."

"All right."

I cruised past the Buckman Bank Tavern toward the flashing squad car lights south of Buckman. As I slowed down, I watched the Hummer take off down the road, and I followed in hot pursuit. I called him back, "Pull over!"

"They're going to kill me."

"They won't unless you give them a reason. It's just me, Lorenzo. Pull over. I'll go to you before the squads catch up."

The Hummer pulled over once again.

Still on the phone, I said, "Get out of the vehicle and put your hands on the roof. I'll come to you."

Lorenzo stepped out of the vehicle wearing a baby blue Christian Dior polo shirt and Ralph Lauren jeans, which cost somewhere in the neighborhood of fifteen hundred dollars. Each. As I approached, he worriedly glanced my way and then took off into the darkness. He might be the stupidest man on the planet. *What did he think was going to happen? Did he honestly think that country folk would open their doors and embrace a hysterical stranger in designer clothes who was running from law enforcement? They'd be more likely to shoot him.*

Squad cars pulled in from both directions. I told the officers, "Lorenzo's headed straight west." I sprinted into the darkness. Chasing criminals in the dark was dangerous, but fall was a bad time to escape into a field. The corn had been chopped nearly flush to the earth, so Lorenzo was trying to escape, running on wide-open, barren ground where he could easily be spotted a football field away. He might be the stupidest guy on three or four planets.

Squad cars turned perpendicular to the road and lit up the field. I let my anger kick in. I thought about Lorenzo standing outside my house with a rifle. If he had killed one of my kids, I don't know that I would have bothered chasing him. I might have just taken out my gun. The dark thought bothered me. I don't want to be that guy. Fueled by my rage, it wasn't long before I caught up and tackled him hard, forcing him face down into the ground.

Officers quickly surrounded us. I got up and stepped back.

An officer yelled, "Stay lying face down on the ground. You have the right..."

I was too angry to be the one who cuffed him. I watched as he was read his rights, restrained, and pulled to his feet. I turned to the officers and asked, "Was anyone else in the car?"

"No," an officer answered. "There was a sniper rifle."

Lorenzo turned to me. "Let me explain. I didn't do anything."

An officer patted him down and said, "No weapons."

I turned to the officers. "Please step back. I need to talk to him." After they stepped away, I asked Lorenzo, "Do you know your parents' Escalade was blown up?"

He didn't respond, but he clearly knew.

"So, you were part of it," I suggested.

"I would never hurt my parents! Not for any amount of money—ever!"

"You just lost your online celebrity status. People on the internet will assume you went after Eliana with a sniper rifle to kill her. When people hear about this, they're going to suspect you originally went to Eliana's home in St. Paul to kill her and just happened to kill McBride instead."

"I didn't, I swear." Lorenzo studied me nervously. "You're going to kill me out here in the middle of nowhere."

"It's tempting," I remarked. "You're going to be arrested for harboring a fugitive. Aiding and abetting, to be exact. Where is Carmel Cano?"

"I don't know. She left me tied up and disappeared. I swear, I wasn't involved in any of it. I killed McBride, but only to protect Ellie. All the rest of that crap is on Carmel. I came to your dad's place tonight to protect Ellie. Carmel was coming here to kill her. I brought the high-powered rifle and was going to kill Carmel myself if she came close to Eliana. It didn't appear Eliana was home, so I left after Carmel did."

"Did you ever consider calling the police?" I questioned.

"No," he responded with a shrug.

"Did you meet the ambulance when you were driving away?"

"What was that about?" Now Lorenzo was worried.

"Did you see Carmel fire all those shots into the hayloft?"

"Nobody was up there, so I thought it was harmless."

"Well, there was a police officer in the hayloft. And right now he's in intensive care and we don't know if he's going to make it."

"Fuck!"

"And you were hiding her out. How bad do you want to go to prison?"

"I can't. What can I do?"

"You need to deliver Carmel."

"She damn near killed me." Lorenzo theatrically waved his hands in the air. "She was going to castrate me. I was lucky to get out of there alive."

"You sound like she did castrate you."

He lowered his hands and faced me. "What the hell is that supposed to mean?"

"Don't you get it? Carmel can't afford to kill you. Carmel is nothing without you."

"She's pregnant with my child."

"But Carmel wants to be the Godmother—matriarch. Having a baby doesn't give her that. Lots of mobsters have illegitimate kids. You're the one who inherits the estate. She has to be with you. If she miscarries, she has nothing. Carmel would never take that chance after all the work she has done to trap you. The door hasn't closed on your cage yet. Carmel will contact you. She needs your resources and your money. Grow your balls back and take control of this situation."

"What should I do?" he asked.

"You need to get her to talk about the murders." I raised an eyebrow and taunted, "Are you telling me you've lost your ability to charm women?"

"Don't be ridiculous."

"If you can bring Carmel to me, I'll keep you out of prison. You're still going to have to go to court for harboring a fugitive, but I should be able to have you placed on probation if you hand over Carmel. We're taking your sniper rifle and any other weapons out of your vehicle for now."

"That's bullshit. You're going to get me killed."

That's a chance I'm willing to take. I said, "Open your eyes. Every officer here would love to see you in jail tonight for trying to flee. I'm willing to let you walk, but you have to deliver. You know as well as I do, there is no running for you. The Twin Cities are your playground. I imagine you have a waiting list of women you're anxious to start working your way through."

"All right," Lorenzo said. "I'll get Carmel to come in."

"Call me as soon as you know." We walked back to the road, and I handed Lorenzo over to an officer. "Write him a ticket for fleeing."

"What the hell?" Lorenzo exclaimed.

"I'm letting you go after you get the ticket. If you deliver, I'll get this charge dropped. If you don't, I'll have you prosecuted to the max on all charges." While the officer had Lorenzo sidetracked, I put a tracker on his Hummer.

When I checked in with Sean at the BCA, he insisted I complete paperwork on everything that had transpired and send him a report before I went any further. I told him, "We can't afford to lose Lorenzo."

"You have a tracker on his Hummer, right?" Sean responded.

"I do."

"When you're done with the paperwork, run it down."

2:30 A.M., WEDNESDAY, OCTOBER 23, 2024
PIERCE STREET NORTHEAST
BELTRAMI, MINNEAPOLIS

I followed the trail of Lorenzo's vehicle to his parents' home. When I arrived, the Hummer was parked in front of the house, which was dark inside. Not trusting Lorenzo, I had the phone company search for his phone's location, and it placed Lorenzo here. It was late, and his Hummer and phone were here. There were two possibilities. Either Lorenzo was inside sleeping, or Lorenzo had ditched his phone and vehicle and disappeared with Carmel. I went to the door and rang the doorbell. No answer. After a second try, my gut feeling was Lorenzo had ditched his Hummer and phone and gone rogue. I had the option of ramming the door open or getting my blunt keys out of the trunk and picking it open. I opted for the second choice, more out of respect for my shoulder than for the dwelling.

Once inside, the alarms went off, but I didn't particularly care. I had to find his phone. A half-eaten dish of pasta sat on the counter. He had microwaved leftover marinara but didn't have time to finish it. The bowl was lukewarm. The phone wasn't in the kitchen, the living room, or the bedroom. From the wet towel in the bathroom, it was clear Lorenzo had recently showered, abandoning his phone on the bathroom counter. I tried to see who had called, but the phone was locked. With phone in hand, I quickly departed before security arrived. Security employed by the Mafia doesn't handle intruders gingerly.

3:00 A.M.
FEDERAL BUREAU OF INVESTIGATION
1501 FREEWAY BOULEVARD BROOKLYN CENTER

I headed to the FBI office in Brooklyn Center. I called ahead and asked to use their Cellebrite program, an Israeli-owned cybersecurity program. Cellibrite purchased Cyber Technology Services Inc., or CyTech, in July of 2024 and took over our federal contracts. The Feds have some fantastic technology. Following the assassination attempt on Donald Trump this past summer, Cellebrite had the shooter's phone unlocked in forty minutes.

Even though it was late, I texted Serena and let her know where I was. I found a couch in a relatively quiet corner and slept while the agents worked on the phone.

5:30 A.M.

My boss, Sean Reynolds, woke me and told me the phone had been opened. We were quickly on our way to the location linked to the last number Lorenzo had called.

6:30 A.M., PONY HILL GLAMP
DANCING WATERS
19485 ESTES ROAD, CLEARWATER

Liz Dwyer and Curtis Weinrich provide a "glamping" adventure where a couple can camp in a full-size tent and sleep in a comfortable double bed in the woods near an organic farm. The adventure is complete with a fire pit and everything needed for a moonlit meal.

As we pulled into the area, Sean reiterated our plan. "I'll sit in the car focusing on the GPS and coordinating with the Wright County Sheriff's Department as they arrive."

"I'll try to catch Lorenzo alone and have him get a confession out of Carmel. Keep the troops out of sight for an hour. If he still doesn't emerge, I'll text."

"What if Lorenzo comes out shooting?" Sean asked.

"I'll wear a vest. My main concern is not having enough evidence to prosecute Carmel."

"You get him to carry in the mic, and I'll listen in from the car. I'll send deputies your direction as soon as they arrive. You sure you don't want to wait?"

I got out of the car and left. I was angry that Lorenzo had run. I should have known. You give a stupid person a task, and what do they do? Something stupid. Unlike the brain, the stomach alerts you when it's empty. My brain gets sarcastic when operating on little sleep, making it essential that I keep my mouth shut. We have had a very warm fall, and it was already pushing seventy degrees this morning. You could say, I didn't have this case solved, but I was getting warmer.

I followed the coordinates of Lorenzo's last phone call through the woods. The wind helped cover the crunch of my footsteps through the leaves. It wasn't long before a large white tent was in front of me. I cautiously approached and knelt by the west side of the tent so my shadow wouldn't be visible on the inside.

7:05 A.M.

I finally heard someone stirring inside. I moved to the opposite side of the opening. The tent unzipped, and Carmel stepped out in flannel pajamas. When she started to turn my way, I slipped down out of sight. *Had she sensed me?*

I heard her reenter the tent. I took a deep breath and waited. At any second gunfire could rip through the canvas in my direction. I listened carefully.

Finally, Carmel said, "Lorenzo, you need to get a fire going so we can have some hot coffee."

I could hear rustling followed by Lorenzo stepping out into the cool morning air. He wore only boxers and a T-shirt.

I emerged with my finger on my lips.

He silently mouthed, "Shiiiit."

I whispered, "There is a net of law enforcement circling this place, slowly closing in. Either you get a confession out of Carmel, or you're going to prison. This is your last shot. What do you think your folks would say about you protecting Carmel?"

"What do you want me to do?"

"Set this mic anywhere in the tent and get her to talk." I handed him a small circular mic.

"She doesn't trust me."

"Then get her to. Humiliate one of your girlfriends on the phone for her. Carmel isn't going to trust you until you give somebody up for her. You're going to have to sever the ties to another woman in front of her. Carmel's a narcissist. She's dying to tell you what she did; you need to make her feel safe enough to do so."

47

LORENZO TURRISI
11:30 A.M., WEDNESDAY, OCTOBER 23, 2024
PONY HILL GLAMP
DANCING WATERS
19485 ESTES ROAD, CLEARWATER

I went back into the tent and set the mic on the stand by the bed. I wasn't going to prison over this crazy bitch. Time for me to convince Carmel that I was done with Ellie once and for all.

Carmel had snuggled back under the blankets. She moaned, "It's freezing. Did you get the fire going?"

"Cold? I was good in a tee and shorts," I teased as I crawled under the blanket and kissed her.

Carmel snuggled against me. "C-c-cold." She shivered playfully. "I don't smell smoke. Are you sure you got the fire going?"

"The fire is here," I said. I was still holding my phone. "I have a plan so you can get your revenge on Ellie, but then you have to promise to leave her alone. I'll call her right now, and we can pretend we're having mad passionate sex while she's listening."

"You'd do that for me?" She kissed me eagerly.

"Yeah. I'll pretend it's a butt dial. We're partners now, okay? My parents ran the organization flawlessly because they worked in unison. We need to be the same. Flat-out honest with each other." I couldn't stop thinking about her comment, "I'm holding the scepter to the throne." Me and my stupid dick cost me the best relationship I've ever had. For a moment with Eliana, I was proud of myself. My parents knew Carmel was no good from the onset, but I didn't listen.

With a sly smile, Carmel said, "Okay. Dial up McBride's bride. Remember, he had her on your engagement night," she gibed.

I picked up my cell phone, called Eliana, and put her on speaker.

"It's early," Eliana complained. "Did something happen?"

In a low, soothing voice, I crooned, "Carmel, you are the best piece of ass I've ever had. Pants down, you're number one."

Grinning ear to ear, Carmel panted out, "Ah! Ah! Ah! Ah!" followed by a long moan. "Mmmmmm. Oh, Lorenzo, you are so—"

"You called to let me know you were having sex with Carmel?" Ellie said in disgust. "You are such a pig."

"I'm preggers, Eliana," Carmel chimed in. "Whoops, sorry. Heard you can't carry a baby anymore. By the way, Lorenzo, did you ever tell Eliana we made love in her bed after you showed her you could patch up the bullet hole in her wall? Ellie burned rubber leaving the driveway, and we stayed and burned passion in the bed." The line went dead, and Carmel burst out laughing.

I never told Eliana about that. She wouldn't understand. I was mad that Ellie left without saying goodbye. Carmel walked in and was eager to give it up, so I took her to the bedroom, had her slip into Ellie's clothes, tore them off her, and had revenge sex right in Ellie's bed.

Carmel told me, "I'm never putting on Eliana's clothes for you ever again. You have to be done with her."

"I just slammed that door shut," I assured her. "I'm down for this—together. All of this. But if we're going to run this family, I need to know how you did it."

"What?" she asked slyly as she lay by me in bed.

"Let's start with Cheri. Why did you kill her?"

"I didn't kill Cheri. McBride did. He was pissed she wouldn't have sex with him, so he raped her."

"Why did you jump up and down on her body?" It was a hunch, but I thought I'd take the shot.

She laughed. "I told you; there's consequences for being unfaithful."

Larry must have told Carmel about the mile-high adventure I'd had with Cheri. And then it hit me. Carmel believed *we* were in a relationship all along, but I saw her as a side piece during my relationship with Eliana. "How did you know where Cheri lived?"

"Larry and I followed her home from work."

"Whose idea was it to brand her?"

"That was Larry's craziness. I thought if he wants to put the target on himself, fine. It'll save my ass in the long run." Carmel wondered, "How do you know so many of the details?"

"I've been interrogated multiple times." I scratched my hip. "When did you decide to kill Eliana?"

"When she told me you were going to propose." She carefully studied my reaction and said, "I'm not completely heartless. I gave her the entire weekend to reject your proposal and walk away. If she didn't, I was going to let her have her night and blow up her car after she left the arts and crafts fair. Larry placed the bomb in her car before she left St. Paul. I was surprised it didn't explode when she smashed that bike into the Jeep. Evidently, the impact was just below the threshold. After we were done with Eliana in the woods, Larry had to go back to the hotel and get the bomb out of her car. I told him he could keep it, but he said I paid for it; it's mine. Larry showed me how to hook it up to a vehicle's electronics. Ended up working out perfectly."

"How do we explain the bomb?"

"We'll never have to. Who would ever suspect me of having a bomb? I can't make a bomb," she said with a sly grin. "That's a mob thing."

"So, they would have suspected me."

"Absolutely not. You just gave Eliana a ring. More likely, they would have suspected you were the target. As for your parents, Roan and Cat have more than enough enemies to keep you off the list. Everyone knows you loved them."

"Why take a hammer to Ellie? That was insane."

"While I was pouring my heart out to you on the phone, she was getting you off. Eliana deserved to be violated for that." Picking up on my disgust, she added, "You know your mom would have done the same thing. You mess with the bull; you get the horns."

Mom was a respected matriarch because she kept it about business. She would torture someone for hurting her family, but she didn't kill people over heartbreak.

Carmel was becoming progressively more excited as she spoke. "Larry was supposed to put Eliana out of her misery, but he insisted on using his homemade zip gun. His failure to kill her opened a whole new can of worms. When Cat asked me to bring Larry to her, I thought she would take care of him for me. I gave him a drink laced with ketamine and later convinced Larry that Cat had roofied both of us. Instead of killing him, Cat had him tattooed."

"Where did you get the ketamine?"

"I had a friend who was prescribed it for depression. She said she couldn't remember anything, not even taking it. I told her I'd get rid of it for her, and I did."

"So, you talked me into killing Crazy Larry. How did you know Ellie was home?"

"She called me. And Larry called me. Told me he got out."

"You thought she was alone, so you invited me over. Then you told me Larry was released from custody and talked me into checking on her."

"Slow down." With a coquettish grin, she reminded me, "You talked your way over to my house."

Carmel was a master manipulator. She knew exactly how to play me. I thought I was saving Ellie. I said, "You needed Larry dead."

"Eliana called and told me she was alone and asked me to stay with her. Larry was supposed to kill her. Ellie didn't tell me Jon was at her house. He's the only reason Ellie isn't dead."

"And then I killed Larry. Cleaned it all up for you."

"Do you regret saving Eliana?" she asked with a bit of excitement.

"No. And I don't regret killing Larry. Why did you kill Londyn? She was no threat to you."

"Are we being honest, Lorenzo? You see, I'm smarter than Eliana. I noticed Londyn was at the Eelpout Festival in Walker. I remembered you were at the Eelpout Festival, too. Are you going to tell me you weren't with her?"

How the hell would she know I was with Londyn? I didn't even tell my friends. I debated lying. Concerned that Carmel might have known someone working at the hotel, I finally admitted, "I was with her. It's not easy to get a woman to meet you for sex when you're fishing. Had to be someone who gets paid."

"Do you need to have sex with someone when you're *fishing*? Honestly, Lorenzo. You belittled me by drilling that eelpout whore. There are consequences every time you disrespect me. I thought it would be years before they found her." She made a gun with her thumb and forefinger. "As much as I wanted to punish her, it was *pop-pop* and gone. No evidence. Like a Mafia hit." Carmel lightly gestured with her hands as if she was saying, "Oh well," and said, "It turns out she did have a heart. I watched it bleed out. And I gave that cunt one solid kick in the twat as she was dying. That was for all the women she pissed off by flashing it to their men."

"I wish you hadn't killed my parents." I sighed.

"I know." She scooched up and kissed me. "But we'll work through it together. We'll sit down with their financial adviser and attorney and look at all our options. We're rich! We can do whatever the hell we want."

Her callousness bothered me. Eventually, when it was financially convenient for her, she'd kill me. I got out of bed and dressed. "I'm sorry, but I'm not in the mood right now. Give me some time, and I'll be all right. It's a lot to digest. I'm going to check the fire."

"Eliana will not be touched. If you call your other puta after we have our coffee, you can have me again before we leave." She got out of bed, pulling her hair into a ponytail, and said, "Back to platinum blond tomorrow."

When we exited the tent, there stood my parents, Roan Caruso and Catania Turrisi. Law enforcement circled the entire tent. The fury in Mom's eyes was frightening, but my relief at seeing them alive was nearly palpable.

Jon Frederick advanced toward us and said, "Carmel Cano, you are under arrest for the murder of Londyn Larson. You have the right to remain silent. Anything you say can and will be used against you. You have the right to an attorney. If you can't afford one, an attorney will be provided."

Carmel turned back, but I blocked her retreat. "Lorenzo, what's happening?"

"I don't know," I lied.

A deputy stepped forward and said, "Lorenzo Caruso, you are under arrest for aiding and abetting a fugitive," and then read me my rights.

Jon explained, "You can be held liable for a crime if you intentionally aid a person who intends to commit a crime."

Confused, I wanted to say, *I did everything you asked.*

When I opened my mouth, Dad quickly interrupted. "The only thing I want to hear you say is, 'I need to speak to my attorney.'"

While I felt helpless and betrayed, Carmel coolly pulled it together and told my parents, "I'm pregnant with Lorenzo's child. Your grandchild."

Mom said with a sneer, "That is the only reason you haven't been wiped off the face of the earth. I dare you to get out of police custody for even a day. I'd take a thick-handled sledgehammer to you."

Dad gently took Mom's hand, like I'd seen him do a hundred times. It was his signal to her to stop talking. Crisis always seemed to calm him.

Mom often swept his hand away, but she didn't today. She directed her eyes to me and said, "We'll meet you at the jail with our attorney."

BCA Superintendent Sean Reynolds told us, "They're being

transported to the Ottertail County Jail in Fergus Falls, where Londyn was murdered."

"I had nothing to do with that," I argued.

"You can explain that in court. Your vehicle was there, and you picked up an additional charge for Fleeing a Peace Officer since then."

Before I could respond, Dad said, "'I need to speak to my attorney.' No other words, understand?"

I nodded and recited the words.

48

JON FREDERICK
3:00 P.M., WEDNESDAY, OCTOBER 23, 2024
BUREAU OF CRIMINAL APPREHENSION
1430 MARYLAND AVENUE EAST, ST. PAUL

I finally had the opportunity to call Serena. I started, "I've said from the beginning, I was curious where the car bomb would turn up. When I noticed a camera in the Carusos' Escalade, I asked Roan why he had a hidden camera above the passenger visor recording the driver. Roan didn't realize it was there. I immediately told him to get out, called the Minnesota Department of Public Safety's Homeland Security department, and asked them to send a bomb squad over."

"I'm glad you're okay." Serena paused, and her voice trembled a little as she said, "I still have nightmares about you being around bombs."

"Roan and Catania were so angry, it was all I could do to contain them. I didn't want Carmel on the run for years, so I talked Roan and Cat into laying low by explaining that if Carmel thought she'd gotten away with it, she had no reason to leave the state. I went to the neighbors' houses and asked them to leave until further notice. At the first house, I was met by an eighty-year-old woman named Beverly. I told her, 'We're asking people to clear out the neighborhood. The Carusos have a gas leak. I'll take your number and call you when you can return.' She turned and yelled. 'Arnold!'" I imitated the woman's crotchety voice, "'I swear the house could blow up, and Arnold wouldn't hear it. We'll go to his brother Stanley's for the afternoon. Living next to Carusos is about as safe as it gets in Minneapolis. No one gets a car stolen in this neighborhood.'"

Serena laughed nervously. "I don't imagine, with Roan's history of executing car thieves."

"Once the neighborhood was cleared, and the bomb was defused, I worked with Homeland Security to recreate what would appear to be an actual explosion on camera. We had Roan and Catania sit in the front seat of the Escalade, and we froze the picture so that when the bomber looked at the phone camera, she would see Roan and Catania. They wired a red light to shine outside the vehicle when the detonating phone call came in. They then flashed a light directly into the camera lens and snipped the camera wire so it would look like an explosion had occurred and destroyed the camera. It mimicked an explosion perfectly. Then the bomb squad left with the unexploded ordnance."

"When are you coming home?"

"I'm not sure." I took a long, deep breath. "Convicting Carmel won't be a slam dunk. After we got back to the office, I listened to the recording of her conversation with Lorenzo. She didn't directly admit to killing anyone. Carmel was storing electronics somewhere, and I had to find out where. She needed Lorenzo's laptop to set up the meeting with Londyn, and Carmel could have only gotten it on the night Eliana was assaulted. Carmel also had to have Londyn's phone and computer to send messages to herself and Lorenzo.

"Come home," Serena pleaded. "I need you here, even if all you do is sleep."

"All right."

49

ELIANA CASTILLO
1:00 P.M., WEDNESDAY, OCTOBER 23, 2024
ST. GABRIEL'S HOSPITAL
815 2ND STREET SOUTHEAST, LITTLE FALLS

I wasn't allowed into Mike's hospital room to visit him since I wasn't family. I felt so alone. Mike could have been dying, and I just sat there, in the sterile white waiting room, all by myself, waiting for news that never arrived.

During the night, an officer stopped by and took me into a room for a long interview. He was kind enough, but I wanted to be done talking to the police about being a victim of crimes. Once we had gone over every detail multiple times, my statement was finished. I explained that the gun hadn't been fired, and he told me he had already checked. I offered to store Mike's gun for him until he returned to consciousness. The officer laughed and told me that wives can't even get an officer's gun back without completing a significant amount of paperwork first.

The conversation reminded me that I had packed a gun when I came to Pierz, which I never unpacked. Lorenzo had bought me a lightweight handgun for home protection on nights he wasn't around. It was time to dig it out. After sitting by myself in the waiting room for the rest of the night, all I had was a report that Mike was unconscious but stable. Early in the morning, I called Serena, and she gave me a ride home. She offered to stay and talk, but I told her I wanted to try and get some sleep, and I'd greatly appreciate her returning home to her family and my son. Her mom was watching the kids, and she was good, but I could rest easy if Serena were with Luis.

PIERZ

But of course, I couldn't sleep. Instead, I sat like a depressed zombie watching "breaking news" reports. A seventy-nine-year-old woman died riding a bicycle south of Bowlus after a semitruck hit her. Bowlus isn't exactly on a major highway. That story just raises a lot of questions. Mike Jeffries, the former CEO of Abercrombie & Fitch, was arrested on federal sex trafficking and interstate prostitution charges. Jeffries is accused of luring financially vulnerable men to the Hamptons and hotels for commercial sex acts. His attorney claims Jeffries is suffering from dementia and is unfit to be prosecuted. Of course. The American justice system at work. Even if he was prosecuted, he'd probably be pardoned. I hadn't shared the story of my evening with Billy yet, so I retrieved my gun from the gun safe to keep at my side until he returned.

I was sitting on the couch, holding my Smith & Wesson 380 Shield EZ. It was lightweight and stainless steel. I remembered there was a recall on this gun I never addressed. The concern was that when you pulled the trigger once, it would continue to fire like a machine gun. I should get that fixed.

The local news reporter was now saying, "Carmel Cano and Lorenzo Turrisi Caruso are being transported to the Ottertail County court facilities in Fergus Falls for a 3:30 p.m. arraignment hearing today." I aimed the gun at Carmel on TV.

A call from Donny broke my trance, and I immediately dropped the gun on the coffee table. Donny didn't even bother to introduce himself. "I heard a cop was shot at your place last night. I'm getting an attorney and taking Luis away. Your life is ridiculous and certainly not safe for a child. If I weren't so committed to my own family, I would have taken Luis years ago. The biggest joke is that you think you're a decent mother. Instead, you're a melodramatic, self-absorbed jejune teen who is no better at parenting now than you were when you got yourself knocked up."

He needs to retake health class. I hung up without saying a word. I didn't have the energy to argue. Melodramatic—I can see that. Self-absorbed—perhaps, although it's less of an option once you have a kid. Bad parent—not true. I'm a shell of the woman I used to be, and I'm losing everything. I'm damaged goods. I'm going to lose my wonderful child and am not capable of having another. I'm also losing Mike—the one true love I've known. And it was all on Carmel, my former best friend. The person who knew my deepest, darkest secrets. It wasn't enough that she destroyed my body. The vengeful bitch was going to cost me my relationship and, ultimately, custody of my son. My body still winced every time I thought about what she did with that hammer. It was cruel. How long had Carmel hated me? She enticed McBride into raping me. And then Carmel promised to stay with me my first night home from the hospital and sent McBride instead. I think she hoped that McBride would kill me, and Lorenzo would kill him. She spent that night with my ex, and then later screwed him in my bed. But the straw that broke the camel's back was shooting Mike Haney. The kindest man I've ever met is lying unconscious while she and Lorenzo are being transported to Fergus Falls for court. She came to my house to kill me. Well—maybe. She stood longest on the side of the house by Luis's bedroom. Would she have killed Luis? Knowing how much she hated me, I think she might have killed my son and not me. That's never going to happen. I picked up my handgun and drove to Fergus Falls.

3:00 P.M.
OTTER TAIL COUNTY COURTHOUSE
121 WEST JUNIUS AVENUE #310, FERGUS FALLS

I parked on West Junius Street. I reached under the car seat and pulled out the gun. I was tired, and so sick of it all. Would I do this if I'd gotten some sleep? I don't know. My mind was set. I gripped the gun and slipped it into the deep pocket of my sweater. *How much should I be expected to take? It never ends. People keep coming after me.* I walked to the sally port in the back of the courthouse, where reporters and curious citizens had gathered to see the psychopathic bitch being escorted into the building.

I stood there waiting while people made small talk around me. It was a circus. There were old people, young people, reporters, thrill seekers, and even a Marilyn Monroe look-alike. And me. *What was I doing here?*

The first squad car pulled up. An officer opened the back door, and Lorenzo stepped out. He glanced at me with a bit of confusion.

I was so done with Lorenzo. He didn't pique my interest in the least.

A second squad pulled up. People rushed over to get a glimpse of Carmel—the femme fatale. I squeezed in to get to the front of the crowd and reached into my pocket. *I needed to keep the gun aimed at Carmel. I didn't want to injure any innocent people if the gun continued to rapid-fire.* There were so many people packed around me that I couldn't lift my arm back out of my pocket. In my trancelike state, I gripped the gun tightly. *Be patient. The opportunity will come.* An officer swept the crowd back. In the process, people were separated slightly, giving me a clean shot. "BANG! BANG!"

The noise seemed to awaken me. I was so nervous I could have thrown up.

"BANG! BANG! BANG!" an officer fired back.

People rushed toward me, knocking me to the ground. The crowd fled, and I realized my hand was still in my pocket. I had never gotten the gun out. *What happened?* I looked up to see an unscathed Carmel being rushed into the courthouse by two officers. Lorenzo lay bleeding on the sidewalk.

Ten feet away, an officer wrestled a gun from Molly McBride's hand. She was on the ground, bleeding out. "You killed my son, you piece of shit!" Her words gurgled through her blood as she yelled at Lorenzo. "Die shitbird!"

The officer next to Lorenzo shouted, "We need an ambulance. We're losing him."

A second officer, who was tending to Molly, yelled, "She's going to be dead in short order."

A third officer dropped to one knee and slowly set his gun on the ground, saying, "I'm sorry." He was the one who shot Molly. "I was just trying to get her to stop. Trying to protect people. So no one else would get hurt."

I slowly pulled myself to my feet. People were rushing in all directions. There was nothing to feel good about. I moved toward Lorenzo. Blood was coming out of his mouth. An officer was putting pressure on his wounds and telling him, "Hang in there."

He looked scared. I was scared, too.

I glanced back at Molly and remembered what Jon had said about her. "She's not as crazy as you think—she's crazier." I looked at her body one last time and realized that it could have been me. Luis could have lost his mother. *What the hell was I thinking?*

Realizing I could be in a lot of trouble if I were searched, I briskly left the scene. As I approached my car, I received a call. "Hi, this is Emily. I'm a nurse at St. Gabriel's Hospital. Is this Eliana Castillo?"

"Yes. Is something wrong?"

"No. Mike has just returned to consciousness, and he wanted to notify you first. I think he was kind of hoping you'd come in."

"Of course. I'm almost two hours away, but I'll come right there." *I need to get into therapy.* This was a grave error—almost disastrous for Luis—and I felt overcome with shame. On my way out of Fergus Falls, I stopped at Lake Alice. It's right in town and, fortunately for me, there were few houses on the lakeside. I ran to the shore, threw my gun as far as I could, and watched it splash into the lake. I am never touching a gun again.

6:00 P.M.
ST. GABRIEL'S HOSPITAL
815 2ND STREET SOUTHEAST, LITTLE FALLS

Mike Haney was lying in a hospital bed. I had to set my foolishness aside for the time being. Being a mom had honed this skill. This moment wasn't about me. I sat on the edge of his bed, leaned over him, and teased, "Blink once for *yes* and twice for *no*, okay?"

He gave me a gentle shove with his good arm. "You know I can talk."

I couldn't stop smiling. I had gone from depressed anguish to giddy elation. Mike was coherent, and he was going to be okay. I was so worried he was going to die. Death has been at my doorstep, and I can't get it off the damn porch. "Tell me what happened."

"I was shot in the shoulder, but I tried to refrain from making any noise. It was my right shoulder, and I dropped my gun. And then Carmel must have hit that weathervane hanging above us, and it knocked me out cold."

"I saw the arrow sticking in the wood. I didn't realize it hit you."

"The arrow didn't, but the big metal rooster delivered the knockout punch. The EMTs were not sure how I ended up with blood all over my face."

"I might have done that." I squirmed in my seat. "When I realized you were bleeding, I rolled you off of me, and your arm kind of went up by your face."

Mike's parents entered the room. His mother declared, "Thank God you're okay!" She immediately went to Mike, and I stepped aside. "What were you doing in a hayloft in the middle of the night?"

"Mike, I should let you talk to your parents." Embarrassed, I started inching away.

"It would be great if you stayed right here." He grinned at me. "Mom and Dad, meet Eliana. We were studying celestial bodies."

I don't remember much of what was said after. I hugged Mike's parents and sister, and after they left, I crawled next to him in his hospital bed and crashed. Mike had shared some of my story with the nursing staff, and they let me sleep. I was told I slept soundly for ten hours straight.

50

JON FREDERICK
1:30 P.M., FRIDAY, OCTOBER 25, 2024
DELANO SELF STORAGE
1100 MCKINLEY PARKWAY, DELANO

I should put James Weber on speed dial. "I have a warrant for a Mazda MX-5 Miata Sport. I need you to access the data recorder and let me know if it stopped at a storage place."

"I can't just drop everything every time you need something, Jon," James complained.

"Actually, you can." James was self-employed.

"Look, I have a project I need to finish. I can begin in a couple of days. Sorry, it's the best I can do."

"All right." Not being particularly patient, I decided to see if I could figure this out on my own. I called Bina Kaplan from the electronic crimes unit, and she helped me get out pictures of Carmel Cano to the owners of rental units around the metro. We shared that she drove a red Miata Sport. The value of the technology team can't be overstated. Within two hours, Bina had notified every owner of a rental unit within an hour of Carmel's home. I believed Carmel had Londyn's cell phone and Lorenzo's computer in storage. Lorenzo would have recognized his laptop if he had come across it.

I was presented with the same problem I faced when I wanted the geofence warrant: I wouldn't be granted a general search warrant. In this case, they wouldn't allow me a warrant for an entire facility. I had to find the exact container. After showing my BCA identification to storage facility owners who rented to someone who met Carmel's description, they shared the list of renters at the sites. There was no Carmel Cano at the first three sites.

My fourth stop was at Delano Self Storage, a new storage facility that is both clean and has high-resolution security cameras. I met with Julie at the Delano site, and the list of renters generated some interesting names. Julie was a pleasant and athletically fit woman in her thirties. I asked, "Do you allow people to rent with nicknames? Like Lemonjello and Orangejello?"

"Those are real names, and they're pronounced, *leh-MON-juh-lo* and *or-AHN-juh-lo*. I checked their IDs," Julie laughed. "They're sisters. And believe it or not, there's one more, Cherryjello, pronounced *shuh-REE-juh-lo*."

There was one name on the list that caught my eye: "Dana Owens." It was Queen Latifah's name before she was Queen."

"Can I see some footage of Ms. Owens at the storage unit?"

"Sure."

The two of us leaned over a computer screen to review security footage. We watched a young woman, wearing sunglasses and her hair tucked under a baseball cap, bring a bag of items in and out of the storage unit. The hair that was visible appeared to be blond. I asked, "Can I see the footage from the parking lot cameras on the days she was here?"

Julie was able to pull up footage of the woman getting in and out of a Mazda MX-5 Miata Sport. She informed me, "They call that color Soul Red Crystal."

"Thank you!" While it was parked so the license plate was never visible, it sure looked like Carmel Cano's car. I had enough for a search warrant.

4:20 P.M.

Sean Reynolds had a judge on his phone's Favorites list, so he was able to get a warrant in a relatively short period of time. Within two hours, Sean was in his black suit and tie at the storage unit with me. Julie opened the door and left us to do our work. Sean had contacted Homeland Security, and one of their officers walked a bomb-sniffing dog through the unit before we entered. When nothing was detected, Sean and I put on our gloves, turned on our cameras, and entered. I had picked up a bolt cutter at the BCA office while waiting for the warrant.

Once inside, we found clothing and furniture of no particular interest to our investigation. We were intrigued by a large wooden steamer trunk about three feet long and two feet high, secured with a Master Lock. I quickly snapped the lock with the cutter, and Sean opened it. We smiled at the sight of a laptop and a cell phone side by side. On top of the laptop was a four-by-three-inch planner. When I paged through it, I found lists of passcodes, including the codes for Lorenzo's computer and Londyn's cellphone.

Sean suggested, "Let's close this trunk and set it in the back of my Yukon. We'll haul it back to headquarters and have the electronic crimes unit go through it."

I nodded and then, for the sake of the recording, said, "Okay."

Sean spoke as we moved the chest. "We are loading a chest of electronics from a unit at Delano Self Storage. The rental unit was paid for in cash by a woman who identified herself as Dana Owens."

1:30 P.M., MONDAY, OCTOBER 28, 2024

I sat with Bina Kaplan, looking at Lorenzo's computer. Bina had a bit of the androgynous Kristen Stewart vibe, and I sometimes vaguely wondered if a Mrs. Kaplan was waiting for her at home, through it made no real difference to me. We had pulled Carmel's fingerprints off both Londyn's cell phone and Lorenzo's computer. Bina was far better with electronics than I was. Carmel had apparently impersonated Lorenzo and set up the date with Londyn.

Bina said, "Show us the magic!" as she pulled up the September 13 conversation on Lorenzo's computer.

Lorenzo: Babe, I've missed you.

Londyn: Do you want to FaceTime? I have some new lingerie.

Lorenzo: No. This time, I want to be with you. I need to feel that what we have is real, for one moment, and then we can go back to FaceTiming.

Londyn: Isn't that why I met you at the hotel in Walker during the Eelpout Festival?

Lorenzo: This time in my Hummer, in the woods of northern Minnesota.

Londyn: I'm more of an indoor gal.

Lorenzo: If you can't do it, I'm closing my account. I like you, Londyn, but there are a lot of women on OnlyFans I could be talking to. If you can't do this for me, I'm moving on. But if you can do it, you won't need another customer.

Londyn: Financially?

Lorenzo: Yes. This is the coup de grâce of our relationship. You can even pick the site, but it has to be isolated. I've got a family reputation to protect.

Londyn: Believe me, I have no desire to be caught, but I don't think you know what coup de grâce means.

I couldn't help thinking Carmel knew precisely what it meant—a death blow to a mortally wounded person.

Bina looked up from the screen at me. "Carmel's playing with her. Like a cat with a maimed mouse."

Lorenzo: This is the moment that takes our relationship to another level.

Londyn: Okay, I'll do this for you, Lorenzo. That's how much you mean to me. But it needs to be daylight. I'm not driving deep into the woods in darkness.

Lorenzo: How about high noon?

Londyn: Perfect. High noon on Friday, September 13, Minnesota Street, New York Mills. I'll drop a pin and text it to you. Promise me you'll be there. I'll be dressed for pleasure, so if you're not there, I'm going home.

Lorenzo: No worries. I'll be there.

I asked Bina, "How did Carmel unlock Londyn's phone? Carmel had to open it to send texts to herself and Lorenzo."

"My guess is she held the phone to Londyn's face to open it and then changed the password. The password was changed at 12:25 p.m. on September 13, 2024." Bina looked up at me. "You're getting a ton of evidence from the phones and laptops. What are you charging Carmel with?"

"First-degree murder for killing Londyn Lust. Aiding and abetting murder for the death of Cheri Wilde, aiding and abetting attempted murder for the assault on Eliana Castillo. Arson for burning her own house down."

Bina placed her forefinger on her chin and thought out loud, "I see a lot of circumstantial evidence, but it's not a slam dunk. And keep in mind, they'll tear Eliana apart on the stand."

"You're right. I don't know that Eliana can stand up to it. She's in a much more fragile state than you see on the surface. I need to find a way to get Carmel a life sentence without Eliana's testimony." Carmel was a fighter. *How was she going to attack?*

51

JON FREDERICK
9:00 A.M., MONDAY, NOVEMBER 19, 2024
DAKOTA COUNTY DISTRICT COURT
14955 GALAXIE AVENUE, APPLE VALLEY

It was ultimately determined that we'd first prosecute Carmel Cano for Aiding and Abetting in the murder of Cheri White, then follow up by prosecuting her for the murder of Londyn Larson. We had a pretty solid case with Londyn, as we had the electronic messages, a video of Carmel with the Hummer in Detroit Lakes, and Carmel's recorded confession. If Carmel were sentenced to life without parole on those cases, we wouldn't put Eliana through the process of testifying. We could always charge Carmel for attempting to kill Eliana later.

The prosecution of Carmel Cano for aiding in the murder of Cheri White was pivotal. If we could get a conviction here, the Londyn Lust case would be an easy win. The State of Minnesota vs. Carmel Cano was now in its third day, and the case could go either way at this point. We didn't have texts or electronic messages in Cheri's killing like we had in the other cases. We had the support of Dakota County Prosecutor Kathryn Loch on our side, which was a plus. Still, defense attorneys have a way of twisting the truth to make it look like law enforcement has engaged in a conspiracy against their client. Carmel's attorney, Ben Grafton, had a reputation for saying anything to win.

Sean Reynolds asked me to meet him in an interview room just off the courtroom. I assumed he wanted to go over my testimony with me. Instead, he dropped down in the wooden chair across from me and said, "You have been charged with witness tampering, and you are to be suspended, pending an investigation. Were you ever sexually involved with Eliana Castillo?"

"No. Never." I hadn't seen it coming, but perhaps I should have. Carmel needed a way to discredit my testimony.

"Yeah, I didn't think so." Sean leaned back in his chair and said, "The spin is you were sleeping with Eliana, and you set up Carmel for her because Carmel had betrayed her."

"And what would I gain from doing this?"

"The theory is you did it out of love. I know it's ridiculous. They just need to convince one jury member."

"Suspended with pay?" I asked. There was nothing I could do about the lie, so I'd go home and enjoy time with my family.

"Yeah."

"Can I go?"

"No," Sean clarified. "You still have to testify. Carmel's attorney got wind of a conversation you had with Dr. Ho. Apparently, you told her you suspected Carmel had been framed."

"I postulated that McBride could have been framing someone. We throw out tons of possibilities when we're working a case."

"I know. But anticipate that this conversation is going to come back to haunt you."

10:00 A.M.

After being sworn in, I took the stand.

Ben Grafton was a round man with thick, gray hair combed back like a mobster. He started with, "I've heard there has been a complaint filed against you for your work in this case. Is that

281

accurate?"

"Yes, I just learned of it this morning. I'm assuming you filed the complaint." It was difficult to hide my irritation. I hated it when attorneys manipulated ethics complaints to bolster their cases.

"Please confine your answers to the questions asked," Grafton directed.

The Honorable Caroline McCartney was presiding over the case, and she nodded in agreement. With her short, straight blond hair, Judge McCartney looked younger than both the defense attorney and the prosecutor.

Grafton continued, "According to the police report, you were at Eliana's house on the night Larry McBride was killed there. Were you planning on spending the night with her?"

"Eliana called me and asked me to stay after Carmel Cano said she wouldn't be showing up."

"It's a yes-or-no question," Grafton cut me off.

"I was there to provide protection."

"*Yes* or *no*?" He turned to the judge, putting on a pained expression. "Could you direct Frederick to just answer the question?"

"Objection." Prosecutor Kathryn Loch stood. Her long, blond hair brushed the shoulders of her dark suit jacket. "Please let Investigator Frederick respond. Mr. Grafton is suggesting something illicit was taking place. Mr. Frederick should be allowed to explain his presence in the home."

"Jon Frederick will be allowed to explain his answer," Judge McCartney acquiesced.

"As I stated, Eliana Castillo had informed me that her friend, Carmel Cano, had initially promised she would stay. When Carmel called and said she wouldn't be arriving as expected, Eliana asked if I would stay with her. I thought this was wise as I had concerns that her life was still in danger. My concerns proved to be warranted."

Grafton was irritated that the judge had allowed me to explain my answer, so he paused for an uncomfortably long time before asking, "You done?"

"*Yes*," I answered.

"Wait a minute." Grafton dramatically waved his hands in the air in front of the jury. "I'm pretty sure Eliana couldn't speak at that time."

"She texted," I responded. "I have no romantic interest in Eliana, and I've never cheated on my wife."

"Your Honor," Grafton exclaimed. "He's making a mockery out of this hearing."

Judge McCartney directed the jury, "You will please disregard the last statement about his wife."

I'd said what I needed to say. It's hard for a jury to "unhear" things.

"I think we need to get back to yes-or-no questions." Grafton nodded to the jury as if agreeing with himself. "Is Eliana staying with your family?"

"Yes," I responded.

"Is it typical to have witnesses stay with your family during investigations?"

"No. I contacted my supervisor, Sean Reynolds—"

"*Yes* or *no*," he cut me off.

"Objection," Prosecutor Loch stated. "He is not letting his witness answer the question."

"It's a yes-or-no question," Grafton argued.

Judge McCartney said evenly, "You may explain your answer."

"I contacted my supervisor and asked if we could provide Eliana a safe place to stay. He told me it wasn't in the budget. My father lives by himself in a farmhouse, so I asked if Eliana could stay with him for a bit. My concern for her safety was legitimate. Larry McBride came after her in her home, and a police officer who was protecting her was shot in my father's home."

"But that has nothing to do with this case," Grafton quickly interjected. "Has Eliana been sexually active since she's been in your family's home?"

"Objection. Relevance." Prosecutor Loch stated.

Grafton turned to the judge. "Jon Frederick is accused of tampering with a witness by being romantically involved with her."

"Objection overruled," the judge stated.

"I don't know," I responded. "I have never asked her about it."

"I don't believe that," Grafton muttered.

"Objection," the prosecutor stated. She raised her hands as if to signal *What the hell?* "Counsel is testifying and making improper character attacks."

Judge McCartney turned to Grafton. "Consider yourself warned, Mr. Grafton, that I will not tolerate further outbursts."

He nodded to the judge. "I'm sorry, Your Honor. I'm establishing his history of poor boundaries with Eliana." Grafton asked me, "Has Eliana ever been inside your house?"

"Yes."

"Has Eliana ever played with your children?"

"Yes."

Grafton studied me and paced as he mulled over asking his next question. It was a risk for attorneys to ask questions when they didn't already know the answer. He decided to chance it. "Have you ever hugged Eliana?"

"She was a victim of a violent assault. I hugged her because we were at the scene of her assault, and Eliana almost collapsed talking about it."

"From your perspective," Grafton remarked as he pompously grinned at my affirmative answer. "And then a complaint was filed about your unprofessional involvement with her. Do you know if Eliana made the complaint?"

I hated the question. I'm sure Eliana didn't, but the accused is not told who originates the complaint. "No."

"Let's talk about this case. There is a video of you discovering a shirt belonging to a woman in Larry McBride's home. In the video, you and the officer postulated that this was the shirt of another victim. Wasn't it your conversations with Eliana that changed Carmel from being a victim to the accused in this case? You went after Carmel even though you have no evidence that Carmel had any contact with Cheri."

"We have Carmel on a recorded statement reporting she was present when Cheri was murdered. It was Carmel's statement that convinced me she was involved." I had suspected this, but the recording assured me I was right.

"Wait a minute," Grafton said as though he'd just remembered something. "Didn't she say on that recording that Larry McBride killed Cheri White?"

"She did. But Carmel had information that hadn't been made public. Such as knowing Cheri had been branded."

"McBride could have told her that, correct?"

"Yes."

"And didn't you suggest to Medical Examiner Dr. Amaya Ho that McBride might have dripped blood on the shirt to set someone up?"

"Yes.

"No more questions. I would like to call Dr. Amaya Ho as my next witness. She will attest that Carmel Cano was set up."

"Objection," Prosecutor Loch stated. "Counsel is testifying. Again."

"Sustained," Judge McCartney ordered. She glared at Grafton and then turned to the jury. "Please disregard Mr. Grafton's last statement."

Once again, it would be hard for the jury to disregard what they'd heard.

Judge McCartney pounded her gavel. "Let's take a fifteen-minute break before we start Dr. Ho's testimony."

The Dakota County Courthouse is a large brick building that houses a variety of government agencies, including a community corrections center. I strolled to the office during the break and called Serena.

"How's it going?" she asked.

"Carmel's attorney, Ben Grafton, accused me of having an affair with Eliana. He's saying I set up Carmel to please Eliana."

"That's ridiculous. I hate attorneys who attack caring professionals simply because there is no way to defend their client's behavior. What evidence do they have?"

"Grafton questioned my boundaries. He brought up that Eliana's been to our house and she's living with my dad."

"Is there anything else?"

"I hugged her when we were at the crime scene."

"How did Grafton know about that?"

"He asked and I told him."

"Jon, sometimes I wish you weren't so honest. Carmel's going to walk on this," Serena worried. "One by one, she'll get out of every charge."

"She's not getting out of the murder charge on Londyn. We have too much evidence from too many sources. And this case isn't over yet."

"People watch too much TV," Serena remarked. "On a crime show, she'd be living with you, and you'd be having a torrid affair. I'm sorry you have to deal with this, Jon. I trust you, if that's any consolation."

"It's what matters most. I have to head back into court. Love you."

"Love you, too."

11:00 A.M.

Dr. Amaya Ho and I had been sequestered, which meant we were ordered not to share information about our respective testimony. I sat in the galley, anticipating that Amaya's testimony would only serve to damage the prosecutor's case further. Being used by Ben Grafton to support his case had to be infuriating for her. She disliked him more than I did.

After Amaya was sworn in, she took the stand. Amaya wore a gray blazer with a white cashmere sweater underneath. She sat with perfect posture.

With an affectation of respect, Grafton started, "There have been some complaints about the Hennepin County Medical Examiner's office, but none of this had anything to do with your work, correct?"

"That is correct," Amaya responded.

"As a matter of fact, your work is held in the highest regard by the Bureau of Criminal Apprehension. Isn't that right?" Grafton added.

"They request my work frequently," she responded.

286

"And you recall an occasion where Jon Frederick brought a woman's T-shirt into your lab for you to analyze."

"Yes. The owner of the shirt was unknown at the time, but I was able to determine who wore the shirt."

Surprised, Grafton asked, "Did Jon Frederick suggest who owned the shirt?"

"No, I was able to extract DNA from the shirt. I didn't have a match until Carmel Cano was arrested. The DNA matched Carmel Cano."

"So, the shirt had been rubbed against Carmel or something in her home," he stated.

"No," Amaya corrected him, "Carmel wore the shirt. The DNA was extracted from sweat that had accumulated under the armpits and breasts, as it naturally would if a woman were wearing this shirt."

"It could have been taken out of her laundry, correct?" Grafton suggested.

"Yes."

"For my last question, I simply need you to confirm that Cheri Wilde's blood was dripped on the shirt—exactly as Investigator Frederick postulated—and that Larry McBride was setting Carmel up."

"That's not true," Amaya responded and, for a second, glanced at me. "Investigator Frederick was wrong."

"It wasn't Cheri Wilde's blood?"

"It was Cheri's blood. But it wasn't dripped on her shirt. It spattered the shirt while Carmel Cano was wearing it."

"My understanding is that there was blood on both the front and back of the shirt. If Carmel was watching the murder, wouldn't the blood have only been on the front?"

"True," Amaya said.

Grafton rubbed his forehead as he debated asking the next question. "So, are you saying Carmel wasn't present when Cheri Wilde was killed?"

"The only way this pattern of blood spatter could have occurred was if Carmel Cano was wearing the shirt and striking Cheri Wilde with a hammer."

Shocked, Grafton tried to recover, saying, "This is your opinion." Grafton realized he had just buried his client and opted to bail. "No further questions."

Prosecutor Kathryn Loch stood. "I'd like to redirect the witness." The judge nodded, and Prosecutor Loch asked Amaya, "Tell us about the additional testing you did on the shirt?"

"Objection," Grafton shot to his feet. "This is beyond the scope of redirect."

Prosecutor Loch smiled. "You opened the door by questioning the blood spatter."

Judge McCartney smiled. "She's right. Objection overruled. Dr. Ho, you may answer."

"I worked with the forensic serology department to analyze the bloodstain pattern on the shirt. We conducted controlled drip tests from multiple heights and angles, but were unable to replicate the pattern. Passive drips form circular stains with smooth margins, but the stains on this shirt exhibited radiating spines, satellite spatters, and elongated shapes—features consistent with cast-off patterns. Cast-off occurs when a blood-covered object is swung in an arc, flinging droplets; the 'tails' or elongated ends point in the direction of the motion. This is similar to what you'd see if you snapped a paint-loaded paintbrush at a wall. You can tell by the pattern of the paint which direction the paintbrush moved. In this case, the shape, elongation, and distribution of the stains indicated the bloody object was swung back and forth, and the pattern suggested multiple blows."

Prosecutor Loch pursed her lips as she contemplated this new information and then asked, "How do you explain the blood spatter on the *back* of the shirt?"

"When you strike the hammer down, you have to draw it back to strike again." Amaya moved her right arm forward and back, simulating a hammering motion. "When Carmel pulled the hammer back, she created the blood spatter pattern on the back of the shirt. We tested various implements and confirmed that the only way to create this precise pattern was for the person wearing the shirt to strike someone bloody with a hammer. We can share our videos of the experiments."

Prosecutor Loch asked, "Wouldn't it be bizarre for Investigator Frederick to both set up Carmel Cano and suggest she is being set up at the same time?"

Grafton shot to his feet again. "Objection. That question is beyond the scope of the Medical Examiner's expertise."

Prosecutor Loch smiled. "I'll withdraw the question."

Ben Grafton argued, "I want it stricken from the record."

Judge McCartney calmly replied, "Your objection is sustained. I've given you considerable latitude. I think Dr. Ho has demonstrated the hammer swings both ways."

Ben Grafton thought Dr. Amaya Ho's testimony would free his client. Instead, it backfired, and Amaya buried her. I was never happier to be wrong about a theory. Amaya was dismissed as a witness, and she gave me a fraction of a smile as she strolled confidently out of the courtroom.

I couldn't help thinking that Amaya might have been the one who leaked my suggestion that McBride was setting someone up. Grafton never would have called Amaya to the stand if he'd had any idea that she was sitting on evidence that would bury his client.

52

ELIANA CASTILLO
10:00 A.M., TUESDAY, DECEMBER 3, 2024
MINNESOTA CORRECTIONAL FACILITY—SHAKOPEE
1010 6TH AVENUE WEST, SHAKOPEE

I paid Carmel one last visit at the women's prison in Shakopee to help bring closure to the brutal assault she had perpetrated on me. After being seated in the very white waiting area on a vinyl-covered chair, I nervously reconsidered this choice. I was the only one in the waiting area, and it almost felt like I was the one incarcerated.

A stocky guard entered and told me, "They've called for an unscheduled count, so you might be sitting here for an hour." The metal door slammed as she exited.

Jon told me random counts occur at least daily, and inmates are stuck in place until every prisoner is accounted for. I would have to leave my phone in a locker when I went in for the visit, but since I still possessed it, I decided to call Roan Caruso and check on Lorenzo's status.

Roan was laughing heartily as he answered, "Hey girl, it's great hearing from you."

"I wanted to check in and see how Lorenzo is doing."

"Lorenzo had a ruptured lung and lost his spleen, but the boy is healing. He's going to survive. Tough kid. Bullets do a lot of damage. You should give him a call."

"I'll think about that. It's hard, knowing he was cheating on me with Carmel the whole time we were together."

"Yeah, I get it. Every time I want to jack that kid up, there's another reason to feel sorry for him," Roan grumbled. "Wasn't there something in the Bible about forgiveness?"

Roan knew my Catholic faith was important to me. "In Ephesians it's said, 'Be kind to one another, tenderhearted, forgiving one another, as God in Christ forgave you.' But I'm not ready to forgive him." It also states in Proverbs, "Let the wise hear and increase in learning." In other words, don't keep making the same stupid mistakes. Thinking Lorenzo would change was a mistake.

"I've always thought forgiveness was overrated," Roan remarked. "Put it in the past and move on. But you don't wanna forget it. You might get burned again, so you gotta be ready."

"I'm glad Lorenzo's healing. I never wanted anything bad for him, or for your family." I scratched my arm as I thought, *I wish I hadn't made this call*. Wanting to be done talking about Lorenzo, I commented, "I heard Molly McBride is dead, and someone burned her trailer."

"That was a work of art," Roan laughed. "If I'd known how it would go down, I would have recorded it. After Molly shot Lorenzo, I needed to send a message that messing with the Caruso-Turrisi family comes at a cost. I lit the place up. There were multiple explosions, blowing pieces of that trailer fifty feet in the air. Turns out, Crazy Larry had dynamite stored beneath the trailer. It was a glorious sight! Better than the 4th of July."

"Thank you for being supportive of me, Roan. I need to go. I'm glad it's good news with Lorenzo." I wasn't going to call Lorenzo. I was done with him.

The guard returned to the visiting room, and I told Roan, "Got to go. I have an appointment."

"Take care, girl."

"Goodbye."

The guard said, "You can visit now. Lock your phone up, and I'll pat you down."

I did as instructed. Carmel Cano had received a sentence of life in prison without the possibility of parole for the murder of Londyn Lust and aiding and abetting in the murder of Cheri White. I learned that a prosecutor can't alter the charges once the trial begins, so even with new evidence tying Carmel to Cheri's murder, they couldn't upgrade her charge. However, the new information impacted Carmel's sentencing—aiding and abetting a murder can still carry a life sentence.

Carmel's assault on me wasn't included in the charges, for which I was grateful. Testifying would have been horrifying for me, and I didn't need the additional trauma. I needed to speak to Carmel one last time for my own sake. She was once my best friend. I wondered if she'd try to apologize, even though it wouldn't mean anything. What can she say? It was an accident?

I was escorted to a drab, four-foot square room and seated behind inch-thick plexiglass to wait for Carmel. She entered on the other side and sat across from me. Carmel wore an orange jumpsuit. Her hair was short and dark for the first time in years. She looked hard and angry, and I realized that this transition began years ago. Her left eye was healing but still had some purple around it. She picked up the phone on her side and signaled for me to pick up mine.

Carmel started coldly, "If you're looking for an apology, you might as well leave now. I gave you chances to redeem yourself. I even had Donny call you, hoping maybe your old flame could get you to step back, but you just had to keep taking."

"I never knew you were dating Lorenzo. And you were right; I was oblivious to how my behavior was impacting everyone else. But I didn't deserve to be raped. When did that become okay?"

"You always said it didn't matter to you if the guy had money, as long as he was decent, but it *did* matter to me." Looking bored, Carmel sat back and said, "Why couldn't you let me have him?"

"I wish I had. But you would've ended up here anyway. You killed Cheri before I was assaulted. For God's sake, girl, you hammered her teeth out."

"Have you ever done something horrible, and after, just felt fucking ecstatic?"

"No," I assured her.

"Not even when you wrecked Donny's life? You cost him the support of his family."

"I thought I loved him at the time." I stopped myself. I didn't need to explain myself to her. "I guess I wasn't thinking."

"Make whatever rationalizations you want, girl, but his family abandoned him, and when you were all he had left, you dumped him. You can be a hard bitch, and I respect that. It's the reason you're still alive, and I'm in here. If you hadn't survived, nobody would give a damn about Cheri."

"I didn't dump Donny. He had his chance, but he refused to talk to me if I didn't get an abortion. Some things aren't negotiable."

"I get it," Carmel said with a shrug. After a beat, she added, "Want to hear a classic? My mom called Catania and offered to sell her the grandparent rights to my baby."

"What did she say?" Knowing Cat, I can't imagine that went well.

"Cat told her, 'You raised that bitch-ass killer. I would bury you alive before I'd give you a cent. If I ever see you near my grandchild, I'll end you.'"

For a long time, I thought Carmel was okay despite her parents. She wasn't okay. "What happened to your eye?" When she didn't respond, I said, "I thought Roan and Catania would take care of you, since you're carrying their grandchild."

"You've met Cat. Nothing's free with that witch." She sighed and said, "Fine, I'll tell you—since I know you want to hear it. You deserve that. A couple of hags assaulted me, and then my roommate announced, 'Camel's mine.' That's another thing; they insist on calling me 'Camel' now that they know I'm carrying a baby. Anyway, she yelled, 'Nobody touches her. She's mine.' Then she made me hold the back of her shirt and follow her through the meal line so everyone would know I'm her bitch."

"So, what do you have to do for her?"

Carmel smirked. "I don't get the hammer, but I'm on call

nightly. When I told her I wasn't attracted to women, she told me, 'I don't care who you're attracted to. Total humiliation is my jam.' At least she doesn't touch me."

"I'm sorry. Can you report this to someone?"

"Me and my baby are protected. That's all I need. Give me a year, and I'll be the one in control."

I knew Carmel. If you wanted to get her to talk, all you had to do was compliment her. "I can't believe how well you had it all planned out. You almost pulled it off."

"You don't know the half of it," Carmel bragged. "The hammer was yours. I got it out of your garage after you left my place to spend the weekend in Detroit Lakes. And I returned it after. I thought if by some reason you'd survive and come after me, I was going to argue that you were a freak who faked the rape yourself. When they searched your house, they'd find the hammer in a drawer in your garage, unwashed. The thought of you one day opening the drawer and finding that bloody hammer still brings a smile to my face. You can find that hammer, just where you left it, tonight. The only evidence on that hammer is your DNA and your fingerprints. I pressed it into your hand before I bagged it."

Psychopath was the thought that came to mind.

Carmel continued, "But you would never have the balls to stand up to me. You knew you were no match. I wipe the floor with rags like you."

"In prison," I added. "Then why did you need McBride?"

"Lorenzo would always be disgusted by the fact that Larry had you. Involving Larry guaranteed me that Lorenzo would get over you. If I'd have just assaulted you, I'd still be free."

"Even after Jon Frederick told me he thought you were the one who assisted McBride in my rape, I didn't believe him. You wouldn't do that to me."

"You're still the same as you were in high school. Naive and ignorant." Carmel stood up to leave. "We're not friends, Eliana. You stole my man, and I got my revenge by hammerin' your money maker. That's what we are to each other." And she left.

I sat for a minute and decided I was good. I don't believe that

I benefited from being assaulted. But I do think we can take terrible things and make ourselves better. I am stronger, and today, I am *Victoriosa*! Conversations in the visiting booth are recorded just like phone calls, and I've just handed the investigators Carmel's confession to her assault on me. I will call Jon Frederick and ask him to send a CSI team to my garage to retrieve the hammer. After they hear what she just said, I will never have to testify. I'm done with Carmel. The chingona in me—the unapologetic badass—has emerged, and she'll be on call from now on.

53

ELIANA CASTILLO
1:00 P.M. FRIDAY, DECEMBER 6, 2024
MALL OF AMERICA
60 EAST BROADWAY, BLOOMINGTON

Donny requested a visit with Luis. I consulted with an attorney who encouraged me to agree to the visit. There was no custody battle in play yet, and it was to my advantage to avoid court if possible since I had total control of Luis. All the way to St. Paul, I told Luis that Donny was a good person who hadn't been ready to be a father until now. Donny was busy with his own family and knew I was capable of caring for Luis, so he left us be. And the two of us were great together!

Donny agreed to meet at the climbing wall at the Mall of America at 1:00 p.m. He would pay to take his son climbing, and I could shop until they were done. For my own sake, I needed to stay close. My dark-haired little Luis nervously squirmed in his seat as we waited. He was worried his dad wouldn't like him.

I crouched by his chair. "You're perfect, okay? No worries." It was fifteen minutes after one, so I suggested, "Let's get the climbing gear. I'll help you put it on so you're ready to go when your dad gets here."

As we approached the desk, Luis said, "I wish Mike could be my dad, and I wouldn't have to visit Donny."

I smiled and kissed his forehead in response. *Me too. But that's a complicated decision—and I'm finally giving myself the time to make it.*

1:30 P.M.

Luis was completely in gear, so I told him, "I want to see how high you can climb." He wanted to climb the Lincoln Memorial wall to the seated Abraham Lincoln. Luis climbed, and I cheered.

My phone buzzed and, dreading the message, I pulled it out of my back pocket. Donny texted, "I've tortured myself over this. I simply don't have time for another child. Please let him know I'm not a bad person. Even if I saw him today, it might be another year or more before next time."

I texted back, "At least he would know for a moment that you cared."

"I'm sorry. My family needs me. You have no idea of the commitment it takes to maintain a normal family."

"Miércoles," I muttered under my breath. *True, Donny, but that's on you. I wanted to be a normal family.* I put my phone away, thinking, *If you can't man up and parent, don't torture your son by telling him you're going to be there and not show up. I am so done with bad men.*

I texted Mike and told him Donny had let Luis down once again.

Luis had reached Honest Abe and yelled down at me, "I did it!"

Tears poured down my face. I begged them to stop, but they wouldn't. I told myself that part of getting healthier means being more emotional.

Luis jettisoned down the wall like a pro and came running to my side. "What's wrong, Mom?"

"I'm so happy, I'm crying. You are so amazing, and I get to be with you."

He studied me curiously for a moment, then said, "Dad's not

coming, is he?"

"No." I pulled him into a tight hug. "I love you!" After a deep breath, I told him, "Some of the cruelest people think they're good people. Instead of being a responsible father, Donny thinks we're better off without him. He thinks he's doing us a favor."

Luis smiled. "Then he is."

Out of the mouths of babes. *He was right.*

"I don't want to spend time with him," Luis added.

"And I don't want you to." I kissed his head.

Embarrassed, he pulled away. "Stop kissing me. I want to keep climbing."

"Then climb you shall." I was proud of myself. Some people mistake assertiveness for being an intolerable bitch, but to me, it simply means saying what needs to be said to get what you want and need in life. I spoke up for Luis, but not to the point of shaming Donny into his life. My amazing son shouldn't have to spend time with a man who doesn't treasure him. So, I'd quietly let Donny walk away. We were done, and I felt good about it. Adios, Donny!

Mike Haney came walking in. "Do you have room for another climber?"

I did a double-take, then stood, dumbfounded. "What are you doing here?"

"Call it a hunch." He smiled. "I thought—just in case, maybe I should catch a ride here. Could I ride home with the two of you?"

"Of course." I pulled Mike into a tight hug.

Mike waved for Billy to leave.

I watched Luis and Mike climb one wall after another. The past few months, I'd been through hell. I was also incredibly lucky. If I had shot Carmel like I'd planned, Luis wouldn't have a parent to help him through the trying emotional events he'll face in life. I almost let my selfish pride take me away from this incredible gift of a son. I addressed my fleeting thought of killing Carmel with my therapist. She told me I should never make major decisions when tired. My PTSD brain falters into crazy mode and puts me at risk of undoing all the good I've done. I don't care enough about Carmel to think about her anymore. I'm glad no one was hurt, and I'm better than that now. The love of my parents, friends, and perhaps mostly Luis and Mike has softened my heart once again. Mom and Destiny remain a stable, loving force. Mike is living in Sauk Rapids and working full-time, but he's with me three nights a week. It's always when I sleep best.

I was infatuated with Donny as a teen and Lorenzo as an adult. I loved them because they loved me. "Puppy love," I guess. I love Mike because being with him melts my defenses, and my love flourishes when we're together. I'm deeply enamored with Mike, and what we have is pragma—an enduring, steady love that develops with patience and trust over time. There's a tender adoration Mike and I share that's built on a solid foundation and is quickly growing. The metamorphosis wasn't all voluntary, but from an anxious people-pleasing girl emerged a strong, determined woman.

54

JON FREDERICK
8:00 P.M. SATURDAY, DECEMBER 14, 2024
PIERZ HEALY HIGH SCHOOL
112 KAMNIC STREET, PIERZ

Serena decided to do our "chance encounter" date at a high school wrestling event. At home events, Pierz has a center light that drops down from the ceiling to spotlight the wrestlers, so the rest of the gym is dark during the match. It provides an opportunity for fans to be anonymous. Pierz was hosting Grand Rapids tonight, which packed the gym. The last time these two teams wrestled was for a chance to enter the state tournament. The match was so close that it ended in a tie and was ultimately settled by the seventh tiebreaker. We squeezed in among a group of visiting adult Grand Rapids fans to give ourselves a group of unknown observers. Serena sat two rows in front of me. It was difficult for me not to cheer when Jayden Zajac pinned his man and Pierz took the lead.

There was a break in the action when the officials were forced to tend to a bloody nose. Serena turned in the bleachers, looked up at me, and said, "Jon?"

"Here I am." I raised my hand.

"You picked a packed wrestling match for a blind date?" she shouted.

"If the date's not entertaining, the match will be," I returned.

We had the attention of the fans packed in around us, and heads turned back and forth as we spoke.

"You don't look anything like your profile picture," Serena scoffed.

"My daughter drew it when she was mad at me."

"Do you really work for A-Hunk Movers?" she teased.

It was a line I didn't expect, but I went with it. "I didn't name the company," I shrugged. "Just needed a job."

Serena stood and looked me up and down. "Fits. I was worried it was one of those creepy OnlyFans sites, but apparently, it's a legitimate moving company. How many children do you have?"

"Two great kids. The verdict's still out on the third."

Serena's eyes widened. "I can't believe you said that."

"Kidding. I have three great kids."

"Three may be a little more than I can handle. My ex and I couldn't have kids. Not the way we did it."

People around us snickered.

"So—" I hesitated. "Why did you agree to meet? You don't like my picture, you question my work, and you don't want my kids."

Serena worked her way up the bleachers to my side. She turned to a nearby couple and said, "Excuse me," then nestled in next to me. "Sorry, this probably should be said in private," she said to the folks surrounding us. The result was that they all leaned in close to hear. She continued, "My primary reason is that your name is Jon. I was infatuated with this guy, Jon, and I kept saying his name at the most inopportune times. It cost me relationships. I decided, if I can just find a guy named Jon, it won't be an issue anymore."

Snickering could be heard all around us.

"So, you want me to be your Jon?"

"Well, you don't have to say it like that."

"Regardless of what you call me; I still get to be with you."

"And I with you. Remember, a rose by any other name would smell as sweet." I had embarrassed her, but she surged on. "Tell me something interesting. I mean, there is no point in being with you if you have nothing to offer."

"Okay, I have some seasonal Grand Rapids trivia. Did you know Judy Garland changed the lyrics to 'Have Yourself a Merry Little Christmas'?"

"I did not." Serena raised an eyebrow and smiled.

"She refused to sing the original line, 'It may be your last,' to child actress Margaret O'Brien in the movie *Meet Me in St. Louis*. Margaret was only seven years old at the time and very fond of Judy. The line was changed to—"

When I hesitated, a woman two rows in front of us filled in, "May your heart be light."

"M, yes, that's much better." Serena pointed to the woman. "Thank you!"

The woman smiled in quiet satisfaction.

Serena turned back to me and said, "Judy was talented, and I'm a fan of a light heart. Mine's been heavy for too long." She prodded, "Okay, now tell me something funny."

"Who was the roundest knight in King Arthur's Knights of the Round Table?"

"Hmm…Sir Bors," she said with a coy grin.

"Nice try. Sir Bors the Younger *was* one of the knights in Arthur's court. But the answer is—Sir Cumference."

"That's terrible." She rolled her eyes and giggled.

"You smiled," I pointed out. I loved seeing the fire in her eyes again. "Okay, I'm offering you obsessively annoying trivia. What are you bringing to the table?"

"So, it's like that. I lay it all out on the table, or the date ends right here in the bleachers."

"Well, I don't need it all, but I do need something."

"And having a lover who calls out someone else's name isn't enough?" Serena quipped. "Let's see, I can be fun—but I can be depressed for periods of time."

"Did you know that shock therapy is the gold standard for treatment-resistant depression?"

"I did not." Serena's eyes glistened. She is so expressive. It was all I could do to keep myself from pulling her into a hug.

"I'm still in love with the mother of my children," I quickly interjected.

"Why would you say that?" she asked with feigned surprise.

"Shock therapy. What are you feeling right now?"

"Angry. Jerk!" Her back straightened as she leaned away from me. "What am I supposed to do with that?"

"Thank me. You were depressed. Now you're angry. See, it works," I casually added.

"Are you serious?" Serena asked.

"Yes."

"You're still in love with the mother of your children?"

"Yes."

"Okay. Hmmm. I think I'm okay with that." She calmly tapped her chin with her pointer finger as she thought out loud, "Shows some level of commitment, although I'm starting to wonder if I should be committed for liking that about you. No more shock therapy. Anything else work?"

"CBT."

"I've heard it's the treatment of choice, but I don't understand how it works," Serena softly responded.

"Caressing with Blissful Tenderness—CBT."

"I don't think that's what CBT stands for." Serena cocked her head to one side.

"It's more effective when combined with exercise. I can work that into our CBT. I promise you'll get a workout."

"I don't know if I can trust you," she sighed. "Does it have demonstrated success?"

"I feel happier just thinking about it."

"Okay." She glanced back at the people around us, who were shaking their heads to discourage her. "Then I'd be a damn fool not to do it. Could you love a depressed woman?" she asked with complete earnestness.

"Absolutely." Her honesty caught me off guard, but I responded in kind.

"You have captured my—"

"Heart," I offered.

"Curiosity." Serena stood and bowed dramatically. "Let the

treatment begin." She took my hand and escorted me down the bleachers while the people around us observed our departure in wonderment.

8:45 P.M.

Jackson was staying with Eliana and Luis tonight at Dad's. Nora and Cami were staying at Serena's parents' for the night. It was possible we could be called to retrieve Cami before the night was over, but I anticipated we'd have until at least midnight. Nora was good with Cami, which would help.

As I parked in our driveway, Serena grinned. "Follow to the hollow." She took my hand and led me through the snow into the forest behind our yard. She stopped in an opening surrounded by tall maple and oak trees. We read in this nook with the kids by a campfire on warm nights. She pulled me into an embrace, and our lips warmed in the cool air as we kissed.

"This is who we are," I whispered.

"Forest creatures?" she teased.

"Explorers. It's why we investigate. It's why we read."

"I love that we read in the woods together." She grinned.

She picked up a stick, pointed it at me, and said, "*En garde!*"

I raised my hands in mock surrender. Serena dropped the stick, stepped toward me, and took my hand. "To paraphrase *The Legend of Sleepy Hollow,* 'My heart was like a fortress that had been captured, sacked, abandoned, and left desolate. But you rescued me, Jon Frederick.'" With genuine sincerity, she said, "I will never forget that you stood by me during my darkest times. Thank you, honey."

I followed with a second line from the book. "I profess not to know how women's hearts are wooed and won. They have always been matters of riddle and admiration."

"My feet are cold." Serena stepped into me and nuzzled her cheek against mine. "How does a warm blanket in front of the fireplace sound?"

"Perfect."

As we strolled to the house, Serena kicked up powdery drifts.

"My shoes, socks, and pants are all wet with snow. I'm going to have to take them off."

"Mirroring the behavior of the client is a tool used in CBT." We entered our quiet home, and I offered, "I'll get a fire going."

"I imagine you will," she deadpanned.

11:30 P.M.

As we spooned in exhausted elation in front of the flickering embers, Serena closed her eyes and said, "This CBT is wonderful, but I've had all the emotional and physical therapy I can take for one night." With a mischievous smile, she proudly shared, "I'm back, alive, and in color. As a mother, I'm back to feeling heart-warming pride when Cami manages a word, when Jackson helps out of pure kindness, and when Nora goes out of her way to teach her younger siblings. But as a woman, this moment of bliss is the best. There is no bliss in depression." She nuzzled into me. "The bliss I missed. Maybe I should write a song." Eyes still closed, but now emitting a radiant grin, she countered, "Or maybe I'll just enjoy it. We got through this."

"We did." The tender warmth of her body was all I needed at this moment. Our greatest Christmas gift to each other wasn't written or purchased. It was simply loving each other day in and day out. The certainty that someone is going to be there, determined and unwavering in their love, is everything.

The End

ABOUT THE AUTHOR

Frank was raised in rural Minnesota and is the 6th of 10 children, named in alphabetical order. Frank was raised with a hard work ethic, in a family of musicians and storytellers. He became a forensic psychologist specializing in homicide, sexual assault and domestic abuse cases. He uses his unique understanding of how predators think, knowledge of victim trauma, and expert testimony in writing his true crime thrillers. Frank has been interviewed on investigative shows and profiled cold case homicides. His novels have earned numerous awards. Frank is the 2024 recipient of the Outstanding Achievement Award from Minnesota Psychological Association and received the President's Award from the Minnesota Correctional Association for his forensic work.